Praise for Anna Durand's Books

"I have enjoyed this whole series, but Emery and Rory [from *Scandalous in a Kilt*] have stolen my heart and are now my favorites!"
The Romance Reviews

"[*Scandalous in a Kilt*] is beautifully written with a heavy emphasis on the actual romance and sensuality experienced by [the] two characters. [...] I've found each of the [Hot Scots] books to have entertaining and original plots and marvelous characters."
Readers' Favorite

"[*Insatiable in a Kilt*] smokes from the very first pages. [The] plot works on a number of levels, giving this story suspense and drama as well as sizzle, and her characters are well-defined and credible. Durand's Hot Scots family saga just keeps on getting better."
Readers' Favorite

"[*Notorious in a Kilt*] is the book I have been waiting for! A great second-chance romance and one of my favorites in this series."
The Romance Reviews

"I loved the Scottish in Ian and the strength of Rae, but the love of one little girl makes [*Notorious in a Kilt*] something to behold."
Coffee Time Romance

"*Gift-Wrapped in a Kilt* is a marvelous continuation of the author's Mac-Taggart family saga. Durand's story has an entertaining plot, and her steamy interludes are well-written...a celebration of healthy relationships between loving adults written in a tasteful and compelling manner."
Readers' Favorite

"An enthralling story. [...] I highly recommend the writing of Ms. Durand and *Wicked in a Kilt*, but be warned you will find yourself addicted and want your own Hot Scot."
Coffee Time Romance & More

"*Dangerous in a Kilt* by Anna Durand delivered! [...] It was the journey, characters, and smoking hot sex scenes that kept me turning the pages."
The Romance Reviews

Other Books by Anna Durand

Dangerous in a Kilt (Hot Scots, Book One)
Wicked in a Kilt (Hot Scots, Book Two)
The MacTaggart Brothers Trilogy (Hot Scots, Books 1-3)
Gift-Wrapped in a Kilt (Hot Scots, Book Four)
Notorious in a Kilt (Hot Scots, Book Five)
Insatiable in a Kilt (Hot Scots, Book Six)
Lethal in a Kilt (Hot Scots, Book Seven)
Irresistible in a Kilt (Hot Scots, Book Eight)
One Hot Chance (Hot Brits, Book One)
One Hot Roomie (Hot Brits, Book Two)
One Hot Crush (Hot Brits, Book Three)
The Dixon Brothers Trilogy (Hot Brits, Books 1-3)
Natural Passion (Au Naturel Trilogy, Book One)
Natural Impulse (Au Naturel Trilogy, Book Two)
Natural Satisfaction (Au Naturel Trilogy, Book Three)
Fired Up (a standalone romance)
The Mortal Falls (Undercover Elementals, Book One)
The Mortal Fires (Undercover Elementals, Book Two)
The Mortal Tempest (Undercover Elementals, Book Three)
The Janusite Trilogy (Undercover Elementals, Books 1-3)
Obsidian Hunger (Undercover Elementals, Book Four)
Willpower (Psychic Crossroads, Book One)
Intuition (Psychic Crossroads, Book Two)
Kinetic (Psychic Crossroads, Book Three)
Passion Never Dies: The Complete Reborn Series
Reborn to Die (Reborn, Part One)
Reborn to Burn (Reborn, Part Two)
Reborn to Avenge (Reborn, Part Three)
Reborn to Conquer (Reborn, Part Four)

Scandalous IN A KILT

Hot Scots, Book Three

ANNA DURAND

JACOBSVILLE BOOKS — MARIETTA, OHIO

SCANDALOUS IN A KILT

ISBN: 978-1-934631-95-9 (paperback)
ISBN: 978-1-934631-96-6 (EPUB ebook)
ISBN: 978-1-934631-94-2 (Kindle ebook)
ISBN: 978-1-934631-80-5 (audiobook)
Library of Congress Control Number: 2018939071

Manufactured in the United States.

Jacobsville Books
www.JacobsvilleBooks.com

Publisher's Cataloging-in-Publication Data
provided by Five Rainbows Cataloging Services

Names: Durand, Anna.
Title: Scandalous in a kilt / Anna Durand.
Description: Lake Linden, MI : Jacobsville Books, 2018. | Series: Hot Scots, bk. 3.
Identifiers: LCCN 2018939071 | ISBN 978-1-934631-95-9 (paperback) |
    ISBN 978-1-934631-96-6 (EPUB ebook) | ISBN 978-1-934631-94-2
    (Kindle ebook) | 978-1-934631-80-5 (audiobook)
Subjects: LCSH: Man-woman relationships--Fiction. | Scots--Fiction.
    | Highlands (Scotland)--Fiction. | New Orleans (La.)--Fiction. |
    Romance fiction. | BISAC: FICTION / Romance / Contemporary. |
    GSAFD: Love stories.
Classification: LCC PS3604.U724 S33 2018 (print) | LCC PS3604.U724 (ebook) |
    DDC 813/.6--dc23.

Chapter One

oft piano music drifted through the room to surround me where I slouched at the bar, my butt parked on a scuffed wooden stool. I took a sip of my drink—a rum-based concoction known as a Hurricane—wriggled on my seat cushion, and clasped both hands around the tall, curvy glass. I twirled the twin straws, watching the ice cubes dance within the red liquid. The drink had been garnished with a lemon slice and a cherry, but both lay on my napkin. All that remained of the cherry was the stem. I took one more sip of my Hurricane, leaning back in my stool to savor the sweet, fruity flavor of the drink, eyes closed. As the cool cocktail slid down my throat, I opened my eyes to survey the room.

I'd come to the piano bar at Pat O'Brien's, one of the most famous bars in New Orleans, in search of relaxation after a long flight from Colorado Springs. The brick walls and aged-wood ceiling lent the place a historical feel, while the beer mugs hanging on the wall behind the bar made it clear this was a place for imbibing. Giant mirrors hung on the far wall, projecting images of the room. People occupied every one of the thirty or so tables behind me as well as every bar stool, save for the one between me and the wall.

Past the adjacent, empty stool, I spied the entrance doors and the dim lighting in the alley beyond, where artificial bulbs gave in to the darkness of the night. On the other side of the alley, another doorway led into the main bar of Pat O'Brien's. Groups of people meandered down the stone-paved carriageway in various states of revelry. A few laughed too loud, stumbling on the paving stones, obviously drunk. At ten o'clock? Sheesh, they'd gotten an early start. Everyone seemed to be having more fun than I was, but I'd resigned myself to an evening of one drink and then back to my motel for bed.

Stifling a yawn, I fought the urge to scratch my scalp. Airline travel always left me feeling grimy and itchy, in desperate need of a shower. I'd opted for alcohol instead of cleanliness, though, and hadn't even bothered to change out of my travel clothes. Everyone ignored a girl in a ComicCon T-shirt and worn blue jeans. Tonight, I preferred solitude. Tomorrow, I planned on a wild night of dancing with strangers and diving into the NOLA nightlife. The slinky dress I'd bought specially for this trip hung on a hanger hooked onto a post of the bunk bed in my motel room. Yep, I shared a room with three other ladies, the cheapest and friendliest way to stay.

My dress would come out to play tomorrow. Tonight, I needed to rest up for revelry of my own. If I still had it in me.

Of course you do. You're Emery Granger, the fun-loving crazy chick who won the award for skimpiest costume at the office Halloween party.

Yes, I remembered how to cut loose—and I had two more days and another night before I headed home. *Ugh.* Home to what exactly, I still didn't know. Unemployment sucked, but the nine-to-five grind inside a cubicle in a windowless office had cramped my style big time.

My phone warbled, indicating a new text message.

Luke. I knew it was him before I wrestled my phone out of my hip pocket and saw my ex-fiancé's name on the screen. We'd stayed friends, like I had with all my exes—except for one, whose name I refused to even let into my thoughts. Might wreck my weekend vacation. Instead, I focused on the text from Luke.

How's NOLA?

With one finger I typed my response. *Awesome. The ten feet of it I've seen so far.*

Show me?

Everybody knew I loved a good selfie. What the heck. I held my phone at arm's length, elevated above my line of sight, and smiled broadly for the camera. I texted the image to Luke with a caption: *Emery rocks the Big Easy, geek style.*

Luke's reply came seconds later. *Cool! Love the shirt.*

He included two emojis—a winking smiley face alongside a cocktail glass. We exchanged a few more texts, then said goodbye. I promised to send more pictures once my New Orleans adventure really got going tomorrow, then I stuffed my phone in my back pocket, wriggling to get in a position where it wouldn't dig into my tailbone. The rectangular shape of my driver's license in my front pocket pinched me a little, and the movement caused the bills stuffed into my bra to shift. Heedless of the crowd around me, I shoved my hand inside my shirt to reposition the twenty-dollar bills I'd stashed in the safest place available to me.

With my loot secure, I grabbed my drink and ignored the straws this time, swigging a big mouthful. Sighing, I closed my eyes again. The fruitiness of my drink lingered on my tongue as the warmth of the alcohol suffused my body. I'd never sampled a Hurricane before tonight. *Mm, yummy.*

"May I take this seat?"

The rumbliness of the deep voice posing the question made my eyelids flutter open.

I sprang upright, feeling a sudden urge to fluff my hair and check my makeup. My pulse beat faster as blood raced down my veins to enliven my skin.

A man stood a couple feet away behind the adjacent stool. Not a mere man, oh no. His head nearly bumped the wooden ceiling above the bar, and even through his dark-green dress shirt, I glimpsed enormous muscles. My gaze traveled downward as I admired his muscular calves and honey-brown leather boots. A kilt concealed his thighs.

My attention stalled there. I stared at the plaid garment draped around his hips. I'd seen a lot of strange clothing choices tonight, but no one else had worn a freaking kilt.

"How old are you?" he asked.

I tore my gaze away from his kilt. "You must not get lucky very often if you ask women that question."

He tilted his head left, then right, studying me. "You look young, but your manner is mature."

"Oh, I get it. You're worried I'm jailbait. Relax, I'm thirty-four." People often thought I was younger, so I'd gotten used to this treatment from guys. I lifted my glass. "Ask the bartender. He carded me."

"I'll take your word for it." The stranger eased between my stool and the vacant one. "Well, would you mind having me?"

I latched onto the sight of lightly tanned skin, exposed by the undone top two buttons of his well-tailored shirt. The scent of his cologne, woodsy and spicy, enveloped me and warmth rushed through my body again, though not from booze this time.

"Have you?" I mumbled, distracted by his flexing muscles as he rotated the stool toward me. I'd love to have him—pressed against me, lying on top of me, any way he wanted.

"As a neighbor," he said, his lips curving into a sexy smile. He patted the empty stool. "May I?"

"This is a free country. Be my guest."

My new friend perched his taut ass on the stool, sliding in until his body bumped the back of the stool. He laid an arm atop the copper bar and aimed his brandy-colored eyes at me. "Being the guest of a bonnie lass appeals to me."

Bonnie? I blinked rapidly, struggling in vain to clear the haze from my brain. His voice…He spoke with an accent.

"Are you Scottish?" I asked.

Those rich, amber irises glowed in the subdued lighting. His smile turned teasing. "What gave me away?"

"Can't fool a college graduate." I leaned forward to wrap my hands around the glass of my Hurricane, needing the cool-down. Not that it helped. The iced drink chilled my hands but left the rest of me flushed with a tempting warmth. "You have a kilt and an accent. Even if I were stoned, I could've figured that one out."

He slanted forward a touch, and the light gleamed on his short, light-brown hair, setting off golden highlights. "College graduate, eh? I found an intellectual woman to bide my time with. What was your field of study?"

Ech. This was where I lost a lot of guys. Supposed I could've lied, but I preferred to tell the truth, even to a gorgeous stranger from another country. Besides, I wasn't embarrassed. I didn't want to scare off a hot prospect, though.

I sat up straight, hands on my thighs. "Computer programming."

"Ah," he said, drawing out the single syllable as if he relished the taste of it. "You expect me to be less than impressed."

"My occupation isn't the stuff of men's wet dreams, now is it?"

His throaty chuckle shivered along my skin like a physical touch. "I prefer professional women. And anyway—" He bent toward me, so close his breaths whispered over my lips. "You'll be featured in all my dreams tonight."

My throat went thick, my skin tightened. I'd come to New Orleans for excitement and adventure, an escape from my boring life, to shed my corporate skin and let my wild side out to play. Why not flirt with a stranger? Naughty flirting, no less.

Excitement zinged through me, an electric current like nothing I'd experienced in a long, long time. *You're overdue, girl, go for it.*

"Tell me," he said, "what is a beautiful, intelligent woman doing all alone in a bar? You should have a horde of men slavering to do your bidding."

"I got into town this evening. Haven't had a chance to drum up a horde." I wiggled on my seat to angle toward him. Our faces hovered deliciously close, and I pulled in a deep draft of Scot-scented air. Crossing my legs, I lay an arm on the bar while my other hand rested on my thigh. "Would you do my bidding?"

The part of me that conformed to expected behavior winced. The other part of me, the one I kept quiet most of the time out of necessity, thrilled at the prospect of…whatever I was doing with this man.

"Ah, lass," he purred, fingering a lock of my pale, ash-blonde hair. The lighting had imbued it with an almost ethereal glow. "For you, I'd go down on my knees and do whatever is necessary to make certain you feel nothing but satisfaction."

Holy shit. This guy was a master of dirty flirting.

With a soft groan, he shifted his mouth to my ear. "I love your eyes. They sparkle like topaz dusted with emerald flecks. A man could drown in those eyes of yours, and he'd never want to come up for air."

Couldn't speak. Couldn't catch my breath. My fingers crooked into my thigh, and my mouth went dry. When he moved one hand onto the back of my stool, I stopped breathing altogether.

His voice rumbled in my ear. "Let's go somewhere more…intimate."

"I'm not that easy."

A chuckle resonated in his chest. "I am."

"Telling me you're a man-whore is supposed to turn me on?" Damn if it hadn't, but really, I had never gone off with a stranger. I shouldn't do it.

I burned to do it.

"You are aroused," he said, his voice husky, "I can see it. We're adults, and I willnae do anything without your consent."

"Damn straight you won't." My breathless tone sapped most of the oomph out of that statement, and my traitorous body melted from the inside out at the thought of what he might do to me. Excitement? Oh yeah, I'd found it all right.

The stranger nuzzled my throat, just below my ear. "I want to kiss you."

His statement, spoken in that sultry voice, triggered a deep, wet throbbing between my thighs. Somehow, I mustered the breath to reply. "I'd like that."

"Good." He skimmed his lips along my jawline, then dragged them across my cheek to the corner of my mouth. His tongue flicked out to taste my skin.

I sucked in a sharp breath.

His tongue explored the seam of my lips as he repositioned his mouth over mine, not quite touching me. My lips parted of their own accord, my body acting without my conscious thought. *Screw thinking.* I'd done enough of that at work, slaving over line after dreary line of code. I let my body sag toward him and floated my palms up to his broad, firm chest. The silky texture of his shirt—was it actual silk?—teased my sensitized skin.

When he brushed his lips over mine, I let out a breathless little moan.

He pressed his mouth to mine, his lips warm and soft and oh-so-inviting.

I clenched his shirt in my fingers, my heart pounding at the expectation of what was to come, my mouth opening more for him.

The Scot licked at my tongue. Delicate, teasing laps that had me dissolving into his hard body, stretched across the distance between our stools, our knees grazing each other. His free hand found my back and glided upward until his big palm landed on my nape, rippling a shudder of need through my entire body. His fingers slid into my hair to cradle my head.

Wildfire. Consuming my skin. Scorching through my sex.

His tongue plunged inside my mouth. I met his velvety thrusts with my own, our tongues locked in an erotic dance, the flavor of him infusing my mouth as I moaned into his. My nipples shot hard, and my body ached in ways I'd only dreamed of before tonight, before this moment with this man.

The Scot severed our kiss, staring at me with glossy eyes, his chest heaving. "How much have ye had to drink?"

"What? Two sips and one gulp of this one drink. Why?"

"Yer still thinking clearly, then." He ghosted the backs of his fingers over my cheek. "Come with me to my hotel. Stay the night."

Every good-girl alarm in my brain clanged at the suggestion, but I was so fucking sick of playing by the rules. This man ignited my desires like no one else.

Adventure. Excitement. Embodied in a stranger.

Gazing into those brandy eyes, I spoke a single word that rushed out on a sigh. "Yes."

Chapter Two

The door to the room clicked shut behind us. The word "room" seemed inadequate to describe this huge suite in the Ritz-Carlton. I had set foot in a luxury hotel for the first time ever. Though we stood in a short hallway, beyond it I glimpsed a spacious and luxurious living room. Other doorways opened off the hall, leading into rooms I couldn't quite see. My hot Scot had brought me to a suite that would've dwarfed my apartment back home.

He settled his hands on my hips and backed me into the wall, his hooded gaze riveted to mine, hunger sizzling in his expression and tautening his muscles. His eyes shimmered a luscious, golden amber reminiscent of brandy or whiskey, and I spiraled down into their intoxicating depths.

I would've melted then and there if my insides hadn't already liquefied. He'd made certain of that during our cab ride from the bar to the hotel, with his tantalizing kisses and talented hands.

Those hands, the ones that had just eased me up against the wall, roamed down to my buttocks to splay over my flesh in a possessive gesture. He molded his body to mine, his solid muscles flexing against my soft body, his hard-on a rigid line against my belly.

Head spinning, heart pounding, I craned my neck to behold his face. His eyes searched my face as if seeking an answer to a question he hadn't asked yet, even as his hands massaged my behind and he ground his hips into me. I rocked mine forward, seeking the contact. He drew my earlobe into his mouth to suckle and nip at the tender skin, then laved a path down my throat with his lips and tongue.

I floated on a cloud of anticipation and disbelief, my scalp tingling and my body crackling with fervent energy. A one-night stand? Never in my life had I done anything like this. I'd always been a free spirit, but this was beyond crazy, even for me. After years of living as an office drone, I needed to break out.

This would be a huge adventure. A huge risk.

Maybe I should've been disturbed by how fast I'd agreed to go with a stranger to his hotel room for a one-nighter. Maybe I should've backed out.

Not this time.

"I haven't changed my mind," I said. "In case you were wondering."

"Mmmm," he murmured against my skin. "Ahmno doubting ye want me."

"Who are you?"

"Does it matter who I am?" He feathered his lips over mine. "We'll have one night and only one night."

One night only. An electric tingle chased through my body. One scandalous night with a stranger. No names, no strings, nothing but one smoking-hot man and the pleasure we might give each other.

His hand dived under my T-shirt and swept up to close over my breast. When he thumbed my nipple, my neck arched. God, I wanted our clothes off. *Now.* The torture of his flesh separated from mine by a thin layer of cotton drove me mad. My skin had become hypersensitive to the whisking of fabric and the deliberate flicking of his thumb. He grasped my ass in both hands again as his mouth sealed over mine and his tongue plowed deep inside, his invasion fierce and voracious and irresistible. I moaned into his mouth and flung my arms up to encompass his neck, my fingers tunneling into his short, silky hair.

He lifted me onto my toes, bringing our faces closer, and tore his mouth from mine. A ruddy pinkness tinged his cheeks. "For you, ahmno rushing. Plan on savoring every moment with ye, my wicked little angel."

Surrounded by him, I felt small, my five feet six tiny compared to his massive body. He made me feel naughty and ravenous, but somehow safe. *Insane,* my rational brain warned. I no longer gave a damn about being rational.

He eradicated my thoughts with his supple lips on mine and the velvety swipes of his tongue. Determined fingers kneaded my ass, pushing me forward into his waiting erection. I hooked a knee around his thigh, desperate to expose my flesh to him. He rubbed his hard-on into my cleft, and shocks of pleasure ricocheted through me, propelling a rush of cream that soaked my sex and my panties. My jeans, his kilt, they barred me from what I craved with a blistering need.

The Scot dipped his head to my breast and swallowed my nipple through my clothing, sucking it hard and fast. I bowed my back and clutched his head to my chest. My head lolled against the cool wall, and I reveled in the sensations, in the natural high brought on by hormones and lust and the dampness of his mouth saturating my shirt and bra.

"More," I pleaded, my voice so throaty I hardly recognized it as my own. "Oh God, please, more."

With a raspy growl, he gathered me in his arms and carried me into the living room. With heavy-lidded eyes, I glimpsed a pool table upholstered in crimson felt and a sofa with chairs arranged in front of it, one of the chairs upholstered in the same crimson as the pool table. I caught sight of French doors and a terrace outside, but then my Scot set me on my feet behind the red armchair and, with his hands on my hips, urged me to lean back into the chair.

A gauzy white curtain shielded a floor-to-ceiling window in front of me—until *he* moved between my body and the wall. His erection tented his kilt, though dammit, not enough for me to see what lay beneath it.

He caged me to the chair's back with his hands at either side of me, kissing me again, kissing me like he'd die without my breaths feeding into him through our fused mouths. His hands on my hips, he tugged me into his hardness and compelled me to arch into him. I clamped my hands on the chair, in need of an anchor, my knees wobbly and my tummy fluttering even as the weight of desire settled low in my belly. He nibbled at my lower lip. I went boneless against him, grateful for the chair that prevented me from falling to my knees at his feet.

An image flared in my mind, of me kneeling before him, naked and willing. Heat lightning ripped through me, and my knees threatened to buckle.

He skated his lips along my jaw.

"Want ye naked," he breathed into my ear. "Need to bury myself inside yer sweet little body."

Oh yes, please. I couldn't utter the words, speechless from a heady rush that overpowered my senses. Maybe I should've been shocked by how badly I wanted to do this, but I'd skidded straight past reason into a crushing need for his cock inside me.

His tongue penetrated my mouth, hot and deep and demanding, while his hands worked at his shirt, fumbling to unhook the buttons. I pushed his hands away to take over the task, frantic to speed through this part and get to the good stuff. With my eyes closed, mindless from his kiss, I freed the buttons without any conscious thought for what I was doing. When I'd freed the last button, he shrugged out of the shirt.

Both his hands lunged under my shirt, whisking it up my skin. Cool air set off a flurry of goosebumps as he peeled his lips away for only a second to pull the shirt over my head. He unzipped my jeans and stripped them off me along with my panties, without even a hesitation in his ravishing of my mouth—until he inclined his head as if to latch onto my nipple.

His brow furrowed, then smoothed out, his attention riveted to the twenty-dollar bills sheltered between my breasts, inside my bra. A slight smile curved his lips as he hooked one finger inside my bra to pull it out a smidgen, peeking into the valley between my breasts. He raised his head to lift one brow at me.

I shrugged. "Don't like to carry a purse in crowded places."

Amusement crinkled his eyes and dimpled his cheeks. He plucked out the wad of cash and tossed it onto the table beside the chair, then looped his arms behind me to unhook my bra.

The last shred of my clothing crumpled to the floor. I stood naked before a stranger, my ass against the back of a plush armchair, every inch of me exposed to the air and his molten gaze.

He took one step back. His eyes drank me in, his tongue moistened his lips.

My gaze landed on his chest, and my jaw dropped. *Holy mackerel.* Acres of mouthwatering male flesh had been sculpted into rigid lines of muscle, from his impressive biceps and pecs down to his exquisite six-pack abs. A trail of fine, tawny hairs dusted his skin, tapering down toward his groin. And there...

The kilt still obscured my view.

He unfastened the leather belt that secured the kilt. With a swift tug, he shed the garment. The plaid fabric fell into a heap on the rug.

I pulled in a shaky breath, my legs trembling again at the sight of his nude body, the full expanse of him revealed at last. Darker hairs dusted his powerful thighs, but my gaze inexorably gravitated to the region between his thighs.

Oh. My. God.

His engorged penis swayed in front of him, curving up toward his belly, the head glistening with a rosy blush. I marveled at the long, thick shaft and the sleek skin unblemished by even a single vein. His cock jumped as if my attention excited him. I envisioned his length impaling me, filling my body to the hilt, and the thought of it stole my breath. Had I picked the right guy for a one-nighter or what?

The Scot stretched out his hand, fingers bent into his palm, and hovered it an inch from my chest. He touched his middle finger to my breastbone. His tongue darted out to lick his lower lip, and his dick twitched. With that solitary finger, he traced a line down my breastbone onto my belly.

My breaths shortened into soft pants.

His gaze snapped to mine, pupils blown. His breaths grew labored.

That finger dipped into my navel, then moved downward until it grazed my mound.

Clinging to the chair, I bucked my hips toward his finger.

He groaned, long and low and carnal, then scooped me up and strode back to the hall, through a doorway into a spacious bedroom. With amazing strength and dexterity, he hugged me to him with one arm while he tossed the covers off the king-size bed with his other hand. He laid me down on the mattress on my back, my head cushioned by a fluffy pillow.

I couldn't resist frisking my palms over the satiny white sheets. My motel was decent enough, but this place was a whole other universe. Gossamer curtains veiled the windows, and a tall mirror showed me a full-frontal view of my own body sprawled across the length of the mattress—as well as a side view of the highly aroused man beside the bed. I got a peek at his backside, at his taut buttocks and the flowing lines of his back muscles.

Seeing myself in the mirror, I had the inexplicable impulse to rearrange my body so my Scot could get a better view. The impulse proved irresistible, and I stretched my arms above my head to caress the wooden headboard. I sloped my back up just enough to boost my breasts, with my nipples jutting toward the ceiling. My knee bent, I spread my thighs.

He hissed in a breath, his eyes narrowed to slits. A drop of moisture beaded on the tip of his penis.

I writhed on the sheets to make my breasts jiggle.

The Scot ripped open the top drawer of the dark-wood dresser beside the bed. He snagged a condom packet, slammed the drawer shut, and sheathed his length faster than I'd ever seen a man accomplish the task. Dressed in nothing but a condom, he towered over me with his lips parted and his erection waving.

Wriggling my butt, I laid my hands on the sheets at either side of my body.

He scraped his tongue across his bottom teeth, inside his lip.

I gave him my best seductive smile. "Come and get me."

The man growled the way he had earlier, eying me like a predator sizing up his prey. "Yer the finest work of art I ever laid eyes on. A masterpiece of sensual beauty."

Work of art? Masterpiece? Man, this guy knew how to talk to a woman.

And I wanted him like I'd never wanted anyone.

He climbed onto the bed on all fours to position his body over me, our faces aligned.

I fanned my palms over his broad chest.

Arms bent, he devoured me with his mouth, his tongue raking over mine, licking at the roof of my mouth, swirling around my tongue until I was breathless and burning for him. Each greedy swipe of his tongue wound a coil of need tighter in my belly. Though we'd kissed and kissed and kissed for the entire ride to his hotel, that experience paled compared to this moment. Possessed by a wild urge, I closed my hand around his shaft.

He choked back a groan, his mouth glued to mine, his tongue faltering only for a second.

I lost myself in the sensation of tongues on tongues, teeth gnashing against lips, his hand on mine as it palmed his cock. He grasped my hip, pulling me closer, and still our mouths ravaged each other.

I stroked my hand up and down his shaft.

Propped on one arm, he grasped my hand and eased it away from his erection. While I made a disappointed noise, he lowered his body onto the bed to lie on his side with one arm above my head and his front snug against me. His hard arousal prodded my hip as he laid his free hand on my belly, skating his palm down, down, down to the thatch of hairs between my thighs. I clenched my fingers in the sheets as he toyed with those hairs, making me squirm. The second my legs opened, he delved his fingers between my slick folds.

His fingers glided up and down my cleft while the heel of his hand settled over my clit. As his gaze pored over me, the golden glow of the bedside lamp transformed his eyes into a shade of dark honey. His fingers tormented my swollen flesh, and the heel of his hand chafed my nub. I clenched his biceps. His fingers began to pet me with sure strokes, faster and harder, a relentless onslaught of pleasure that had me digging my nails into his arms.

"Ah!" The exclamation burst out of me as I bucked my hips up, half crazed for the release building inside me, the pressure almost unbearable. "Please, oh God, please."

He thrust one finger inside me, then another.

My sex tightened around his fingers, as desperate for him as I was, and my body tensed.

The heel of his hand kneaded my clit in quick, rough circles. His fingers burrowed in and pulled out, scraping my cleft with each movement. He sank his fingers inside me to the last knuckle, kinking them to caress me in a secret spot.

I cried out, thrashing under his hand.

He forged his tongue deep inside my mouth, its thrusts synchronized with the motion of his fingers.

An orgasm detonated inside me, stunning in its power, robbing me of my voice as he tore his lips from mine. I clung to him, my mouth wide on mute cries, my nails scratching his skin as I clawed for an anchor amid the crashing waves of ecstasy. He watched my face, his features tight, shifting his fingers to rub my clit mercilessly, milking every last ounce of pleasure from my body.

He brushed stray hairs from my face. "Ye come like a volcano, so wild and explosive. It's…maddening."

I felt my brows scrunch. Maddening?

He withdrew his hand, wiping his fingers on the sheets, and smiled at my confusion. "I meant it's maddening how much it arouses me, seeing you come this way."

"Oh." I couldn't muster any more words than that. What he'd done to me, the sheer power of my climax, it had vaporized my ability to think.

He ran his tongue over my bottom lip. "We're not done yet."

Chapter Three

Not done yet? I'd realized as much, but the thought of what he might do to me next set my head to spinning again. Already, he'd rendered me defenseless, a willing slave to his desires.

Reclined on his side, he raked his gaze over my body, admiring me with an intensity that made warmth bloom in my belly, sliding lower and lower. He rested his hand on my collarbone, his fingers fanned over my throat.

Eyes half closed, I absorbed every sensation. The silken texture of the sheets. The weight of his hand. The draft kissing my skin.

He smoothed his hand down my breastbone, over one breast and then the other, rolling my nipples between his thumbs. Goosebumps dappled my arms, and a delicious shiver sizzled along my skin. He frisked his hand down to my belly and circled his palm around my navel. I fought to catch my breath, my tummy rising and falling with every labored inhalation. His eyes followed the path of his hand, and his lips had compressed with a deep concentration on his task. That hand ventured lower, but when it dipped within millimeters of my mound, he diverted his track to my hip and cupped it, his thumb massaging the hollow.

My lids flickered and closed. I wanted nothing more than to immerse myself in the feel of his hand exploring my body and the lazy arousal it engendered in me.

Sighing, he skated his hand down my thigh, over my knee, along the side of my calf and down past my ankle. His fingers danced over the top of my foot and around to the sole. The delicate touch of his fingertips tickled in the most erotic way, and I squirmed with pleasure. He rubbed my sole with deft yet leisurely strokes, as if he planned to spend all night on this languorous exploration, as if he planned on memorizing every contour of my body.

He shifted his hand to my other foot, lavishing the same attention on its tender underside.

I exhaled a breathy moan, every muscle in my body slackening, even as my body readied.

The lusty man beside me coasted his hand up the inside of my leg until he reached my inner thigh. His longest finger grazed the outer folds of my sex.

He pulled in a long breath, groaning with profound satisfaction. "Yer scent drives me mad, it's like whiskey and honey and musk." He combed his fingertips through the curly hairs of my mound. "The scent of lust."

The hunger in his voice made me open my eyes.

His head poised over my sex, he swept his hand down my leg and glided it back up slowly.

I fisted my hands in the sheets.

With his hand curled around my thigh, he pressed his lips to my belly. His mouth left a damp warmth on my skin as he kissed his way up to my breasts, where he paused to nuzzle my cleavage.

I flattened my hands on his back, where the muscles rippled beneath my palms.

He darted his tongue out to moisten the peak of one nipple.

"Yes," I murmured, my fingers sinking into his flesh.

My Scot swallowed my nipple and swirled his tongue around the tip. A jolt of pleasure shot down my body, from my breast straight into my sex. He released my nipple, only to latch onto the other to repeat his ministrations. The cool air on my damp breast made the nipple pucker, and combined with his mouth on the other breast, worked me into a fervor once more. I plowed my hands into his hair.

He let go of my nipple and lay beside me as he had before, his head near mine and his hand on my hip. He drew me snug against him, rolled me onto my side, and tucked my head under his chin. He slid his hand off my hip, down to my thigh, lifting my leg to expose my core.

I stretched my arm over his torso to hold him close.

He hooked my leg over his, spreading his palm on my ass, and pulled me toward his erection. His shaft brushed my flesh.

My pulse thundered in my ears.

He penetrated me with one slow, smooth stroke, consuming me with his cock until it seemed I couldn't stretch any further.

"All right?" he rumbled in my ear.

I buried my face against his neck. "Yes. Don't stop."

"Willnae."

He gripped my behind as he began a measured rhythm, his pace unhurried, his shaft plunging inside and then abandoning my body, over and over until I was clinging to him and whimpering against his neck. His muscles rippled around me in time with the movements as the firm length of him glided in and out of my swollen flesh. He blew out a breath with each thrust and sucked in air each time he pulled out.

I locked my leg tighter around his, pawing at his back, wordlessly begging for more.

As if he understood my desperation, he rolled us both over so I lay flat on my back with his body above me, held up on one straight arm. Never wavering in his momentum, he ran his free hand up and down my side, from my ribs down to my thigh. He bent his supporting arm to lower his head near mine until our foreheads touched. His eyes, so close to mine, enraptured me. I rolled my hips up into each of his thrusts, opening my legs more with my knees drawn up to bracket him.

"Ah, lass," he groaned. "Come for me now, come for me again."

Hands bolted to his arms, I fought a losing battle for breath and sanity. "Faster, please, faster and harder."

Bracing himself on both elbows, he pulled his hips back and slammed into me with so much force my body bowed up and my mouth fell open on a strangled cry.

"More," I pleaded.

He raised onto straight arms, driving into me again and again, faster and faster, his hips pumping and his cock pounding into me like an out-of-control machine. Our bodies slapped together with each punishing thrust, eliciting a wet sucking sound from my sex. I fastened my legs around him and gripped his arms like I'd fly off into space without him to ground my body. He grunted with every lunge, sweat slicking his skin.

And I came for him.

Every muscle snapped tight for an instant, then the orgasm seized me, and my head thrashed on the pillow. My frantic cries spurred him to unleash a hoarse shout as he pummeled my sex once, twice more. He threw his head back and roared.

His release pulsated inside me, and I came harder.

Two more thrusts and he was spent, collapsing onto the bed next to me, on his side. Between gasping breaths, he said, "Thank ye for that."

Ohhh-kay. I'd never been thanked after sex before. Was it a good thing or a bad thing? If he plunked a couple hundred-dollar bills on the table and sauntered out of here, I'd hunt him down and—

"Relax," he said, cradling me to his body, frisking his hand over my back. "It's a compliment. You are a passionate, spirited woman."

"Thank you." I snuggled into him with my face against his neck, enjoying the lovely afterglow of scorching-hot sex. "This was unexpected, but I'm glad you asked me to stay with you tonight."

"I'm glad too." He threaded his fingers through my hair and kissed the top of my head. "A pleasant surprise. Most of my lovers aren't as enthusiastic as you."

His lovers? Plural? I drew my head back to look at him. "Are you saying you do this kind of thing a lot?"

"Aye." He squinted at me, then kinked his lips into a slight smile. "Well, not a lot. I indulge in the occasional fling, but it's not a long-time habit."

Had I been screwed by a lothario? Well, what had I expected? I'd wanted a one-nighter as much as he had, so I couldn't complain. Excitement, check. Shaking up my life, check. Mission accomplished, I should relax and enjoy my time in this bed with this man.

Whose name I didn't even know.

"No more talk," he said.

I didn't object when he lay back on the bed and pulled me half onto his body, one of my arms over his chest and one of his arms around my shoulders. He reached over to shut off the light on his side of the bed, leaving only the lamp behind me for illumination. As he tugged the sheet and blanket over us, he made sure to cover me up to my shoulders.

"Sleep," he whispered. "I've worn you out, haven't I?"

"Mm" was all I could manage, because a deep weariness had overtaken me. The unease that had frosted through me when I realized the extent of what I'd done, sleeping with a stranger, evaporated when he began to caress my arm with his fingertips.

I drifted down into sleep, ensconced in the arms of a mysterious Scot.

Chapter Four

Muted sunlight glowed behind my eyelids as my mind surfaced from sleep. I cracked my lids first, adjusting to the brightness before daring to open my eyes all the way. A clock on the bedside table told me it was a quarter to seven. I stretched and yawned, the sheets soft and slippery on my bare skin. Above my head, the bed's canopy coiled into a rosette as if someone had clenched a giant fist in the fabric.

My hands. Fisting in the sheets. A stranger thrusting into me, again and again, until we both climaxed with exultant cries.

I bolted upright, my heart racing at the memory of what I'd done last night. A one-nighter with a guy whose name I didn't know. I'd slept with a complete stranger, after a few minutes of naughty flirtation in a bar. Sure, I prided myself on being adventurous, but this…I hadn't even checked for hidden cameras.

My one-night lover hadn't seemed like the type to humiliate me, but then, I didn't even know what to call him. I hadn't let the past affect my present, not until I leaped into a crazy fling with a foreigner.

Relax, Emery.

Miraculously, the mental command helped. Sitting there on the enormous bed, I assessed the luxurious bedroom. The gold curtains hung open, revealing a view of the city from high above the streets.

A realization shuddered through me on a chill. I was exposed from the waist up, right in front of a window. I pulled the sheet up to cover my breasts. The air cooled my backside, but at least nobody in a neighboring high-rise would be posting photos of a bare-breasted blonde on Instagram.

Scoping out the room again, I comprehended a couple more facts. I was alone, and my clothes lay neatly folded at the foot of the bed.

On my knees, I scuttled across the bed with the sheet clutched to my chest and managed to get dressed while keeping the sheet over me. Once I was decent, I hurried to the bathroom to check for my bedmate and make use of the toilet. Nobody there. A giant bathtub occupied a good portion of the room, and though I would've loved a nice hot soak, after satisfying nature's call I returned to the bed.

That's when I noticed something else.

On the table on my side of the bed—uh, the side I'd woken up on, that was—I spotted my phone and a piece of ivory-colored notepaper, folded in half. My phone I'd forgotten about, but luckily, it had survived impact with the floor when my one-night lover chucked my jeans. After checking for messages and finding only one text from Luke, asking how I'd liked the bar last night, I shoved the phone in my back pocket.

The ivory paper beckoned me.

I picked it up, revealing several twenty-dollar bills beneath it. I bit my lip, suddenly queasy. Money on the bedside table? Unwilling to jump to conclusions yet, I unfolded the fancy piece of paper. It seemed like linen, maybe.

The note, scrawled in a masculine hand, read, "Thank you for last night."

I stared at the sentence for a moment, not blinking or comprehending. Finally, I noticed the second sentence written at the bottom of the page—"Don't forget your money."

The twenty-dollar bills. They were rumpled, though someone had tried to iron them out so he could stack them in a tidy pile. The man I'd slept with last night had a fetish for order, I guessed. He wouldn't have let his cash get wrinkled, which meant these must be my bills, the ones I'd stashed in my bra. I picked up the money and counted it. One hundred dollars, exactly.

Relief flooded through me, sagging my shoulders. Well, at least he hadn't paid me for services rendered. He'd returned my cash.

I read the note again but couldn't figure out how to feel about it. No man had ever written me a thank-you note after sex.

Resigned to never understanding my onetime lover, I dropped the note on the table and tucked my cash in my bra. Then I hustled through the bedroom and out into the hallway. It dead-ended at the suite's primary door to my left and opened onto the living room to my right. Across the hall, I spied the unoccupied dining room.

I swerved right, stopping at the edge of the living area.

No one here either.

My shoulders slumped again. Had I really hoped he might still be here? He wouldn't write a note and then stick around to say good morning. He'd told me it would be one night only but skulking out in the pre-dawn hours without saying goodbye…Not cool.

I rubbed my eyes, rubbed my neck, rubbed my chest. So, I'd done it. I'd had a one-night stand. Time to move on.

Last night, I'd had little chance to absorb the full splendor of this huge suite, which I'd guessed measured four times the size of my little apartment back in Colorado Springs. With nothing else to do except slink out of the hotel, I decided to explore my surroundings before I left. I might never again find myself in a suite at a five-star hotel.

I'd already seen the sofa and the three upholstered chairs arrayed before it, but now I took note of a fireplace to the right of the furniture. Floor-to-ceiling glass windows admitted the sun's illumination. The crimson-upholstered pool table took up the left side of the room. Lamps and flowers adorned dark-wood tables in strategic locations.

Shuffling across the living room, I peered out the French doors at the terrace.

Nobody there.

Why did I keep looking for the jerk who'd taken off while I was sleeping? Figured the guy I picked for my first-ever fling would turn out to be a worm.

He hadn't seemed like a worm last night. He'd been so attentive, so concerned with my pleasure, so tender—and so damn hot. He'd woken me in the middle of the night for another round of powerfully sensual sex. Why would he do that if he intended to abandon me?

Oh yeah, I should've known. Hot guys who wanted anonymous sex had to be jackasses.

Lesson learned, check.

Maybe I could order up a whole bunch of room service, a four-course breakfast or whatever, and have it charged to his room. Or I could steal the towels. Or—

Ugh. Who was I kidding? I was no thief, and revenge wasn't my style.

I smoothed out my ComicCon T-shirt and combed my fingers through my hair. It stayed a tangled mess. The comb in my purse could undo the tangles—if I'd brought my purse, which I hadn't. *Rats.* With a last glance at the suite, I turned toward the hallway and the door at its end.

Acid churned in my stomach.

I supposed this was what they called a walk of shame. My first one. *Yay, what a milestone.*

The door to the suite pivoted inward.

My one-night lover marched inside, shut the door, and made it halfway down the hall before he noticed me. The Scotsman froze. He stared at me blankly for several seconds before he regained his manly composure and waltzed down the hall to stop an arm's length from me. His expression betrayed nothing.

The sun streaming in through the windows and glass doors glimmered in his eyes.

"You're still here," he said.

"Duh." I folded my arms over my breasts. "Did you forget your wallet and had to slither back here to get it?"

"No," he said slowly, eying me like he worried I had a hatchet hidden in my bra. "I thought you'd be asleep."

"Sorry to disappoint."

"I'm not disappointed. I—" He shifted his weight from one foot to the other and back again. Scratching his neck, he adopted a pinched expression. "I am sorry for, ah…"

"Skulking out in the dead of night like a slimy worm?"

A big, sexy worm. But a worm nonetheless.

Sighing, he gave me a tight smile. "It wasn't the dead of night. I left at dawn."

"Are you expecting applause for waiting until sunrise?" I tapped the toe of my sneakers on the floor. "You could've, gee, maybe woken me up to say goodbye. And by the way, who leaves a thank-you note after sex? It's bizarre."

Kind of endearing, but yeah, bizarre.

Don't you go all gooey and forgive the hot Scottish worm. Not allowed, Emery.

Shoulders bunched, he averted his attention to the wood floor. "I'm afraid that's what I do. Find a partner for the evening and satisfy our mutual needs with an hour or so of uncomplicated sex."

"Uncomplicated?" I narrowed my gaze on him as the rest of what he'd said sunk into my brain. "Wait a minute. An hour? You stayed until dawn."

"Ah, yes." He winced, shoving his hands in the pockets of his slacks. "I hadn't intended to stay, but…Donnae know."

"Hmmm." I stalked to the nearest chair, the one he'd backed me up to last night when he stripped me naked. I flopped onto the cushioned crimson seat, my hands on the arms, and drummed my fingers. "With those other women, the ones you bang for an hour, do you say goodbye before you scurry off?"

"Yes." He meandered to the chair opposite mine, a striped armchair with wood trim, and settled his bulk onto it. Perched on the chair's edge, he wedged his elbows on his thighs and scrutinized the spiffy rug at his feet. "I indulge in the occasional fling with a stranger. I'm not interested in relationships anymore, but I have…needs."

"Uh-huh." I swung one leg up to cross it over the other. "You're a big old horndog, I get it. You prey on women you think are desperate and lonely."

"No." He spoke the word in a harsh tone, but his anger seemed more self-directed than aimed at me. He turned his head to the side. "I choose professional women."

A spike of cold lanced through me, and the leg raised on the other dropped to the floor. "You thought I was a hooker?"

His face blanked briefly but then amusement dimpled his cheeks—and he chuckled.

I huffed. "You think that's funny? Listen up, buddy, I am not for sale."

"You misunderstand." He leaned back in his chair, smiling at me like I'd told a good joke. "I meant women who have successful careers, the kind who have no time for relationships and want what I want. A casual encounter with no strings and no future."

Oh. That kind of professional. I remembered now he'd talked about "professional" women last night, when I'd told him what I did for a living. Maybe I was still a bit touchy about the anonymous-sex-and-abandonment thing. Not that I wanted a relationship with this guy. I did not like players. They were trouble with a capital T and a flashing exclamation point.

I glanced down at my shirt. "If you like professional women, why'd you pick me last night? A geek in a ComicCon T-shirt."

"You aren't a geek."

"I am a proud geek, a computer programmer who loves fantasy and science fiction movies. I don't have a high-powered career. I love to dress up in sexy costumes for Halloween or just to go to the Renaissance fair." I clasped my hands on my lap, suddenly wondering why the hell I'd told him all that. "The point is, I'm no professional in search of a quick fling."

He gave me an appraising look. "Do you often follow strangers to their hotel rooms?"

"No, of course not." I slouched in my chair. "I've never had a one-night stand before. Certainly never had sex with an anonymous stranger. I like to have fun, be wild and crazy, but even I've got my limits."

Oversharing again, but I couldn't seem to shut my mouth. Anxiety did this to me, always had. I'd blab away until I'd expelled all the nervous energy.

He observed me for so long, without blinking, that my skin itched from the magnitude of his concentration. At last, he gusted out a breath, slapped his hands on his thighs, and heaved his body off the armchair. He strode to my chair, offering me a hand.

"Up," he said.

Seriously? Up? I frowned. "I'm not a dog, you know. I don't heel on command."

"I'm aware of that." He took hold of my right hand. "Please stand."

"Why?"

"Are you always this suspicious?"

I raised my eyebrows. "Only of men who won't tell me their names."

He knelt before me, his eyes at my level and his gaze steady, then held out his hand again—this time as if to shake mine. "Rory MacTaggart."

"Emery Granger." I slipped my cold palm into his warm one, and he gave mine a gentle shake, his long and sinewy fingers curling around my hand. A little shiver of awareness rippled through me, but I refused to allow another flashback to last night. So, I cleared my throat. "Nice to meet you."

His luscious mouth formed a faint smile. "Nice to meet you too, Emery. You have a lovely name."

"Thanks." My hand enveloped by his, I swallowed against a disconcerting tightness in my throat and blurted out the next thing that popped into my brain. "Why were you wearing a kilt last night?"

Today, he wore gray slacks and a gray dress shirt that conformed to his sensual body. No matter what he wore, he looked classy and entirely lickable.

Rory gave a little half shrug, tipping his head to the side. "I like wearing kilts. They're quite comfortable, and they represent my heritage. Of which I am very proud."

I bit the inside of my lip, unable to prevent my gaze from wandering over his broad chest. "You look good in a kilt. But I like this businessman kind of stuff too."

He lifted my hand and touched his lips to my knuckles. "I know I said it would be one night but…May I see you again?"

I straightened in my chair, wishing to hell I'd brought my purse so I could comb out my hair. Did I want to see more of Rory? He wasn't my usual type, not being a geek—and I prayed he wasn't obsessed with Internet porn—but he must have some kind of problems. No man this hot and this charming could be playing with a full deck.

But dear God, I did want to see more of him. Badly. Something about him intrigued me, in ways I'd never experienced before. More than sex. More than his gorgeous bod. I wanted to know the man underneath the delectable surface. If we stuck to public places with lots of other people around…Then again, if he'd wanted to hurt me he could've done it while I slept.

And besides, I could always bolt at the first sign of nutso behavior.

His breaths whispered over my knuckles, sultry and inviting.

"Do you have plans for today?" I asked.

"Not yet."

What kind of wild child would I be if I shunned an opportunity to spend the day with an alluring and intriguing man?

"Okay then," I said. "Come sightseeing with me."

"Sightseeing?"

"Don't you have that in Scotland?" With one finger, I tickled his lips. "Sightseeing is when you go to various locations to stare at a bunch of old junk or to admire the scenery, or maybe to make fun of goofy little niche museums. It's corny and cheesy and all that jazz. Geeks like me live for it."

He released my hand, placing both of his on my knees. "All right. Let's go sightseeing."

"Awesome." I moved to get up and he rose too, stepping backward to give me room. I gave him a playful smile. "Hope you're ready to party hearty."

His restrained smile tightened his closed lips and sparkled in his mesmerizing eyes. "One question first."

"Shoot."

Rory waved a finger at my shirt. "What is ComicCon?"

Chapter Five

I kicked back on the sofa cross-legged and barefoot, tucked into the corner but angled toward my new…friend…companion…whatever. Rory sat straight and tall at the opposite end, facing forward with the soles of his shiny loafers planted on the rug. He held a plate of praline pancakes in one hand, while with his other hand he brandished a fork, intent on eating with dignity.

Me? I gobbled up my pancakes without worrying about mess or decorum. Rory monitored my progress with odd fascination while I hacked up the short stack, slathered the whole pile of bite-size chunks with an abundance of real maple syrup, and shoveled them into my mouth. The whipped cream on top smeared on my lips, but I licked it off with long glides of my tongue.

When syrup dribbled down my chin, he asked, sounding rather bemused, "Why do you eat this way?"

"Because I'm starving," I replied mid-chew. Swallowing, I swiped away the syrup on my chin with a cloth napkin. "Never got around to eating dinner last night. My flight was delayed, and after checking in at my motel and taking a cab to Pat O'Brien's, I barely had time to taste my first Hurricane before a certain foreigner seduced me."

Rory winced as if it were his fault I'd skipped dinner. Before I could assure him it wasn't, he asked, "What is a Hurricane?"

"The signature drink at Pat O'Brien's. It was invented there. Didn't anybody tell you?"

"I wasn't interested in the bar's history." He fidgeted at his end of the sofa, and his as-yet-untouched plate of pancakes wobbled. Steadying it with one hand, he said, "I walked into the main bar at Pat O'Brien's ten minutes before I approached you. I was looking for company, not a strange red cocktail."

"The Hurricane is yummy. You missed out." I scarfed down another mouthful of breakfast and swigged my glass of whole milk. What a bad girl I was, flouting the rules of healthy eating. I dabbed my mouth with the napkin. "By company, you mean you were on the hunt for a professional woman to screw."

"Uh, yes." He fidgeted again, and his plate almost tumbled off his lap. He caught it deftly before the pancakes could spill over the fancy-shmancy sofa on which we sat. "I saw no one who interested me. Then, as I was stepping out into the carriageway, I caught sight of a bonnie lass in the piano bar."

"What happened to her? She turn you down?"

He must've recognized the teasing tone of my voice, because his lips twitched upward at the corners, but only for a second. "Once I saw you, I lost interest in every other woman."

"Mm, I get it." Spearing a bite of pancake, I pointed at him with my fork. "You've got a fetish for geeks wearing ComicCon T-shirts and worn jeans, and who haven't showered or brushed their hair."

Hadn't brushed my teeth either, or shaved my legs, or put on make-up. While waiting for our breakfast to arrive, I'd taken a shower, shaved, detangled, and brushed both teeth and hair. Rory had called someone—a concierge, I guessed—and asked for "toiletries for a woman," which turned out to include everything I needed.

"I have a fetish for beautiful women with stunning smiles and even more stunning eyes." He swept his gaze over my body, his eyes alight with sizzling interest. "And a breathtaking body I couldnae wait to plunder."

"Plunder? You sound like a pirate." Though I joked with him, and I did find his language peculiar at times, I couldn't deny the response from my body. It softened and warmed at his compliments, and from the desire evident on his face. "Seriously, why pick me? You could've hooked up with any one of the hot little numbers strutting their stuff in that bar. I'm confused about why you'd pick me, the girl who'd just stumbled off an airliner. I hadn't even shaved my stubbly legs."

Why oh why did I tell him that? In his presence, I lost the ability to filter my thoughts before blurting them out.

He shrugged one shoulder. "Your legs seemed fine to me when I was fondling you from head to toe."

Oh, I remembered that with vivid detail. His hands, everywhere, mapping out my body with delicate, sensuous movements. And he hadn't noticed the light stubble on my legs? Sure, I'd shaved Thursday, but—*Stop obsessing, woman, that's an order.*

I gave up on worrying about his opinion of my girlie grooming, or lack thereof, since he didn't seem to give a hoot.

Rory began to eat the plate of pancakes balanced atop his thigh. With the precision and efficiency of a surgeon, he cut the short stack into square pieces of equal size, stacked them on one side of the plate, and poured a small puddle of syrup onto the other side of the plate. After that, he proceeded to consume the meal one bite at a time, dipping each piece into the syrup without dripping any of it. He tapped his fork on the plate to make sure no excess syrup clung to the bite, then he slid the fork into his mouth and withdrew it, empty, without getting one tiny speck of gooey liquid on his lips.

Watching him distracted me from all other thoughts, because I'd never seen anyone eat that way. I pulled out my phone to snap a picture of him.

He noticed, his mouth warping. "Are you taking my picture?"

"Uh-huh. Gotta document this. Never seen anybody eat the way you do." I peeked over the screen at him. "Do you mind?"

"Do what you want."

I took the picture. "You're very photogenic."

He grunted.

Once I finished my breakfast, I settled in to watch him. After a couple minutes, when he'd taken his fourth bite of food, I said, "You're fanatical about not getting even one molecule of food on your spiffy clothes, aren't you?"

"Messes are unpleasant," he said. "Though not to you, clearly."

"Are you implying I'm a slob?"

"Not at all. I admire your enthusiasm."

"Thank you." I scuttled across the sofa on my butt until my knees nudged his leg. "I admire your efficiency, the way you eat with surgical precision. It's so cute." Though he opened his mouth, I didn't give him a chance to balk. "But you're kind of missing the point of eating pancakes."

"Am I?" He slid another mouthful between his lips.

"Definitely. If you don't spill any syrup on yourself, how can I lick it off?"

He froze with the fork lifted to his lips, a pancake square pierced by its tines, his unblinking gaze on me. "What?"

"Let me show you."

I plucked the fork from his fingers and dunked the pancake piece into the syrup. Heedless of the sticky liquid threatening to dribble off the fork, I raised it to his mouth and skimmed the drenched bite of food across his lips to glaze them with sugary goodness. A drop of syrup rolled off the fork onto his chin. I held the fork out to the side and sloped toward him.

He kept so still I wondered if he'd stopped breathing.

I thrust my tongue out to rake it over his lips and then drag it down to lap up the syrup on his chin.

Rory stared at me, eyes wide.

I licked away the last iota of syrup. Leaning back, I raised the loaded fork to his mouth. "Eat up, Rory. You'll need lots of carbs to keep up with me today."

He stared at me some more, his breaths growing heavy.

I waggled the fork. "Don't you want another bite of soft, succulent flesh drenched with liquid?"

From the way his pupils dilated, I knew he'd understood my double entendre. My thoughts flashed back to last night, when he'd plunged into my soft, succulent, drenched flesh. I'd burned for him to taste me, but he never had. Now, he looked like a man desperate to lunge his head between my thighs and devour me.

My clit pulsed at the mere idea of it.

Rory lunged his head forward, but not to devour me. He opened his mouth and enclosed the entire pancake square and all the fork tines, sealing his lips around them. I pulled the fork away, leaving the food in his mouth. He chewed with the fervor of a man starved for days.

He swallowed—without completely chewing up his food, it seemed— and all but tossed his plate onto the coffee table. It smacked down, the perfect squares of pancake jiggling. He slung an arm around my waist, stunning a gasp from me, and silenced my startled exhalation with his mouth. Those lips, sticky and faintly sweet from the syrup, fitted to mine and I surrendered to the pleasure of his tongue forging deep into my mouth. I moaned, going limp against him, answering every lash of his tongue with my own, even as my hands rose to bracket his face and my breasts mounded against his chest.

His hands whisked down to my ass and wrenched me closer.

My ears rang from lack of oxygen, what with him consuming me this way, stealing my breath and scattering my thoughts. I swung a leg out, excited by his groping hands as they guided me onto his lap. Straddling him, our mouths still joined, I crushed my body against his and moaned again at the sensations of his hardening erection between my legs, my breasts mashed against his muscles, and the firmness of his thighs beneath me. His fingers kneaded my ass, their tips plunging between my cheeks with each inward thrust.

On instinct, I tipped my hips up so his fingers dived down to graze my sex through my jeans.

Rory grasped my upper arms and pushed me away.

Panting, hot all over and half off his lap, I gaped at him. "Why'd you stop?"

He hooked a finger under my chin. "Didnae want to."

"Then why? It was just getting good."

"Aye, it was." He rested his hands on my hips. "Losing control is not my strong suit."

"On the contrary, you excel at shedding your inhibitions."

He ran a hand over his jaw, switching his attention to a far corner of the room. "I don't normally behave like a randy virgin." One corner of his mouth twisted downward. "Until last night. Twice I've lost control with you, and twice I…didnae want to stop."

"Why did you stop? If you liked it."

"Told ye. Cannae abide a loss of control." With an ease that delighted a secret part of me, he took hold of my waist and hoisted me off his lap to set me down beside him. He glanced at my ComicCon T-shirt. "We should get you to your hotel. You must want a change of clothes."

Change of underwear, for sure. "Yeah, I would."

With a solitary finger, he traced the outline of the ComicCon logo on my shirt.

Earlier, after he ordered our breakfast, I'd attempted to explain Comic-Con to him. First, Rory had tried to define it himself.

Brows furrowed, he'd asked, "Is it a gathering of comedians?"

"Not that kind of comic." I'd wandered to the pool table, running my fingers over the felt surface. "It started out as a convention for fans of comic books, but these days it includes various kinds of popular culture not directly related to comics. Sci-fi and fantasy are popular topics. And there's a cool contest for masquerade costumes."

Rory's lip curled, even as he continued to appear baffled. "Costumes. I cannae fathom why grown men and women want to dress up in silly outfits."

I smiled. "Everybody could use a bit of silly in their life."

He pulled a face, then straightened as if a steel rod had been shoved up his spine. "Do you wear costumes?"

"On Halloween and at ComicCon, yes." I sighed wistfully, recalling my last Halloween costume. "At the office party, my co-workers gave me a rinky-dink certificate declaring my costume the sexiest and skimpiest of all."

"Sexy and skimpy?" His voice had gone husky, full of unrequited thirst.

"Absolutely. Halloween is my favorite holiday because dressing up is so much fun." I stroked my fingers over the crimson felt, imagining I was caressing him. "If you're super nice to me, I might show you photos of my costumes."

He gulped, his Adam's apple bouncing. "You place a high value on fun, don't you?"

"Sure do." I grabbed the eight ball, rolling it between my palms as I leaned a hip against the table. "I'm getting the impression you don't."

"It's a waste of time."

Wow, that had to be the saddest thing I'd ever heard. Or at least in the top ten.

I touched the eight ball to my cheek, its smooth surface cool on my skin. "What's your favorite thing to do? Favorite in the whole wide world?"

"Work."

My jaw must've dropped, because a sudden breeze rushed in to chill my teeth. "You've got to be kidding."

"No." His mouth slid into a suggestive smirk. "Fucking is a close second."

"Only second?" I placed the eight ball on the table. "Seems to me that ought to be first on your list. I mean, you were so into it last night."

"Yes, but work is my passion."

Beg to differ, Mr. MacTaggart. I'd experienced his passion at length, and it had nothing to do with earning a living.

"That is so sad," I told him, and flicked my finger to set the eight ball rolling across the felt. "Why are you in New Orleans? Business?"

"I'm visiting an American friend who's in the same line of work."

"Which is?"

He coughed and glanced out the windows at the view of Bourbon Street below. When he returned his gaze to me, he conspicuously evaded my question. "Why are you in New Orleans? For fun?"

"Naturally." I sashayed up to him, so close I had to bend my head back to behold his eyes. "I got enough work at work. This is a vacation. According to everyone but you, vacation is defined as traveling with no useful purpose, solely to have a good time."

"I see." He tapped a fingertip on my lips. "How long are you here?"

"Leaving on the red-eye tomorrow night."

"Then I have two days with you." He touched his puckered lips to mine, the kiss chaste and tender. "Two days to plumb the depths of the mystery that is Emery Granger."

So, I mystified him as much as he mystified me. Mutual mystery-plumbing sounded like a spectacular way to spend my two days and one more night in New Orleans, a city as exotic and captivating as the Scotsman hovering inches away from me.

"Plumb away," I said in the sultriest voice I could muster.

He leaned in as if to kiss me but only teased my lips with his breath. "I look forward to it."

Back in the here and now, Rory unfolded his brawny yet lithe body from the sofa and offered me his hand. "To your hotel."

"Um, it's more of a hostel than a hotel." I accepted his help in getting up off the sofa. "Nowhere near as swanky as this pad."

He shrugged. "Money isn't important."

"Says the guy who probably has his own private Fort Knox."

He pressed his lips together and hissed a breath out his nostrils. "I need a change of clothes before we leave."

"Yeah, you're not really dressed for a freewheeling day of sightseeing. Of course, a billionaire can get away with wearing anything, I guess."

"I'm not a billionaire." He moseyed toward the bedroom door. "Only a millionaire several times over."

I tried to speak but eked out nothing more than a croak.

He disappeared into the bedroom.

Last night, I'd slept with a multimillionaire. The thought kept me glued to the spot where he'd deposited me after lifting me off the sofa.

Rory emerged from the bedroom several minutes later wearing deep-blue jeans that sported sharp creases indicative of a professional pressing and a champagne-colored T-shirt that complemented his eyes. The clothing clung to his taut body, accentuating the lines of every muscle.

He cocked his head at me. "Are you ready?"

I nodded, unable to speak. Not only was he rich, but he always looked good enough to lick, nibble, and pet for hours and hours.

Rory clasped my hand and led me out of the suite. As we strolled into the elevator, he bent his head to whisper in my ear. "I'm yours for the weekend. What will you do with me?"

My brain revved up at last, and I smiled. "Show you how to loosen up and have fun."

"An impossible task. I dislike what most people consider to be fun."

"Lucky for you, I like a challenge."

Chapter Six

Spending the day with a man I'd met last night, a man from another country who prized control and order above all else, proved an unusual experience. Not bad. Just unusual. Rory had at least two, possibly three, distinct facets to his personality. Though they intersected, one took precedence at any given time—though not always the same one. Last night, I'd gone to bed with the irresistible Scot who refused to tell me his name, a master at pleasuring a woman. This morning, I'd met what seemed like the dominant side of his personality, the regular guy who'd forgotten how to relax and enjoy life.

I'd also glimpsed another side of him, the serious and laser-focused multimillionaire. With only a glimpse of that man to go by, I couldn't quite figure him out. My paranoid side wondered why he wouldn't tell me what he did for a living, even after asserting work was his number-one passion in life. As for the seductive side of him, I understood what that part of Rory wanted. Uncomplicated sex, over in less than a night.

Except he'd stuck around this time, with me.

Which led me back to regular Rory, the most fundamental part of him. That guy had no clue why he'd come back to the hotel room hoping to see me again. He also couldn't comprehend the real me. Emery the silly. Emery the slightly crazy. Emery who mystified a big, hunky Scot.

Did I really want to get tangled up with a guy this complicated?

No tangling going on here, no way. I would fly home tomorrow night and never see this man again. Sightseeing was more fun with a friend. Nothing else going on here, just a little companionship for the weekend.

Our visit to my "hotel" stretched Rory's slender adventurous streak to the point of snapping. The Quisby was an offbeat hostel that occupied a historic building with the original Audubon Hotel sign on its front. Rory developed a semi-permanent crease between his brows, right over his nose, when I took him to the room I shared with three other women, a room equipped with two bunk beds.

When I told him two of my roommates were called Stevie and Ronnie, his jaw went slack. "You share a room with men?"

I shook my head, struggling not to laugh. "Chill out. This is a girls-only dorm. Besides, I'm not into orgies."

Though he seemed relieved, he resorted to pacing the length of the room while I retreated into the bathroom to swap out my clothes. I returned a few minutes later to find Rory examining the room from his position near the door, his hands linked behind his back. His expression brightened from uncomfortable to interested. Very interested.

I raised my arms and twirled for him. "Like my duds?"

"Aye," he said, his voice deep and decadently sensual. He strode toward me, his long legs spanning the distance in two steps. "I like it very much."

Figured he would. My denim shorts exposed most of my legs, and the neon-pink T-shirt I'd selected featured short sleeves and a low neckline. An image of brightly colored flowers sprayed across the shirt's front. Sneakers and pink ankle socks completed the ensemble. I'd pulled my hair back in a ponytail, secured with—what else—a pink scrunchy.

Rory glided the back of one finger up my arm, from my wrist to my shoulder, where the extra-short sleeve of my T-shirt ended. "I liked the ComicCon shirt, but this one suits you better. It's full of color and life, like you."

A rush of warmth weakened my knees, and all I could think of was how desperately I wanted him to take me. Right here, right now. On the bunk bed.

He wouldn't have fit on the bunk bed, though.

Rory hooked a finger inside the neckline of my shirt and peered down into the space between my breasts. "No cash?"

I held up my pink clutch. "Got a purse today."

"Ah." He traced my neckline with the tip of his finger. "Stay with me tonight. You'll have more room and privacy."

"I don't know." *Yes, oh God yes, I'd love it*, my body screamed. He didn't seem to notice the outburst from my raging hormones.

"Please. I have no expectations, for sex or anything else." He cleared his throat. "I would very much like to have another night with you."

"I'll consider it."

He linked his hands behind his back again and nodded. "Good."

Five minutes later, we climbed inside his luxury rental car. Rory navigated the sedan down the streets of NOLA with the same focus and precision he'd applied to eating pancakes. We'd rounded one corner when I piped up with the answer I'd known all along, though my stubborn streak had kept me from saying so.

"Yes," I said, "I'd love to stay with you tonight."

His lips peeled back from his teeth, but he squelched his grin before it had a chance to take hold. Composure reasserted, he spoke in a matter-of-fact tone. "I'm sure you'll be more comfortable at the Ritz-Carlton."

I hadn't missed his almost grin, or the exultation it implied. The goofy, girlie part of me loved knowing he wanted me around so much the desire threatened his cherished self-control.

Despite that need for control, he let me pick the destinations for our sightseeing tour. I whipped out my phone periodically to photograph his bafflement. The voodoo museum in the French Quarter tested his ability to adapt, or at least to mask his unease, especially when we explored the display of fat candles in glass holders, which bore images of voodoo deities with names like Elaggua. After that, I took pity on my stuffy Scot and suggested we stop in at a less-exotic museum, the Historic New Orleans Collection.

The assemblage of seven historic buildings seemed more his speed, and he took to the exhibits with a fascination that twinkled in his beautiful eyes. We surveyed the displays of period clothing and weapons, oohed and ahhed at the restoration work on the buildings, studied the artwork on display, and got our exercise strolling from one building to another. Rory grew more at ease the more we explored the buildings and got rather animated when discussing the nifty period furnishings. My guy had a thing for old-timey swag. It was totally adorable.

Not my guy. Why on earth had I thought of him that way? My companion for a day or two, that's what he was.

After a trip to the National World War II Museum, where Rory regaled me with stories of his grandfather's aerial exploits during the war, I needed a break from the past. As much as I dug history, the time had come for fun of a more tangible variety.

Outside the war museum, I stopped him with a hand on his arm.

He gazed down at me, brows lifted.

"We've done the history thing," I said. "Are you up for something a bit more audacious?"

"This would be your attempt to make me have fun."

"Yep." I slipped my arm under his, looping it around his bicep. "Think you can handle it?"

"I can." He ducked his head to meet my gaze. "If you're expecting me to become more like you, I'm afraid you'll be disappointed."

"Like me?" I nudged him with my elbow. "What am I like?"

"You are open and free, unafraid of what anyone thinks of you. I admire that, but I will never be like you."

"Do you want to be?"

He raised his head, lips working as if he were mulling his answer. After a moment, he resumed his collected demeanor. "I'm comfortable the way I am."

I noted he hadn't said no. Being comfortable with the status quo didn't mean he wanted to stay that way. As we headed for his rental car, I wondered if Rory had invited me—silently, even subconsciously—to show him the benefits of being like me.

With some effort, I convinced Rory we should have lunch at SoBou, a Cajun restaurant in the French Quarter. I cajoled him into trying gumbo with me, though I'd never had the soup before. Rory seemed to like it, grudgingly, but when I offered him a bite of my oyster taco, he reared back as if I'd shoved a rotting squirrel corpse in his face.

Lip curled, he said, "No thank you."

I waved the taco in front of his mouth. "Come on, Rory, live a little. One bite won't kill you."

"Oysters can be appealing, but not in a...taco." He spoke the word with a disdainful tone, then barred his arms over his chest. "Again, no thank you."

"This is a vacation day. Take a risk." I touched the taco to his lips. "One teeny bite."

He rolled his eyes heavenward, sighed, and lowered his arms. "All right."

Leaning forward, he took a dainty bite of the taco and chewed with extreme care, like he thought the food might explode in his mouth. He swallowed and sank back in his chair. "Happy?"

"Yes. Wasn't awful, was it?"

"Not entirely." A mischievous glint sparkled in his eyes. "You do realize oysters are thought to be an aphrodisiac."

"Guess you'll find out later if that's true."

I'd gotten Rory to try something new. Check off one box on my to-do list for getting him to loosen up.

A new question occurred to me. "How old are you?"

"Thirty-nine. I'll be forty in a month or so."

I gave him an assessing glance. "You don't look forty, but you act ninety."

"Thank you," he said crisply, the twinkling in his eyes a contrast to his tone.

"Don't worry," I said, "your stuffiness is cute, and kind of a turn-on."

"I feel the same way about your silliness."

Once we'd finished our meal, I hopped up from my chair. "Buckle up, we're off to our next stop."

Rory got up and stretched. "What now?"

"I want to drive a Lamborghini at over a hundred miles an hour." I grabbed his hand. "Come on, there's a place where you can do that."

His eyes bulged, and his face went slack.

"Relax," I said. "You can sit and watch while I take all the risks. Or, you could be my copilot. How brave are you, Mr. MacTaggart?"

"Not that brave."

Chapter Seven

I reclined on the sofa in Rory's suite, my feet propped on the coffee table, my tummy full of good food—meaning everything a nutritionist would label as unhealthy. Rory had gone the boring-health-food route, ordering a Cobb salad. I chose an enormous ribeye steak, and to my surprise, Rory made no comment on my selection.

His salad lay half eaten on the table.

My plate was empty, both because I'd been starving and because he had eaten a good portion of it. Stealing my food might've qualified as shunning propriety, except he'd politely asked my permission to taste my steak. Ah well, at least I'd gotten him to eat something other than salad. I liked a nice salad as much as anybody, but after a day of walking and seeing the sights and driving a supercar, I needed serious protein.

For dessert, we'd shared a large piece of cheesecake. Two forks, of course. And he wouldn't let me feed him.

Now I lounged on the sofa waiting for him to return from the bathroom. Our trip to the Xtreme Xperience had left him shell-shocked, I decided. While he'd observed from the stands, I'd donned a helmet and strapped in behind the wheel of a genuine Lamborghini. After a half-hour training session, I'd taken the supercar for a wild spin on the racetrack, with my instructor in the passenger seat. Three laps. *Zeee-oom. Zeee-oom. Zeee-oom.* When I'd finished, Rory had looked sick.

I'd patted his shoulders and said, "You weren't even in the car, and you look like you're about to throw up."

"You were driving very fast," he'd said, his voice a little shaky. "I was sure you'd crash into the wall and die in a hellish explosion."

Rory had feared for my well-being? A warm glow spread through my chest, and I couldn't stop myself from saying, "You are so sweet to worry about me."

He scowled. "I'd worry about anyone as reckless as you."

"It's adorably sweet, Rory."

"Stop calling me adorable and cute and sweet." His scowl had mutated into an exasperated look. "I'm a man, not a kitten."

When the man-not-kitten at last emerged from the bedroom doorway, I was in the midst of a big yawn.

"Long day," he said, leaning against the doorjamb. "Time for bed."

I stretched my entire body, arms above my head and toes extended. "Mm, yes, bedtime sounds good."

He drank in the length of me, from my bare arms and cleavage to the exposed expanse of my legs and my socked feet. His tongue darted out to slicken his lips, but when he looked at my face again, he maintained a neutral expression. "No sex tonight. You're exhausted, and so am I."

"We can perk each other up." I waggled my toes, lifting one foot to point my big toe at him. "Unless you're afraid you'll lose control again."

"I won't." He crooked a finger at me. "Come, lass. Time for sleep."

The way he'd amended the statement from bed to sleep might've disappointed me, if I weren't yawning again. This day had proved invigorating—and yes, fun—but I'd gotten more and more tired the longer I sat here. He was right. We both needed sleep.

Sharing a bed without any steaminess involved felt more intimate than getting down and dirty together.

Rory crooked his finger again.

I rose and stretched one more time, boosting up onto my tiptoes, and slapped my heels back down on the floor on another yawn. "We spent the day together, and now we're spending the night together with no sex. Sounds an awful lot like dating, wouldn't you say?"

"I don't date anymore."

Hands on my hips, I canted my head. "What do you call this?"

Rory scratched his cheek. "A casual fling, I suppose."

I strolled across the room to him and laid a hand on his shoulder. "Nothing about today was casual."

He speared me with a sharp look. "For me, it was."

Bullshit, my inner voice said. But if the guy needed to dismiss our day of fun and bonding in order to make himself feel safe, I wouldn't begrudge him his crutch. I'd met the real Rory today, and that man wanted to come out and play more often. The mystery of why he retreated into stoic mode intrigued me more than seemed healthy. I wasn't dumb enough to believe I could change him. His desire to spend a day with me, possibly two days if we stayed together tomorrow, suggested to me he wanted to shed his uptight facade.

I couldn't change him, but maybe I could help him.

The question was, should I?

My mouth gaped open on yet another yawn. I'd answer that question tomorrow. Right after I figured out whether he really wanted my help.

A fourth noisy yawn overtook me.

Rory swept me up in his arms and carried me to the bed, plunking me on my feet beside it. "Get ready for bed. For sleep."

"Aye-aye, sir." I saluted, earning a tiny upward tick of his lips.

He marched around the foot of the bed, yanked the drapes closed, and dug his wallet out of his pants pocket to toss it on the bedside table. Sitting down on the edge of the bed, he began to untie his shoelaces.

While he carefully removed his sneakers, I took hold of my shirt's hem to slide it up and over my head.

Rory bolted up off the bed. "What are you doing?"

"I sleep naked." The truth, plain and simple. But I might've been trying to tweak him a little, since he'd declared our day together had been casual and, by extrapolation, meaningless to him. Not that I bought his statement for one nanosecond.

He flung up his hands. "Ye cannae."

Interesting, I thought, how he spoke in a more casual way when he was excited or upset, or very relaxed. Right now, he was panicking.

Dressed in my bra and shorts only, I shook my head. "Honestly, Rory, how can you be such a prude after last night? We were both naked. All night. In this bed."

He shifted his weight from one foot to the other, grasping the back of his neck. His gaze flickered down to my lacy pink bra, his nostrils flared, and he veered his attention to the pillow nearest him.

"Please," he said, "wear something to bed."

"Like what?" I flapped my arms. "Forgot to pack a nightie."

"You were planning to sleep in the nude in your communal hotel room?"

Rory gaped at me like I'd threatened to streak through his upper-crust hotel while screaming his name.

With a frustrated growl, I flung my hands up. "My roommates didn't care. Why should you? For pity's sake, we've had our hands all over each other's naked bodies."

His lips compressed into a slash as he stared at the wall behind me. After a moment, he whipped off his T-shirt and chucked it at me. "Wear this."

I caught the shirt. "Okay, but I have to take off everything else. Not sleeping in my bra, no matter how uncomfortable it makes you."

"Fine." He turned his back to me. "Undress quickly."

"I prefer sleeping naked, anyway. Hard to believe you're the same guy who tore my clothes off right there in the living room last night."

"That was different."

"Because you wanted to get in my pants then."

"I—" He made a noise that was part growl, part hissing sigh. "Change yer bloody clothes, would ye?"

I shimmied out of my shorts and panties, then unhooked my bra and lobbed it at him. It flopped onto his shoulder.

His entire body flinched. He took the garment between his thumb and forefinger with the delicacy of someone handling toxic materials, plucked it up, and dropped it on the floor.

Oh, he was no fun at all tonight. I must've burned out his frivolity circuits today.

I slipped into his shirt, loving the way it smelled like him. "Fit for viewing now, Mr. Fussy Pants."

Rory spun around. He zeroed in on the hem of the shirt where it hung halfway down my thighs.

I plunked one foot on the bed and rolled my sock down, cast it aside, and repeated the procedure with the other foot.

His eyes stayed trained on me the whole time.

I crawled under the covers and stretched out on my side with my head on the pillow. Rory stripped off his jeans and climbed in beside me wearing only his boxers. He fidgeted until he'd situated himself on his side of the bed, facing me, with a gap of a foot between us. I tucked my hands under my cheek on the pillow.

He lighted a fingertip on my upper arm, trailing it back and forth along my skin. "You mentioned you're a computer programmer. What is it you do?"

"Programming, duh." I resisted the impulse to wiggle, despite the way his fingertip stimulated my skin. "It's technical and very, very boring."

"I'd like to know. Do you create software?"

With a restraint that amazed even me, I didn't point out wanting to know about me proved this hadn't been a casual thing today. "I work for Travellis Games, a company that makes software for everything from the latest Kor the Space Viking game to online poker and digital slot machines. I don't really create anything, though. I fix what other people create. Debug code, rejigger scripts, that kind of thing. It's mind-numbing at times and always tedious."

"Why do it if you hate the work?"

"In college, I loved writing code. But the jobs I got after graduation were all programming, not actual creative coding." I sneaked a hand out from under my cheek to pick at the seam of the pillowcase. "Being trapped in a cubicle forty hours or more every week, fixing someone else's creation, it gets to be a real drag after a while."

"You could find another career."

"Not that easy for us non-millionaires. Getting the training for something else takes time and money I don't have." I bit my upper lip to stave off a breathy moan as his finger painted an invisible line of tantalizing sensations up to my shoulder. "My last job paid well enough, but I spent most of my income paying off my student loans. When the bosses ordered everyone to work longer hours, having fun became a rarity in my life."

He moved his hand away from my arm to close it over my fingers where they picked at the pillowcase. "You said your last job paid well, past tense. What about your current job?"

"Don't have one. Got laid off—downsized, as they say." I cuddled deeper into the pillow, and my chin grazed his knuckles. "I'd worked there longer than most of my coworkers, but I was the first to go."

"I'm sorry, Emery." He extended one finger to stroke my chin. "You deserve better."

"Why?"

His brows knit together. "Why? Because—You do, that's all."

Did he like me? I saw no other reason for his behavior.

A dangerous desire flickered in the back of my mind, a craving to spend more than a weekend with him. Yet I knew next to nothing about the man beside me.

"What do you do for a living?" I asked.

He pulled his hand away and rolled onto his back to inspect the bed's canopy. "Nothing interesting."

I tapped his nose until I'd reclaimed his attention. "If you won't tell me your occupation, at least tell me how many times you've had one-night stands."

"Not often," he said in a measured tone.

"How often?"

"Four times." He rolled onto his back. "Including you."

"Only four? I got the impression you do it a lot."

"Why would you think that?"

I shrugged one shoulder, all I *could* shrug while lying on my side. "You were so skilled at seduction, I figured you take strangers to bed all the time."

"No." He pinched the bridge of his nose with his thumb and forefinger. "My brother Aidan has convinced my entire family I travel the world seducing hapless women. No one should ever believe Aidan, though. He thinks it's humorous."

Ahhh, so Rory had at least one sibling. A brother named Aidan. I felt outrageously victorious at discovering this tidbit.

I poked him with my knee. "But you were looking for a professional woman to whisk away to your suite last night."

He punched his pillow in a violent attempt to fluff it. "I meant to have a whiskey, enjoy the music at the bar, and find a companion for the night. I'd given up on the latter. None of the women I met interested me." His gaze flew to mine, his eyes simmering with desire. "Until I saw you."

I couldn't think of a blessed thing to say. Out of all the sexily dressed women in that bar, all the women he might've bumped into on his way there, he'd chosen me. "Why did you come back this morning?"

We stared at each other for a long moment, until he coughed and swerved his gaze to the window. "I have no idea why I couldn't walk away from you."

My curiosity peaked, but I realized he didn't want to talk about this anymore. I changed the subject. "I'd like to hear more about your family."

Rory punched his pillow again. Linked his hands over his belly. Squirmed. Smacked his hands down on the sheets.

"If you'd rather not talk about it," I said, "that's okay."

He rubbed his forehead. "It's all right. I have two brothers, Aidan and Lachlan, as well as three sisters. They are Fiona, Catriona, and Jamie. Lachlan is the oldest, and Jamie is the youngest. I'm second, after Lachlan."

"What about your parents?"

"Alive and well. Most of my family lives in and around the village of Ballachulish in the Highlands, where we were born and raised." He moved only his eyes to look at me. "What about your family?"

"My parents moved to Australia ten years ago, for my dad's work. My sister, Hadley, got married four years ago and moved to Germany. She has beautiful twin girls."

"You must not see your family often."

"Haven't seen any of them since Hadley's wedding."

Rory brushed the back of his hand over my cheek. "I can't imagine never seeing my family. Must be difficult."

"I get by. But yeah, I miss them a lot." A pang pulsated in my chest, behind my ribs. "Since losing my job, I feel more alone than ever. I know they didn't want to leave me, but sometimes I feel like an abandoned child. God, I have no idea why I'm telling you this."

He twined his fingers with mine, studying our joined hands. "Maybe you sense we have something in common. For quite a while, I've felt…lonely. You've provided a welcome distraction, if an unusual one."

"Is that a compliment or an insult?"

"A compliment. You are unusual in the very best way." He lifted an arm and patted the bed between us. Once I'd snuggled up to him, my head on his chest, he placed his arm around me. "You're also beautiful, brave, sensual, ridiculous at times, and you have a wonderfully strange sense of humor."

That lovely glow fired up in my chest again. He'd complimented me in a personal way that belied his claims we had nothing besides casual sex between us.

Right, because I knew him so well after twenty-four hours. *Get a grip, Emery.*

If I had woken up earlier this morning, I would've fled before Rory came back. We wouldn't have been here tonight, and I wouldn't have suffered from delusions of a fairytale romance with a wealthy stranger from a foreign land. One-night stands did not turn into love, except in the movies.

"Sleep," he said.

"Like I can do it on command."

"Try." He sifted his fingers through my hair, soothing me more than any sedative.

I listened to his heart thumping beneath my ear, letting the rhythm of it lull me. "Admit it, you had a teeny bit of fun today."

"Perhaps a little." He skimmed his free hand up and down my arm, nestling his face in my hair. "Rest, Emery."

He began to sing softly in a language I didn't recognize, his voice deep and soothing. "*O chì, chì mi na mòr-bheanna, o chì, chì mi na coireachan, chì mi na sgoran fo cheò.*"

"What is that?" I murmured. "Doesn't sound like English."

"It's Gaelic. A song my mother taught me, called 'The Mist Covered Mountains.' It's about how bonnie Scotland is."

"Sing to me some more, please. You have a wonderful voice."

He hugged me tighter and crooned for me, his voice deep and velvety, masculine yet imbued with a tender longing.

My eyes drifted shut, my body went limp, and my thoughts dwindled into a mental silence broken only by his voice and the achingly beautiful melody he sang to me.

Chapter Eight

When I woke in the morning, the sun had risen high enough in the sky I wondered if I'd slept through the whole morning. A glance at the clock on the bedside table assured me I hadn't. It was eight thirty, though, and I rarely slept this late. Slumbering in the arms of an odd and enticing Scotsman had proved enormously restful.

Rory had left a terrycloth robe at the foot of the bed for me. I ditched his shirt, the one I'd slept in, and donned the robe before ambling out into the living room.

He sat in a high-backed, upholstered chair adjacent to the terrace doors, wearing charcoal slacks and a pale-green dress shirt, his attention focused on the laptop computer balanced on one thigh. Brows lowered, mouth tight, he studied whatever the screen displayed to him. Glasses perched on his nose, reflecting the light from a nearby lamp. So intent was he on his task that he didn't notice me until I crouched in front of him and laid my hands on his knees. Without lifting his head, he glanced up at me.

"Good morning," he said. "Sleep well?"

"Yes, very." I squeezed between his knees, but his computer blocked me from getting as close as I wanted. "Why are you doing boring things on your computer? You should join me for a bath instead."

"How do you know what I'm doing is boring?"

"Because you look tense. If it was interesting—or heaven forbid, fun—you'd look more relaxed." I pushed up on the corner of his mouth with one finger. "Might even smile."

"I'm not on holiday, Emery. This is a work-related trip."

"Come on, it's Sunday. Spend another day with me before I have to go home."

He watched me for a moment, his expression unreadable. Then he tipped his head down to peer at me over the tops of his glasses. "As much as I would enj—appreciate the company, I have to finish this contract."

I sank back on my heels. "Contract? What kind of business are you in?"

"Later, I will explain. You have my word."

"Ugh. It's always later with you." I picked up his computer and set it on the floor. He held motionless while I wriggled between his thighs to twine my arms around his neck. "Be spontaneous, just this once. For me. I'll beg if you want."

His lips twitched, and his eyes sparkled, but he didn't reciprocate my embrace. With his hands on his thighs, he gave a small shake of his head. "Later is the best I can offer."

"What are we going to do later? At least tell me that."

He caught me around my waist and stood up, hoisting me with him. I landed on my feet, and he eased me away from his body. *Spoilsport.*

"Have a bath," he said. "I'll be finished soon."

"And then you'll join me?"

"I will come to you in the bathroom."

Why did I get the feeling he was sidestepping my question? Joining me in the bathroom didn't mean he'd get in the tub with me. I could not understand his reticence to get naked with me again. We'd had sex, for crying out loud. A bath was going too far?

Helpless to resist the chance to tweak him, I undid the sash of my robe and let the terrycloth fall open.

Rory's focus snapped to my breasts. He inhaled a long breath, his body relaxing as he released it. His gaze wandered down to the hairs at the apex of my thighs. He cleared his throat and met my eyes. "Have your bath, Emery."

No mistaking the roughness of his voice or the faint blush in his cheeks.

"I'll do that, Rory."

My robe flounced around me as I spun on my heels and sashayed into the bedroom. I veered around the bed, heading straight into the bathroom. While I got the tub filling, I considered the situation. Before this weekend, I would never have believed a man with Rory's seduction skills could be so uptight outside of the bedroom. He wanted me, but he wouldn't take me even when I all but threw myself at him. I'd told him I would beg if he wanted me to. The disturbing part was I'd meant it. I would beg. I wanted him that much.

A one-night stand, as hot as it had sounded at the time, would've left me feeling empty inside. I'd realized the truth when I woke yesterday to find Rory gone. A full day and another night with the man had made me curious—fascinated, actually—about the mystery that was Rory MacTaggart.

So what if I might've begged him to take me. I would've done it in a sassy, entertaining way that would've made him cringe. In the end, though, I would've gotten my way, because he wanted me with a lust as all-consuming as mine.

I lost track of the time while I soaked in the jacuzzi with bubbles swirling around me. They tickled my skin, and when I raised my knees to spread my legs, the bubbles tickled my sex. I let my head fall back, loving the arousal that burgeoned within me. A memory replayed in my mind, of Rory's hand on my sex and the skillful way his fingers propelled me toward release, the pleasure building like an ocean swell cresting.

Well, if *he* wouldn't touch me...

I snaked a hand between my thighs. My fingers delved between my folds where I was already wet and aching for Rory's touch. I moved my fingers in slow, sure strokes—the way he had done to me the other night, with those strong fingers. The image of him poised above me took hold in my mind, a vivid recollection of his naked and muscular body, and my lust cranked up higher and hotter on a new surge of liquid need. Arching my back, I rubbed my clitoris hard and fast, my breaths shortening into breathy grunts.

Someone rapped on the bathroom door.

I froze, my hand motionless though pressed to my swollen flesh, and struggled to catch my breath. "Yes?"

"May I come in?" Rory asked.

Panic iced through me, but then I realized I had nothing to hide. If he took one look at me and figured out what I'd been doing, maybe he'd jump in the tub with me after all.

"Yeah, come on in," I said, removing my hand from my groin. I rested my arms on the tub's sides, my legs outstretched.

The door swung inward, and Rory stepped inside the bathroom. He halted alongside the tub, near my feet. Unlike last night, when I'd shocked him with my intention to disrobe in his presence, this morning he gave my nude body an assessing glance. His lips kinked into that repressed smile of his, a barely perceptible indication of interest.

He ran one fingertip along the tub's rim. Slowly. Sensuously.

Oh yeah, it was more than interest.

"Enjoying the amenities?" he asked.

"Absolutely." I raised one knee, swishing it to make the water splash high enough to lap at his finger. "What's the point of staying in a luxury hotel if you don't avail yourself of its pleasures?"

He tipped his head to the side, his focus gravitating to my sex, visible every time my knee swished to the right. The rich brown of his eyes seemed to darken and smolder with desire. Though he lifted his head to stare at the opposite wall, his gaze kept flitting to my body.

"Out of the tub, please," he said gruffly. "I need to speak with you."

"We can talk here." I braced my ankle on the tub's rim, poking his leg with my toes. "Hop on in."

"No thank you." He leaned his leg against the tub, probably an unconscious action, and folded his arms over his chest. Those thick biceps bulged a little more. "I will wait for you in the dining room."

I feigned a pout. "You're no fun."

"Yes, I stipulate that fact."

Stipulate the fact? I squinted at him for a moment, wondering for the umpteenth time what kind of job he had. He talked in such a formal way sometimes.

I lifted my leg, stretching my toes in an attempt to reach his arm, but I couldn't quite get there. Foiled, I wiggled my damp toes in the air near his hip. "I'd rather have a conversation in this tub. I think better naked."

He choked on what sounded like a laugh that he managed to squelch. "I rather doubt it. Even if it's true, I will not think properly while naked in a tub with you."

I smiled, reveling in his admission. "You're that hot for me. Wow, I'm super flattered."

Rory snared my foot with his hand, and his thumb traced circles on the ball. "As tempting as you are, I need to discuss a serious matter with you." His thumb drifted down the side of my foot, following the sensitive flesh at the edge of my sole. "We'll talk in the dining room."

With another fake pout, I let my arms splash down into the water. "If you insist."

"I do." He released my foot and moved to the door. "And put on some clothing, please."

I admired his gorgeous backside as he strode across the bedroom to the doorway. His sculpted ass flexed under his slacks, but I lost my view of those fine glutes when he exited the bedroom. I climbed out of the tub, dried off, and strolled into the bedroom to dig some clothes out of my suitcase. Since we were having a "serious" conversation, I chose indigo-blue jeans and a sunny yellow peasant top.

No cleavage exposed, so Rory could concentrate.

What he wanted to discuss with me, I couldn't even guess.

In the dining room, I discovered him seated at one end of the rectangular wood table. Though a golden-colored chandelier hung suspended above the table's center, most of the light came from the two windows. A white pot in the middle of the table held pretty purple flowers.

Rory had placed a little stack of papers on the shiny tabletop. A small, rectangular black box beside his laptop spit out more sheets.

A portable printer. *Nice.*

The printer completed its task, falling silent. Rory added the newly printed sheets to his perfect stack.

"Have a seat," he said, waving toward the chair at the opposite end of the table.

Okay, I wasn't allowed to sit beside him. *Whatever.*

I pulled the chair out, plunked my butt onto its cushioned seat, and propped my feet on the table. My elbows on the chair's arms, I linked my hands over my belly.

Rory's mouth scrunched up, but he made no comment on my pose.

"What's up?" I asked.

He tapped his fingers on the table but avoided looking at me. "What were you doing in the bathroom when I knocked? I heard noises."

"Oh, that." I grinned. "Since you wouldn't join me, I decided to have a good time all by myself. I was seconds away from my happy ending when you interrupted."

He did a double take. "You were touching yourself?"

"Bingo," I said. "You must've suspected as much, or you wouldn't have asked what I was doing."

He squared his shoulders, re-stacked his perfectly stacked papers, and reasserted his impenetrable expression. "I simply can't understand why you would do that in the daytime."

I clamped my teeth over my lips in an attempt to keep from laughing. He'd take it as an insult, but really, I found his discombobulation to be the cutest thing ever. "It's okay, Rory. I like your hang-ups. Makes me want to nibble them away one by one with my teeth, my tongue, my lips, my—"

"Enough. I've deduced your meaning."

Damn if his stuffy language didn't make me want to crawl across the table to start that nibbling campaign right away.

"Is this what you wanted to talk about?" I asked. "Whether I masturbate in the tub, in the daytime, while you're standing outside the door. Bet you were listening at the keyhole."

"There is no keyhole on the bathroom door."

"Don't be so literal. I'm cool with you being a lech."

"I am not—Never mind." He snatched up a pen and twirled it around and around his middle finger.

"Out of curiosity," I said, "what do you do for a living?"

"I'm a solicitor."

Wow, he'd answered this time. "That like a pimp?"

He slapped the pen down on the table. "No, it's like a lawyer."

"Chill out, I was kidding. I watch BBC America, I know what a solicitor is." I relaxed into my chair. "And you are a very solicitous solicitor."

Harrumphing, he picked up the papers, rapped them on the table to make their well-aligned tops extra-even, and set the stack down again. "I have an offer for you."

"What kind of offer?"

"One I hope you'll consider." He shut the laptop's lid with a soft click and fiddled with the papers a bit more. "You seem as if you'd be amenable to this sort of—"

"Spit it out, Rory."

He repositioned his hands on his lap and leaned back against his chair. "I want us to marry."

Chapter Nine

Everything seemed to stop moving, from the draft from the air conditioning to the atoms of my body. I must've misheard him. Right? Nobody proposed after thirty-six hours of acquaintance. Did they? And of course, I had to say no. This was insane, and even I had enough sense to turn down a proposal pitched from left field. Didn't I?

Deep down, beneath the surface shock, I kind of wanted to consider it.

Either he'd hypnotized me while I slept, or I'd lost my mind.

"Perhaps I should explain," Rory said.

"Yeah, I think you really should."

Head bowed, he flattened a palm on the tabletop, kinking his fingers and then spreading them. He studied his own reflection on the polished surface of the table. "I've been divorced three times, and I have no desire to marry again."

"So naturally, you propose to me."

His fingers tensed into a claw-like position. "I said I have no desire to marry, but circumstances require that I do."

"This isn't the Middle Ages. People aren't required to get hitched."

"You don't understand." He slumped forward, elbows on the table, hands atop the skinny stack of papers. "In the past two years, both my brothers have married. First Lachlan, then Aidan. This has resulted in my family insisting what I need to set me right is another wife."

"Set you right?" I tipped forward, crossing my arms on the tabletop. "You mean because you're so uptight and pent-up and determined to make yourself miserable when you could be having a rollicking good time?"

Rory stabbed his tongue into the inside of his cheek. "Yes."

"You've decided they're right, and that marrying a stranger is the solution."

He scratched his head. "This will not be a love match. It will be a business arrangement."

"Better explain in more detail, before I run for the phone and call nine-one-one to report a man is kidnapping me for sex slavery."

He rolled his eyes, and with a huff, threw his body against the chair's back. "No slavery of any sort. You are intelligent enough to consider my offer and decide whether to accept it."

"Gee, thanks. But you haven't explained your offer yet."

He steepled his fingers under his chin, elbows balanced on the chair's arms. "I need a wife, to appease my family. As I said, they've grown rather insistent marriage is the cure for what they believe ails me, to the point they've begun to contrive seemingly accidental meetings with eligible young women every time I go out in public. They convinced my housekeeper to bring her divorced daughter to work with her in hopes I'd find her appealing."

"You didn't."

He rested his forehead on his steepled fingers. "She's bonnie, but I'm not interested. Besides, she was a wee bit frightened of me."

"Frightened? Of you?"

"I realize I have no such effect on you, but some people find me intimidating." He glared at the papers he'd left on the table. "The salient fact is this. I tried marrying for love three times, and three times I was...disappointed."

By the way he said it, I got the feeling disappointment was an understatement.

"This time," he continued, "I will marry for pragmatic purposes. If I go home with a new wife on my arm, my family will have no choice but to stop blethering about my personal life. You and I would remain married for one year, then you will leave, and I will tell my family our marriage is over. There will be a legally required one-year separation after that, but you will receive generous compensation as soon as you move out."

"How generous?"

"Five hundred thousand American dollars."

I drew back, most likely slack-jawed, as my arms tumbled off the table onto my lap. "You're paying me half a million bucks to be your wife for a year."

"Precisely. I have more conditions, however." He reached for his papers but changed his mind and took up his pen, twirling it like a gunfighter. "You will live with me, and we will have sexual relations on a regular basis."

My mouth definitely dropped open then.

He raised a placating hand. "Of course, you're free to say no if I want sex and you don't. But I will require it at least twice a week."

Sex. Twice a week. With him. As much as the idea appealed to me, the rest of his cockamamie offer rang alarm bells in my head. The loud, grating kind.

Before I could muster the brainpower to voice my concerns, he went on. "Sex with strangers has been less than fulfilling, and even the risks involved couldn't provide enough stimulation for me. A monogamous arrangement seems the most prudent alternative."

I gripped my chair's arms. "We were strangers the other night, which means you're saying sex with me was less than fulfilling."

"That's not—I meant the others, not you."

"Mm-hm." I glanced at the windows and then at him, confounded and intrigued at the same time. "This is sounding an awful lot like I'll be your live-in prostitute."

"Donnae be ridiculous." A muscle jumped in his jaw. "You will be my wife, with all the benefits of such a relationship."

"Like what?"

"Free access to my financial accounts and the freedom to do whatever you wish." He stood, gathered up his papers, and stalked down the table's length to where I slumped in my chair. Poised on the table's corner, one leg bent, he held the papers facedown on his thigh. In a voice far too enticing for my sanity, he said, "You told me you've spent years working hard to pay off your student loans, and that you had little opportunity for the fun you value so highly. It sounds to me as if you've been stifled by responsibility. For a woman like you that must've been torture."

Damn, he was good. He'd listened to everything I blabbed to him, but more than that, he'd figured out what it all meant.

"Not torture," I said. "I got sick and tired of working forty hours a week—often fifty, sixty, or more—to make my employer rich while I lived in a teeny apartment and never took a single vacation day."

He nodded in understanding, his entrancing eyes fixated on me.

Maybe he did understand me. Rory MacTaggart had to be the most stifled person I'd ever met, but he seemed to have done it to himself. Could that be the real reason he wanted to marry me? Did he hope I'd encourage him to break out of his iron shell?

"What I offer," he said, slanting his body down toward me, "is liberation from those responsibilities. With my wealth, you can do anything you want. Consider it an extended holiday or start your own programming firm if that's what you like."

"Oh no, I've had it with that stuff."

"Discover what you do want. Even after we separate, you'll have a significant amount of money and no need to rush to find employment." He settled a hand on the back of my chair, his face inches above mine, the scent of his spicy aftershave enveloping me. "I'm offering to fund your search, so you can take all the time you need to find your passion."

Gazing up into his eyes, feeling the heat of him so close, I couldn't stop my body from responding. Heat suffused me, from my skin down to the depths of my sex, where he'd claimed me two nights ago and shown me passion and pleasure like none I'd ever known. I had trouble catching my breath, and my body hummed with awareness of him.

Rory dragged a fingertip down my jaw to the corner of my mouth. "Who else can offer you this sort of freedom?"

Ohhh, he was beyond good at this. He was like the devil seducing me into selling him my soul.

"How do I know you'll stick to the bargain?" I asked. "What's to stop you from using me and throwing me away when you get tired of my silliness?"

"This." He proffered his papers to me. "A contract."

"A—huh?" I blinked rapidly, my gaze flitting from the papers to his face several times before I managed to freeze my attention on him. "I don't understand."

"These papers include two documents, a prenuptial agreement and a marriage contract. Combined, they detail our arrangement." He set the papers on my lap. "Read them. Carefully."

"Should I have a lawyer look at this?" Not that I could afford one.

"For the prenuptial agreement, yes. As for the marriage contract, a lawyer would tell you it's unlikely to be enforceable."

"How is the contract different from the prenup?"

"You'll see when you read it."

I looked down at the papers on my lap. "If the contract's not enforceable, what's the point?"

"The contract is a promise between us." Rory ratcheted his spine straight, still perched on the table's edge. "Essentially, these documents obligate you to remain my wife for one year and to perform your marital duties at least twice a week. You will have access to my financial accounts, as I've said, but you are free to open your own accounts should you wish to do so. You further agree to attend social functions and to maintain the pretense we are in love."

A frantic laugh spurted out of me, accompanied by a light spray of spittle that missed Rory by a hair. "Are you serious? I have to pretend we're madly in love. You better hire an actress because I don't think I can be that convincing."

"I believe you can."

He inclined his body to hover low over me, cupping my cheek with one hand. The other palmed my breast through my clothing.

My mouth opened in a silent "oh." I pushed up on the chair's arms, lifting my butt off the seat a fraction.

His lips curled into a hint of a smug smile. "You won't have to fake your reactions to me."

"That's lust, not love."

"No one will notice the difference." He flicked his thumb over my stiffening nipple, shooting a jolt of pleasure straight down to my core. "If you need a bit of encouragement to fulfill your social duties, I can provide it."

Oh great. I'd walk into every family gathering and holiday party so turned on I'd be on the verge of orgasm. But hey, at least his family would buy our story about instant true love.

"I'm still not sure," I said. Waving a finger in a circle in front of his face, I added, "As far as I can tell you've got at least three people living inside that pretty little head of yours. Not sure I can handle psychological bigamy."

"There's no one else in my head. Only me."

"I don't mean actual split personalities. You have these distinct facets to your personality, and they come and go like flipping a switch."

He frowned. "If you think I'm insane—"

"No, that's not what I mean either." I searched his simmering eyes for the answer but failed to find it. "You're very complicated, Rory."

"I've been told as much before. By my family."

A realization iced through me at the mention of loved ones. "What about my family? What am I supposed to tell them?"

"The same thing we tell mine."

"A lie, you mean." I squirmed, uncomfortable with deception but also enduring a sudden, wet ache between my thighs, instigated by his enticing voice and his palm on my breast. "Would you please remove your hand?"

He complied, resting one hand on his thigh and the other on the table.

Sure, my family knew I was unhappy with my life. If I announced I was marrying a man I'd met Friday night, they'd probably jump on the next plane to America and kidnap me, spiriting me away to the nearest mental hospital.

I didn't have to lie. Part of the truth might satisfy them.

Oh shit. I was seriously contemplating his offer.

My mouth went dry. I clenched the marriage contract in my hand. "I need to think about this."

"Take all the time you need." He rose to tower over me. "I can wait in the other room."

"No." I shoved my chair backward and sprang to my feet. "I need to think while I'm away from you, away from your crazy-hot sexiness and charming little idiosyncrasies. I'll change my airline ticket and fly home as soon as I can today."

His head drooped, his shoulders caved in.

"I promise I will think about your proposal." Since he blocked my path to the door, I laid a hand on his chest and pushed. "Please move. You're in my way."

Rory enclosed my hand in his much bigger one. The feel of his sinewy fingers around mine stimulated me in the most distracting way. My Scot was the antidote to rational thought.

Not mine. But he could be. All I had to do was say yes.

He kept my hand caged in his as he backed me up to the table, forcing me to brace my behind against the edge. His knee eased between mine to part my thighs. I gripped the wood in one hand, but nothing could ground me when he was this close.

He pressed my other hand to his chest. "What can I do to convince you?"

"I-I don't know. You're suggesting I marry you for sex and money." I pitched backward but couldn't move far with his hand around mine and the table behind me. "The money I get. But the sex...We only did it the one time. Maybe it'll stink from now on."

His chuckle rumbled in his chest, soft and erotic, vibrating against my palm. "It won't. And for the record, we fucked more than once."

"Twice in a single night. I'm counting that as one time."

"You came three times."

My body softened more the longer he lingered inches away from me. His knee between my thighs had my hips longing to thrust into his blossoming erection. How did he do this to me so easily? One minute he was Mr. MacTaggart, solicitor general of the world. The next he'd transformed into the scorching Scotsman who'd beguiled me into spending the night with a man whose name I hadn't even known.

I wrestled my hand free of his, despite my racing pulse and the ever-growing slickness in my sex. "What did you do, make a spreadsheet to keep track of our sexual encounters? Bet you like spreadsheets. You're so...meticulous."

His lips tightened into a naughty smirk. With his mouth a breath from mine, he murmured, "You make 'spreadsheet' sound filthy."

And just like that, a vision blasted through my mind. Me spread across a sheet with Rory on top of me. A crimson sheet. Silk. Slippery.

His lips teased mine as he spoke. "Stay until the red-eye tonight. I'll show you how meticulous I can be."

Molten heat flooded over my skin, and a mindless hunger pulsated inside me. Helpless to resist, I flung my arms around his neck and slung my legs around his hips. My heels dug into his ass. "Why wait? Show me now."

"Can't."

"Excuse me?" I pulled my head back. "Why not?"

The pained look on his face evinced a deep inner struggle. "It's daytime."

"Huh?" I pulled back a little more, narrowing my gaze on him. "Oh Rory, you have got to be joking."

"No joke." He disentangled himself from me and shuffled backward a few steps. His arms hung stiffly at his sides, and his fingers twitched. "It's daytime. Sex is a nighttime activity."

"Uh-huh." I pushed away from the table. The contract he'd given me lay strewn across the floor where it must've fallen out of my hand when he backed me into the table. "Listen, I better go home right away. Your hang-ups are cute and all, but I need to seriously consider whether this is a good idea for either one of us."

I gathered up the papers in a messy bundle and hurried past him toward the doorway.

"Emery."

Something in his voice stopped me. I half turned to glance at him.

His arms hung limp, his face had become a stony mask. "If the answer is no, tell me now and be done with it."

"I'm not saying no. I'm saying give me a little time and space." I hugged the haphazard sheaf of papers to my chest. "When do you go home?"

"Wednesday."

"You'll have my answer by then."

Preoccupied with the papers I held, he twitched his fingers again. "Where do you live?"

"Oh. Sorry." A nervous laugh bubbled out of me. "Forgot to tell you, didn't I? Colorado Springs."

"I'll wait until Wednesday." He motioned toward the papers. "Those must be out of order."

"Yeah, I'll sort them out later." I tilted my head. "You really, really want to come over here and straighten these papers yourself, don't you?"

He hissed what sounded like a curse in another language. "I'm not that uptight."

"Glad to hear it." I tapped the pages against my chest. "One more question. Why me? Out of all the women in the world, why pick one who drives you crazy?"

"I loved my previous wives. You're nothing like any of them, nothing like the sort of woman I've been attracted to in the past." He shoved a hand in his pants pocket, then removed it. "There's no danger involved. I can't love you."

Rory MacTaggart was, I decided in this moment, the living embodiment of denial. His attraction to me had been proved beyond any doubt. I'd begun to wonder if he wanted me because I was different. Because I challenged him. Because he thought he could love me one day.

Dangerous thoughts, for sure.

"Better call the airline," I said, "and change my reservation. I'm leaving as soon as possible."

Though I couldn't see him as I exited the room, I sensed him watching me. The poor guy seemed oddly hell-bent on marrying me. And I, for some bizarre reason, was tempted to say yes. More than tempted. I had a burning itch deep inside compelling me to sign on for a marriage of convenience. I must think about it.

No more thinking, Emery the wild whispered in my ear. *Seize the Scotsman and run with it.*

I ordered my inner voice to shut the hell up.

Then I walked out the door.

Chapter Ten

Tuesday morning, I leaned against the low wall of a cubicle inside the windowless offices of Travellis Games with an envelope in my hand, tapping the envelope's corner on the cubicle. My elbows were balanced on the wall, my hands hanging off the edge, as I stared into space.

Today, I'd signed the final papers to end my employment with Travellis, laid off after six years here. The envelope I held contained my severance, the equivalent of two paychecks, as well as a letter of recommendation from my former boss. I hadn't told him I was done with programming. Done with tech jobs, period. I needed a change, something drastic that might lead to a more fulfilling life. I had no clue what my passion in life might be, but I knew how to find out.

Accept Rory's offer.

Ever since I'd left him Sunday morning, I'd thought about it—thought longer and harder than I had about any decision in my life. I preferred the "jump first and get the details later" approach to life. After some serious cogitating, I'd reached a deceptively simple conclusion.

Nothing tied me to Colorado Springs. Nothing tied me to this country, even. Oh, I loved America and I'd miss it, but nothing meaningful kept me here. My sister lived in Germany, my parents in Australia. I had no other family. With my job gone, I could either stay here and search for another programming position I didn't want, or I could take a gigantic leap of faith and maybe find the excitement and adventure my life had lacked for too long.

I'd always picked the safe guys, the ones with gainful employment and steady personalities but no joie de vivre. There hadn't been anything wrong with them, really. I'd loved the man I almost married, and yet I hadn't experienced any regret about calling off the engagement two weeks after accepting his proposal. Six months had gone by since that day, and Luke and I had returned to the friendship we'd known before we tried to remake it into a romance. I realized after our split I loved him as a friend and only a friend. He seemed as unaffected by our breakup as I had been. Something had been missing in the relationship. Something vital.

The zing.

Maybe it was a silly term for a lack of passion, but it embodied the missing element better than any other word. Luke and I had no zing, in bed or in any aspect of our relationship. With Rory MacTaggart, I'd found the zing.

And I'd decided to marry him.

"Em, are you sleeping standing up?"

The voice of my coworker—former coworker, that was—jerked me back to the moment. Sabri Yilmaz stared at me with uplifted black brows, his dark eyes obscured by the fluorescent lights reflecting in his glasses. I hunched on the opposite side of the cubicle wall from him where he sat upright in a half-back office chair with no armrests.

I hated those chairs.

Sabri waved a hand in my face. "Earth to Emery."

"Ha-ha. I'm awake."

"That trip to NOLA must've been wild to leave you in a trance." He folded his arms over his chest, hiding the logo of his ComicCon T-shirt. Yeah, we'd ventured to San Diego together, along with another cohort from Travellis. Sabri sighed. "Man, I can't believe we won't be working together anymore. I'll miss you, Em."

"I'll miss you too."

A head popped up from the adjacent cubicle, a head fringed with blue-streaked brown hair.

"What about me?" Pamela Figueroa asked. She feigned a pout. "Guess you've already forgotten me."

"Of course not," I said. "I'll miss you too, Pam."

"Aw, Em, it won't be the same without you." Pam glanced around the office space at all the empty cubicles. "It's like a tomb in here."

I may have been the first to go, but downsizing had claimed a lot of others after me. Sabri and Pamela were the only ones left in this office, though the company had more cubicles in another space down the hall.

More drudge workers. I wouldn't miss the long hours of a daily grind that never seemed to end.

"I may be leaving the country," I said.

"Going where?" Pam asked, hurrying out of her cubicle to stand near me.

"Scotland."

Sabri's eyes went wide. "Awesome. Will you wear a kilt?"

"Maybe."

"Awesome." He grinned. "Text me a pic. And make sure the kilt is good and short."

I stretched over the cubicle wall to tousle his hair. "Behave, kid. I'm old enough to be your…well, not your mother. Your older stepsister, maybe."

"Super-hot stepsister." He picked up a photo frame that rested on his desktop, a picture of the three of us at last year's Halloween party. Sighing wistfully, he said, "I'll really miss your costumes."

"You need a girlfriend, sweetie."

He winked. "Tried, but you turned me down."

The kid was seven years younger than me and totally incorrigible.

Pam laid a hand on my arm. "ComicCon will suck without you and your Princess Leia homage."

Ah, yes. My costume inspired by the skimpy slave-girl outfit worn by Princess Leia in *Return of the Jedi*. I'd gone to ComicCon once, and I'd had a blast. Part of the reason was my friends.

"Let's not lose touch, okay?" I said. "Email, text, social media, whatever. We've got no excuse for losing each other in the digital age."

"We won't lose anybody," Pam assured me.

"No way," Sabri said with a decisive shake of his head.

Pam's gaze wandered around the empty office, her expression turning somber, but then she froze, and her face lit up. "Hello, kitty. Who is that?"

Sabri rose halfway up from his chair, squinting in the direction Pam looked. "We got a bigwig coming in today? Nobody told me."

I turned—and my heart thudded.

Striding across the room, deftly navigating the maze of vacant cubicles, Rory MacTaggart held his head high and his shoulders square. His charcoal suit complemented his physique, but he'd forgone a tie in favor of leaving the top button of his crisp, white dress shirt open. His golden-brown hair and brandy eyes almost glowed in the fluorescent lighting.

Only he could look good under artificial lights.

And damn, did he ever look good. Mouthwateringly, lickably good.

Rory spotted me and made a beeline for my position. Muscles strained the fabric of his suit as he moved, the picture of surety and resolve.

He'd come for me. And I was about to leap into his arms.

Not literally.

Well, maybe.

"There you are," he said in that sensuous voice, the one that made me liquefy inside.

"Here I am," I concurred.

Sabri had gotten a peevish look on his face. "Who's this guy? You know him?"

"I do." Unable to resist the impulse, I placed a hand on Rory's bicep and gave it a little squeeze. Firm. Solid. Powerful. Reining in my lust as best I could, I spoke to my friends. "This is Rory MacTaggart. My fiancé."

Rory seemed as surprised as my friends were.

"Fiancé?" Pamela said, then broke into a huge grin. "Congrats, Em. Why didn't you tell us you were seeing somebody? You sly puppy."

I hated lying, and I stank at it anyway, so I relied on partial truth. "Um, it just happened. We met in New Orleans."

"Love at first sight? That's so romantic."

Sabri screwed up his face. "I asked you out four times, and you turned me down cold. You meet this guy a few days ago and decide to marry him?"

"Yes." I hooked my arm under Rory's, cuddling up to him. To show my friends how close we were. Not because I loved the feel of his hard body. Nope, not that. *Bad liar, Em.* "You know how spontaneous I am. When I met Rory, we clicked and I ran with it."

Sabri shook his head, but a slight smile tugged at his lips. He stood and offered a hand to Rory. "Congratulations, man. Em's an amazing girl."

Rory shook Sabri's hand. "I'm well aware of how fortunate I am."

He sounded like he meant it. Either I was about to marry a world-class actor, or he was genuinely glad I'd accepted his proposal.

My friends besieged me, tearing me away from Rory to suffocate me in a group hug, blubbering like I was heading off on an interstellar trip to another galaxy and they'd be long dead by the time I returned.

Pam released me, spun around, and flung herself at Rory.

Like a true gentleman, he caught her and accepted her embrace.

"Take good care of her," Pam said.

"I will," Rory promised.

Sabri let me go, and I sidled up to Rory. We both bid my friends good-bye and then strolled out of the office arm in arm. Once we'd exited the one-story building onto the sidewalk, Rory stopped us. He rotated me to face him, his expression grim.

"Did you mean it?" he asked. "You called me your fiancé. Are you accepting my proposal?"

"It's more of a proposition than a proposal." I splayed a hand on his chest, fingering his lapel. "But yes, I'm accepting your offer."

He *almost* smiled.

"I have two conditions, though," I said.

"Name it. Whatever you want, it's yours."

"First, I need total honesty. No secrets, no lies. This is nonnegotiable, and I'll do the same for you."

He directed his gaze past my shoulder, seeming pensive, then zeroed in on me. "The other condition?"

"Sex and money is great, and of course I love the freedom you're offering." I patted his chest, bracing myself to explain. "But I need to be useful."

"I don't understand."

"Being your trophy wife isn't enough for me." I rolled my shoulders back, lifting my chin. "While I search for my true calling in life, I need something to keep me busy. I need a mission, and I've picked one."

His brows knit together. "What is it?"

"You."

He blinked slowly. "What?"

"Think of me as your private therapist." I smiled brightly, bouncing on my toes. "I'm going to help you remember how to enjoy life, Rory."

He groaned. "You want to change me. Do you think my previous wives haven't already tried it?"

"I don't want to change you. Only you can do that. I want to help you."

"There's a difference?"

"Absolutely. I'm not dragging you kicking and screaming into the fun zone. I'm illuminating the path for you." I inched closer, tipping my head back to see him. "You've gotten a taste of what I'm like. You understand I'm no wallflower, and I won't be the trophy wife you trot out at parties and put away in a closet the rest of the time. Are you sure you want me?"

He studied me for a long moment, giving away nothing on his face. Then he grasped my upper arms. "I'm certain. And I accept your conditions."

"Good." I wrestled with my purse, slung over my shoulder, and extracted the contract he'd given me. I held it up. "Signed and delivered."

He dragged me into his body, his arms coming around me as he crushed his mouth to mine. I welcomed his invasion, thrusting my tongue in concert with his, teasing the roof of his mouth, savoring the indescribable flavor of him.

Stepping back, he snagged the contract. He glanced at it, then folded the papers in half and tucked them into an inside pocket of his suit jacket.

"Are you going to sign it?" I asked.

"Later. We marry today and leave for Scotland in the morning."

"Today?" I shook my head. "Don't know how it is in Scotland, but here we've got licenses and blood tests and whatnot."

"Not in Colorado." He gave me a quizzical look. "Didn't you know that? You've lived in this state for how long?"

"Six years. But I've never been married. Engaged once, but never married. I didn't have a reason to learn about the marriage laws."

"I researched the process last night."

"Of course you did." I hesitated, a thought occurring to me. "How did you find me here?"

"You mentioned Travellis Games and Colorado Springs. I didn't expect to find you at work, but I hoped your colleagues might point me in the right direction."

"Impatient, huh?"

"Today is Tuesday. I leave tomorrow." He fiddled with his shirt collar. "I needed your answer."

"You've got it."

He checked the time on his phone. "We should hurry if we're going to do this today."

"What's the rush? Don't you want to have a wedding in front of your family?"

"No." He slipped a hand under his jacket, his forehead crinkled, and he withdrew his hand. "Are you sure you've read the entire contract and understand it fully?"

"Yep." I boosted onto my toes and pecked a kiss on his lips. "I'm a smart girl. I know what I'm getting into."

Sort of. It enhanced the adventure aspect of this to recognize the risks and the unknown variables.

I had read the prenup and the contract, three times each. He gave as much as he required from me, mostly asserting all the transgressions that would mean I'd forfeit the half million bucks. Things like cheating, embezzling, damaging his professional reputation, failure to provide "sexual congress"—oh yeah, he used those words—at least twice a week. Sex with Rory would hardly be a trial.

Though I'd told him the sex might stink from now on, I didn't believe that. The way my body reacted to his presence assured me we'd have good sex at the very least, and I had every reason to believe it would be fantastic.

I wouldn't marry him for sex, or money, no matter what he thought. This would become my biggest, wildest exploit ever and the source of as-yet-untold thrills. I would help Rory as much as he'd let me. At the very least, when I left after a year he might be less rigid and more open to love in the future.

What if you fall for him? a small voice whispered in my ear. *What if you love him, and he won't love you?*

A bridge I'd cross when it materialized in front of me. This leap of faith, it promised great rewards and a kind of freedom I'd never had in my entire life. Find a new career I loved? Get to know an intriguing and outrageously sexy man? Walk away a rich woman? I couldn't turn it down.

If I found I couldn't stand to live with him, I'd walk away with nothing.

A chance worth taking. I'd decided that before he showed up at my former workplace. Something about him lured me closer, like the cliché about a moth and a flame.

Then again, maybe he was the moth and I was the flame beckoning him toward the brilliant light of liberation. We'd find out together.

Rory guided me to a limo parked along the curb, swung the door open, and waited for me to climb inside.

A gentleman. A seducer. An uptight lawyer. Rory was all those things and more.

I climbed into the limo, sliding across the seat while Rory lowered his big body onto the cushioned leather beside me. A couple days ago, I'd wondered if I could handle the distinct facets of his personality. As I sat here beside him, our hands inches apart on the seat, I realized why I was doing this.

Whatever might come of our marriage, I needed to find out if Rory the hunk of unrefined carbon could become a shining diamond. I needed to know if we could have something more than sex and money shared between us.

This wasn't how I'd ever imagined getting hitched, but I'd take it.

Chapter Eleven

One good thing about marrying an uptight lawyer? Rory steamrolled his way through the American legal system, doing whatever it took to ensure we tied the knot today. I'd acquired a passport yesterday in preparation for our departure from the land of my birth. Rory took care of everything else, including the acquisition of wedding rings. Never rude, but always determined, he'd employed a kind of jet-powered mixture of politeness and ruthlessness that got the job done.

Though he made a snooty face at the idea of buying rings off the shelf, instead of ordering custom ones, I'd reminded him of his self-imposed deadline for marriage today. He'd sucked it up to get through the ring selection.

"Uptight and kind of a snob," I teased while we studied the options inside the glass case in a swanky jewelry store.

"I like quality and originality," he said, his impassive expression never wavering as he examined the rings lying on velvet cushions.

"Originality, hm? Is that why you wore a kilt Friday night?"

"No." Rory waved to the clerk. When the baby-faced guy approached, Rory indicated a pair of simple gold bands that cost more than several months of my rent. While the clerk retrieved and packaged up the rings, Rory angled toward me with a hip braced on the jewelry case. "I told you why I wore a kilt."

"You fed me a mouthful of BS, and being a polite lady, I let you get away with it." I moved closer, gratified when he rested a hand on my hip. "Seeing as I'm about to uproot my entire life for you, I think the least you owe me is the truth about your choice of clothing that night. Why a kilt?"

He exhaled a long-suffering sigh. "Aidan."

"Your brother?"

Rory nodded, his mouth crimped, though I detected a hint of humor in it. "Aidan dared me to wear a kilt in public, in a location where no one else would be wearing one and no one would expect to see a man dressed that way." He scratched his jaw, his lips spasming with an amusement he couldn't quite let out. "Aidan thought it would be funny."

"Because you're...you."

"Aye. The dare turned into a wager."

"You won. What do you get?"

"A favor from Aidan. Whatever I want, whenever I want."

"Wow, that's quite a wager. What are you going to make him do?"

"Haven't decided yet."

I insisted on taking a picture of us in the jewelry store, and Rory acquiesced with a roll of his eyes. Once we'd bought the rings—well, once he'd bought the rings—we drove to my apartment so I could pack. I'd barely stuffed one suitcase when he announced it was time to go.

"But—" I flapped my arms in a vague gesture. "All my stuff. I can't live out of one suitcase for the next year."

"You can buy new things."

"What's the big rush?"

He shoved his hands in his pants pockets, shoulders hunched. "I want to go home."

Was I hallucinating? Nope. Rory the stoic solicitor had admitted he was homesick. He looked so forlorn and so embarrassed by his confession, I couldn't help myself. I rushed forward and threw my arms around him. "You miss your family, I get it. We can rush, and maybe I can get my friends to pack up the rest of my stuff and somehow get it shipped to me."

He wore that bemused expression, the one he only ever displayed when I'd done something impulsive and harebrained. I kissed his cheek and released him, backing up a couple steps to give the poor man space.

He surveyed my tiny, one-room apartment. "I'll hire someone to take care of your belongings."

I assumed he meant he'd get my stuff packed and shipped. No idea how long it would take to transport my things to Scotland, but I'd make do in the meantime.

Yet another impulse overtook me, and I rushed at him to plant another kiss on his cheek. "Thank you, Rory. You're a real sweetie-pie."

"Donnae say that in front of my family, or Aidan will be calling me 'sweetie-pie' for the rest of eternity."

"I will try to restrain myself, but no promises. I'm impulsive, you know, which you really ought to like since it's the impetus for me marrying you."

He said nothing for several seconds. "I can live with your outlandish enthusiasm."

"Thanks a bunch, sweetie-pie."

Rory grumbled, snatching up my lone suitcase.

He'd been so honest with me, admitting he missed his home, I wanted to reciprocate. I had told him I required total honesty. Time to fulfill my end of the deal.

My gut twisted.

I took a breath and forged ahead. "There's something you should know before we tie the knot, in case it changes your mind."

"Nothing will change my mind."

"You haven't heard my confession yet."

Rory set down the suitcase. "Tell me, then."

Where to start? A pain tightened the back of my throat. I'd start with the abridged version.

"Remember how I said I hate secrets and lies?" My gaze flitted around the room, everywhere except to Rory, and I couldn't seem to stop it. "That's because my ex took naked pictures of me and posted them online without my knowledge or consent. I mean, I consented to him taking pictures of me. But I had no idea he'd post them on social media. He swore they were just for him to look at. After I broke up with him, he got revenge-y."

Rory squinted. "Revenge-y?"

"It's called revenge porn." I felt weak all of a sudden, like I might pass out. "I'll spare you the details. The gist is I got the photos taken down from his social media accounts, but there's always a chance the images had been propagated elsewhere. Our contract talks about moral obligations, and I don't want you to be humiliated if nudie pictures of me turn up somehow, somewhere."

He glanced down at my belly.

I followed his gaze and realized I was wringing my hands in front of my stomach.

"I won't be humiliated," he said, his tone soothing. He squeezed my shoulder, then folded his hand around both of mine. "And I haven't changed my mind."

The tenderness of his actions triggered a pang in my chest, but I couldn't shake the fears I'd sworn wouldn't affect my future. They never had, until now. Until I decided to marry a stranger.

Rory, seeming to perceive my inner turmoil, ducked his head to look into my eyes. "I don't treat women that way, no matter what they do to me. Do you believe me?"

I couldn't speak, that pang hitting my chest harder, so I nodded. I did believe him. God help me, I trusted him. Maybe I'd plunged into a bottomless pool, but I couldn't deny the truth.

He separated my hands, letting go of one, keeping hold of the other as he laced his fingers through mine. "All of that is in the past."

I let him lead me out of my apartment. My former apartment. Rory had taken care of terminating my lease, of course. My landlord had gaped at us both when I told him I was marrying Rory and running off to Scotland, but eventually, he'd offered us both his congratulations and wishes for good luck.

No luck required. I intended to force good things to happen through sheer willpower and, as Rory called it, outlandish enthusiasm. *Think happy, be happy.* Why the hell not?

A few hours later, a magistrate solemnized our marriage. Yeah, I learned a new word. Rory wore the same suit without a tie, but I'd changed into a knee-length, cream-colored sundress with a modest neckline. It was the most wedding-appropriate thing I owned. My strappy heels added another three inches to my height, but I still had to crane my neck to meet Rory's gaze. Not that he looked at me during the ceremony. He maintained his stoic expression throughout the solemnization whatchamacallit, even when he slipped the ring onto my finger. The whole thing happened so fast I had no time to process the event until we were back in the limo, headed for the Garden of the Gods resort for our wedding night. In the morning, we'd fly to Scotland.

My brain, though addled, had reminded me to take a photo of us in the magistrate's office.

I was married. *Married.* To a man I met slightly more than four days ago. Tomorrow, I'd be in another country. On the other side of an ocean.

At least I'd be closer to my sister, since Hadley lived in Dusseldorf.

But I was…a wife. Rory's wife. I had a husband. One who swore he couldn't love me and wanted me for sex and to trot me out at family functions.

Oh suck it up, woman. You knew what you were getting into.

Did I know?

The question taunted me as we crossed the resort's lobby.

Rory, his body strung tight as a rubber band stretched to its limit, clapped the door shut behind us and announced, "I need to ring my family in private."

"Ring them?"

He articulated each syllable with painstaking care. "Call them on the telephone. To explain what—what I've done."

"You make it sound so romantic."

"This is not romance, it's a business arrangement."

"Yeah-yeah, I know." I flung a hand in the direction of the balcony and its sliding glass door. "Go make your call in private. I won't listen at the keyhole like a certain someone did when I was having a good time in the jacuzzi."

He made that exasperated face for at least the tenth time today.

I ran my hands up his lapels. "You are so easy to tease. And so much fun to tease too."

Rory raised his eyes to the ceiling and then marched out onto the balcony, jerking the glass door open and shut. He dropped into one of the chairs positioned around a circular table, his back to me.

I needed to call my family too, but I had no idea what to tell them. The truth. Part of the truth, anyway. I dug my phone out of my purse and dialed my parents' number in Sydney. When my mom answered with her usual cheerful greeting, I dived right in.

"Hi Mom," I said, yawning as I settled onto the sofa. Ahead of me, I could see the balcony and Rory. "I, uh, have some news."

"Did you find a new job?"

The hopefulness in her voice made me cringe inside. Would she be as happy about my actual news?

"Not exactly," I said. Bite-the-bullet time had come. "I got married today."

Silence. Only the faint noise of a TV in the background told me we were still connected.

"You've been seeing someone?" she asked, the hopeful tone replaced with confusion. "You never mentioned it."

"The last time we talked, I wasn't seeing anyone." Since we'd last talked five days ago, she must've been calculating the maximum duration of this courtship. "It happened fast. His name is Rory MacTaggart, he's from Scotland. Tomorrow, we're flying to his home near a village in the Highlands called Ballachulish."

"Y—You're moving to Scotland?"

"I'm excited about it. A new country, a fresh start. You know I was sick of programming, and now I can find something else to do with my life.'"

"You can do that in America. Or come to Sydney and stay with us."

Another silence echoed between us for several seconds. I could imagine her struggling to absorb this information and collect her wits before speaking again.

"I'm sorry," Mom said. "Of course we're happy for you, if you're happy. Do you love him?"

Ack. How to answer honestly without giving away the game? "Rory is a good man. He's smart and kind, very determined, not to mention gorgeous and sexy. He's also, um, a multimillionaire lawyer."

"Are you marrying him for sex or money?"

Rory thought I was.

"This is what I want," I said. "Rory offers me the change I've needed in my life."

"You could've shacked up with him for a while. What's the rush to get married?"

How many mothers would recommend their daughters shack up with a guy instead of getting married? These days, I supposed some might. My traditionalist mom never would have before, but I'd shocked her so much she was clamoring for any alternative. She wouldn't have liked me moving in with a stranger, either.

"You know me," I said, aiming for the only truth I could offer. "I'm impulsive, and when I decide what I want I go for it."

A click indicated someone else had joined our conversation.

"What's going on?" my dad said in his gravelly voice. "Your mom's white as a sheet. Emmy, what the blazes have you done this time?"

"I married a Scottish man, and I'm moving to the Highlands with him."

"What?" Dad all but shouted. "Who is this guy? Gimme his name so I can get on the Internet and order a full background check."

"Dad, honestly. Rory is a good guy." I squirmed on the sofa's edge. "Besides, it's too late. I'm already married to him."

"We can come get you anytime."

"Ted," my mom said in her best chastising tone, "stop haranguing Emmy. She's a grown woman capable of making her own decisions, whether we understand them or not."

How could they understand? I wasn't so sure I did.

Dad snorted. "We haven't even met this guy."

The glass door slid open, and Rory strode back inside. When he caught sight of me, he lifted one brow in a silent question.

"Mom, Dad, please," I said, "try to be cool about this, okay? I know you haven't met Rory but—"

Rory commandeered my phone. "Mr. and Mrs. Granger, this is Rory MacTaggart."

He spoke in a calm, pleasant tone that did not match his tight expression.

I tried to speak, but my voice had died.

"Please accept my apologies," Rory said, "for sweeping your daughter off her feet with a whirlwind courtship and marriage. I need to go home tomorrow, and I couldn't bear to leave without her. However, I should've spoken to you first so this wouldn't have been such a shock. I hope you can forgive me."

He listened intently, nodding.

I pushed up off the sofa, scrutinizing his facial expression but gaining no insight from it.

"You have my word," he told my parents. "I will do everything in my power to ensure Emery is happy. She will not be alone in a foreign country. She has me—and my family. But you should visit as soon as possible. I'm certain you'll feel more comfortable with the situation once we've met."

The idea of seeing my parents in Scotland, soon, made my heart swell.

"Never mind the expense," Rory assured my parents, "I'll send my jet for you. And of course, I will have Emery's sister and her family flown in as well. Let us know when you can take a holiday, and I'll arrange everything."

Holy shit. He was flying my whole family to Scotland? Just to make them feel better?

It was a smart move. Placate the family, placate the wife.

This intelligent, cunning, determined man had set his sights on making my family happy. If I'd learned anything about Rory, it was that once he'd set a goal for himself, he would stop at nothing to achieve it. All that intensity and iron resolve, it was...sexy as hell.

The room had grown hot, and my breaths quickened.

Oh, it wasn't the room. I'd grown hot and tingly inside, desperate to rip his clothes off.

I tore the phone from his hand. "We'll be in touch to talk travel details. It's our wedding night, so forgive the rude goodbye but—goodbye."

I hung up and tossed my phone on the coffee table.

Humor crinkled Rory's eyes.

"Thank you," I said, "for handling my parents like that. Once they calm down, they'll be stoked about getting a free trip to Scotland."

"I look forward to meeting them."

"One more thing." I jabbed a finger toward his chest. "Don't ever butt into my life again. I don't like being bossed around, even if it turns me on big time the way you take charge and get things done."

With a deliberate casualness that indicated sarcasm, he retrieved his phone from his pocket. "Should I order dinner?"

"Later." I seized the lapels of his suit jacket and hauled him closer. "Take me into the bedroom and fuck me."

He hit me with a devastating, erotic smile. "Whatever my wife desires."

Chapter Twelve

I sprawled naked on a large bed, waiting for my new husband to recover his pride. Rory slumped at the foot of the bed in the nude with his feet on the floor, elbows on his thighs, hands slack between his legs. For ten minutes, he'd stared down at his hands in silence. I raised my left hand, fingering the plain gold band on my third finger. We'd gone from betrothed to be-married in a matter of hours.

"You okay?" I asked.

He flashed me a dark look that said *are you nuts.*

I sat up. "This is completely normal. It happens to everybody."

"Not to me." He dropped his face into his palms. "What have I done?"

Whether he meant his inability to perform or his decision to marry me, I didn't know.

Everything had started out so good. Lots of kissing, plenty of fondling, and by the time we undressed we were both ready to go.

Then something had changed. He'd swept me up and set me down on the bed, his lust obvious in the glossiness of his eyes and the strong curve of his erection. I had smiled at him, entranced by the vision of my gloriously naked husband—and he had frozen. His eyes bulged. He swallowed hard enough I could see it and hear the little gulp. While I lay puzzled on the bed, he had stumbled backward.

And his arousal flagged like a flower pummeled by a rainstorm.

"What have I done?" he repeated, his voice hardly a whisper but rife with self-recrimination.

I crawled to him and knelt at his back, laying my hands on his shoulders.

His head shot up, and he stiffened.

"Take it easy, baby," I said, twining my arms loosely around his neck, my hands over his collarbone. I held my lips to his ear. "I know you don't have a physical problem, which means this is emotional. We can work through it together."

"Cannae."

I nuzzled his cheek. "You're awfully morose for a man who got what he wanted today."

He drummed one knuckle on his thigh.

"What is it you're afraid you've done?" I asked.

"Doesnae matter."

Translation: *None of your business, Emery.*

Maybe he regretted our quickie marriage. Maybe…*Gah.* I could drive myself bats worrying about what he'd meant, but I would never know until he decided to tell me. My best option was to deal with the more immediate issue.

I floated my hands down his chest, swirling my palms over his pecs. "The night isn't a bust yet. We had a weird, stressful day. That's bound to make you anxious." I coiled my tongue around his earlobe. "Let me help you relax."

"Ye can try, but it willnae work."

"Don't be such a pessimist." I pressed my lips to the pulse point on his throat, while my hands moved ever lower, caressing and exploring his abs. "I have skills too, ya know."

He pulled in a ragged breath.

I dragged my mouth down his throat, tasting his skin with light licks as I moved.

The knuckle drumming his thigh went motionless. He'd stopped breathing, his lips parted.

"Mmmmm," I said as I curled one hand around the base of his shaft. "I love the flavor of your skin."

While my hand glided along his penis, I sank my teeth into his shoulder.

A breath exploded out of him.

My chin on his shoulder, I watched my hand moving along his cock. "I can feel your enthusiasm growing."

He pried my fingers from his hardening shaft. "You first."

"Me first what?"

Rory turned his head to peek at me. "Lie down and you'll find out."

Powerless to resist, and with no desire to anyhow, I reclined on the silken sheets.

My husband crouched at my feet, his hands on my ankles, his focus on my groin. "Yer so beautiful, ye make my *bagais* ache, *cho cinnteach is a tha bod's an each.* I want my face in your *camas,* my mouth on your *brillean.*"

I had no clue what he'd said, but the huskiness of his voice made my body ache for his.

Any thoughts of asking for a translation scattered when he leaned in to spread his hands on my thighs.

"*Leannan*," he said, "I wanted ye in the tub the other day when ye tickled me with your wee bonnie toes. I wanted to give ye the happy ending ye needed, but I held back." He slid his hands under my thighs and lifted them to bend my knees slightly. "Ahmno holding back tonight."

His hands shifted to my inner thighs, easing them apart. As he settled in between my legs, he kept his hands on my inner thighs. His tongue stroked across his lower lip, slowly, as if he were envisioning savoring my flesh. He brushed his lips over the hairs of my mound.

My fingers curled into the sheets.

With the index fingers of each hand, he parted my outer folds, exposing my clitoris and the pink inner folds of my sex.

I held my breath, transfixed by the hunger on his face.

He skimmed his fingers up and down my folds, exciting my flesh so deeply I bit down on my lip and breaths blustered from my nostrils. Eyes half closed, he puckered his mouth and blew a stream of cool air across my rigid clitoris.

"Please," I moaned.

With a crooked smile, he flicked his tongue over my clit with feather-light pressure, the pace languid and steady, the delicacy of his ministrations propelling me to the brink of orgasm. I threw my hands above my head, clenching the pillow so tight my fingers hurt. His fingers whisked along my folds, teased my opening, and his tongue swirled around my clit in that maddeningly gentle way.

"Oh God," I said, my breaths coming in sharp bursts. "Please don't stop, please."

He chuckled, and tiny wisps of his breath tormented my skin.

I closed my eyes, lost to the pleasure.

"Stop," he snarled. "Donnae close your eyes."

My lids flew open, but I couldn't quite focus on him or what he'd said. "What?"

"Donnae close your eyes." He compressed his lips and then, with a visible effort, relaxed his features. "Please."

Another hang-up? Christ, I wanted an orgasm, not a lecture on the rules of Rorydom. With my mind scrambled by thwarted bliss, I said in a breathless rush, "Okayfinewhatever."

The tension in his body melted away.

"Just don't stop, Rory. For heaven's sake, don't stop."

"Donnae say my name either."

I gaped at him with my heart pounding and my clit pulsating. "What, like, ever?"

"Not while we're being intimate."

I hoisted my head up and tried to puzzle out his expression, but he didn't seem to be joking. "What should I call you? How about 'asshole'?"

"Anything but my name."

I flopped back onto the mattress and whimpered—not with lust, but from the sheer agony of needing to climax. "Why did you have to tell me these crazy rules right in the middle of things, when I was about to—to—"

Tears blurred my vision, tears of extreme frustration.

"Donnae cry," he said, his voice as soft as the look in his eyes. "I'm sorry for shouting."

"I'll get mad at you later. Finish what you started before I rip my hair out."

His gaze tethered to mine, he lowered his mouth once more.

The instant his tongue lapped at my clitoris, I came. My back flattened into the mattress, my hands gripped the pillow, my teeth clamped together even as desperate cries erupted from me. He licked and licked my flesh through so many waves of pulsating pleasure that black dots popped out in my vision and my ears rang.

When he raised his head at last, I went limp, dazed from the unbelievable strength of the climax he'd given me.

"Oh God," I breathed. "That was…you are…"

My words trailed off. I couldn't form a coherent sentence anymore.

Rory crawled up my body to crouch on all fours over me, his face above mine. "Have I exhausted you?"

"In a good way."

His erection bobbed between our bodies, sheathed in a condom.

I sealed my hand around his cock and swept it up to the base. "When did you put this on?"

"While you were coming down from the clouds. You had your eyes closed."

I winced. "Oops. Sorry, I meant to keep my eyes open."

"Donnae worry." He lowered his head next to mine, our cheeks touching. "You looked at me when I was pleasuring you and when you came. That's what I needed."

He needed me to look at him during sex. I longed to ask why, but the answer must've formed the crux of his anxieties about love and marriage. Reluctant to push that button yet, I satisfied myself with knowing I'd given him what he needed tonight.

I folded my arm around his neck while I methodically pumped his shaft. "We're not done yet, are we?"

His cheek lingering on mine, he grasped my wrist to halt my hand. "We are nowhere near done."

"Good," I murmured into his ear, "because I can't get enough of you."

He held stone-still for a moment, then pulled his head back, his wary gaze on me. "I want you more than I should. We have a business arrangement, not a traditional marriage. Sex for us should be a mutual satisfaction of needs and nothing more."

"Stop making this so complicated." Though his hand on my wrist prevented me from pumping his length, I rubbed my fingers over his engorged flesh. "I'm your wife. Kiss me."

His mouth arched into his patented sensual smirk. He lunged his head to within millimeters of my mouth.

I parted my lips, alive with anticipation.

He planted a kiss on my shoulder.

"You rat," I said, slapping his arm.

My husband chuckled. "Rat is better than 'asshole.' "

"You might earn the asshole designation soon enough."

He nipped my chin. "Patience, my sweet wife."

"I want to be fucked, not appeased."

"Of course." He raised onto one straight arm. "I promised to deliver anything my wife desires."

His free hand plunged under my bottom. He elevated my hip until I lay twisted at the waist with my shoulders on the bed. His hand coasted over my hip and down the side of my thigh, while he fluttered his lips over the back of my knee, urging me to bend it with light pressure from his hand.

"Not quite sure what you're doing," I said, "but I'm game for anything."

"One of your most endearing qualities."

Had he called me endearing? I had no chance to consider his statement, because he shifted one of his legs to jam it between mine. My bent knee wound up hooked around his hip.

This was…interesting. None of my ex-lovers had been creative in bed. I watched his every move, enthralled by whatever plan he'd concocted.

He lodged his knee firmly on the mattress, my body between his legs, and his erection brushed against my sex.

I shuddered with need, helpless to stop my hands from reaching for him.

Rory captured my wrists in one hand, pinned them above my head, and braced his other hand alongside my shoulder. "Ye want to be fucked, aye?"

"Oh yes, please."

He drove into me with a single, all-consuming thrust—and paused there, buried inside me to the hilt.

My protest came out as a squeak.

That grin, the one imbued with wicked intention, flashed across his face and devastated my willpower. I surrendered to him completely, relaxing into his hold on my wrists, awaiting anything he might do to me.

He rolled his hips in a circle, his cock penetrating me deeply, his un-hurried motions connecting with parts of me no one had touched before. Bound by his hands, I couldn't clutch him with my hands, so I clutched him with the leg I had locked around him. Mindlessly, I rocked my hips in time with his movements, luxuriating in the feel of this new position, how it seemed to unite our bodies with exquisite intimacy.

I nestled my face against his neck and inhaled the masculine scent of him, mixed with the scent of sweat.

With a groan, he impaled me in lush, vigorous strokes. His pace accelerated as he thrust harder each time, pounding into me until we both bounced on the mattress from the force of his passion. I shut my eyes, helpless not to, grateful my face was mashed against his neck where he couldn't see. The need for climax tortured me, the promise of bliss a magnificent agony.

He pistoned his hips, his flesh scraping my clitoris.

My body went rigid. I came like a firework bursting in the sky, scorching and brilliant, ripped apart by explosions of color. My body convulsed, my muscles pulsating around him, frantic to milk his release. His climax hit while I thrashed under him, my orgasm rolling on and on, and he kept thrusting lazily until, at last, the riot of pleasure calmed inside me.

He disentangled our bodies to lie beside me.

My heart thudded, and I gasped for air.

"Shh," he whispered to me. "Breathe slow and easy."

His chest heaved against my side, rendering him as breathless as I was, yet somehow, he managed to speak. I couldn't have mumbled, much less formed intelligible words. Unlike our first time together, he hadn't lost control. Yes, he'd taken me with the same passion and vigor as before. Yet he'd retained dominion over his senses.

Unlike me. My sanity had flown through the roof, spiraling out into the universe.

I enjoyed the loss of control, whereas he saw it as a character flaw in himself.

He rubbed my tummy, the gesture achingly sweet.

Little by little, I gathered my wits and calmed my breathing. "I love your ingenuity. That position was amazing."

"I'm not ingenious." He ceased rubbing my belly, fanning his hand over my skin. "That position appears in numerous books about sex."

I shot him a sidelong look. "You read sex manuals?"

The most adorable blush tinted his cheeks. "I, ah…bought a few of them over the years."

For his ex-wives? Maybe I'd ask him another time, when the question might not embarrass him. If I'd printed out my list of questions about his previous wives, it would've outweighed an unabridged dictionary.

I wriggled to lie on my side facing him. "Nothing wrong with looking for ways to spice up your love life. I've read sex books too, even the Kama Sutra."

He raised his eyes to peek at me through his thick lashes. "I wasn't brave enough to read that one."

"It's not as lewd as most people think." I placed a light kiss on his lips. "We could look at it together sometime. If you want."

"Perhaps," he said cautiously.

"No rush." I skipped my fingers along the rippling curves of his bicep. "Are we done for the night?"

"Aren't you tired?"

"Nope."

He draped a hand over my hip. "Should we go again?"

"Oh yes, baby. Yes indeed."

Chapter Thirteen

I woke to the fluttery sensation of Rory's lips on my throat and his hair tickling my cheek. As my lids struggled to open, I noticed his hand on my belly and the silky texture of his long-sleeve shirt on my skin.

Shirt? My eyes popped open. He was fully clothed.

"You're dressed," I said, a tad peeved about it. I lay on my side while he leaned over me from behind.

He trailed the backs of his fingers across my belly. "I don't generally board an airplane in the nude."

"Maybe I will." Laughing at his horrified expression, I slapped the back of my hand on his chest. "That was a joke. I'm not an exhibitionist." I toyed with a button on his shirt. "Unless you want me to exhibit myself for you."

"Not at the moment." He sat up and spanked my behind. "Time to get dressed. We leave for the airport in thirty minutes."

"Thirty—" I sprang into a sitting position. "I need a shower and breakfast and—What time is it?"

"Five o'clock. You can freshen up in flight." He rose from the bed and flapped his hand. "Up, Emery."

Mumbling curses under my breath, I clambered out of bed and reached for the robe laid over the foot. As I pulled it on, I gave him a mulish look. "Just so you know, bossiness at five a.m. does not turn me on. Why the stampede to get outta Dodge?"

"I want to take you home, and I'm not known for dawdling."

I rubbed my forehead. "Jeez, Rory, it's still dark out. I need a shower to wake me up and food to keep me from passing out from hunger."

He fisted his hands, then stretched his fingers taut. "I will feed you on the jet, which has a full bathroom. A bed too. Please, may we get on the plane quickly?"

"You're super anxious to get home, hey?"

"Aye."

"Why is that?"

He dropped onto the foot of the bed, slumped forward, and rested his elbows on his knees. "I've been gone for ten days, the longest period I've ever been away."

My heart melted at his miserable expression, and I took a seat beside him. "This seems like more than missing home. What else is bothering you?"

He frowned at the floor. "My family is anxious to see you. I convinced them not to meet us at the airport, but they insist on coming to the house tomorrow."

"They want to check out the trophy wife."

"You are not a trophy."

What was I, then? Not his soul mate, for sure.

"I can deal with meeting your family," I said. "And I promise not to embarrass you if that's what you're worried about. Your family will meet a well-behaved American."

"Not worried about you." He unfolded his torso to the upright position as if preparing for takeoff. "You can handle yourself. My family...They don't understand what I've done."

I supposed it didn't help I wasn't the kind of girl an uptight solicitor would take home to his mama.

His words from last night echoed in my mind. *What have I done?* he'd muttered.

"Do you regret marrying me?" I asked. "This wasn't exactly a well-thought-out decision. You were lusting after me, and you got this crazy marriage idea in your head. I'd understand if you have buyer's remorse."

"I haven't bought you."

"You kinda did. Half a million dollars after a year, remember?"

He ground his teeth. "I haven't bought you. All of my ex-wives received generous settlements when we divorced."

But you loved them, I wanted to point out. I swallowed the words.

"My family can be overly protective," Rory said, "particularly my brother Lachlan. He almost frightened away the woman Aidan married. He terrified my first two wives, and the third kept her distance from him."

A smile tugged at my lips, though I tried to suppress it. "Are you afraid your big brother will have me fleeing in terror? Your concern is adorable but unnecessary. I'm not that easy to get rid of, baby."

His mouth cinched up at one corner. "Why do you keep calling me that?"

"What?"

"Baby."

"Don't know. Didn't realize I was doing it." I bumped my shoulder into his. "Guess it means I like you. Which is a good thing since we'll be living together."

Rory launched his body off the bed. "You'll change your mind about that soon enough."

He stalked out of the bedroom into the living area, out of my sight.

Did he mean I'd stop liking him? I couldn't see that happening. The more time I spent with him the more I liked my husband. He must've liked me too, despite swearing he would never care for me. Why did he think I'd wind up disliking him?

Maybe I'd find out he was a perv with a sex dungeon full of medieval torture devices.

Rory? Mr. Law and Order? Nah, I couldn't believe it.

I cleaned up and got dressed, then headed into the living area.

Rory perched on the sofa with his computer on his lap, typing away. When he noticed me, he clapped the laptop shut. "Ready?"

"Yep." I ogled his muscles as he levered his body off the sofa while holding the laptop in one hand. My thought from a few minutes ago resurfaced, and I had to ask. "We don't know each other very well, so I need to ask you something. Are you a pervert who's into BDSM—bondage, sadism, that kind of thing?"

"No." He made a face that said *dumb question, you silly American.*

"It's not a ridiculous thing to ask," I said. "You told me I'd change my mind about liking you, and I couldn't help wondering if that means you've got a tawdry secret at home. Maybe you'll lock me in your sex dungeon."

He rolled his eyes, Rory-style. "I may live in a castle, but I don't have a dungeon."

"So, you're not into the twisted shit."

"I am not." He stowed the laptop in its carrying bag. "Time to leave."

He snagged my suitcase and wheeled it toward the door where his bag waited. When he swung the door open for me, I hesitated.

"You live in a castle?" I asked, dubious.

"I do."

He had to be pulling my leg. He had to.

With a hand on my back, he compelled me to move.

The journey to the airport rushed by in a blur of activity and motion. As we approached the jet, I stumbled to a halt. The plane was enormous and spiffy and shiny white, with a pointed nose. I'd been on airliners before, but this was something else.

Rory touched a finger to my chin. "Your mouth is hanging open, lass. Insects might fly in there if you're not careful."

I shut my mouth, but I did not miss the sarcastic slant to his lips or the gleam in his eyes.

His ex-wives must've done a number on him to make him so afraid to show his emotions.

"This is yours?" I asked, pointing toward the elegant monstrosity.

One of his brawny shoulders lifted and fell again. "I share it with Lachlan. After he married Erica, he wanted a private means of getting wherever he might need to be." The slant of Rory's lips kicked up a little higher into the closest approximation of a smile I'd seen yet. "I think he wanted a flying bedroom so he could ravish his wife up in the clouds."

"I'm sure you have no such plans." I cozied up to him, looping an arm around his waist. "Did you guys go halfsies on the plane?"

"It's a jet, but I'm not sure what you're asking."

"Did you each pay half the cost."

"Ah, no. Lachlan insisted on buying the jet himself. I do pay for the fuel, and I tried to convince him to let me pay a portion of the cost. He wouldn't agree. This was the first of two jets he bought."

"Two jets?" I rested my chin on his arm, my face turned up toward his. "How rich is your brother?"

"I'm not certain, but I'd wager it's at least ten times more than I have."

"Ten times? I suppose your brother Aidan has twenty times more."

"Aidan is not wealthy," Rory explained, "though he has rebuilt his construction business into quite a success. He nearly lost the company after he was injured in a rock-climbing accident, but he's worked like the devil to bring it back to life."

His tone conveyed pride in his little brother's accomplishments.

Rory ushered me up the airstairs into the plane—pardon me, jet. Well-cushioned seats lined both sides of the cabin, their ivory-colored leather pristine. One group of seats faced each other with a table between them, and a sofa occupied one space along the right-hand side. Beyond that, boxes filled up an empty area. Past that, I glimpsed more rooms.

"Through there is the bedroom, bathroom, and galley," Rory said, gesturing into the jet's bowels.

"What are those boxes?"

He looked at me like I'd asked what that yellow ball in the sky was. "Your belongings."

My gaze flitted to the boxes and back to his face. "You said you'd hire people to pack up my stuff and get it to me. I assumed that meant shipping it. How did you get anybody to do it this fast?"

"I paid them a great deal of money." He curled his hands around my upper arms. "I'm spiriting you away to a new country and a home you've never seen. You'll feel more at ease if you have your belongings."

"Thank you. That's unbelievably considerate."

"Don't thank me. I've asked a lot of you, and this was the least I could do in return."

A yawn erupted out of me, stretching my jaw to its full extent.

Rory picked me up, cradling my body in his thickly corded arms. "My wife needs a lie-down."

I lay my head on his chest as he carried me away to the bedroom.

He was nuts if he thought I'd get sick of him. How could I ever tire of this man?

Never going to happen.

Chapter Fourteen

I slept during the three-hour drive from the Inverness airport to Ballachulish, waking up in time to see the village zip past my window. Even on this cloudy day, Scotland looked lovely. Rory seemed at ease behind the wheel of his Mercedes S-Class, his hands steady and his focus squarely on the road ahead. A large lake stretched close to the road for a long ways, with more land visible in the distance across the waters.

Popping upright, I squinted at the scene around our car as the village dwindled in our rearview mirror. "What was that lake?"

"Loch Leven."

"Where are we going?"

"Home."

"Gee, you're so helpful with the details." I fell back against my seat. "We passed the village. I thought you lived in Ballachulish."

"I said I was born and raised there. I live an hour from Ballachulish, near a village called Loch Fairbairn."

"This house of yours, is it out in the boonies or close to town?"

He made a pained face, squirming in his seat. "I suppose that depends on your definition of boonies."

"Rory, honestly." I twisted in my seat to see him. "Why are you avoiding my question? Will I be living in the middle of nowhere or not?"

"You will. In a way." He made that face again. "I don't think of my home as remote, but you may have a different perspective."

"Are you afraid I'll be horrified when I see where you're taking me and flee as fast as I can?"

"Some women would."

I analyzed his face while he concentrated on guiding the Mercedes down the winding road. We went over a bridge, with Loch Leven on the right and another lake on the left, or maybe it was still Loch Leven.

"What's that?" I asked, pointing out the window. "Is it still Loch Leven?"

"No, that is Loch Linnhe." He sighed with melodramatic annoyance. "Are ye planning to question me for the entire trip? Why donnae ye go back to sleep?"

Ugh. He'd brought me to a strange land, triggering my voracious curiosity. He'd better get used to my craving for knowledge.

"What's got you so grumpy?" I asked. "Worried about seeing your family tomorrow?"

He squashed his lips while trying to pucker them, resulting in a goofy combination. "If I promise to point out every notable place we pass by, will you cease talking?"

"Absolutely not." I slanted in until my breasts grazed his arm. "If you wanted a wife who doesn't speak unless spoken to, you shouldn't have picked me. You knew damn well what I was like when you practically begged me to marry you. I talked plenty over the weekend in New Orleans."

"Incessantly, yes."

"Watch it, buster. I'm this close—" I held my hand before his face, my thumb and forefinger a quarter inch apart. "— to forfeiting that half million bucks by refusing to do you for at least two weeks."

His nonchalant shrug didn't fool me one bit. "I survived without sex for thirteen months before I met you."

"Thirteen months?" I slouched into my seat. At least the new fact explained some of his pent-up state. "It was six months for me. How many women have you slept with, total?"

"In my life? Twelve, including you."

Twelve. Okay, that wasn't an outrageous number for a man his age.

"What about you?" he asked. "How many men?"

"Five." I tapped a finger on my leg, mulling his number. "You mentioned before you've had four one-nighters."

"Three."

"Four including me."

He threw me an irritated glance. "I've spent more than one night with you."

"So, three one-nighters, me, three wives...That's seven. You've had five other lovers." Why was I prattling on about his sexual history, tallying the numbers like it mattered? Three of the women he hadn't cared about, hadn't known their names even. At least three he'd loved. "Um, those other five women—"

"Christ, Emery. What the devil is it you want to know?"

"Not sure." *Tell me about those other five, what they meant to you.*

Rory huffed and steered the car off the left side of the road, alongside a field lined with trees. Mountains hemmed in the valleys and the dark, glassy lochs, but Rory's foul mood distracted me from appreciating the scenery.

He squinted his face and massaged his forehead with his thumb and forefinger. "You want my full history? I fucked a girl in high school, but she preferred my brother Aidan, not that he'd have her. Even Aidan was never that callous. I fucked three more girls in college before I met my first wife. After she left me, I fucked one woman, but she threw me over. Satisfied?"

I reined in my compulsion to get annoyed at his offhanded listing of past liaisons. His tone had conveyed exhausted irritation with a hint of shame. He was upset about something, but not the question I'd asked.

"Listen," I said, keeping my voice even, "if you're trying to make me feel like an idiot for asking, forget it. I'm not that easy to cow. For your information, I've had five lovers in my life. One I almost married, another who humiliated me, and two who just didn't give a damn. Oh wait." I waved a hand in his direction. "Make that three who didn't give a damn."

The squinty expression on his face crumbled away. Moaning, he slumped forward to rest his head on the steering wheel between his hands. His entire body sagged.

He mumbled something.

"Didn't catch that," I said. "Take your face out of the steering wheel if you want me to understand."

Rory heaved his head up as if it weighed a ton.

Without looking at me, he said, "I don't regret marrying you, but I suspect you'll regret marrying me soon enough. If you don't already."

A shaft of sunlight broke through the clouds, streaming down on his face, revealing the dark circles under his eyes.

"When was the last time you slept?" I asked.

"Last night."

"For how long?"

He hesitated. "Two hours."

"No wonder you're so testy." I combed my fingers through his hair, caressing his cheek with my thumb. "Let me drive for a while."

"You have no idea where you're going." He eyed me askance. "And you'd need to drive on the left side."

"If you can handle right-side driving, I can manage the wrong way."

"Driving on the left isn't wrong in the UK."

"But it's unnatural." I tickled his cheek with my fingertips. "Why do you think they call it driving on the *right* side?"

He grumbled a wordless complaint, then said, "I'm fine to drive."

"At least take a nap." I nodded toward the dashboard. "The car's got GPS. Punch in the address, and I'll drive for a spell."

He wrung the steering wheel with his hands. "All right."

I clapped once. "Yay. My first driving experience in Scotland."

"You will wake me in twenty minutes. I need your word."

"Fine, I'll wake you up."

"In twenty minutes."

"Yes, Mr. Bossy."

We clambered out of the car and switched sides. I had to move the seat forward to accommodate my much shorter body. After a brief instructional session—during which he told me things I already knew, like which pedal was the gas and that I should avoid running into trees or lochs—Rory let me pull out onto the road. Onto the left side. With the other lane to my right. It felt weird, but I'd get used to it.

This was my home now. I needed to get used to a lot of things.

Rory fell asleep in two minutes flat.

I drove through the town of Fort William without crashing into anything or mowing down any pedestrians. The road signs were written in English and Gaelic. *So cool.* Though I would've loved to stop there to visit the museums I glimpsed, I knew Rory wanted to get home.

A few minutes after departing Fort William, I realized my twenty minutes were up. I pulled over to the left side of the road and roused my husband. Once we'd switched places and resumed our journey, I observed the view out my window in silence—until Rory began announcing landmarks and towns along our route, sometimes offering tidbits of information and sometimes simply reciting the names. He was trying, and at least he seemed more relaxed after his nap.

The further we traveled, the more we retreated into the wilds. A house here, a house there, no more villages. When we made our last turn, onto a dirt two-track, Rory announced, "Almost there."

"Where?" I bent forward but saw only the two-track unfolding ahead of us, carving a line through the woods.

"Home," he said without inflection. "This is the drive."

"You're saying this is your driveway, and we're almost to your house."

Rory nodded. "If you insist on repeating everything I say, yes."

"I'm excited."

"We'll be there shortly."

I whipped my head this way and that, craning my neck. "You said there was a village, Loch Fairbairn."

"Can't see it from here. The village is past the mountain, Beann Dealgach, behind my home. Our home."

"Beann Dealgach?" I said, probably butchering the name. "Is that Gaelic? I can't keep up."

He placed a hand on my thigh. "Easy, lass, we'll be there soon. And yes, most of the names are Scots Gaelic or Anglicized versions of the Gaelic."

I tapped my foot on the floorboard, hands pressed to my thighs, my gaze riveted to the driveway as I searched for a glimpse of my new home. Minutes elapsed on the dashboard clock while Rory maneuvered the car around potholes. My pulse kicked up a couple notches, and I gnawed at the inside of my lower lip. Why should I be this excited about a place I'd live in for a year, at most? It was dumb, but I couldn't shake the jittery anticipation.

The drive had segued into gravel that ticked on the undercarriage.

Just when I'd decided he was kidnapping me to a cave, we broke out of the trees and the house came into view.

House? The word fell woefully short of describing the place. I gripped the dashboard, tipped so far forward my head bumped the windshield. I twisted my head up and to the side to gape at—Oh lord, I'd thought he was kidding. But no.

My husband lived in a castle.

Not the fairytale kind with pretty, rounded turrets capped with cone-shaped roofs. This castle hunkered on the landscape, boxy and molded from grayish-brown stone. The main section soared three or four stories high, though I had trouble differentiating floors based on the uneven arrangement of windows. Three thingies jutted from the roof, two of them turrets and the third possibly a chimney. A blue flag emblazoned with a white X flew above the middle turret.

"Is that the flag of Scotland?" I asked.

"Yes," Rory replied as he steered the car ever nearer to the castle.

"How much land do you have?"

"One hundred acres."

A structure resembling a wall or a covered walkway joined the central, tallest structure to the shorter one behind and to the side of it. That rectangular building, narrow and only two stories high, featured a chimney but no turrets. An old wooden fence extended from the covered walkway, past the smaller building, and around the backside of the compound.

From the central building, a wall stretched to the left and concealed all but a glimpse of the top of another, much smaller structure one story high. A massive wooden gate embedded in the wall hung open like a monster's mouth ready to swallow us, and beyond it, the driveway curved around the castle's rear. Or front. I had no idea which was which.

Rory parked the car behind the main building, near the jutting section.

My eyes grew so big they burned from my inability to blink. A draft parched my mouth, thanks to my jaw going slack.

I was moving into a genuine castle, complete with a wall and a gate.

Beyond the driveway, opposite the freaking *castle*, a lavish garden filled a walled space connected to the exterior wall, and a broad entrance afforded me a splendid view inside. Plants flourished in a natural way, their wildness curbed only enough to keep them from overflowing the outer walls and the paths within the garden. Flowers in a multitude of colors flowed out of large, bowl-shaped containers or spilled from the branches of green bushes. Rectangular beds that curved in graceful, random shapes housed more brilliant buds, interspersed with decorative greenery. Even more flowers covered the wooden latticework of a small arbor.

My door swung open.

I yelped and jerked upright, thumping my head on the windshield for the second time. While I'd gawped in mute awe at my surroundings, Rory had climbed out of the car and crossed to my side.

He offered me his hand.

I accepted his aid to climb out of the car, stumbling on the gravel as I rubbernecked some more, transfixed by this glorious place. I shook off his hand, wheeling in circles to soak in a three-hundred-sixty-degree view of the castle compound.

"Holy shit," I said, sounding as awestruck as I felt. "This is amazing. I assumed you were pulling my leg when you said you live in a castle, but this…" I threw my head back and whooped. "I love Scotland!"

Rory's mouth warped and crimped, but his sparkling eyes gave away his mood. He was, once again, fighting off a smile.

"The garden," I said, swinging an arm in that direction. "It's so…freewheeling. Did you design it?"

"I gave Tavish, the groundskeeper, a few instructions. Then I told him to do what he wanted and have at it."

"The garden is gorgeous. This whole place is stunning."

"It's home," he said casually, shutting the car door. "Come inside. You'll have plenty of time to explore the grounds later. Let's get you settled."

My mouth seemed incapable of shutting itself. I lagged behind him on our way toward a wooden door situated where the jutting-out section fused with the central building, which itself stuck out to the left. The turret I'd spotted from outside the walls was attached to the right-hand corner.

The door burst open. A stout, middle-aged woman with curly gray hair dashed out to clinch Rory in a bear hug.

He patted the woman's back. "Hello, Mrs. Darroch."

She released him, grabbing his face in both hands. Her blue eyes twinkled in the light of the partly sunny day. "Rory, ye naughty *chuilein*. Sneaking off to America to bring home a bride and not telling anyone until the deed was done."

He ducked his head, shoulders slumped. "Well, I…"

The woman cowing him wore a plain denim dress and a white apron, with sensible shoes. A white substance, maybe flour, smeared her cheek.

Rory seized my hand, hauling me against his side. With his arm latched around me, he cleared his throat. "This is my wife, Emery Granger."

"MacTaggart," I corrected, earning a surprised look from my husband. "I may be unconventional in many ways, but I have a traditional streak. My mother raised me to believe a woman should take her husband's name."

He stared at me, unblinking, then nodded toward the other woman. "Emery, this is Mrs. Evelyn Darroch, my housekeeper."

I held out my hand to Mrs. Darroch. "Pleasure to meet you."

She took my hand in the firm grip of one callused hand. When she beamed at me, the expression etched deep lines around her eyes. She didn't strike me as old and worn, though. Rather, she had the air of a jolly older woman who might've married Santa Claus. The motherly sort, based on her interactions with Rory.

"Lovely to meet ye, dearie," Mrs. Darroch said. She wrested me away from Rory and into an enthusiastic hug. When she let go, she clasped my upper arms as she sized me up. "My, ye are a bonnie wee thing."

Wee? I was taller than the woman speaking to me.

"Emery is intelligent," Rory said, his tone a tad defensive, "and very… adventurous. She was a computer programmer, but she's taking time to find a new vocation."

"No need for excuses, *mo luran*," Mrs. Darroch said. She winked and added, "Ye must love her, or ye wouldnae have made sure to tell me how clever and adventurous she is."

Rory hugged me to his side again and planted a solid kiss on my cheek, gazing at me like he sincerely adored me.

My stomach fluttered. *Stupid tummy.*

The housekeeper snared my hand. "I'll show you around your new home, Mrs. MacTaggart."

"Call me Emery."

"What a charming name." She gave my hand a little tug, drawing me away from Rory. "Come, lassie. Cannae have ye getting lost your first night here."

Rory nabbed my other hand, forcing me to stop after I'd gone a mere one step.

"Mrs. Darroch," he said, "I will show my wife the house. You should be home in bed."

"Tosh," Mrs. Darroch said as she relinquished my hand. "It's early evening, and my home is behind the garden, not in Devonshire. Thought I should stay to be a neutral party, considering."

Rory stopped on the threshold. "Considering what?"

She gave him the kind of look only a mother could pull off, one that said he was a good boy but kind of an idiot. "Ye've forgotten, haven't ye? Jamie's here."

"Jamie—" He squashed his mouth into a pale line, muttered an oath, and turned his attention to me. "My sister Jamie has been living with me for over a year."

No wild sex in every corner of the house, then. *Bummer.*

At his bulging-eyed expression, I tried to hold back a smile. He looked so disarmingly flustered. "It's no big deal, Rory. I want to meet your family. Might as well get started today and test the waters with one sibling, since I'll be meeting the whole gang tomorrow."

"Are you sure? Jamie can be…energetic."

"Oh, you mean like me." I tickled the underside of his chin. "If I can handle being me, I can handle your energetic sister."

He gazed at me with appreciation and a hint of surprise. "I imagine you can."

Mrs. Darroch retreated into the house, waving for us to follow. "Ye'll be wanting to see your new home. It's called Dùndubhan."

"What's that mean?" I asked as Rory shepherded me inside.

Rory answered my query. "It means fortress of the black water. Either that or fortress of the fishhook."

"Fishhook?" I said with a laugh. "Not very imposing."

He harrumphed. "You're in the vestibule of the not-imposing castle."

We followed Mrs. Darroch past a spiral staircase into a long hallway.

Someone shrieked.

I whirled to the right, into the path of a young woman barreling down the hallway. Her long hair, the same shade as Rory's, flew wild around her face. She had the same angelic features as Rory too but lacked his studied composure. The girl shrieked again as she descended on me.

Her arms flung around me, and she babbled excitedly in my ear.

"You must be her," she said. "Rory's wife, the one he met in America and couldn't wait to marry so he went on and did it and never told us until yesterday but—Oh! You must be exhausted from the trip, but how romantic and—"

"Jamie!" Rory hollered.

Unfazed, Jamie relinquished me only to snatch up my hands and beam at me with all the joy of someone unfettered by fears of what others might think. I liked her already.

"Don't be a humbug," Jamie told Rory. "I want to meet your wife."

He ground his teeth and offered terse introductions. "This is Emery. And this is my youngest sister, Jamie."

I grinned, because I couldn't not grin with Jamie beaming at me. "I kinda figured that one out, but thanks for the super-friendly intro."

He barred his arms over his broad chest.

"Ignore him," Jamie said. "I'm friendly enough for both of us. And I'm sooooo happy to meet you, Emery."

"Likewise, Jamie."

My sister-in-law grabbed me by the arm. "Let me give you the tour. This house is really a castle, do ye know? Built in the Middle Ages."

"I knew it was a castle, yeah, but Rory hasn't been forthcoming with the details."

Jamie dragged me down the hall. "We'll start the tour here."

"Stop," Rory said, his stern voice reverberating in the hall. "I will show my wife our home, if you please, Jamie."

"No need to shout at me. Ahmno deaf, Rory."

"Why don't you go to bed?"

Jamie snorted. "Ahmno five years old. It's only seven o'clock."

Rory glowered at her, without any real punch to the expression.

"All right," Jamie said, hands raised in surrender. "But I want to talk to my new sister over dinner."

"Fine," Rory hissed. "Stay down here. The top floor is for myself and my wife alone."

Jamie saluted, clicking her heels together. "Aye-aye, admiral. I willnae step a toe on the third floor, so you and Emery can make all the noise ye want when you're shagging."

My husband flashed his sister a frown, then towed me down the hall.

Jamie and Mrs. Darroch laughed softly and retreated into the vestibule.

"This is the ground floor," Rory said. "The house has four levels."

"Cool."

Despite his frazzled state, he continued with the tour. "We have a land-line, and every room has a telephone. You can dial out, but you can also ring the kitchen, my office, or the master suite."

He took me on a forced march through the castle, pointing out various rooms on each level. The ground floor boasted a large bathroom with a claw-foot tub and a separate shower, as well as a laundry room, dining room, cloakroom—aka one huge coat closet—and an exercise room. The dining room opened into the guest wing which housed bedrooms, bathrooms, the kitchen, and a sitting room. We passed windows here and there, but this wasn't a well-lit abode. I supposed castle-builders cared more about security than southern exposure.

When we tromped up to the next level, Rory said, "This is the first floor."

"Downstairs isn't the first floor?"

"That's the ground floor," he said with immense patience. "This is the first floor."

"But it's upstairs."

"You will adjust to the oddities of castle living."

The first floor, known to any normal human as the second floor, contained a cavernous room called a "great hall." Beyond that lay another room, its door closed.

"At our right is the library, my office," he said. "Inside that is the old study I've converted into a file room."

"Your law office is in your castle?"

"I work from home quite a lot, but I do have an office in Loch Fairbairn. I go there for client meetings."

Up the stairs we slogged, my thighs complaining about the unexpected exercise. I'd get strong legs after a year of traipsing up and down four floors.

"Is there an elevator?" I asked.

"No. This is a castle, not a shopping mall."

"Just asking, sheesh."

On the second floor, we paused so Rory could point out the gigantic "long gallery," a space that made the great hall seem cozy, and a bedroom in "the tower." My head spinning, I jogged to keep up with Rory as he ascended to the third and final floor. Which was actually the fourth level.

Rory halted in a long hallway. "Our bedrooms are up here, along with a shower room, bathroom, and dressing room. There's also a third bedroom accessed through yours, with stairs leading down to it."

"Um…" I rubbed my eyes and my temples. "The last bedroom is actually on the second floor, but its door is up here?"

"No, it's between floors."

"I'm never going to get any of this, am I?" Something he'd said a minute ago finally registered in my brain. "What do you mean the third bedroom is accessed through mine? You mean our bedroom, right?"

"You'll sleep in that bedroom." He pointed toward the door at the right end of the hall. "I sleep in the master bedroom, there."

He hooked a thumb toward the left end of the hall.

I nailed him with a hard look. "Separate bedrooms? That wasn't part of the deal."

"We hadn't discussed sleeping arrangements." He walked toward the door at the left end of the hallway, and I followed in his wake. He opened the door enough for me to glimpse what lay inside. "The dressing room. My bedroom is accessed through it. When the boxes of your belongings arrive tomorrow, you can store any you don't need here. We share a bathroom, there."

He gestured toward another doorway.

Considering him, I cocked my hip with a hand balanced on it. "What happens when we have sex?"

"I don't understand the question."

"We screw, and then what? Do you scamper back to your master bedroom, leaving me alone in my hole in the wall?"

"Your room is not a hole in the wall."

"Well, this explains why you ordered Jamie never to come up here." I narrowed my gaze, trying to spear him with it, but he seemed unaffected. "Wouldn't want your sister to find out you don't sleep with your wife. A quick roll in the hay, and you're off to your private suite for the night."

"You make it sound unseemly."

"What about Mrs. Darroch? Does she know?"

Head down, he scratched his brow with a fingertip. "She does. Mrs. Darroch cares for the whole house, and I had her prepare your room for you. I told her we'll sleep in separate rooms because you snore."

"I snore? Thanks a bunch, Rory."

"Everyone knows I don't snore."

"Guess that was a fly snoring in the car while I was driving."

Totally deadpan, he said, "It must've been."

Rory never smiled at me except as an expression of sexual hunger. He would smile for me one day soon, though, I'd make sure of it. A real, joyful smile.

I envisioned a smiling, exuberant Rory. He'd be devastatingly gorgeous if he graced the world with a genuine grin. Maybe he'd pull me into his arms and spin us around and around, laughing all the while.

"What's wrong with you?" he asked, shattering my beautiful fantasy.

"Huh?" Yanked back to reality, my brain fumbled to readjust. Ah, that fantasy had been so nice. "What do you mean? Nothing's wrong."

He eyed me with suspicion. "You looked...dazed."

A half-suppressed laugh snorted out of me. "Dazed? Guess you only know how to sweet talk a girl when you want to get lucky."

I hadn't been dazed. I'd been dreamy.

He glanced up at the ceiling, then gestured toward the stairwell. "Jamie's waiting for us to have dinner with her. We should go."

Deciding not to argue, I let him lead me away from our rooms.

Chapter Fifteen

An hour later, the three of us lounged in the sitting room having enjoyed a yummy meal of locally produced sausage with potatoes and turnips. Mrs. Darroch, who'd rustled up the dinner, called them tatties and neeps. I fell in love with the housekeeper when I learned she'd left us a blueberry tray cake coated with sugar and coconut. After my second piece, I joined Jamie in sipping hot cocoa, a beverage Rory refused. My sister-in-law claimed cocoa would soothe our jet lag and help us sleep better. Rory denied ever experiencing jet lag, calling it "a mental state, not a physical condition."

I'd yawned my way through our dinner, despite having taken a nap on the jet and another one in the car. Soothed by the cocoa, I yawned again and slumped into my cushy chair, eyes half closed.

Jamie occupied one end of an adjacent sofa, legs tucked under her and hugging a pillow to her belly, smiling in a knowing way as she switched her attention back and forth between me and Rory.

My husband sat upright in a high-backed chair angled to face halfway toward the windows. He drank whisky from a tumbler, his gaze on one of the three tall windows overlooking the castle compound. Sunset ignited the sky and wispy clouds with a pinkish glow.

Tonight, I'd learned the Scots spelled the word whisky without an E, and that Rory preferred Ben Nevis single malt. The brand originated in Fort William, the town we'd passed near Ballachulish. His brother Lachlan had a weakness for Talisker single malt, made on the Isle of Skye, and his brother Aidan had no real preference. Apparently, he would drink any brand. As for his sisters, when I'd asked what they liked to drink Jamie had pretended to gag and told me she and her sisters hated whisky.

"Men have no taste buds," she informed me. "They'll drink anything. I like Irn Bru."

"That's not a real drink," Rory said with disdain. "It's orange soda."

"I'd like to try it sometime," I told Jamie, who nodded her approval.

My hubby made a disgusted noise. "Donnae think I'll kiss ye after ye drink it."

Another yawn overtook me, and I glanced at the grandfather clock in the corner. The time was nine o'clock. That equated with two in the afternoon, Colorado time. I shouldn't be tired, yet I was.

"You two are so sweet," Jamie said.

Rory cast her a sideways glance. "My wife would say I'm grumpy."

"She'd be right. I meant overall, the way you are together." Jamie absently rubbed circles on the pillow over her belly. "When will you have bairns?"

Rory sputtered and coughed but managed to keep from spilling his whisky.

"Bairns?" I asked.

Jamie gave me an impish smile. "Babies."

Ah, no wonder Rory had gone into apoplexy over that one. We hadn't talked about children because our marriage was a one-year farce.

"Mind your own business," Rory snapped.

His sister looked pleased with herself, as if she knew a wonderful secret. Something related to his ex-wives? Had he wanted children with any of them? How had he behaved with those women? He'd told me he loved his previous wives.

Jamie tossed her pillow aside and hopped off the sofa. "I'm for bed. You can go upstairs to your king-and-queen's bedroom and make all the noise you like. I can't hear a blessed thing down here."

Rory made an exasperated face as Jamie skipped out of the room humming.

Once the sitting room door clicked shut, and Jamie's humming faded into the distance, I wandered over to the windows. Choosing the middle one, near Rory's chair, I took a seat on its broad sill.

"Do you want kids?" I asked.

He didn't sputter this time because he'd just lifted his glass to his lips and hadn't imbibed yet. Appraising me over the tumbler's rim, he tapped a finger on the glass. "Why do you ask?"

"Curiosity." I folded one leg to lodge my foot on the windowsill and wrapped both arms around my raised knee. "You're on your fourth marriage. Did you want kids with your ex-wives?"

He swirled his whisky, peering into its amber depths that mirrored the color of his eyes. "Doesn't matter."

"I'd like to know, please."

He slouched back in his chair and stretched out his legs, crossing one ankle over the other. His attention remained on his drink, though he'd stopped sipping it. "I tried with my first wife, Isobel, but it never happened. Lilias, my second wife, wanted to wait until she felt more settled in her position as a schoolteacher. She divorced me nineteen months later. Left me for someone else and they had a baby. Una never wanted children, but she didn't tell me until after we were married."

"That was rotten."

He shut his eyes and sighed. "I should've asked before marrying her. Turned out Una didn't want a bairn with me, but she was happy to have one with her next...partner."

Though I sensed his carefully worded answers hinted at deeper stories, I didn't want to push. Still, I had to point out the obvious. "You haven't answered my question. Do you want children?"

He cracked one eye open. "Leave it alone, Emery."

No point in pushing anymore. He wouldn't tell me.

I yawned again, big and thorough and noisy.

Rory tossed back the last of his whisky, surged up from his chair, and reached me in one long stride. With a hand on the window frame, he slanted in—close enough I felt his exhalations whispering over my skin and scented the whisky on his breath.

"Time for bed," he announced.

I slid off the windowsill and landed flat on the floor in my bare feet. I hoisted up onto my toes, leaning in, and tilted my head back to meet Rory's gaze. His breaths shortened. The lust in his eyes made my skin tighten. I splayed my hands on his chest, loving the feel of his silky shirt on my palms.

"Yes, please," I said. "Let's go to bed."

"To sleep, Emery." His hooded gaze told me otherwise, the way his eyes smoldered. His voice had gone rough, but he insisted, "You need rest, to recover from the jet lag."

"So do you." I glided my hands up to his shirt collar, pressing my body against his, my nipples hardening as they raked over his muscles. "Might as well lie down together."

"I doubt either one of us would sleep that way." He dipped his head, as if to nuzzle my cheek or neck, but caught himself. "We will lie down. You in your room, and I in mine."

My hands roved up and over his shoulders, and I linked them behind his nape. "Your perfect grammar makes me so hot."

"Behave, Emery." Despite his chastising words, he sounded ready to tear my clothes off, a conclusion his growing erection confirmed.

"You like it when I misbehave." I twirled my fingers at his nape, rewarded by his sharp intake of breath. "Never asked me what kind of whisky I like."

"Try Ben Nevis. I think you'd like it."

"I'd love to taste it." I feathered my lips over his, licking at the seam of his mouth, detecting a hint of the whisky. "Think I'll sample it now."

My fingers spread over his scalp, I clasped the back of his head in both hands and fused my mouth to his. He parted his lips, inviting me to take more, and I delved my tongue into the silken depths of his mouth, exploring with leisurely strokes, teasing the roof of his mouth and coiling my tongue around his until he responded with hungry thrusts. His hands came around my waist, and he pulled me into him while plunging deeper into my mouth.

The whisky. Oh God, the flavor of it mingled with the hints of the cake we'd both eaten, transforming it into a heady concoction. The whisky was rich, smoky, imbued with a touch of nut and even chocolate, with an undercurrent of fruitiness. So decadent. So tantalizing. So…Rory.

"Mmm," I moaned into his mouth, then retreated from the exquisite pleasure of kissing my husband, reluctantly separating our mouths. Relaxed and aroused at the same time, I massaged his nape and felt my lips curve into a lazy smile. "Delicious."

He stared down at me, lips slightly swollen from our kiss. His eyes scorched into mine, and his hands bound me to him.

I danced my fingers over his cheek.

He blinked rapidly as if coming out of a trance. "To bed, Emery. You in your room—"

"And you in yours. Yeah, I heard you the first time." I let my hands fall away from his shoulders and rocked back on my heels. "I'm not crazy about this separate-bedrooms thing."

"Once you've lived with me for a while, you'll be glad of the privacy."

That stopped me. Back in Colorado, when I'd said I liked him, he told me I'd change my mind about that soon enough. Tonight, he assured me I'd want my own bedroom so I could get away from him. Jesus, he really believed I'd get sick of him and want out.

Hence, the half-million-dollar bribe to stay for a year.

One puzzle piece clicked into place in my mind, but a thousand more lay scattered around it. Knowing more about his ex-wives might help me sort out the mess, but I didn't dare push too hard to get him to tell me. We'd made progress today, and I wouldn't screw it up.

To keep him from panicking, I needed to acquiesce to one of his directives.

"You are my husband for the next year," I said. "I'd rather share a bed with you, but if separate bedrooms makes you feel safer, I'll go along with it. For the time being."

"Thank you."

"You're welcome."

He spun on his heels and headed for the door. "Upstairs, to bed."

I hurried to catch up, following him down the hallway and through the door to the dining room, out into the main hall and up the winding stairs to the top floor. At my bedroom door, he halted with shoulders stiff and chin elevated.

"Sleep well," he said, turning to leave.

I laid a hand on his arm to stop him. "No good-night kiss?"

Face averted, he said, "You had your kiss downstairs. Good night, Emery."

My husband hustled down the hall to his bedroom door—far, far away from mine at the opposite end of the hall. The door shut behind him.

Oh Rory, what will I do with you?

Succumbing to another yawn, I shambled into my room and sagged against the closed door. I knew exactly what to do with Rory. On the day I accepted his proposition, I'd informed him that he would be my mission. Loosening him up might prove harder than I'd ever imagined.

I pushed away from the door, rolling my shoulders back. When did I ever give up on a task because it was difficult? I may have languished in corporate hell for too long, but I hadn't lost my gumption.

"Rory MacTaggart, you are in trouble now. I'm coming for you."

A small smile stretched my lips. One day soon, Rory would cave and allow himself to have a good time. With me. In every way I could dream up, and any he dreamed up. In bed, out of bed, in the daytime or at night, anytime and anywhere.

Warm tingles swept over my skin, raising the hairs up and down my arms. Rory unleashed would be awe-inspiring. Magnificent. Earth-shattering.

The hairs all over my body shivered erect at the thought of him grinning and laughing and scooping me into his arms to twirl us around and around.

Aw, shit. I was pining for my husband. Not in love with him, not yet, but definitely pining for a day when he might harbor some glimmer of feelings for me.

I slapped the heel of my hand on my forehead and groaned. *Emery, you damn idiot.* Maybe I was an idiot, but I'd made a promise to myself and to Rory. I would get him to enjoy life if it killed me.

Or if it broke my heart.

I shuffled to the bed, stripped off my clothes, and climbed under the covers of my big, four-poster bed in my big, high-ceilinged bedroom inside a ginormous castle in the middle of Nowhere, Scotland.

And I prayed for sleep.

Chapter Sixteen

The next morning, I loitered in the vestibule in the shadow of the spiral staircase, immobilized by the thought of what awaited me outside the main door. The front door, I supposed, even though it opened into the courtyard-type area behind the house. Or maybe the part facing the long driveway was the front. My brain couldn't wrap itself around the layout of this fortress, or the simple idea I lived in a castle.

Simple. *Hah.* Nothing about my new life was simple.

I smoothed my pale-blue cotton shirt, skipping my fingers over the buttons to make sure I'd done them up right. Meeting my in-laws with misaligned buttons would make them wonder whether I was merely a total ditz, or if I'd sprinted outside after a quick roll in the silk sheets with my husband. Couldn't decide which conclusion would be worse.

Sheesh, I felt like a wreck this morning. A night of tossing and turning would do that to a girl.

As I checked my clothes again, panic jolted me. Were jeans the right image to show my in-laws? Maybe I should've worn a skirt—except most of my skirts had high hems and/or revealing slits up the side. I'd worn pants to work every day, but Travellis Games had encouraged a casual environment with jeans or cargo pants as the standard. Though I owned eight pairs of jeans in varying colors and styles, I owned no dress slacks. The jeans I'd pulled on this morning were dark blue, not stonewashed or ripped. Though they featured a low-slung waist, my shirt covered my belly.

My shirt. *Gah!* I slapped a hand over my cleavage, exposed by the deeply plunging neckline.

I whirled around, intent on sprinting up three flights of stairs to exchange my shirt for a more demure option. Instead, I collided with Rory.

Yelping, I flailed backward.

He caught me around the waist and held me tight.

Though I couldn't see all of him, I took in enough of his appearance to realize I was doomed. He, of course, looked perfect—put together and neat, dressed in a tan, long-sleeve shirt with the top button undone and a pair of khaki pants, not to mention his smooth and shiny leather boots. He'd shaved and showered, as evidenced by his damp hair.

I'd had no time for a shower. My crummy night's sleep had concluded with me falling into a near-coma around four a.m. I hadn't woken until twenty-eight minutes before his family was set to arrive.

Plastered to his delectable body, I inhaled in an attempt to clear my head. *Aw, shit.* He smelled good too, his aftershave enlivening my senses with hints of wood, spice, and musk. My brain, overloaded by anxiety, shut down in the face of his yumminess. The only thoughts I could muster were *man smell good, lick man, crawl under man's clothes.*

Rory watched me with a neutral expression. "Are you all right?"

"Yeah, sure." I unleashed a pitiful moan. "No, I'm not. Jeez, I was never this nervous for job interviews. I'm a disaster. Why do you have to look so good and smell so good? It's not fair."

"Emery." He dropped his hands to my ass. "You are beautiful, but my family doesn't care about superficial things. They want to know who you are, and you have no reason to be fashed about that. Jamie worships you after one evening in your presence."

In addition to his perfect appearance, he calmed me with the perfect words. Damn confusing, since half the time he was terse and tense. This time, however, he'd hit the mark. I dissolved into him, everything inside me warm and liquid.

"Your sister worships you too, you're her hero." I considered the door to the hallway. "Where is Jamie?"

"She went out to keep the family from storming our castle."

The blood seemed to evacuate my whole body. "They're mad? Oh God, I—"

His mouth sealed over mine, silencing my panic. With his lips lingering on my mouth, he said, "No one is angry. Relax, Emery. I've never seen you frantic before."

"You've known me for less than a week." Our lips scraped each other when we spoke, a distractingly sensual contact. "To be fair, I've never been this frantic before. Never had to meet the in-laws, seeing as I called off my last engagement. And considering your opinion of me, I'm not sure what your family will think. Jamie might be an aberration."

Those big, strong hands on my ass squeezed gently. "What do you think my opinion of you is?"

"I'm crazy and annoying."

He nibbled on my upper lip, his tongue flicking against the tip of mine. "You're wrong."

"Then what do you think..." My voice trailed off as two of his fingers dipped between my legs to rub me through my jeans. I stifled a moan but clamped my hands on his biceps, my knees suddenly weak.

Those fingers caressed me while his breaths whispered into my mouth. "We can discuss that later."

He hefted me up onto my tiptoes, devouring me with a rough, demanding kiss. My body came alive, every nerve sensitized to the pressure of his hands on my ass and his fingers tormenting my sex and his tongue thrashing against mine. My breasts ached, and little jolts of electric lust fired through my nipples straight down to my core.

A moan vibrated in my throat.

He set me down and peeled his hands away, then patted my shoulders. "You're ready."

"I'm—huh?"

"You're not nervous anymore," he said, with self-satisfaction in his voice and on his face.

Oh, you sneaky bastard. He got me wound up so I wouldn't think about the gauntlet to come. Well, he had vowed he knew how to relax me. I hadn't believed he'd actually do this to me, though.

"Terrific," I said, straightening my shirt and staggering backward a step. "I get to meet your family while I'm on the verge of orgasm."

"At least no one will doubt we married for love." He tapped a finger on my nose. "You look like the adoring bride."

Because I was dazed, which could easily pass for dreamy adoration of my husband. Maybe I did adore him, on occasion, but right now I could've smacked him.

Instead, I jabbed a finger into his chest. "Don't ever do that to me again."

He arched one brow.

Smoothing my shirt, I tried for composure but fell short. "Unless, you know, I ask you to do it."

"Of course," he said. "Only when you beg me for it."

No point in arguing. My body thrummed whenever he touched me, and we both knew I wasn't above imploring him to take me.

A fist banged on the door.

I jumped. Rory withdrew his hand from my hip, his body went rigid, and his gaze sharpened on the door.

"Rory!" A man shouted. "Are ye coming out to see us? Or should we let ourselves inside?"

My husband stomped to the door, ripped it open, and confronted the man waiting on the doorstep.

As tall as Rory, the stranger boasted a body even more muscular than his brother's. His lustrous blue irises glittered in the sunlight, and humor glinted in those eyes as he took in the sight of me, pink-cheeked and flustered. The stranger resembled Rory in many ways, though his chestnut hair was a shade darker than Rory's and lacked the golden overtones.

Rory made an exasperated noise. "Aidan, what the bloody hell are you doing? We'll come out when we're ready."

"When you're ready," Aidan repeated with a sly smile. "Would that be before or after you have a quick poke in the vestibule?"

He enunciated "vestibule" so carefully, and with a smidgen of sarcasm, that I wondered if Rory was a stickler for making everyone use the correct term for this entryway.

Yeah, he would be.

Rory made a sound between a growl and a huff. "I don't have a poke anywhere."

I raised my hand. "What's a poke?"

Aidan's lips split into a mischievous grin. "It's a word for sex."

I stepped up beside Rory, though his arm blocked me from Aidan, what with his hand on the doorjamb. "We weren't doing that."

"What a shame," Aidan said, still grinning. He thumped his fist into Rory's shoulder. "I see why ye married her so fast. She's bonnie and braw."

"I'm what now?" I asked.

"Braw means fine, and bonnie means beautiful."

I'd known what bonnie meant, but braw was a new one on me. "Thank you for the compliment, then. I'm Emery, by the way, since my husband won't introduce us."

Ducking under Rory's arm, I squeezed in front of him and proffered my hand to Aidan. He shook it, his smile deepening when Rory squinted and compressed his lips.

My brother-in-law turned sideways, motioning us to come outside. "Everyone's waiting."

A gaggle of people—men, women, and two babies—observed from the other side of the courtyard, near the garden.

Rory grasped my shoulders, anchoring me in place.

Aidan waggled his eyebrows. "Willnae let her out of the house, eh? From what Jamie said, Emery's not the sort to let you lock her indoors."

"I'm also not the sort," I said, "to do whatever my husband says."

"Aye, Jamie said that too." Aidan's eyes glittered with more than sunshine. "A strong-willed, feisty American. Just the sort of woman Rory needs, whether he knows it or not."

That was when I decided I liked Aidan. Without a thought for what Rory or anyone might think, I hopped up to give Aidan a quick hug. "What a nice thing to say. Thank you, Aidan."

When I dropped back onto my heels, sideways to Rory, my husband rolled his eyes. "You can stop thanking my brother for being an erse."

"He means ass," Aidan explained.

"Rory, your brother is not an ass," I said. "Now, let's go greet the rest of your family."

Like a king and queen receiving guests, Rory and I stood in front of the little arbor in the garden as his relatives filed past to greet us. The fragrance of roses wafted from the vines that climbed the arbor's latticework, while huge rhododendron bushes blossomed at either side of us. Nine MacTaggarts shook my hand, and each one expressed happiness about my marriage to Rory. The kindness of their words touched me so deeply I couldn't restrain myself.

I hugged all of them.

Rory's older brother, Lachlan, slapped my husband on the arm and said, "Did ye kidnap her, Rory?"

His wife, Erica—a pretty American with brown hair who held their toddler son, Nicholas, in her arms—shook her head. "Give the poor girl a break. She's not used to the MacTaggart tradition of incessant, well-meaning harassment."

Rory ignored his brother's comment, though Lachlan seemed thoroughly entertained by Rory's harried expression.

Aidan breezed past Lachlan towing the lovely Calli, his redheaded American wife, in his wake. He secured her delicate hand with his big one. She cradled a baby in a sling-like doohickey that crossed diagonally over her chest and abdomen.

"Out of the way, Lachie," Aidan said briskly. "Donnae get to hog the new girl."

Lachlan scowled at his brother's use of the diminutive Lachie.

Rory came soooo close to smiling.

The procession included Gavin Douglas, the brother of Aidan's wife. He seemed uneasy at this family gathering, but we exchanged comments about getting used to a new country. I learned he was also Jamie's boyfriend, and that they had a long-distance romance. He would fly back to America later today.

I got a bit queasy when Rory introduced me to his parents. Niall and Sorcha MacTaggart treated me like a longtime member of the family, but I felt weird keeping up our farce for them. Fooling his siblings was one thing. Tricking his mommy and daddy was quite another.

Sorcha latched her arms around me and said, "Welcome to the family, Emery. We couldn't be more pleased to meet anyone."

Rory snorted out a poorly stifled laugh. "Don't let Lachlan or Aidan hear you say that. They think their wives are the bonniest, most charming women in all the world."

"They are," his mother said. "All our American daughters are equally bonnie and sweet and welcome. But Emery is a wonderful surprise."

"Aye," said Niall, his face betraying nothing in a Rory-like fashion. Like father, like son. "We were afraid those other ones had put Rory off marriage for good."

"Niall," his wife chastised, "we agreed not to mention the others in front of Emery."

He made a dismissive noise. "Sorcha, ye cannae treat him like a bairn. Rory's a grown man who can abide hearing his ex-wives mentioned."

Rory had gone stiff, his face blank, his eyes trained on me.

Was he worried how I'd react to the mention of his exes? Or did talk of them upset him? Maybe he still loved one of the women who'd wrecked him. I had no illusions I could fix Rory, but I could sure as hell challenge him to enjoy life a bit more.

Rory's sisters herded their parents out of the way, determined to corral me. Jamie I'd met yesterday, so I greeted her with a hug. Fiona offered a friendly introduction and assured me she agreed with Aidan that I was perfect for Rory, inspiring me to hug her as well. Catriona hung back until both her sisters ambled off to mingle and Lachlan called Rory away.

Catriona inspected me for a moment, seeming to gauge my worthiness. Then she nodded, satisfied, and glanced past my shoulder. "I have to thank you for that."

"For what?" I peeked over my shoulder, to where Rory hung out with his brothers. My husband was laughing and smiling, gesticulating to illustrate whatever he'd said. I swallowed against a lump in my throat. He seemed happier with his brothers than with me.

"He's never been this happy before," Catriona said. "The last time I saw him laughing this way was at Lachlan's wedding. You're clearly good for him."

I wanted to be good for him, I tried to be good for him. Catriona's confirmation I'd succeeded, in whatever small way, made tears prick at my eyes. If his family thought he'd found happiness with me, maybe I had a chance after all.

Naturally, I threw my arms around Catriona. "Thank you. That's the nicest thing anyone has said to me."

She patted my back, muttered something polite, and left to find her sisters.

A bit later, Calli and Erica tracked me down to offer me advice on living with a Scotsman.

"If your husband says something that sounds like gibberish," Erica told me, "call me or Calli. We can translate for you."

"And if your husband mentions a caber," Calli said, "that's a big wooden pole. Scottish men like to throw them around."

"Good to know," I said.

We agreed to get together one day soon, just the American wives. When I referred to us as the American Wives Club, both women laughed and agreed it was the perfect name for us.

A few minutes after Calli and Erica left me, Sorcha towed Rory back to me with Niall hurrying to catch up to them. Rory's mother shooed him toward me as her husband jogged up beside her.

Sorcha claimed both my hands, sandwiching them between her warm palms. "Rory told us you haven't seen your family in a long time. I hope ye donnae mind, but I asked for your parents' number and Rory gave it to me. I had a good chat with your mother last night."

How had Rory gotten my parents' number? I'd grill him about that later.

I smiled at my mother-in-law. "That's great. I imagine you and my mom commiserated over being left out of the loop on this marriage thing. I really have to apologize—"

"Hush, lass." Sorcha squeezed my hands. "I'm happy to see Rory awake to the world again. He's been hiding in his castle keep for too long, like the ghost of a medieval laird."

I couldn't prevent my smile from broadening. "That's a perfect description, Mrs. MacTaggart."

"Och." She waved a dismissive hand. "Call me Sorcha."

Sorcha looked at me like I was the answer to her prayers.

Man, Rory hadn't exaggerated. His family must've *really* wanted him to get married again.

His mother freed my hands. "Penny and I had a wonderful idea. Since you and Rory eloped, neither family had the chance to witness your marriage."

Rory secured an arm around my waist. "Mother, what are you on about?"

With a decisive little nod, she said, "We're having a wedding for you. A proper, traditional ceremony."

Rory sighed. "If it'll make you happy, we can plan it for a few months out."

"No." Sorcha anchored her hands on her hips. "It'll be Saturday two weeks."

Chapter Seventeen

"Bod an Donais," Rory hissed. "Ye cannae order us to—"

"Rory Niall MacTaggart, don't you curse at me," Sorcha said in that tone every mother perfected. "You decided to sweep the lass off her feet and bulldoze her through a marriage ceremony in a magistrate's office, in another country. This wedding is for Emery as much as for me and Penny and our families."

Rory moaned, with a hint of a whine. "Mother…"

She arched one brow exactly the way he did sometimes. "Lachlan and Aidan gave us weddings."

Ah, the guilt card. *Well played, Sorcha.*

Rory's shoulders slumped. "I gave ye three ceremonies. How many do ye need?"

"One for every marriage. Lachlan didnae complain about another wedding."

"He's only had two."

Out the corner of my mouth, I whispered to him, "Let her have this."

He shut his eyes and hung his head for a moment, then pulled himself up. "You can have your wedding. In *three* weeks."

"It's your wedding, Rory," Sorcha said. "And you will pay for it, won't you."

Not a question. A declaration.

He grimaced ever so faintly. "I will."

"Then you can have three weeks." Sorcha winked at me.

I loved this woman.

Rory's mother grasped his face and planted a firm kiss on his cheek. "Good lad."

He shot me a resigned look.

Sorcha kissed my cheek next. "This is for you, Emery. We willnae do anything you don't want."

With that, she led Niall away to inform everyone of the upcoming nuptials. He glanced back at Rory and shrugged in the universal male acknowledgment that a man couldn't argue with a determined woman.

"I like your parents," I said.

Rory grunted. "You want a posh wedding."

"No, but this will make our mothers feel better. Don't you want your mom to be happy?"

Another grunt. "Arguing with women about weddings is a futile endeavor."

I debated whether to ask but decided to go on and do it. "Did you have big weddings the first three times?"

"Not extravaganzas. Tasteful ceremonies."

"I'm sure our mothers won't go hog wild with this one."

He pinched his lips. "I should speak to Lachlan and Aidan. Maybe their wives can help us keep this bloody wedding under control."

Ah yes, control. He needed to believe he held the reins. An illusion, of course, with two enthusiastic mothers involved, but I'd let him hold on to his fantasy.

"You do that," I said, and kissed his cheek.

I hung out under the arbor, alone. Observing the MacTaggarts made me miss my family all the more, but I'd already made friends with Jamie and possibly Catriona, so I couldn't complain. After a while, I caught sight of Rory near the rhododendrons, engaged in conversation with his brothers and their wives.

My heart stuttered.

Rory was *grinning*. He looked younger and more relaxed than I'd ever seen him.

When he glanced my way, his smile faded into a slight frown. He averted his gaze.

Oh great. I made my husband *stop* smiling.

I meandered away from the arbor, a cold pit forming in my stomach, and chose a position near the garden entrance away from the crowd. Rory frowned when he saw me. Catriona claimed I made him happy, but his actions contradicted her assertion.

A few minutes later, Aidan approached me. "You're looking lonely over here. Where's Rory?"

"Not sure. I think he's mad about the wedding plot."

"He'll be fine," Aidan said. "After he figures out he cannae stop two mothers."

"I think he knows that already, but he's waging a desperate battle to avoid an onslaught of taffeta, puffy sleeves, and doves flying over our heads while dropping rose petals on us."

Aidan laughed softly and sidled closer, lowering his head as he spoke in a sardonically conspiratorial tone. "Maybe you can solve a mystery for me. Why do women like Rory? He's got a caber up his erse."

He's a sex god in the bedroom, that's why, I mused. But I said, "Afraid I can't divulge confidential information."

Aidan glanced around as if concerned someone might overhear. "He's a devil worshiper, isn't he?"

I smacked his chest with the back of my hand. "Calli warned me you're a rascal."

"Cannae deny it." Aidan rubbed his chin. "Lachie and me, we were trying to advise Rory about how to handle motherly interference. But he kept looking at you, like he couldn't bear to be separated from you by even a few meters."

Oh sure, Rory couldn't bear to be separated from me. That's why he slept in his own bedroom at the opposite end of a very long hall.

"We all agree," Aidan said. "Rory's gone doolally for ye."

I decided that meant crazy. The notion was itself nuts. Rory liked having sex with me, but he'd exhibited no signs of anything "doolally."

Despite doubting his statement, I suffered an irresistible impulse to hug Aidan. I clamped my arms around his broad torso and said, "You guys have all been so sweet. I feel like part of the family."

"Ye are family," Aidan said, his arms coming around me. "You're our sister."

"Aidan, unhand my wife, if you please."

Rory's tone brooked no nonsense yet was tinged with humor.

I pulled away from Aidan to find Rory watching us from ten feet away.

Aidan bunched his shoulders, hands spread wide. "What? She hugged me, Rory. Would've been rude to shove her away."

Rory crossed the distance to me, slinging an arm around my waist to haul me into his body. "Maybe I should wrap myself around your wife, Aidan."

His brother grinned at me. "Doolally, see?"

Aidan clapped Rory on the shoulder and moseyed off in the direction of Lachlan.

Rory massaged his forehead. "Must you fling yourself at everyone you meet?"

"I was expressing gratitude. Aidan said I'm part of the family, which was very sweet of him."

"The pair of you were having an intimate discussion, by the look of it."

Tangled in Rory's embrace, I had to wriggle to get turned around and face him. "Aidan wanted to know why women like you."

"I see. What did you—"

A sight past my shoulder stole his attention. His face went slack. He didn't blink. Didn't move. Didn't breathe as far as I could tell.

Rory brushed past me to stop a few feet from the opening in the wall.

A rangy man occupied the garden entrance, a stranger of average height with gray-peppered brown hair and crow's feet around his eyes. He seemed a bit older than Rory, but the saggy skin under his eyes and his uneven coloring suggested he was a smoker prematurely aged by his habit. He dressed in rumpled khakis and a polo shirt, his longish hair unkempt.

"What do you want?" Rory asked the man in a flat voice. "You weren't invited, and you are not welcome here."

"I'm a journalist, MacTaggart," the man said. "Your new bride is big news in the village. Everyone wants to know if your taste in women has improved, or if you'll be a victim of another failed marriage."

The man's smug look implied he liked the idea of Rory losing another wife.

Rory scoffed. "You are a journalist as much as I'm a sheep farmer. At least sheep shit washes off your clothes. The stench of being a *bod ceann* can't be cleansed."

The rest of the MacTaggart clan gathered behind us, with Aidan and Lachlan alongside me.

"Graham Oliver," Lachlan said, his tone making it clear he disdained the man. "Rory told ye to leave, so go on. Before I skelp your sorry hide raw."

The eldest MacTaggart brother cracked his knuckles.

Unfazed, Graham jutted his chin, thumbs stuffed in his waistband. "Is it my fault ye donnae have security? I've got journalistic privilege, at any rate." He switched his attention to me, his eyes bright with interest. "Mrs. MacTaggart, what a pleasure to meet ye."

Rory cast me a worried glance.

I responded with a small, encouraging smile.

"Need your wife's permission to speak?" Graham said. "Ye married her so fast, she must've put a hex on ye. Led around by the short hairs, MacTaggart?"

Rory shook his fist at Graham. "*Falbh dàirich fhein*, ye bawbag."

What on earth had he said? Must've been Gaelic, I supposed.

Lachlan stepped up beside his brother, laying a hand on his shoulder. "He's not worth the sore knuckles, Rory. Donnae let this wee shit ruin a family celebration."

Graham sniggered. "Ahmno staying, Lachlan. Stopped in to give my congratulations to your brother. Let's hope the fourth time is the charm, and this one can stand ye for more than eight months. Isobel must've had an iron constitution to stay all those years, but the others—"

"Shut up," Rory snarled.

The self-described journalist moseyed out of the garden, swinging his hands at his sides and whistling a bouncy tune. Through the entrance, I could see Graham climb into a black sedan marred by scratches and dings. Once his car rolled down the drive, Lachlan thumped Rory's shoulder and wandered back to the crowd, waving for them to disperse. Our guests fanned out around the garden once more, and Rory came back to me.

"Who was that?" I asked.

"Graham Oliver."

"Am I supposed to know the name?"

"Only locals know him. Graham fancies himself a publishing magnate, but his newspaper is nothing more than a muck-raking scandal sheet on the verge of collapse." His lips twisted into an ugly smirk. "Graham is as rotten as the smut he peddles."

"Don't hold back, honey." I winked. "Tell me what you really think of him."

"He's a right scunner." Seeing my confusion, he explained, "It means he's a bloody nuisance. His newspaper is the *Loch Fairbairn World News*, but everyone calls it The Bletherer."

"Kinda seemed like he has a grudge against you."

Rory grasped the back of his neck. "He does. I represented his wife in their divorce last year. Negotiated a generous, and well-deserved, settlement for her. Graham's financial fortunes have taken a tumble since then, mostly because he's a boozing gambler."

He had seemed like the hard-drinking, hard-smoking type.

I nudged Rory with my elbow. "You've been speaking a lot of Gaelic today, haven't you? Care to enlighten your American wife? Your mother said you cursed at her."

"*Bod an Donais* means the devil's penis, and it's a curse I picked up from Aidan." Rory's lips took on a wry twist. "Aidan's a bad influence, but I've developed my own favorite insults. *Falbh dàirich fhein* means go fuck your-self, and *bod ceann* is dickhead."

"What about bawbag?"

"It's a reference to a man's...ah..." He gestured vaguely downward. "You know."

I stifled a laugh. "Are you pointing to your balls?"

"Aye."

"You can say dickhead, but not balls. You're the cutest." I bounced up on my toes to kiss him on the mouth. "Let's go mingle with your family and forget that bawbag was ever here."

Chapter Eighteen

Hours later, I flumped backward onto my bed in my private room on the third floor. The lunch Mrs. Darroch had insisted I eat clunked around like a big old rock in my gut. The appearance of Graham Oliver had left me with a gnawing curiosity about the man and his past with Rory, but the encounter had affected my husband more than he'd let on at first. Gradually, he'd become more withdrawn in his stoic way, and I warranted no more than a cursory glance as he collected up his relatives and politely convinced them to leave.

Every MacTaggart, and even Gavin Douglas, had given me a sympathetic look as they filed out into the driveway and piled into their vehicles. Whether because of Graham's intrusion or because of Rory's standoffish behavior, I couldn't tell.

My husband hadn't spoken to me since we parted ways in the ground-floor hall. He'd gone to his office. I'd schlepped up the stairs to my bedroom.

Ich. My bedroom. The quarters of the sex-toy wife.

I cheered up after an intercontinental video chat with my parents and my sister. Hearing and seeing them proved to me they weren't mad about my quickie marriage, and my mom displayed surprising enthusiasm for planning my wedding with Sorcha MacTaggart. I told her they could do whatever they liked. I didn't really care about the wedding. What mattered to me was seeing my family in person for the first time since Hadley's wedding four years ago.

After the chat ended, I went back to lounging on my bed thinking about Rory. I allowed myself one minute of self-pity, not a second more. After that, I freshened up and got my exercise skipping down the stairs to the first floor, the one above the ground floor, intent on finding my husband. Over breakfast, Mrs. Darroch had clued me in to the fact Rory spent the better part of every day in his office, aka the old library connected to the tower. I remembered Rory showing me the door to his office, but it had been shut.

Although the tower stretched up all four levels of the building, the only access to his office from the top floor was in his bedroom.

When I reached the office door, I knocked twice.

"Come," Rory said, his deep voice penetrating the thick wood of the door.

Summoning my brightest smile, I opened the door and waltzed into the library-office.

Dark-wood paneling covered the walls, and shelves packed with books filled three of the four walls from floor to ceiling, including the wall behind Rory's desk. A trio of tall windows admitted sunlight into the room, with an upholstered bench positioned beneath them.

Rory hunched over the dark-wood desk. The size of the desk echoed his bodily presence. Though he occupied a high-backed leather chair, it looked less like an antique than a pricey version of a typical executive chair. A computer resided on one corner of the desk, but Rory was focused on the papers spread out across the desk's center. He slouched forward, arms on the desk, forehead cinched into deep lines.

Two smaller chairs, antique or a good approximation, were positioned in front of his desk at a respectable distance from it. A spiffy rug sheathed most of the floor space.

I grabbed one of the chairs and dragged it across the rug toward Rory's desk.

He glanced at me over the tops of his reading glasses. "What are you doing?"

I plunked my butt in the chair. Folding my hands on my lap, I propped my sock-clad feet on the desk and crossed my ankles. "Oh yes, my darling husband, I'm so pleased to see you too."

My breezy, overly sweet tone earned me zippo in response. Even my brilliant smile seemed to leave him unaffected.

Or so he wanted me to think. The way he regarded me with keen interest suggested otherwise.

Rory nudged the bottom of my foot with one finger. "Your feet are on my desk."

"Yep."

"What do you want, Emery?" He aimed a pointed glance at his papers. "I have work to catch up."

"I have questions."

Rory slumped back into his chair with a defeated sigh. "Go on, then."

"First of all, have you seen my phone? I can't find it. Had to do a video chat with my family on my laptop."

Eyes downcast, he opened a desk drawer and produced my phone. He set it on the desk, pushing it toward my feet. "I went into your room while you were asleep and borrowed your mobile. Only so I could switch it to local service."

I clasped my hands on my lap. "You sneaked into my bedroom while I was sleeping to steal my phone?"

"To switch it to local service," he said, enunciating each syllable with knife-like precision. "It was a favor."

"One I didn't ask for. Is that how your mom got my mom's number? You snooped on my phone?"

He played with the papers on his desk. "Yes. My mother asked me for the number, so she could surprise you."

"Did she ask you to steal my phone?"

"No, I—" He shoved a hand inside the back of his shirt collar. "I didn't know another way to get the information."

"Rory, honestly." I pitched my head back and made a frustrated noise. When I focused on him again, I managed a calm tone. "Let's forget that for the moment. I have more important questions."

He braced his elbows on the desktop, head supported with a hand on his cheek.

"Erica asked if I'd applied for my spouse visa yet." I wiggled the toes of one foot in the air. "Told her I had no idea what that is. She and Calli explained it's an immigration thing, and I'd better take care of the formalities ASAP. Am I going to be deported for not doing that right away?"

"No." He plucked up a pen—a fancy-shmancy one, gold and shiny— and twirled it around his fingers, rapping it on the desktop with every third revolution. "I'm handling it. Started the process before we left America."

"You—" Flummoxed, I could do nothing more than stare at him. "Let me get this straight. Without telling me, without consulting me at all, you took it upon yourself to secretly apply for a visa for me. Meanwhile, you skulked into my room in the dead of night—"

"Not the dead of night. It was daylight, but you were asleep." He shifted uncomfortably in his chair. "I planned to tell you about the mobile service change, but I didn't have the chance yet. Then you flounced in here asking your bloody questions."

"Flounced in?" I laughed, shaking my head. "You are so weird. Lucky for you, I like your weirdness. It's kind of hot."

One side of his mouth quirked. "Am I meant to thank you for the compliment?"

"No, you're meant to apologize for your stealth mission to get me a visa."

He tossed the pen across his desk where it bounced and rolled into his computer keyboard. "I was trying to spare you the stress."

"You should've told me what you were doing."

"You were exhausted from jet lag and worried about meeting my family." He flattened his hand on the desktop and examined my feet. "As I said, I was trying to spare you the added stress of dealing with immigration issues. I should've consulted you, I'm sorry."

My indignation deflated like a popped balloon. I couldn't stay mad at him when he'd been doing me a favor, though I didn't like languishing in the dark about legal stuff.

"Okay," I said, "I forgive you. What you did was thoughtful and efficient. Thank you."

He jerked his head back. "You—thank me?"

"I do."

Wary, he leaned over his desk again. "But I invaded your privacy."

"If you're talking about the phone incident, don't worry about it."

"You should still be angry."

I stretched a leg out to tap his nose with my socked big toe. "Lighten up, Ror. I'm over it. You get a one-time free pass on keeping secrets."

He pushed his glasses down to peer at me over them again. "Ror?"

"Yeah, I'm trying out a nickname for you."

"I don't require a nickname. And 'Ror' is bloody ridiculous. I'm not a lion." He caught my big toe to stop me from waving it to and fro. "My name is Rory. Say it with me. Ror-ee."

I wiggled my toe in his grip. "I knew you had a sense of humor, baby."

"Must you call me 'baby'? I am not a bairn."

"Don't worry. I'll find a good nickname for you." I smiled. "But it might include the word baby."

"As long as it's not 'Ror.' "

"No, that wasn't working for me either."

"Glad to hear it." He released my toe, skating his middle finger down the sole of my foot, setting off a delicious tickling sensation. "Any other questions?"

"Not really a question. More of a request." I plopped my feet on the floor, sat up straight, and rested my hands on my thighs. "Do you remember what I said about needing total honesty?"

He linked his hands on the desktop. "You need to understand two things. I can't discuss my clients or their private legal matters."

"Of course. I get that."

"There are also parts of my past I don't care to discuss at all."

His ex-wives, he meant. "Rory, you can tell me about—"

"No."

My nails dug into my thighs, and my fingers ached. I pried them loose from my leg. So far in our relationship, I'd acceded to several of his hang-ups and demands. This time, I must win a concession from him.

"Total honesty," I said. "It's nonnegotiable."

He fingered his wedding ring.

"This is the deal," I said. "I won't pester you to tell me about your past. I will ask questions, though, and the longer we live together and you don't tell me, the more it'll make things uncomfortable between us. I can't help that. We need to be friends, Rory."

"Asking questions sounds like pestering."

"Not the way I do it." I got up and parked my behind on the edge of his expansive desk. "I'm your therapist, remember? While I search for my true bliss, my mission is to help you relearn how to have fun."

"I assumed it would be sex therapy."

"Sex is a part of it, but you need way more than that."

"I shouldn't be your life's purpose."

A hand splayed over the smooth, dark wood of his desk, I leaned toward him. "You aren't my life's purpose. You're my current mission. I've set my sights on making sure you come out of your office prison for more than sleeping and eating, and that you remember how to enjoy life. I plan on helping you lift that weight you carry around. I'm beginning to suspect it's an ex-wife-shaped burden."

"You mean to save me." He made a face that suggested I would fail.

"I'm not trying to save you, unless you want me to. I told you before, I love a challenge and I love an adventure. You are both."

"I see." He surveyed the room as if it held mystical answers. "May I ask a personal question?"

"Ask me anything you like." I held up one finger. "Be warned, though. It goes both ways."

"Fine." He relaxed into his chair, one ankle propped on the opposite knee. "You mentioned a fiancé. Why did you call off the wedding?"

"I didn't call off the wedding. I ended the engagement." Straightening, I danced my fingers over the computer keyboard near my hip. "Luke and I were together for three years before he proposed, and I took six days to give him an answer. Two weeks after I said yes, I realized if we'd really loved each other, we would've tied the knot a long time ago. So, I broke up with Luke. He wasn't devastated."

"He let you go without a fight?"

"Yep." I bent one knee, tucking my foot under the other leg. "I told him I couldn't marry him, and he shrugged. Literally. He shrugged and walked away. Moved his stuff out of our apartment the same day. Six months later, he's living with a woman who owns a pot shop."

"Ceramics?" Rory said, his face offering no clue to whether he was kidding or actually had no idea what pot was.

"Marijuana," I said. "It's legal in Colorado."

He unfurled his body from the chair, rising up to his full height and angling over the desk toward me. "You haven't said if you were upset when you ended your engagement."

"I wasn't. Relieved would be the best description."

"Why would you stay so long with a man who cared so little about you?"

How to explain this? Only one way, and it required me to lay bare the worst time in my life.

"Luke and I had been friends since college," I said. "Four years ago, I started dating somebody I thought was a nice guy. We got along, and Sebastian was game for any silly thing I wanted to do. Gradually, he became more and more withdrawn, even lost interest in sex. He blamed work stress. About eight months into our relationship, I ran into one of his coworkers. He told me Sebastian had been fired six weeks earlier, for watching Internet porn at work."

Rory hovered nearby but made no attempt to touch me.

I scratched my arm. "When I confronted him, Sebastian admitted he'd been lying to me about a lot of things, not just being fired. Instead of looking for a new job, he'd spent eighteen hours a day watching porn on two dozen different websites. He didn't want to sleep with me because reality couldn't compare to his fantasy women. He liked jerking off while watching them more than he cared about me. I begged him to get help."

"What did he say?" Rory asked gently.

"Flat-out no." I wrapped my arms around myself, suddenly chilled. "I had no choice. I broke up with him."

Rory walked around the desk, sat on its edge facing me, and settled a hand on my knee. "This is where revenge porn comes into the story."

I nodded, unable to meet his eyes. "Six months earlier, Sebastian talked me into posing for nude photos. He swore they'd be for his eyes only, and I was kind of flattered he'd ask. What an idiot, huh?"

"No, Emery, you are not an idiot."

"I trusted him, and he turned out to be a damn liar." I swiped at my eyes, at the tears brimming in them. "He posted the photos on social media. I told you before, I got them taken down. For all I know, some other sleazebag might've copied them."

Rory tugged my hands loose from where I'd locked them over my upper arms. He scooted closer to envelop my hands in his on my lap.

"How does this relate to your engagement?" he asked.

"When the shit exploded in my face, Luke was there to support me." I allowed myself the span of three breaths to enjoy the warmth of his hands. "My family was far away, and I was ashamed to tell them what happened. Luke convinced me I needed to. He sat beside me, holding my hand, when I called my parents. He helped me figure out how to get the photos taken down. I was so grateful to him, I guess I mistook gratitude for love. Three months after the photo fiasco, I moved in with Luke."

"You stayed with him for three years."

"Because it was easy." I inhaled a deep breath through my nose, the scent of him infiltrating my senses. "I swore I'd never let Sebastian's actions affect my future, but I guess they did. I got into this rut with my life. Boring, dead-end job. Boring, dead-end boyfriend. Standing still was easier and safer than uprooting my whole life. Computer programming wasn't my life's passion, and neither was Luke. Both looked good on paper, but all of it stifled me more than I realized until I got laid off and had to reexamine my choices."

"That's why you married me."

"Kind of." I raised my face to him. "You are not boring, that's for sure."

He drew circles on the desk with his finger. "What's the full name of the scunner who shamed you?"

"Sebastian Zegers. Why do you ask?"

With swift and elegant strokes of his pen, he jotted down the name. "I want to make certain he can't hurt you again."

"Are you planning to exact vengeance on my behalf? That's adorable."

"Not vengeance," he said, clicking the pen to retract its tip. "I'd like to hire an investigator in America to check on this Sebastian man. Find out what he's been doing and determine whether he kept those photographs. If so, I will ensure they are destroyed. Permanently."

Holy mackerel. I couldn't believe he'd do all that for me. We hardly knew each other.

"Um, thanks," I said. "That's an amazing thing to do for your trophy wife."

Rory smacked the pen down on the desktop. "Never call yourself a trophy again. You are my wife, full stop."

"And you are a truly awesome husband."

He made that face, the one that usually preceded a statement about how I would get sick of him one day. He kept quiet, though, leaving me to fill the silence.

"My turn," I said. "What did Graham mean about your first wife having an iron constitution?"

Rory coughed, his face pinched. "I'm not sure. Isobel wanted things I couldn't give her, left me because I was boring and—"

He flinched as if he'd revealed too much.

"Is that why you keep telling me I'll get tired of you?" I asked.

He bored his gaze into the darkest corner of the room. "I met Isobel near the end of my traineeship, the final step in becoming a solicitor. I was twenty-five, she was twenty-three. We married six months later, and only after that did she start to complain about my work. She thought being a solicitor was dull and unglamorous, kept telling me I should at least become a corporate lawyer where I'd make more money. Isobel despised the fact I often worked pro bono for those who couldn't afford a solicitor's fees. When she walked out, she told me I would never find a woman who would tolerate the long hours I put into my work, the late-night calls from panicked clients, and what she called the 'pittance income' I earned."

No wonder he assumed I'd dump him too.

A tiny spark of hope ignited inside me. He'd shared a piece of his painful past for the first time.

"How long were you married to her?" I asked.

"Five years."

Oh dear God. Five years with a woman who despised his job and clearly made him feel unworthy? Love had defeated him, I sensed that much. Isobel played a role in the drama, but I was sure the story had more acts.

"Thank you for telling me all of that," I said. "It couldn't have been easy to talk about."

"You are the first person I've told the whole truth."

A tingle rushed through me. I was the first?

"May I ask one more itty-bitty question?" I said. "Not about your exes."

"Go on."

"What's the real reason you got irritated when I hugged Aidan?"

He slithered off the desk and retreated behind it, lowering his body into the chair. "It's ridiculous."

"I love ridiculous. You know that."

He ducked his head, scratched his scalp, and said, "You hugged everyone, even Gavin Douglas. You hugged Aidan twice. But you haven't hugged me today."

"Sure I have."

He shook his head slowly, those luminous eyes assessing me.

"I haven't?" When he shook his head again, I pushed off the desk. "I can remedy that right this minute."

Lickety-split, I circled behind the desk and plopped onto his lap. When I wound my arms around his neck, he stiffened. I rested my cheek on his shoulder anyway.

"What are you doing?" he said.

"I upgraded your hug to a cuddle."

"Hmm." He linked his hands over the small of my back. "Ye willnae do this with Aidan."

"Only you," I assured him.

Here in the library-office, Rory and I held each other for several minutes, his warmth radiating into me, and I snuggled into him even more. It felt so nice to be with him like this, especially after we'd shared our bad memories. I reveled in the closeness, loving the feel of him around me, the softness of his shirt and the tickle of his breaths when they ruffled my hair.

He cleared his throat and tried to sit taller, but my body hindered him.

"Something wrong?" I said, without lifting my head from his shoulder.

"It's about the wedding." He cleared his throat again. "We shouldn't have sex until after the ceremony."

I popped up, hands on his chest. "You've got to be kidding."

"No."

"We're already married. Everyone assumes we're getting it on twenty-four seven."

"Out of respect for our mothers, we shouldn't have sex until after the wedding."

Laughter spurted out between my closed lips and through my nostrils, resulting in an attractive series of piglike noises. "Respect for our mothers? That's the lamest excuse in the history of lameness. You're trying to use our moms as a wedge to keep some distance between you and me. I get you're feeling weird about confiding in me but—"

"Ahmno feeling weird," he said in a somewhat petulant tone. "We should take a break to become accustomed to…well…" He squinted his whole face as he struggled for a lamer excuse. "Until we're accustomed to living together."

I traced a finger along the seam of his lips. "You are full of it, Mr. Mac-Taggart, but I'll make a deal with you. Or rather, a little bet."

"What are the stakes?"

"If I win, you agree to participate in one activity of my choosing. No bitching, no growling, no eye-rolling. Agreed?"

"All right." He tightened his arms around me. "And if I win?"

"The same. I'll participate in one activity of your choosing."

His hand drifted down to my hip, and his fingers probed the hollow. "What is the wager?"

"No sex, like you suggested." I swept a hand up his neck, toying with his earlobe. "I bet you we'll both be naked in my bed inside of four days."

"I can wait until the wedding day."

"Oh sure," I said, making my voice huskier while I worked his lobe with my thumb. "There's no way you'll make it three weeks without at least one good fuck. You're way too passionate to go cold turkey."

His fingers massaged my hip with more ardor, pressing in deeply. Lust darkened his whisky eyes, the pupils large, and his lips parted in preparation for a kiss.

"Do we have a bet?" I asked.

"We do," he said, his voice deep and silken.

I hovered my mouth a breath away from his lips. "Three weeks, Rory."

He rose, picking me up with him, and spanked my behind. "I have work. You'll need to entertain yourself."

"Oh, I'm really good at that." I angled my head up to expose my throat. "Maybe I'll *entertain* myself in my bedroom for a while."

With that, I flounced out of the room.

Upstairs, ensconced in my private chambers, I checked my phone. One text from Luke. He'd heard I got married and was shocked. I couldn't blame him.

As I plunked my phone on the bedside table, shapes in the walk-in closet caught my eye. Pushing up on my elbows, I peered at the cardboard boxes stacked just inside the closet door. The boxes had escaped my notice earlier, what with my moping distracting me—plus, I could only see them from a particular angle, through the few-inches gap between the closet door and the jamb. My belongings had arrived sometime during the day. Rory had promised to take care of it, and he had.

The sight of my possessions should've cheered me. Instead, it left me with a sour taste in my mouth.

My life, all thirty-four years of it, summed up in ten lonely boxes.

Chapter Nineteen

everal hours later, as the sun sank beneath the horizon, I finished the scrumptious meal Mrs. Darroch had cooked up for me. Seated on a stool at the granite island in our modern kitchen, I mulled the day's events. Meeting Rory's family had wiped me out, but I'd taken time to bid Jamie goodbye. The guest wing seemed empty and rather forlorn without her spunky, cheerful presence.

This evening she'd been bummed because her boyfriend, Gavin, had flown back to America. I hoped her new hosts, Aidan and Calli, would find a way to lift her spirits.

"Are ye finished, dearie?" Mrs. Darroch asked, bent over the sink washing the dishes she'd refused to let me take care of for her.

I passed her my empty plate and glass. "Thanks for making me dinner, Mrs. D. You don't need to take care of me, though. I can make my own food and do my own laundry."

"Ye can, but ye donnae have to. I'm the housekeeper. It's my job to care for the honorary laird and lady of Dùndubhan."

"Not used to being waited on." I slid off my stool. "Where might I find my husband?"

"In the office."

"But it's after eight."

She finished washing my plate and glass, drying her hands with a dish towel. "Rory's a darling boy, but he works too hard. Avoiding life, I'd say."

"Yeah, I think so." I smiled. "Better not let him hear you calling him a darling boy."

"He's used to it. I've been with Rory for seven years, since before he married the last one."

The last one? That would've been Una. "Rory's lived in this castle for seven years?"

"Excepting the eight months the last one lived here, he's been alone." She dropped the dish towel on the counter. "Havenae seen him this content in all the time I've known him. You suit him."

"Do I?" I laid a hand on the island, its marble cool under my palm. "Can't quite figure why he bought a big old castle."

"It was a shambles," Mrs. D explained, "and the owner couldn't afford the upkeep anymore, much less the cost of restoration. Rory paid a generous price to save this castle from falling into ruin. His brother Lachlan contributed to the restoration, despite Rory insisting he didn't need charity."

"Sounds like my husband, proud and stubborn." Hands on my hips, I said, "These long hours he works, that's going to change. I'll make sure of it."

Mrs. Darroch followed me out of the kitchen. It resided in the guest wing, and we both turned right down the hallway. When I headed for the door to the dining room, she bid me good night and bustled down the short hallway on the right to the side door of the house.

I breezed through the dining room and out into the vestibule, then up the stairs and through the great hall to the door of Rory's office. I raised my hand to knock but stopped when I heard soft snoring inside the room. I closed my hand around the knob and eased the door inward.

My husband slumped in his chair, asleep.

I tiptoed across the room, behind the desk, and crouched beside him. Rory's head had lolled to the left, cradled by the chair's back, with his mouth open. His left arm lay slack on the desk, his hand weighing down stacked papers, knocked askew. Though his hand blocked my view of the bottom half of the top sheet, I glimpsed familiar words on the top section.

It was our marriage contract.

A tightness burned in the back of my throat. Why had he been examining the contract?

My gaze landed on him again, asleep at his desk, and a pang throbbed in my chest. He looked so at peace, so adorably unkempt with his hair mussed and his shirt wrinkled. I noticed an empty whisky glass next to his computer, and a bottle of Ben Nevis nearby.

Drinking while perusing our marriage contract?

I tried not to draw conclusions from that fact. Only Rory could tell me what he'd been up to in here, all alone, tossing back a glass of whisky while inspecting the document that bound me to him for a year. A legally unenforceable document. A promise between us.

He made a tiny moan in the back of his throat.

My heart melted as I gazed at him. I couldn't leave him like this.

I half stood to press my lips to his cheek.

"Wakey-wakey," I said, cradling his face in one hand. "Rory, wake up."

His eyelids fluttered open, and his bleary eyes sharpened into clarity. "Emery?"

"You got another blonde, American wife stashed in a closet?" I straightened and patted his shoulder. "Get up. You are not sleeping in your office."

He shooed my hand away. "I'm fine here. Have work to—"

"Nope." I seized his hands and leaned back, compelling him to rise. "I decree you shall not spend the night in your office when you have a perfectly good bed upstairs."

He grumbled but clambered to his feet. His mouth split open on a giant yawn.

"Come on," I said, supporting him with an arm under his as I encouraged him to move toward the door. He staggered, and I glanced up at him. "How many glasses of whisky did you have?"

"One."

I clucked my tongue. "Alcohol and jet lag aren't a good combo."

"Ahmno jet-lagged."

"Says the man who was found unconscious at his desk." As we exited the office, I strapped my other arm around his front side. "It's beddy-bye time for Rory baby."

He grunted but kept walking, his steps shuffling though he no longer staggered. Not drunk after all, I deduced, and guided him through the cavernous great hall and up the stairs. We passed the second floor, but he stopped us at the third-floor landing before I could drag him through the doorway into the hall.

Pointing toward a door at our left, he said, "There."

"Where's that go?" I craned my neck to see around him and examine the doorway I hadn't noticed before.

"My room," he said, sounding as exhausted as the shadows under his eyes made him look. "Private entry and exit. Lairds needed a way to escape their wives."

I bit back a sarcastic comment about the fact he made me sleep at the opposite end of the long hallway, so why did he need a separate escape route. Becoming the bitchy, bitter wife didn't appeal to me.

We could talk about the separate-bedrooms thing later.

Rotating us both toward the closed door, I grasped its knob and twisted. The knob didn't budge.

"Locked?" I said. "Is the main door to your room locked too? It wasn't the other day when you showed me around."

"It's locked now."

"Rory, Rory, Rory," I said on a long exhalation. "This extreme need for privacy from your own wife is going to change. Are you afraid I'll sneak in and steal your underwear?"

He fished a set of keys out of his pocket and selected one. As he inserted it into the door lock, he mumbled, "This is how I live."

"No, honey, this is how you hide from life."

Though he stood frozen with the key in the lock, his fingers holding it, his gaze shot to me. For the longest moment, he kept his unblinking eyes pinned to me as if I'd spoken shocking words. Did he seriously not see he was hiding?

He unlocked the door and swung it inward just enough to admit his large body. "Good night, Emery."

My husband shuffled into the bedroom, keeping the door mostly shut so I couldn't see inside.

I wanted to ask him about the contract and why he'd been looking at it, but the discussion could wait until tomorrow.

"Good night, Rory." I hopped up to kiss his cheek. "Sleep late for once. You need the rest."

Uttering a noncommittal noise, he shut the door. A lock clicked into position.

I stared at the door for a minute, maybe longer, struggling to understand why he needed to bar me from so much as peeking inside his private sanctum. At last, I gave up and shambled to my room.

No sign of Rory the next day. He got up before I woke and stayed sequestered in his office through lunch, summoning Mrs. Darroch to bring his midday meal. I whiled away the day exploring the castle, inside and out, discovering the garden wall had a door embedded in the rear section of its wall. Outside the wall, behind the garden, lay a manicured clearing littered with a half dozen wooden posts. They resembled slender telephone poles scattered on their sides. Cabers?

Maybe, but I saved that question for later.

The grounds also included an old carriage house converted into a three-car garage, though Rory kept his Mercedes parked in the driveway. The garage housed a Range Rover, all by its lonesome in the massive space. Both cars cost more than my college education.

My explorations proved to me the only locked room was Rory's bedchamber, accessed by the door in the stairwell or the one at the end of the third-floor hall. He kept both doors sealed tight, wife-proof and vacant.

He couldn't have spent more than six hours a night in that room, given his sixteen-hour work days and factoring in time for bathing, dressing, and eating.

By seven in the evening, I realized he wouldn't show up for dinner.

I ambled into the kitchen just as Mrs. Darroch picked up a tray full of food—intended for my husband, I knew, since the housekeeper had informed me he ate all his meals in his office.

"Ah, there ye are," Mrs. D said with a welcoming smile. "I was about to take Rory his dinner. Yours is ready too, but I cannae carry two trays at once."

I glanced at the other tray waiting on the island's granite countertop. "I can get my own food. Having someone else wait on me is weird."

"You'll acclimate, *gràidh*. Best get Rory his meal."

She made a beeline for the door, but I caught her with a gentle hand on her arm before she could bustle out to serve our laird and master. "I'd like to give him his dinner, if that's okay. Unless I'm horning in on your duties. I mean, you've been with Rory a long time and…um…"

"Ye want to take care of him too." She gave me a motherly smile that made my chest hurt, because it reminded me of my mom. Mrs. D offered me the tray. "Here ye are."

"Thanks," I said as I accepted the tray.

"I'm for bed, then."

With a mental jolt, I realized I hadn't seen any rooms other than mine that looked like anyone slept in them. What if I'd accidentally trespassed, unaware I'd violated her quarters?

I hesitated, considering how to ask. "Do you have a room in the house?"

"No-no, I'm in the cottage." Seeing my confusion, she waved toward the back of the house. "It's attached to the wall at the other end of the garden."

Though I had noticed the stone cottage there, I'd assumed it was empty or maybe used for storage. I did recall she'd mentioned living behind the garden on the day I arrived.

"Before he married the last one," Mrs. Darroch said, "I had a room inside the main house. Una didnae like sharing her home with a servant, though, and I moved into the cottage. Stayed there ever since. It's a bonnie home, cozier than Dùndubhan Castle."

"This isn't exactly homey," I agreed. Especially with my husband forbidding me to enter his bedroom. "Have a feeling I'd be more comfortable in a cottage."

She squeezed my arm. "You'll get used to living here. Good night, dearie."

"Good night, Mrs. D. Thanks for being so nice to the new girl."

"You're an angel, *gràidh*. It's no hardship."

With that, she left.

Rather than taking Rory's meal to his office, I dropped it off in the dining room and then retrieved my tray as well. Once I'd set our meal out on the enormous dining-room table, I went to retrieve my MIA husband.

His office door was shut.

I knocked twice and pushed the door open, traipsing across the room like I owned the damn place. I kind of did, didn't I? Rory hadn't mentioned whether I became a co-owner when we married. He'd called this my home, though.

Formerly absorbed with the papers on his desk, Rory lifted his gaze but kept his head bowed, observing my approach. "What are you doing?"

"You ask me that a lot." Alongside his chair, I dropped into a deep curtsy and said with mock graveness, "Your presence is requested in the dining hall, my laird."

He slapped his pen on the desktop, his mouth warped with his usual effort to defeat a smile. "I eat in here. Mrs. Darroch will bring—"

"Not tonight." I grasped the top of his chair and forced it to rotate toward me. "I'm tired of eating alone. We're having dinner together, in the dining room, like normal people."

With his head at the height of my breasts, he seemed unable to resist admiring them. "I take my meals here."

I bent at the waist to level our gazes. "You take your dinners with me from here on. No arguments. Listen to your therapist, Rory baby."

His brows snapped together. "You called me that last night, but I assumed it was sarcastic."

"It was—then." I bracketed his face with my hands. "I've decided this nickname's a keeper. Rory baby."

"As I've told you before, I don't need a nickname."

"Yes you do." I straightened and held my hands flat, palms up, bouncing them in the air. "Get up. To the dining hall with you."

Grudgingly, he heaved his big-and-sexy self out of the chair. His gaze browsed over my body, his simmering interest impossible to miss. "Why are ye barefoot?"

"I don't wear shoes at home, inside the house."

"You have no socks."

"How observant. I like being as naked as possible at all times."

He gave me an *oh please* look but accompanied me downstairs to the dining room and took his seat at the head of the table where I'd laid out his meal. I settled into the adjacent seat, with my dinner laid out for me there. The bottle of wine I'd pilfered from the cellar was stationed between our plates, uncorked, waiting for one of us to decant it.

Rory picked up the bottle, pouring its ruby-colored contents into my glass first, then his. As he set down the bottle, he said, "I see you found the wine cellar."

"Yep. Hope you don't mind me stealing a bottle."

"It's not stealing, this is your home."

He sipped from his glass, and I did the same with mine—though I took the time to swirl the wine and inhale a deep draft of its layered scent.

"Mrs. D went home," I said, "to her cottage in the garden. We've got full privacy, if you'd rather eat your meal off my naked body."

His fork tumbled from his grasp, clattering onto the plate. "*Bod an Donais.*"

Really, he was so much fun to tease. "It's not the devil's penis I want to suck."

"You're a wicked angel, for sure."

I remembered him calling me his wicked little angel the night we met. Hearing those words meant more to me tonight, since we'd gotten to know each other a bit.

My curiosity peaked, I asked, "Which part of *bod an Donais* means penis?"

"*Bod.*" His eyes glowed in the soft lighting from the crystal chandelier. "Your pronunciation of Gaelic is impressive. *You* are impressive, Emery."

My cheeks warmed at the compliment, and my body followed suit. My husband thought I was impressive. A step in the right direction, I decided.

Rory set into his meal, consuming it with precision and care.

Meanwhile, I dug into mine like a woman starved for a month. Mrs. Darroch's food was always scrumptious, and I couldn't resist pigging out on the T-bone and garlic mashed potatoes. Yesterday, I'd mentioned I loved a good steak. And she'd cooked me one.

I loved that woman to pieces.

Abruptly, I realized Rory had stopped eating to observe me, his expression both curious and fascinated.

I swallowed a mouthful of masticated beef. "What? Do I have food on my face?"

"No." He sat back in his chair, still giving me that oddly fascinated look. "Your enthusiasm for eating continues to amaze me. Isobel ate like a bird, and Lilias was a vegan. Una latched onto whatever diet was most popular at the time."

I sipped my wine. "I've never dieted, unless you count not being able to eat hardly anything when I had the stomach flu. Never understood the appeal of depriving yourself in the hopes other people will like you better if you're thinner."

Holding his glass near his mouth, he roamed his gaze over my body. "You don't need to be thinner."

"Most guys I've dated would disagree. One jerk told me he didn't mind being with a chubby girl, and another one asked if I'd had a baby recently." I took a bite of steak into my mouth, speaking while chewing. "Men these days expect every woman to have a stick figure. With big boobs, of course."

Rory frowned and set down his glass. The intensity of his gaze sparked a warm tingle that raced along my skin.

"Those men are eejits," he said in a voice both soft and decisive. "You're perfect. I love your body, love running my hands over every curve and swell."

The tingle escalated into a full-body fever. "I've never thought I was fat. But thank you for that...compliment."

The word fell woefully short of describing what he'd said, or the way he'd said it, but I couldn't think of a better term. Couldn't think at all, with him staring at me like he really did want to spread my naked body over the table and eat a decadent meal off my skin.

"You're welcome," he said, his voice rough, eyes hooded.

I put down my glass and stretched one leg under the table until my bare foot nestled between his thighs. Every one of his breaths blustered out between his delectable lips. I slithered down in my chair, determined to burrow my foot deeper between his thighs. His leg muscles tautened under my sole, but when I molded my foot over the bulge of his erection, his whole body went rigid.

"What are ye doing?" he said, his voice strained.

"There you go again," I replied, stroking his thickening cock with my toes, the fabric of his slacks smooth as cream against my skin, "asking questions that have obvious answers. If you insist I explain..." I rubbed the length of my foot along the length of his shaft. "I'm trying to get you so hot you'll throw me down on this table and fuck me mindless."

He clapped his hands on the arms of his chair, gripping them so hard I wondered if he'd crack the sturdy wood. "This is your plan to win the wager."

"Partly." I petted him with my toes. "I want you all the time."

His hand cuffed around my ankle, he exerted just enough pressure to force me to bend my knee and retract my foot from his groin. "May I finish my dinner without you...tempting me?"

"I may be shameless when it comes to winning our bet, but I promise." I moved my foot to the floor and sat up in my chair. "I won't tease you, but I can't guarantee you won't feel tempted. I can't be held responsible for your lustful tendencies."

"*My* lustful tendencies?" A smirk tightened his cheeks. "You are the most passionate woman I've ever known. Full of lust and vigor, unafraid of your desires."

"You're full of compliments tonight."

"Well-deserved ones."

Buoyed by his flattery, and buzzed from our erotic interplay, I permitted him to dine in peace while I asked innocuous questions about the castle grounds. When we'd finished our meal, however, I brought up the subject I'd waited all day to discuss.

I thrust my empty plate away. "Last night, when I found you sleeping at your desk, you had a document out. It looked like our marriage contract."

His features contorted.

I turned my chair toward him. "Why were you looking at—"

"Preparing to file it in the proper folder."

"Filing. Sure." I swung a leg over the arm of my chair. "Do I look that gullible?"

He picked at the upholstery on his chair. "Donnae know why I brought out the contract."

God help me, I believed him. Over the past week, I'd come to understand Rory did a lot of things without any comprehension of why. Most of his subconscious actions revolved around me. His decision to go three weeks without sex had cemented my conviction he was afraid to give in to his desire for me completely, afraid of what he might feel if he did.

I was afraid too—terrified I'd made a mistake harnessing my life to his, that leaving him after a year would hurt more than I could imagine—but I wasn't fighting those fears. I confronted them every day.

Rory stumbled through life with his eyes shut.

He fidgeted in his chair, snaking a hand down to adjust his erection. From the way he winced, I gathered the movement didn't ease his discomfort.

Poor Rory. As his therapist, I couldn't let him suffer this way.

I pushed my chair away and got to my feet, one hip buttressed by the table. "You know, we could have sex—right here, right now—and you wouldn't lose the bet."

His brows inched upward.

I sloped my body over the table toward him, supported by a palm spread on the smooth surface. "We're not naked in my bedroom."

His eyes burning into mine, he whisked his tongue back and forth along his bottom lip. Once. Twice. Three times.

"You may be right," he said, "about the bet. But we are not having sex until after the wedding."

Despite his even tone, he looked miserable at the reiteration of his decree. The hard-on straining his pants might've had something to do with it.

"Aw, Rory baby," I purred, crawling across the table, "you look like you need a cuddle."

His body slackened, a silent invitation.

I crawled onto his lap, straddling him. His hands cupped the small of my back as I roped my arms around his neck. His fingers trembled against my back. I fitted my body to his like a second skin, my mouth a hair's breadth from his. "Better?"

"Depends on your definition of 'better.' "

I closed my eyes, pulling in a deep breath, and my lips curved into a contented smile. "You smell so good. I love being close to you."

His hands pressed into my back.

I opened my eyes to spy the surprise in his.

With a breathy moan, I closed my mouth over his. Determined to stop him from saying anything grumpy that might spoil the moment, I plunged my tongue into his mouth.

Rory clenched his fingers in my shirt, crushing me to him while he responded to my foray by curling his tongue around mine in a dance of sensual sweetness. I went limp against him, lost in the intimacy of our kiss, of our bodies plastered to each other. The chair creaked beneath us from every little movement, while he splayed his hands on my back as if desperate to hold me close.

My pulse raced, a lightness fluttered in my chest. This wasn't a lustful kiss. It was…more.

I tore my lips from his, the loss of his mouth aching like the loss of a limb, stirring an emotion that chased a chill through me beneath the heat. This feeling, I recognized it as more than desire. It was more than I wanted to feel, but I wouldn't fight it. I didn't want to. In his eyes, I glimpsed more than the desire darkening them. I found a softness there, a tenderness he would never admit to—not yet, but maybe one day.

Adjusting my position on his lap, I noted a surprising lack of hardness under me. His erection had waned. My desire had lessened too, tempered by an affection I couldn't deny. He wasn't my fake husband. He had become my real husband, the man I wanted to stay with, contract be damned.

The problem? He wasn't ready to hear the truth.

Rory yawned, though he tried to stifle it.

"You need sleep," I said. "It's bedtime."

"Not yet."

He mashed my body to his for a kiss of pure abandon, of possession and dominance, the kind of kiss that branded me as his and his alone, even as the lush glide of his tongue evinced the tenderness he would never acknowledge. I surrendered to him without reservation, reveling in the wildly erotic sensations.

With a guttural groan, he abandoned my lips to drag his mouth down my throat, licking and nibbling at the hollow. His hand claimed my breast, the feel of his muscular fingers no less arousing for the fabric separating our skin. I couldn't catch my breath, could do nothing except let my head fall onto his shoulder, my mouth against his skin.

"Oh," I murmured without conscious thought. "Oh Rory."

We both froze.

"I'm sorry," I hastened to say, afraid to peek at his face. "I forgot the rule—"

"Say it again."

For a couple seconds, I held motionless in his arms, worried I'd misunderstood his request.

"Please," he said, his voice hushed but rife with emotion, his arms lashing me tighter against his body. "Please say it again."

"Rory." His name emerged from my lips as the barest whisper, like a benediction between us.

He buried his face against my neck, his hands fisting in my shirt and loosening again, repeating the motion over and over while his lips peppered delicate kisses over my skin.

The intimacy of this moment robbed me of breath, and something inside me clicked into place. I unbent my body, my hands on his shoulders. "You said I shouldn't speak your name when we're getting sexy together."

"Changed my mind."

"But why?" God, how I prayed for him to say—I didn't know what.

With one fingertip, he charted the lines of the tendons in my hand. "When you say my name, I…like it."

Joy rushed through me, heady as adrenaline. His small admission meant so much to me, I didn't care how silly I was to ascribe deep meaning to it. I loved hearing the words.

I looked up at him through my lashes. "Does this mean the prohibition on me speaking your name during intimate moments is lifted?"

"Aye."

"Hallelujah." I kissed him quick and hard. "It's super hard to make sure I don't accidentally say your name in the throes of passion."

I wanted to get him to throw out the no-eyes-closed rule too, along with the ones about no daytime sex and separate bedrooms, but I didn't dare ruin this moment by pushing for more than he was ready to give.

One rule gone. Progress, for sure.

He turned my hand over to trace the lines on my palm with his finger. "You were right, though. It is time for bed. In our separate rooms."

Shit. He had to go and wreck our bonding moment by reminding me he refused to share a bed.

Rory pushed his chair back, set me on my feet, and stood.

"Good night, Emery," he said, then kissed my cheek and departed.

I would cling to the memory of this night for as long as it took to convince him to open his eyes and embrace life.

A life with me. For more than one year.

God, I hoped I wasn't setting myself up for heartbreak.

Chapter Twenty

On day four in Scotland, day one of Rory's abstinence plan, I resolved to explore the land surrounding the castle compound. Since Rory had absconded to his office before I woke, I'd asked Mrs. Darroch to relay a message to him that I'd be outside all morning. My husband needed a break from me, and I chose to give him the day. We both needed time to decompress after our whirlwind week, when we rocketed through marriage and meeting the family, straight into sharing a home.

Before my explorations could begin, though, I had to fuel my body.

Mrs. Darroch polished the silver while I chowed down on the meal she'd prepared, consisting of oatmeal porridge, smoked salmon, and eggs.

A few minutes later, a scruffy man dressed in denim overalls and well-worn boots trudged into the kitchen doorway. Mrs. Darroch introduced him as Tavish Brody, the groundskeeper and the person responsible for the gorgeous garden.

"It's beautiful," I said. "You have a real flair for gardening."

He grunted, nabbed a muffin from a basket on the counter, and excused himself.

I might've wondered if all Scotsmen were gruff, but Aidan MacTaggart disproved that hypothesis.

After finishing my breakfast, I made my way out the vestibule door and through the courtyard and gate to the front lawn. There, I came upon Tavish trimming the ivy that climbed the castle wall.

"Hey, Tavish," I said, waving to him.

Surprise flashed on his face, but he tromped over to me. "Did ye need something, Mrs. MacTaggart?"

"It's Emery." I rubbed my palms together. "Would you mind telling me about the garden? I'd love to know the names of all the plants."

Tavish perked up at my request, and we spent an hour together in the walled garden.

After a solitary walk in the woods, I returned to the house to unpack my belongings and sort through them. Anything I didn't need in my room could be stored elsewhere, though I'd have to ask my husband where. Ten minutes into my task, I glanced up at the sound of footsteps.

Rory filled the doorway, as hunky as ever, his gaze skipping over the boxes arrayed around me where I knelt on the floor.

"This is a nice surprise," I said. "What's up, honey?"

He did not wince or grouse about my use of an endearment. I squelched the urge to pump my fists in the air, opting for a mental victory lap.

"Mrs. Darroch said you were in here," he told me. "Thought I'd help you unpack."

Giving up work time to be with me? *Fist pump, whoop, fist pump.*

"I'd like that," I said, aiming for cool composure, like I wasn't ready to burst from the joy swelling inside me. I patted the floor beside me. "Have a seat and dig in."

My large husband came over to squat beside me and flipped open the flaps of a cardboard box. One by one, he brought out items of my clothing. Sweaters. Blouses. Skirts. Jeans. The clothing was disheveled from the move. He sat back on his haunches and contemplated each item before folding it with care and placing it in a stack of like items—sweaters with sweaters, jeans with jeans. He even separated cardigans from pullovers.

I sorted my books and sundry knickknacks, keeping some and dumping others back in the box once I'd emptied it.

Rory cleared his throat with deliberate emphasis.

As I chucked a speckled, polished rock back into my box, I glanced his way.

He stared down at an item poised on his palm. A long, cylindrical item with a rounded tip and a battery compartment on the other end. He tipped his head side to side as he mulled the pink object.

"What is this?" he asked.

"My vibrator."

He snatched his hand away, and the device plummeted to the floor.

"Don't break it," I said, picking up the vibrator. "Haven't you ever seen one before?"

"No." Chin tucked, he crimped his lips.

Charmed by his suspicion about a sex toy, I waved the vibrator in his face.

His eyes tracked the object's movement.

"It won't bite," I said, then draped an arm around his neck. "Can't promise I won't, though."

"Yes, I'm aware of that." He touched his shoulder, the one I'd bitten on our wedding night. "You are a she-wolf."

"Salvaged our wedding night, didn't I?"

"You did."

I tossed the vibrator on the bed, but its presence reminded me of something.

"Got a question," I said. "Can you recommend a local doctor? I have a prescription that'll need refilling soon."

Rory dropped the scarf he'd been folding. "Prescription? Are you ill?"

"No, I'm on the pill."

The spot between his eyebrows crinkled. "What pill?"

"Birth control, Rory."

He tugged at the collar of his shirt. "I see. I'll arrange an appoint—"

"Uh-uh. I can do it myself."

Annoyance flickered on his face, but he squared his shoulders and shook it off. "I will give you the number for my GP, Dr. Buchanan. He's in Loch Fairbairn."

I kissed his cheek. "Thanks. You're the sweetest."

He rolled his eyes.

A shape in the box beside me snagged my attention, and I picked up the mini photo album. Its plain gray cover belied the racy content of the photos inside. Flipping through the pages, I got a wonderful idea.

"Catch," I said, chucking the photo album at Rory, who caught it in one hand. "Think of that as your menu for excitement."

With cautious interest, he thumbed through the four-by-six-inch pages. Each held a photo of me in a different costume. Greek goddess. Wonder Woman. Princess Leia, *Return of the Jedi* style. One picture intrigued him, and he stopped to inspect it.

"Like that one?" I asked, leaning over to peek at it. "That's my ancient Egyptian dancer costume."

"Are you naked?" he asked with wonder in his voice.

"Not naked. I'm wearing a flesh-colored body suit." I swirled a fingertip over the image. "For you, I'd nix the body suit. You'd get me wearing nothing but a skinny belt and a long black wig."

In the photo, the braided wig draped down to shield my breasts, the ends of each braid weighted with beads. I also sported a snazzy white headband and sandals, the latter a concession to the hard floors in the nightclub where the picture had been taken. An authentic Egyptian dancer would've gone barefoot.

"You wore this in public?" Rory asked, gawping at me.

"Uh-huh. It was an office Halloween party held at a nightclub, organized by me and my work buddies. The two you met, Pam and Sabri."

"Men saw you dressed this way?"

"You betcha." I dragged my finger up his thigh. "For you, I'll even put on a belly-dance show."

He petted the photo album with one finger. "You know how to belly dance?"

"Sure do, baby." I shut the album and closed his fingers around it. "Look at the pictures. Take your time. Let me know which costume you like the best, and I'll make your fantasy come true."

He studied the album for a moment, then tucked it in his pocket.

We resumed sorting through the boxes. Though he kept glancing at the vibrator, we unpacked the rest of my stuff without incident. Once we'd finished, Rory scurried back to his office. I began the arduous task of finding the proper place for everything we'd taken out of the boxes. Thanks to Rory's meticulousness, I stashed my clothes in the closet in a jiff.

My husband got a surprise that night, no doubt, when he walked into our joint bathroom to find my girlie stuff scattered throughout, including my favorite plush, pink towel hanging on the shower curtain rod and a furry pink bath rug on the floor. If he'd opened one of the cabinets, he would've seen packages of sanitary napkins and my leg-shaving accoutrements. He probably had a minor stroke over that.

Well, he kept saying this was my home too. I had a right to give it the Emery touch.

As I selected the right spots to keep my bedroom things, which drawer or closet space, I stumbled onto a box of condoms in the drawer of the bedside table. A sticky note attached to it, written in Rory's masculine and precise hand, said, "For later."

How sweet.

Not.

Rory must've snuck the condoms in there before he committed to no sex for three weeks.

Day two of our wager passed with no sign of Rory. I could've gone to his office to pester him, but I'd vowed to give him time to decompress. I'd never broken a promise to myself or anyone else, but I teetered so close to the line I might stumble over it any second. The day before, he'd skipped out on dinner with me. On this day, he was a no-show once again, despite me coaxing Mrs. D into reminding him I would partake of my meal in the dining room and would appreciate his presence. She told me he grunted in response without looking up from his desk.

By the following day, the third since we made our bet, I'd gotten damn sick of having an invisible husband and eating meals alone or with Mrs. Darroch, sometimes Tavish as well.

The whole time, I thought about Rory.

He'd helped me unpack my stuff. I longed to believe that thoughtful act meant he cared for me, at least a little. Whatever his feelings, one fact had become undeniable.

I was falling for him. After one week.

Maybe that explained my sudden determination to win this frigging bet, and why I pushed open the door to his office shortly after lunch on day three without bothering to knock first. Dressed in my shortest shorts, the denim ones I'd worn the day after our not-so-one-night stand, I lounged against the doorjamb with a foot braced on it and my arms at my sides. Along with the shorts, I'd selected a powder-blue halter top, and I'd let my hair cascade in loose waves that kissed my bare shoulders.

Rory glanced up from the files laid out on his desk. "No shoes again, I see."

"Told you, I don't wear them in the house." I aimed a pointed glance at his feet, visible under the desk, covered in shiny leather loafers. "How can you be comfortable in those shoes? I mean, aren't you itching to kick them off?"

"I dress for work."

He wore his usual slacks and dress shirt with the top button undone. At least he didn't insist on a tie and jacket.

"You work at home," I said. "Locked up in this office. Nobody will see if you ditch the loafers."

He reclined in his chair, holding a pen between his thumb and forefinger, its tip planted on the desktop. "Did you pop in to chastise me for my choice of wardrobe?"

"No," I drawled. "I'm here to tempt you."

"Are you." He tapped the pen on the desktop, seeming thoughtful but with a canny gleam in his eyes. "You mentioned you're shameless when it comes to winning our wager, but I don't have time to play with you. I have work."

"You always have work." I slid my foot higher up the doorjamb, bending my knee more deeply, and stroked my hand along my exposed thigh. "Do you dream about files and cases and clients? Or do you dream about me?"

The pen ceased tapping.

He nailed his slitted gaze to the hand on my thigh.

With one hand positioned at the hem of my shorts, inches from my sex, I trailed the fingertips of the other hand along the neckline of my shirt, down the inner slope of one breast. "That's a nice, big desk. Have you ever fantasized about stripping me naked, laying me over that smooth wood, and having your way with me right here in your office?"

He gritted his teeth, his hand clenching around the pen tight enough to make sinews stretch taut on the back of his hand. Those amber eyes gravitated to my bosom where my fingers teased my own flesh.

I pushed away from the doorjamb, padding toward him with my hips swaying. "You have. I can tell from the way you're devouring me with your gaze."

His hand flew open, the pen toppled from his fingers. He clutched his thighs, his face tight, as if the erection hardening inside his slacks pained him.

I perched my behind on his desk right in front of him. "Would you like me to sit on your lap the way I did the other night? This time, I'll take your cock in my hand and stroke you while I whisper your name."

"Bloody hell." He ground the words out between his teeth.

I fell to my knees between his legs, wedged inside his thighs. "You can have me anytime you want, anywhere you want, any way you want."

He shut his eyes, gulped hard, and struggled to control his erratic breathing. "Not in the daytime, and not outside the bedroom."

"Okay, baby, whatever you want." I uncoiled my body inch by inch, granting him a close-up view of my cleavage and my naked legs. With his face a couple feet from my groin, I tousled his hair. "If you change your mind, let me know."

I skated my fingers down his cheek, over his chin, across his lips.

He stopped breathing, his attention fixated on the fly of my shorts.

Though my body thrummed with excitement, I could endure my unrequited lust for a little longer. No matter how much I wanted to yank down his zipper and mount him.

Mission accomplished, I walked away from my highly aroused husband, hips undulating. Outside the doorway, my hand on the knob, I paused. "Oh, I forgot to tell you—because I haven't seen you since yesterday morning. Got a doctor's appointment tomorrow. I'm having lunch with Erica and Calli after."

He ripped a sticky note from a dispenser but seemed to have forgotten what to do with it. "Tomorrow. Fine."

"Have a good afternoon."

He mumbled.

I shut the door behind me. He couldn't see my smile.

Chapter Twenty-One

I arrived home the next day in a better mood than I'd known in over a week. The stress of a quickie marriage, the invasion of the Mac-Taggarts, and my ongoing battle to loosen up Rory had trickled away. My appointment with Dr. Buchanan, a surprisingly young man with a kindly demeanor, had gone well. But it was my lunch with the American Wives Club that had reinvigorated my attitude.

Much as Rory might want to, he couldn't understand my situation. I'd uprooted my entire life and become a transplant in a land where the people sort of spoke English. Rory's mercurial moods and numerous hang-ups had proved harder to sort out than I'd imagined.

Sure, I loved Scotland so far. And I might maybe possibly be starting to fall for Rory. I couldn't discuss my relationship with him *with him*. I adored Mrs. Darroch and Jamie, but neither of them could talk me through the chaos of my new life. Only another American, another wife of a complex MacTaggart man, could comprehend my predicament.

Erica and Calli were godsends and great ladies to boot. Lunch turned into the most fun I'd had since that weekend in New Orleans with Rory.

Now, as the vestibule door clicked shut, I made my way upstairs to Rory's office.

The door swung open, and Rory stepped out. He stopped dead when he spotted me.

I trotted up to him. "Hi, honey. I'm home."

He looked like a man caught doing something naughty, though I couldn't imagine what.

"Everything okay?" I asked, peeking around his shoulder. "Were you getting your rocks off in there?"

"What?" He executed a double take, his shock utterly lovable. "Why would you ask such a thing?"

"Because you look guilty."

He shuffled his feet and glanced toward the hall windows. "I, ah, wanted to…watch out the windows for you."

"Waiting for me to come home? Aw, that's so—"

"Do not say sweet or cute."

"Endearing. How's that?"

"Acceptable, I suppose." He turned sideways to the door, gesturing toward the nearest chair inside the office. "Come in."

I flopped into the chair he'd pointed at, the one I'd come to think of as my chair. I expected Rory to retreat behind his desk, but instead, he perched on the desk's edge in front of me with his hands loosely linked.

"Your visa has been approved," he said.

"Wow, that was fast."

"I have a friend at the Home Office. He had your application expedited." Rory did that almost-smiling thing. "Stephen Beckham is an old friend from university, and he was extremely grateful for my help in sorting out his father's estate after the old man passed away. His father had been senile and married an exotic dancer, then tried to amend his will."

"Makes me look like a sane choice, huh?" I rocked back in my chair, the front legs lifting off the floor a smidgen. "Thought you couldn't talk about your clients."

"The details appeared in newspapers. It was quite the scandal at the time."

"Were you mentioned in the stories?"

Rory lifted one shoulder. "A few times, but no one cared about the solicitor. Thanks to his venture capital business, the old man had been a celebrity of sorts even before Graham Oliver defamed him."

"Graham? You mean the *bod ceann*?"

"Very good," Rory said. "Maybe I'll teach you naughty Gaelic later."

"Sounds like fun." Dirty Gaelic? I couldn't refuse that offer. "What did Graham do to your friend?"

"He published a story about Stephen's father. Though there was a kernel of truth to it, Graham perverted the facts into a sordid tale worthy of a Roman emperor. A London tabloid latched onto the story."

I nudged his leg with my sneaker-clad foot. "Never told me you're a famous solicitor."

He closed a hand over the desk's edge. "I am not famous. No one would remember my name, it was years ago. The case did…elevate my financial standing, however."

Elevate? I sat forward, hands on the chair's arms. "Are you saying you made a lot of money off this Stephen guy's case? Is that how you got so rich?"

"In part." He fiddled with the cuff of his sleeve. "Stephen was very grateful, as I said, and generous with more than his money. He recommended me to a few others in need of legal assistance, people who could afford to pay a high price for it and were more than willing to do so. Lachlan advised me on how to invest and grow my earnings."

"At least that's one mystery solved." I leaned back, crossing my legs. "Damn, your first wife must really hate herself for dumping you. If she'd stuck around a little longer, she could've had the rich husband she wanted."

He reached behind his body to retrieve a sheet of paper, which he held out to me. "Information concerning our bank accounts. You can access them online with my sign-in credentials, but you'll need to visit the bank with me in order to become a signatory. We can take care of that whenever it's convenient for you."

"No rush." I took the paper. "Thanks. The way you're so on top of things makes me want you on top of me."

"After the wedding, Emery."

"Whatever you say, Rory baby."

He extricated a set of keys from his pocket. A plain metal ring held them together. He tossed it to me. "For the house doors, interior and exterior. We rarely lock the doors, no need to. You also have keys for the vehicles and the carriage house where they're kept."

"Cool." I stowed the keys in my hip pocket. Then I got up and stretched, extending my arms above my head far enough my shirt rode up and Rory's gaze zeroed in on my belly. "I hope you won't be a grump about the wedding when my family's here."

"I am not a grump."

"You are, but I think it's cute." I eased between his legs, my hands on his thighs. "You could at least try to think of our wedding as a cause for celebration. Do it for me."

He settled his hands on my hips, the gesture seeming unconscious. "I'll try. For you."

"Aw, you're such a sweetheart."

"Emery," he all but moaned.

I raised my hands, palms out. "Sorry, sorry. Can't help it, though, you are adorable. Not a demon at all."

"Who says I'm a demon?"

"It was discussed over lunch." The American Wives Club had a bawdy sense of humor, for sure. I loved those ladies. "Erica said you must be a demon holding me hostage in your dungeon to do naughty rituals with me, and that's why I hadn't left the house since coming to Scotland. Then Calli wondered if you might have a forked penis. After that, we got distracted when Erica started grilling me about what it's like sleeping with an uptight solicitor."

"Forked penis?" He seemed to cogitate on that for a moment until he processed everything I'd said. His hands tensed on my hips. "Did you tell Erica and Calli about—about our arrangement?"

"I wouldn't do that. It's private."

His hold loosened, and he tugged me a little closer. "How did you answer Erica's question?"

"About our sex life?" I scooted even closer, gratified to feel his shaft swelling. "I told her you are a demon, but only in the bedroom. We have mind-blowing, earth-shattering, screaming-hot sex and you do me so hard all night long I can't walk or speak for two days after."

"What?" He gaped at me like I'd confessed to armed robbery.

"Chill, Rory." I pressed my body to his, moving my hand up his thigh and across his hip to cup his erection. "I didn't tell the girls anything private. But I did tell them you're awesome in the sack."

His lips arched into a devilish smirk, and his hands wandered up to my waist. "I'm awesome, am I?"

"Absolutely."

My thoughts drifted back to lunch, when I'd mentioned I owned a copy of the Kama Sutra. Erica had chuckled and said, "No wonder Rory's so happy lately." Though I longed to ask him if he was happy with me, I knew that would be a bad idea.

"I spoke to Aidan earlier," Rory said. "He called me 'sweetie-pie.' Twice."

I winced, baring my teeth. "Whoops. Erica said Lachlan told her you can be a grump sometimes. I told her maybe, but you're also a real sweetie-pie." I bit my lip. "Calli must've told Aidan what I said."

"Heaven save us from blethering wives. I warned you if Aidan heard your silly names for me, he'd be calling me 'sweetie-pie' for the rest of eternity."

"I'll make it up to you, promise." I slithered down his body until my face aligned with his cock, barely restrained by his slacks. The sight of that bulge made my mouth water. "If you'll let me."

His chest swelled on a huge intake of breath.

My hands on his thighs, I took hold of his zipper with my teeth.

The breath exploded out of him.

I pulled the zipper down, down, down.

He grasped the back of my head, halting my progress. "No, Emery."

"Why not? Because it's daytime?"

"Because…Just donnae."

He didn't want to lose control. I understood this, but I couldn't help feeling rejected—again.

My hands on his thighs, I jacked my body up, employing him for leverage. "Okay. Your loss."

Rory stood and slapped my behind. "Off with you. I have work."

As I headed for the door, I waved my fingers at him. "That excuse won't work forever, you know."

Though he said nothing, the resignation on his face answered for him.

Chapter Twenty-Two

That night, I was in my room at ten o'clock wearing only my short, satin robe—pink, of course—and picking out my clothes for the next day. My mood had soured around sunset when I figured out I wouldn't see Rory tonight, the sixth night without him since we'd tied the knot. Damn, he had repression down to a science. I'd gotten him riled up good yesterday, and again today, yet he kept his distance.

After setting out my ensemble for the morning, I ambled to the bed and flipped the covers back.

A knock resounded through the door. Two quick, crisp raps.

Rory.

I glanced at the doorway, my mouth open, but I never got the chance to invite him in. The door pivoted inward, and Rory sauntered inside.

My open mouth tightened into a smile, and a sumptuous warmth rushed through me. He was completely nude, with his erection curving up to bob in front of his lower belly.

He shut the door on his way to me, halting a few feet away at the foot of the bed. "You win."

"Just like that? I mean, you could wait a couple more hours and it'll be day five. You'll have won the bet."

"Donnae care about winning." He caught sight of my legs, and his engorged shaft jerked. His taut expression mutated into pain. "I need to fuck ye, *m'eudail.* Now."

"Oh God, I want you too, baby. So much."

His hands came up to rub my upper arms. "The wager was we'd be naked in your room in four days. Cannae wait another day to feel the heat of your soft, slick body around my cock."

I sagged into him, angling my head up in a silent plea for his mouth on mine.

He skimmed his hands up to my shoulders and down along the neckline of my robe until his fingertips teased my breasts. With one hand, he freed the sash around my waist, and the robe fell open. He pushed the satin off my shoulders, letting it flutter to the floor.

"*M'eudail*," he whispered, "you are the most beautiful thing I've ever laid eyes on." He dragged his hands over my breasts, onto my belly. "Or laid my hands on."

His touch felt so good I spread my hands on his chest. "I want to touch you the way you've touched me, the other times we were together. I want to feel every inch of you."

"This is what you want for the bet?"

"No. This is extra, and you can say no."

Grasping my upper arms, he pulled me into his body. "Have your way with me, *m'eala-fhiadhaich*. Donnae let me fetter your wings."

"My wings?" I hopped up on my toes, twining my arms around his neck. "What was that you called me? It sounded lovely."

"*M'eala-fhiadhaich*. It means my wild swan." His fingers manipulated my flesh, the pressure as gentle as the emotion in his voice. "You are a free and untamed lass, and as elegant and beautiful as any swan."

My throat went thick, my stomach fluttered. An endearment? I wanted to shriek my joy while jumping up and down, but this intimacy between us was fragile. I'd dared to ask what he'd said, and he had confided the truth to me. *Enough for tonight.*

He'd also given me permission to have my way with him. A thrill rippled through me, energizing my skin and electrifying every fine hair.

I moved back a half step, just enough to get more room to admire his body—dear God, I could've licked him from head to toe, especially that glorious erection—and more room to explore him. The golden light from the bedside lamp burnished his skin, except for the red tip of his erection. The whisper-thin, cinnamon-colored hairs scattered over his skin seemed more golden in the muted light, and I placed my palms on his belly to glide them up, reveling in the silky sensation of those hairs brushing my skin and his warm flesh under my hands.

His eyes drifted almost shut, with only a sliver through which he might glimpse me. The slight space between his lips beckoned to me, promising a scorching kiss, but I had my sights set on another goal.

With my hands, I explored and memorized every valley and swell of his muscles, marveling at the contrast between taut sinew and tender flesh. Up his chest my hands traveled, across his shoulders, down his arms and back up his sides to his narrow hips. I moved my palms to his ass, but they couldn't cover the expanse of his firm buttocks. My body flush against his, I ran my hands up his back, feeling the hard curves of his shoulder blades.

He exhaled a jagged breath. His voice gruff with need, he said, "Ye plan on killing me, then, lass?"

"You won't die from lust."

"Maybe not." His body shuddered on a sharp intake of breath. "But I might *caith* before you're done."

Caith? In the instant I wondered what he meant, his shaft throbbed against my belly and I got an inkling. "Do you mean ejac—"

"Yes," he hissed, his cheeks turning a dusky pink.

My poor Rory, all pent up and needy. "I can help with that."

I went to my knees at his feet, my face positioned before his penis. My mouth watered at the sight of it so close, of his smooth flesh stretched tight over his engorged length and at the bead of moisture poised on its rosy head. I leaned in, opening my mouth.

He stopped me with two fingers on my lips. "Don't. Please."

Gazing up the expanse of his body to meet his eyes, I understood he'd made all the concessions he could. His rejection stung less this time, moderated by the knowledge we would share intimacy this evening. Maybe one day he'd let me taste him, but not tonight.

I rose and laid my hands on him once more.

He picked me up and laid me down on the bed. The silken sheets felt so good on my skin, a little shiver of pleasure rippled through me. Rory climbed onto the bed, towering above me with his knees at either side of my thighs.

Gorgeous. No other word seemed appropriate. He was gorgeous.

He moved one knee between my thighs, urging me to part them.

Like I could resist anything he wanted. Naked Rory was a force of nature, one I gladly let sweep me away on the winds of passion. I spread my legs for him as I raised my arms over my head, my hands just above the pillow.

He skimmed his hands up my belly. His fingers molded around each breast while his thumbs pushed under them to rub slow and delicate circles on the undersides.

My body arched into his touch, starved for the sensations he evoked with such ease. Had it only been a few days since he'd laid hands on me? His thumbs swept up to toy with my nipples, and my neck bowed, driving my head deeper into the pillow. Oh God, it felt like forever since he'd touched me this way.

He smothered my nipple with his mouth, saturating my skin with moist heat. The areola pebbled and darkened to a dusky shade of pink.

The breath caught in my throat.

With his eyes trained on mine, he slid his tongue around my nipple like the tongue of an erotic serpent tasting my flesh with aching slowness, unleashing a torrent of pleasure that rippled down every nerve all the way down to my clitoris.

I clenched my hands around the rails of the headboard, hanging on for the tempest to come. *More, please, more.* My voice had abandoned me, so I implored him in my mind as if he might read my thoughts and grant my desperate wish.

His tongue. Licking, licking, licking. His thumbs. Flicking, flicking, flicking. Every movement was deliberate and precise, building the pressure little by little. His erection grazed my belly, and I bucked my hips in mindless need.

My eyelids fluttered half closed.

Panic spiked through my chest. My lids sprang open.

Shit. I'd almost shut my eyes after promising him I wouldn't. But his mouth, the way it tormented my nipple, the impulse to close my eyes intensified every second, the craving to lose myself in the bliss of his touch irresistible.

Oh God. So close to coming, so close, right on the edge. My mouth gaped open on a gasp. *Oh God.*

My eyes tried to shut again.

I forced them open, gripped the headboard tighter until pangs shot through my fingers, and let out a frustrated whimper.

Rory lifted his head, his thumbs going motionless. "What's wrong?"

"I—" The onset of tears stung my eyes and burned in the back of my throat. "I'm trying not to close my eyes, but I don't think I can stop it. I'm sorry, I know I promised, I'm sorry."

He supported his body with one arm, laying a hand on my cheek. "I'm the one who should apologize. Please forgive me, *m'eudail.* I never meant to cause you pain."

With his hand on my cheek and his gentle eyes searching my face, I couldn't deny him what he asked for, couldn't hold on to my anguished frustration any longer. It dissolved in his reassuring presence. A couple much needed breaths soothed my nerves and evaporated the tears.

"It's okay," I said. "You didn't do it on purpose."

He smoothed his hand over my hair. "Forget what I said. Close your eyes if you need to."

"Are you sure?"

His breaths tickled the hairs on my cheek. "Aye. That rule is rescinded."

One more rule gone. More progress. My heart exulted as if he'd declared his eternal love for me though all he'd done was let me close my eyes. Stupid, but I no longer cared if my reactions to him were moronic. Instead of suppressing these feelings, I would marvel at them, relish them, envelop myself in the tempest of emotions this man evoked in me.

And if he never shared my wonder…That was beyond my control.

"Kiss me," I said.

His cheeks dimpled. "I will."

Lighting a kiss on my nose, he shimmied backward down my body until his face hovered over my groin.

I tipped my head up. "You didn't kiss me."

"Ahm about to. Feel free to close yer eyes and scream mah name." With two fingers, he separated my folds. "Mah lass loves pink. So do I, when it's the rosy color of yer succulent, slippery skin."

He skimmed his tongue straight down the center of my cleft, dipping it into my opening only to snatch it away.

"Don't stop," I said. "Kiss me the way you did on our wedding night."

One side of his mouth kicked up, and he placed a soft kiss on my clitoris. "Mah woman needs to come, and ahmno letting ye down."

I lashed my hands around the headboard rails again, my chest heaving with each breath, the weight of need bearing down on my belly.

His lips engulfed my clit, but even as he began a torturously deliberate pace of lapping and suckling, his gaze remained riveted to mine. Those glossy eyes simmered with desire, captivating me so I couldn't have shut my eyes if I'd wanted to. His cheeks caved in as he suckled hard. His lips puckered around my nub, and he rasped his tongue over it. I writhed, my hips bucking every time he pulled on my flesh, only to bounce down on the mattress when he released the pressure for a heartbeat.

I thrashed my head and whimpered, this time in sheer ecstasy.

He wedged a hand between my thighs, and his questing fingers found my entrance.

"Rory," I gasped.

A single finger dived inside me and whisked back out, only to punch in again and retreat. A second finger joined the first, both pushing inside me and then pulling out in a thrusting motion that drove me to moan and writhe with a hunger too intense to deny.

"P-please," I begged between harsh breaths. "Please, oh God, make me come."

His eyebrows eased upward, and his lips tightened as he smiled around my nub. He never let up, not the tiniest smidgen, in his suckling of my flesh. He crooked those fingers inside me, stretching them toward a hidden spot, stroking it so deftly while he nipped at my clit and chafed his thumb along the center of my cleft.

My back arched into the bed, raising my hips, and my knees folded until my heels lifted off the mattress. I clung to the rails, breathless, shocked by the power of what I sensed mounting inside me.

And I did it. I screamed his name.

The climax ripped through me, even as his fingers rubbed that magic spot inside my opening. The exquisite agony of sexual release squeezed sharp cries from me while I flailed like I might fly up to the ceiling if not for Rory's body pinning my hips to the bed.

Spent, I went limp beneath him. My mind seemed to float in a weightless bliss, and the aftermath of unbelievable pleasure shivered through my body.

Rory rose onto all fours and crawled forward until his face was above mine. "Ye didnae close yer eyes."

"Couldn't. You were—" I gulped in cool, delicious oxygen. "Didn't want to stop looking at you."

He fanned his hand over my belly. "I love the way yer always wet and ready for me."

I lifted my trembling arms to clasp his nape. "You make me hot and wet without even touching me, just the look in your eyes does me in."

He nuzzled my throat. "You make me hard as granite with only a smile."

"Really." I freed one hand to wrap it around his rigid shaft. "Oh. You weren't exaggerating."

"Complete honesty, that's what you wanted."

I guided my hand up to the base of his erection, then smoothed it down his velvety flesh. "Honesty can be so hot."

He flailed an arm out, fumbling for the drawer on the bedside table. His big fingers located the metal latch, and he yanked the drawer open. His breaths panted as he grabbed for a condom packet. It slipped from his grasp. With a sputtered curse that must've been Gaelic, he snagged the packet and slammed the drawer shut.

"Let me help," I said, reaching for the foil packet.

He closed his fist around it and growled, "I'll die from lust if ye lay even one of yer wee, dainty fingers on me."

"Told you before, no one dies from lust."

"With you, a man could." He tore the packet open with his teeth and spat out the fragment. "Ye turn me into a bampot, with yer smiles and the way ye move that body."

"What's a bampot?"

"Me." He sprang to his knees, rolling the condom over his thick cock with surprising calmness.

The muted lighting glistened on his skin and highlighted the contours of all those muscles. When he fell to his hands and knees, I frisked my palms over his chest, delighting in the firmness of his pecs and abs.

"Oh Rory baby," I drawled, my voice going husky, "I want you, all of you. On top of me, inside me, any way you want me."

I'd thought those words more than a week ago, back in New Orleans, when he'd approached me in the bar. To speak them now felt like…destiny.

"Emery, *mo leannan*," he said, "I want ye every minute of every day."

He let out the longest, deepest groan, an expression of a need so intense he couldn't speak its name, and lunged his hips down to plow his length into my flesh. He stopped there, arms shaking from the effort of holding still.

I shackled my hands around his biceps.

"Say that again," he whispered.

"What?"

"Call me—" His lips quivered. "Call me Rory baby again. Keep saying it. Please."

That night in the dining room, he'd admitted he liked the nickname. For him to want me to say it while he made love to me…My God, it had to mean something.

I squeezed his arms. "Rory baby."

He pulled out and plunged into my depths, slow and easy, doing it over and over, each stroke a decadent glide of his hardness merging with my tender flesh. My body hugged his length as he possessed and abandoned me. Sweat beaded on his skin, shimmering on the tips of slender cinnamon hairs.

I moaned his name, gasped his name, shouted his name, a litany of "Rory baby" that spilled from my lips one after another.

The pleasure mounted, sweet as honey and rich as hot oil.

Rory gave an anguished groan and bent to cover my mouth with his, swallowing my cry along with his own.

I clung to him through every undulating spasm of my climax. He was my anchor, the center of my existence, the source of everything good in my world. He pumped his hips with enough power to bounce my breasts each time he pounded me into the mattress, until he went rigid and roared with his own release. The universe telescoped down to the two of us, our bodies slick with sweat, our breaths ragged, our bodies bound.

He collapsed on top of me, his head on the pillow next to mine, his face in my hair.

I swathed him in my arms, satisfied in every way, basking in the bliss of climax but also the rapture of his weight atop me and his semi-erect cock nestled inside my body.

Rory let out a sigh of pure contentment. "My Emery, you are irreplaceable."

My Emery. Irreplaceable. The words echoed in my mind, and my heart yearned to accept the deeper meaning they might hold. He called me his, but only in the afterglow of sexual release. I was irreplaceable, but he might've meant as a lover. Christ, I knew I shouldn't let the phrasing get to me.

The glowy sensation in my chest compelled me to believe.

He rolled off my body, robbing me of his heat and weight.

The glowiness receded, though an ember took root in my heart.

I turned onto my side and burrowed against him. When he wound an arm around me, I smiled into his chest. Though I hated to risk losing this wonderful closeness between us, I needed to ask him a question while he was mellowed out.

Raised on an elbow, I asked, "Why did you not want me to close my eyes?"

Though his arm stayed around me, he scrubbed his face with his other hand. "Does it matter? I rescinded the rule."

I felt myself balanced on a thin layer of earth floating on a bog, vulnerable to the slightest movement in the wrong direction that might yank it out from under me. Despite the danger of forging ahead, I might never have him in this mood again, at ease and open to talking.

"I think it does matter, Rory. To you, for sure. And what matters to you affects me."

He covered his eyes with his hand. "My third wife, Una. Whenever we were…intimate, and I would, ah…" Lines cinched tight on his forehead, while his mouth twisted. "When I gave her oral sex, she would keep her eyes shut the entire time. I assumed it was a sign she enjoyed it. Only when she left me did she confess the truth."

No way I would speak or move. Anything might make him clam up again.

After a moment, he went on. "I had noticed she rarely achieved orgasm during intercourse, but she always came when I used my mouth on her." He squirmed but kept his arm wreathed around me and stared up at the ceiling. "On the day she walked out, Una told me she'd made a terrible mistake marrying me. She couldn't be with me or any man because she's gay."

Jesus. No wonder he was skittish about relationships.

"I asked her how long she'd known," he said, "about her preference for women. She said she'd always known, for as long as she could remember. I couldn't understand how that could be, since we'd had sex many times. Una told me she could only have an orgasm during oral sex, and only if she closed her eyes and imagined I was a woman."

Christ, that would've emasculated the most stalwart of men. Why the hell had the woman told him that? For heaven's sake, she could've left it at "I'm gay, Rory."

He shielded his face with an arm over his eyes. "During intercourse, she would pretend to like it when she really wanted it to be over as quickly as possible. Our eight months together were, according to Una, the most painful of her life. She cried while telling me all of this, apologized repeatedly for lying to me."

I wanted to throw my arms around him. Knowing how much he despised talking about his previous marriages, however, I would do nothing that might make him feel embarrassed or exposed. But a question had occurred to me, and the answer seemed vital.

"Um…" I craned my neck to see his face but couldn't.

"Go on. You have a question, ask it."

"You don't have to tell me any more than you already have." I laid my hand over his where it curled over my arm. "I can't help wondering. Why did Una marry you in the first place?"

With half his face concealed behind his arm, he answered in a flat voice. "She believed her family would despise her for being gay. That turned out to be wrong, but she believed it for many years."

I squashed my lips between my teeth, struggling against the impulse to pry a little more.

Rory lowered his arm to reveal his face, but he'd gone stoic, his facade impenetrable. "Say it. Whatever it is, go on and say it."

Damn. How did he know I was itching to say something?

I wiggled around until I was on my knees, sitting back on my heels with my hands on my thighs. "Una caused you a lot of pain, the kind that sticks around for years. Deceiving you like that was mean and selfish."

"Una's not a bad person. She worried about what others thought of her, and I believe she cared for me in a certain way, but her fears were of her own making. Those are the hardest to overcome. I have no ill will toward Una. She did the best she could."

"Fine, maybe Una's not evil." I looked at my hands, twiddling my fingers with nervous energy. "But don't tell me Isobel wasn't selfish and mean, bitching about your job and how much money you made. You're my husband now, and I won't pretend I'm okay with the harm they did to you, whether it was intentional or not."

He hadn't told me about wife number two yet. What damage did she inflict on him?

Rory gave me a strange look, and when he spoke, his tone was guarded. "That sounds rather possessive."

"I stand up for the people I—" *Love.* I cut myself off a nanosecond before blurting out the word, but he'd freak for sure if I said it. Besides, I wasn't positive I meant it yet. Heading in that direction, yeah, but love? Way too soon to know. I started over, saying, "As a rule, I assume everybody's doing their best and doesn't mean to hurt anybody else. But I stand up for my family. We are married, whatever the reason for it, which makes you family."

"That's…generous of you. I have a family of my own, though, so it's not necessary."

Queasiness roiled in my stomach. A family of his own. Sounded like I wasn't included in that group.

"I know you have a family," I said, "and they're amazing. But you haven't told them the whole story about your exes, have you?"

He hesitated. "No."

"Then it's up to me to say 'oh hell no' to what they did to you." I thought for a moment, then asked, "Am I the only one who knows?"

"Yes." He held up a staying hand when I opened my mouth to say more. "I'd rather not discuss this any further at the moment."

"Okay. Thank you for telling me, even though it couldn't have been easy for you."

He rubbed his eyes with the heels of his hands and managed a ghost of a smile for me. "You won the bet. What do you want for it?"

I tapped my chin, pretending to think hard about my options. "Hmm, what do I want from Rory baby?"

His lips scrunched up, but as usual, it seemed more like an attempt to quash a smile than an expression of irritation. Man, I was getting damn sick of his need to *not* smile at me.

Determined to lighten the mood, I swung a leg over him to sit astride his thighs. "I want to see the ocean."

Cinnamon brows shot up. "That's all?"

"I've never seen the ocean, but no. That's not all."

"You have never seen the ocean?"

"I lived in landlocked states. Born and raised in Idaho, moved to Colorado after college. Plenty of lakes, but no seashore."

He clasped his hands behind his head. "What else do you want, then? This was supposed to be one activity of your choice, not a Christmas list."

I raked my nails down his stomach to within inches of his groin. "It will be one activity, Mr. Persnickety. I want to see the ocean as part of a broader tour of the Highlands. And I want you to be my tour guide."

He made a face. "I have work."

"One day," I said, bracing my hands on his shoulders, my breasts dangling in his line of sight, "that's all I'm asking. A day trip."

"Jamie would be a better guide."

I nipped his nose. "No dice. You agreed to our wager, and this is the one thing I want." I sat up and slapped his chest. "Don't be a grouch. Show me your homeland, Rory."

He regarded me in silence as the minutes ticked by on the bedside clock. I shimmied my behind, and he grimaced. Beneath me, his cock stirred.

With a swiftness that surprised a squeak out of me, he surged up and flipped us both. I landed flat on my back with him above me, his knees penning my legs. He strapped my hands to the pillow with his own, at either side of my head. His face descended toward mine, but his lips hovered inches from mine.

"Again?" I asked, and we both knew full well what I meant. My body had come alive the instant he tossed me onto my back. "I'm up for anything, you know that. On our first night together, I loved the way you woke me up in the middle of the night to make love to me one more time."

The desire heating his expression snuffed out.

"What's wrong?" I asked.

He leaped up to kneel over me, stepped off the bed, and walked out of the room.

The door clicked shut.

I pushed up on my elbows, a chill prickling my skin. What the hell had happened? I lay there, mute and paralyzed, while a maelstrom of thoughts sucked me down into oblivion. One inescapable conclusion echoed in my mind.

He wasn't coming back.

Though I'd known he would sleep in his room, the abruptness of his departure hit me harder than I'd imagined it could. A searing pain stabbed straight through my heart into my soul. Nothing but a plaything, that's what I was. A warm body to slake his needs. Worse than a trophy wife, I'd become his whore.

Shit, shit, shit. What an idiot I'd been, rushing into marriage with a damaged man entrenched in his solitary lifestyle. Maybe he didn't want to be helped. Maybe I'd fucked up my life royally, and now I had to live with the consequences of my impulsive and reckless decision.

I pulled the covers over me, huddling with my knees drawn to my chest, knowing I would not sleep tonight.

Chapter Twenty-Three

The next morning, I woke to find Rory had sneaked into my room sometime overnight to leave a note on the bedside table. "Meet me on the green," it said, like I was expected to know what the heck *the green* meant. Since I didn't, I grabbed a quick breakfast in the kitchen, eating the meal Mrs. Darroch had left in the fridge for me, marked with a sticky note that bore my name. I bumped into her in the hallway and asked a vital question.

"Where's 'the green'?"

"It's the grassy area behind the garden," she said, "outside the wall. There's a door behind the hydrangeas."

The wooden door to "the green" hid behind a lavish hydrangea bush with pale-pink, mop-headed blossoms. The shrub, planted beside the doorway, had grown beyond its original location to spill its branches over the exit. I twisted the rusty metal knob and pushed, adding a bit of shoulder force to the effort. The door popped open.

I stumbled through it onto freshly mowed grass, its green scent enveloping me. Though most days had been cloudy, this morning Mother Nature had blessed us with a blue sky marred by only a smattering of clouds.

My husband was in the center of the green, wearing a kilt and leather boots but nothing else. He faced away from me, the sun burnishing his bare back and arms. A long, thin wooden pole lay lengthwise on the grass before him. Its surface had bumps where branches were removed, and its bark had been stripped. The pole must've measured twenty feet long. Five similar poles lay in a pile near the clearing's edge.

These were the poles I'd seen a few days ago when I explored the grounds.

Rory crouched to grasp the pole in both hands, heaved it up, and walked his hands down its length to lift it above his head. When he reached the other end, he had the pole upright.

I sidled up to the wall, fascinated by his actions.

He moved around the pole, keeping it between his hands, so he faced the opposite direction. His attention darted around the green, and when it fell on me, his eyes narrowed and his chest puffed out.

"There you are," he said. "At last."

"What are you doing?"

He slapped the pole. "Practicing my caber toss."

So that was a caber. Calli had mentioned the wooden poles and that Scottish men liked to toss them around. "You're seriously planning to chuck that thing?"

"I am."

A hot thrill shivered through me. He'd invited me out here, implying he wanted me to watch.

Rory shifted his hands down the pole, squatting at its base, and hefted its end up with both hands beneath it. The muscles in his arms and back rippled and flexed.

The caber wobbled the tiniest bit.

I sucked in a breath, unable to release it.

With a harsh yell, he thrust his hands up and out, tossing the caber end over end.

Its furthest end must've landed fifty feet away.

"Holy shit!" I blurted the phrase before my brain filter kicked back into gear.

Rory smirked. "I'll take that as a compliment."

A wicked tingle coursed through me, and I couldn't tear my gaze away from him—away from his broad, muscle-bound chest and his thickly corded arms and his astonishingly powerful thighs. I wanted that body, right now.

I glanced at the caber, that twenty-foot tree, and asked, "Is it safe to practice flinging trees by yourself?"

He rolled one shoulder in a casual shrug. "Safe enough. I used to practice with Lachlan, but I gave up the sport three years ago."

"Why?"

Another nonchalant shrug.

He didn't want to tell me, so I changed tack. "When did you start up again?"

"Last week."

I stuffed my hands in the pockets of my lavender shorts. "After we got married."

He nodded, pretending to examine the grass.

Ah-ha. His renewed desire to chuck trees had arisen post-Emery. The fact struck me as important, though I couldn't fathom what it meant.

"Would ye like to watch me go again?" he asked, his voice warmed by a seductive timbre.

"Love to."

He repeated his raising of the caber and launched the pole end over end.

This time, I pulled out my phone and captured the moment with its camera.

I leaped away from the wall, clapping and whooping. "Go, Rory baby!"

My husband quirked a brow at me, his lips ticking up, eyes sparkling in the sunshine. "Ye like to watch."

Oh yeah. As much as I loved ogling him while he lobbed trees, I wanted more than a sexy spectacle. In spite of the way he'd left last night, I craved him like never before.

I had a fetish for caber tossing. Who knew?

He strode toward me, hips undulating, whisky-dark eyes hooded.

Though I could've reached out to touch him, the arm's length between us seemed way too far. I needed him to mash that body into mine, caging me between the wall and those acres of delectable muscles.

"Wow," I said, "you're like Hercules."

His smirk heated into a darkly erotic smile.

And at last, I got it.

"You invited me here," I said. "You wanted me to see you flinging trees."

He hooked a thumb inside the waist of his kilt.

I cocked my head, leaning into the wall. "Are you showing off for me?"

"Why would I?"

"You tell me." I braced one foot on the wall, my knee bent. "Therapy is a journey of self-discovery, after all."

In a single stride, he erased the distance between us. My bent leg brushed his kilt. He slipped a hand around the curve of my naked thigh to curl it around the underside. "Do I need to prove my masculine prowess to you?"

I settled a hand on his belly, sketching the lines of his abs with my fingertips. "I'm fully aware of your virility and stamina."

He coasted that hand up the underside of my thigh, inside my shorts and panties, his callused skin rough on the soft curve of my ass. As he slanted his body into mine, sinews flexed against me, and my head lolled into the cool stone of the wall. He flattened his free hand on the rock alongside me and rested his chin on my shoulder.

Strong fingers kneaded my ass.

I latched my leg around his, pulling the hard length of his cock into my belly.

His lips painted a hot, damp trail up my throat. "Have ye ever fucked up against a castle wall?"

"Oh yeah, dozens of times."

He tugged my hips into his body. "Liar."

Only he could inflame my lust by calling me a liar.

"Let's go for it," I said.

He went hard as the stone behind me, though not in the part of his body I wanted. He glanced around as if rousing from a bizarre dream.

"*Mhac na galla*," he hissed, and shoved away from me. "We cannae."

Because it was daytime, and we weren't in a bed.

"What the hell is *mhac na galla*?"

"It means son of a bitch." He touched his forehead. "We cannot do this."

"Come on," I said, heedless of the raw frustration in my voice. "Getting me worked up and yanking the rug out from under me again? After the way you sprinted out of my bedroom last night? Not cool, Rory. Not cool at all."

"I believe you're mixing several metaphors."

"Screw metaphors." I rapped my fist on his chest. "Show a little respect, or at least common courtesy. I'm your wife, not your concubine."

He raked a hand through his hair. "I didn't—You're right. I'm sorry, you deserve better, but you knew what I am when you agreed to our arrangement. You said you understood the terms."

Fuck. Our promise in the form of an unenforceable contract had bitten me in the ass, and all I could do was smear antibiotic ointment on the wound. "Thanks so much for reminding me."

The sharpness in my tone seemed to take him aback. He lurched backward, gesturing toward the garden door. "I'm sure you have other things to do. Twirling about on the lawn, perhaps."

"You saw me yesterday?"

"I did."

"That was spinning and skipping, not 'twirling about.' " I flapped a hand in the direction of his discarded caber. "Not any weirder than hurling giant sticks."

"The caber toss is a feat of strength and control," he said. "What purpose does spinning serve?"

"It's fun. And I was soaking up the sunshine." I took a big breath and threw my arms wide as I'd done while lounging on the grass yesterday. "Why don't you come out and join me this time, instead of peeping on me from the first-floor hallway."

"How did you know where I was?"

"Simple deduction. You were in your office, like always, and it's on the first floor. The office windows don't face the front lawn. To see me, you would've had to walk out into the hall."

He gazed at me with approval, tinged with surprise. "My clever wife."

Maybe I hoped for a miracle, but I asked anyway. "Would you come for a walk with me?"

"Can't. I'll be spending the day at my office in Loch Fairbairn." He turned away to roll his caber toward the pile at the edge of the green.

Thus dismissed, I started for the garden door. On the threshold, I looked back at him. "Will I see you for dinner?"

He dumped the caber. It thunked onto the pile. "Don't wait for me."

I slammed the garden door behind me, not entirely because the heavy thing wouldn't close.

It was my turn to watch out the window, though I hugged myself as Rory's Mercedes rolled down the drive and out of sight.

A final cry of ecstasy tumbled from my lips, my voice hoarse from the ruckus I'd made while Rory drove me wild with pleasure. My knees were hooked over his shoulders while his hands were planted on the mattress at either side of my body. He hunched over me, frozen at the apex of his last thrust, our position ensuring he'd taken me deeper than ever before. Droplets of salty moisture from our sweat-slicked bodies dribbled down my side and dripped from his skin to strike my belly. The scent of sex and perspiration permeated the air.

Despite his repeated command I not wait up for him because he'd be back very late, he'd arrived home shortly after ten o'clock. Though I wanted to dash downstairs to greet him, I'd reined in the joyful instinct and waited for him in my bed.

Sure enough, he skulked into my room fifteen minutes later.

No talking. He got straight to seducing me, though his lust seemed tainted with a confusing desperation as if he needed to be inside me to assure himself I still existed. I'd let him seduce me because I needed the same thing—reassurance.

I disliked the separate-bedrooms thing, but I hated his determination to slink out of my room right after sex. I'd resolved to let him do this for a while, though, and try to ease him into a new dynamic. The typical married-people kind. I'd let him into my bed, knowing he'd split the second we finished, for one simple reason. I loved the pleasure he gave me.

Even if that made me a desperate moron.

Rory crawled out from under my legs to kneel at my feet. My knees remained bent, my sex still exposed.

His gaze darted to the door.

Despite the chill of unease trickling through my veins, I understood what I must do for him. "It's okay. You can leave."

He swung his legs over the bed's edge, hesitated, and then leaned over to kiss my forehead. "Good night, Emery."

I forced a weak smile. "Good night, Rory."

Sliding off the bed, he padded to the door.

On the threshold, he paused. "I ran into Graham in the village today. He's developed an odd fascination with you, asked how you were adjusting to your new home. Cannae understand what he wants but be cautious if you see him. Anything you say might be printed in his grimy paper."

"I won't tell him about our arrangement or the contract."

"Graham has a way of wheedling things out of people."

With two fingers, I drew a cross over my heart. "I'm wheedle-proof, promise."

As the door clicked shut behind him, I rolled onto my side and pulled the covers up to my chin. A sour taste tainted my mouth.

In time, he would want to share a bed with me. He had to. If not…Well, his therapist wouldn't let him get away with this for much longer.

During breakfast the next morning, he marched into the kitchen to announce, "I'm having a gate installed at the end of the drive. No car will approach the house without permission again."

A reaction to Graham's intrusion in the garden and Rory's encounter with him in town. Rory needed to reassert control of his privacy.

"The entrance doors are to remain locked at all times," he said. "I'll give you a remote for opening the gate once it's installed."

Without a kiss or a grumbled goodbye, he departed the house.

As he had on the day of the caber-tossing session, Rory avoided me for the next two days by traveling to his office in the village, but by the day after that, he'd gone back to holing up in his home office. I granted him a reprieve from my presence and stayed out of his office unless he invited me, though he never did.

For a week after I'd won our bet, I put up with the mistress-wife treatment. Every night after he left me, I pulled the covers over my head and fought against crying. In the daytime, Rory would seek me out for a kiss— one brief lip-lock at first, but as the days passed our playful kisses became long, luxurious make-out sessions in any and every part of the house, even outdoors under the shade of the larch trees.

I'd begun my search for a new life's purpose, driving to Erica and Lachlan's place to learn about farming and to Calli and Aidan's home to explore the life of a librarian, with Calli as my guide. Catriona let me shadow her for a day while she taught history workshops at local schools. Despite having a

PhD in archaeology, she couldn't get a full-time job with it. Yep, we bonded over our mutual lack of gainful employment.

On the seventeenth day of my acquaintance with Rory, the twelfth day of our marriage, we'd concluded a steamy round of *how far can we go with kissing without going all the way* when Rory surprised me.

He wound a lock of my hair around his finger, spellbound by the strands. "You haven't come to my office lately."

"Thought you'd rather be alone."

"It seems…quiet without your visits."

Crazily, that simple statement made my pulse accelerate. I supposed calling his office "quiet" without me was as close as he'd get to admitting he missed me.

"I'll see you at dinner, then?" he said.

The heaviness trapped in my chest for days disintegrated. We hadn't convened for a meal in more than a week.

"Yes," I said, "at dinner."

He released my hair and nodded. "Good."

With that, he returned to his office.

I hadn't asked him to dine with me, not since the day I'd traipsed into his office and curtsied at his feet. His offer had been his choice. *Hooray,* my heart cheered. My mind took a more pragmatic attitude, unwilling to celebrate yet. We continued to sleep in separate rooms, after all, with no sign he'd ever relent on that dictate. Why was I letting him get away with relegating me to mistress-wife status? I'd allot him two more days of solitude and then…

Watch out, Rory MacTaggart.

That evening, we met in the dining room to share a meal and casual conversation. Afterward, we retired to my room for energetic sex followed by a good-night kiss.

In the morning, I'd stretched my leniency so far the rope had frayed into a flimsy thread. Time to tell Rory how much his nightly departures bothered me, not only because I'd sworn to be honest with him but also because I'd stopped doing silly things like spinning and skipping. This wild swan had forgotten how to fly.

Not acceptable.

I busted into his office, the door slamming shut in my wake.

He flinched, his head jerking up. "Emery?"

The shadows under his eyes matched the ones I must've sported. Maybe sleeping alone didn't agree with him as much as he claimed.

I sprawled in the chair across the desk from him, one leg draped over the arm, foot swinging. "We need to talk about the separate-bedrooms thing."

He discarded his pen, sitting back in his chair. "We've already discussed it."

"No, you issued your decree and I went along with it." I rested a hand on the knee of my dangling leg. "Separate bedrooms isn't in the contract. Did you make your ex-wives sleep alone?"

His lips thinned into a sharp line.

"Well?" I said. "Did you?"

"No."

"Mm-hm." I rapped my knuckles on my knee. "Did you order them not to say your name during sex?"

He fingered the top button of his shirt like he'd forgotten it was undone.

"I'll take that as a no," I told him. "What about your one-night stands? Did you tell them not to speak your name or close their eyes?"

He tugged at his collar and scratched his throat.

"Another no." I scraped my nails on my jeans, eliciting a *scritch* from the denim. "Why do you invent rules for living with me? I'm trying to understand this, Rory, but you've got to help me out. Why am I the special one who gets banished to the other end of a very long hallway?"

I suspected he treated me differently because we'd grown close and it scared him, but I needed him to reach that conclusion on his own.

He fiddled absently with the papers on his desk. "You're not banished."

"Sure as hell feels like it. Either I'm your wife or I'm your mistress. Make up your mind."

He jolted forward, head down, and made a show of stacking the papers on his desk, then putting them in a file folder. "This is our arrangement. You agreed to it."

"I never agreed to these cockamamie rules," I said. "I know you have issues with trusting women, but I'd like to know what I've done to give you the impression you can't trust me. I've been supportive and understanding, right? Haven't I accommodated all your hang-ups?"

"You've done all of that," he admitted without glancing at me.

"Do you trust me?"

He plucked up his pen, hovered it over a page, and set it down again. "I can't sleep with you. It's that simple."

"No, it's this simple." I shoved out of the chair. "Sometimes I'm not sure if you like me, or if you tolerate me because you require the use of my body at least twice a week."

He'd called me irreplaceable and his wild swan, and he often treated me with exquisite tenderness. Though he'd rescinded some rules, others remained—no sex outside the bedroom, no daytime sex, no sharing a bed. I couldn't reconcile Rory the affectionate husband with Rory the damaged and frightened man.

At last, he looked at me. "I have never said I require the use of your body."

"It's in the contract." I slapped my palms down on the desktop. "You require sexual congress at least twice a week. Since you can't bring yourself to spend the night with me, that means you need my body and nothing else."

"Emery."

"Shut up and listen, Rory." I speared him with my razor-sharp gaze, praying I could get through to him. "I tried to be cool with you screwing me and running off to your room, to hide behind a locked door. I tried to be patient and not question your hang-ups, to wait until you were ready to talk. And you have, a few times, and I appreciate that."

His eyes widened a fraction.

"But it's not enough," I said. "You're making me feel like your in-house whore."

"You are not a whore."

"Aren't I? You're paying me half a million dollars to fuck you for a year."

"You signed the contract." His expression hardened, his mouth twisted downward. "If you're waiting for me to fall in love with you, it will never happen."

The bleakness in his eyes contradicted his dispassionate demeanor.

"I'm not trying to make you love me," I said. "A few days ago on the green, after your impressive demonstration of caber tossing, I asked you to show me a little common decency. You stayed with me on our wedding night, for heaven's sake. You fell asleep with me the night we met and only left at dawn. Is it really such a hardship for you to let me into your bedroom?"

Or into your heart, I yearned to ask. Christ, I shouldn't want him to love me. He'd warned me he wouldn't do it, but my stupid heart refused to believe him.

"If you leave me now," he said, "you'll walk away with nothing. Not a shilling of my money."

Despite the flintiness in his voice, something in his eyes and in the tightness around his mouth evinced a deep vulnerability. I'd witnessed this act before—the detached solicitor with no feelings. I hadn't believed it in the past, and I didn't buy it today.

"I know what you're doing," I said. "This is how you keep your distance. You want me to think you're a cold bastard, so I won't like you anymore, but I'm onto you. If you were really a bastard, you wouldn't act like one."

"Your bum's oot the windae."

"I am not talking nonsense." When surprise flickered on his face, I straightened and lifted my chin. "Erica told me what that saying means.

You're the one who spouts nonsense on a regular basis."

He gave me an *oh please* look.

"What I said about bastards," I explained, "means they are bastards, all the time, it's no act. You have to put on a show to convince me you're a jerk, but I see what you're doing and I don't buy it."

He bent his fingers claw-like atop the desk. "Separate bedrooms. That's my final word on the matter."

"Your summary judgment, you mean." My throat had gone thick, my scalp tingled. "I don't want your money, I never did. If you think that's why I married you, then you are the most clueless, blindest man on earth."

I whirled toward the door.

He caught up to me at the threshold, snaring my arm. "Don't love me, Emery. I will only hurt you. Willnae mean to, but..."

Voice trailing off, he let his hand fall away from my arm.

"You are hurting me," I said, "every night when you walk out the door. You'd better think about what you really want, Rory. If we keep going this way, I'll have to do whatever is necessary to protect myself."

I left him standing in the doorway.

Chapter Twenty-Four

I took the stairs two at a time down three flights, veering down the ground-floor hallway to the huge bathroom at the other end, directly under Rory's office. A wall separated the large claw-foot tub from the toilet while the shower lay across from the tub. The toilet area housed a sink with a fancy, curved faucet. All the hardware was a pale bronze-like shade, including the metal racks that held the plush, Rory-size towels.

Bent over the sink, I splashed water on my face until my cheeks stopped burning. A couple deep breaths made me feel less shaky. In the mirror above the sink, my reflection stared back at me, refreshed but not cheery. I looked miserable, maybe because I felt miserable. Rory had thrown the contract in my face. Though I understood his defensiveness stemmed from past trauma, it still stung.

Blame fell at my feet too. I'd done what I swore I wouldn't do, pushing him to give up another of his rules.

I hung my head, hands clamped over the sink's rim. What if he didn't come to his senses?

His ex-wives had done a nasty number on him. Isobel criticized his lack of money and his chosen profession, insisting he wasn't good enough. Una had emasculated him. What had the second wife, Lilias, done to him? He hadn't divulged that bit of his history yet, but I already knew his former wives had wrecked him.

Poor Rory.

I wanted to race back to his office and leap onto his lap to cuddle and kiss him until we both forgot what we'd argued about a few minutes ago. It wouldn't solve anything, though. He would abandon me every night, and I would feel used and empty every time he did.

Fresh air. I needed to fill my lungs with clean, fresh Highland air to clear my head and regain some perspective.

I marched out of the house and straight to the walled garden, where I lay down on the grass beneath the peaked lattice roof of the arbor, on my back with my hands buckled over my belly. Vine roses crawled across the sides and roof of the arbor, coiling around the latticework, transforming the structure into a floral tunnel. Faint sunshine filtered through the spaces between the leaves and flowers, dappling me with shadow and light.

The delicate fragrance of the roses wafted around me.

I shut my eyes, allowing the twittering of birds and the whisper of the breeze through the foliage to lull me into a half-awake state, a lovely place where the world retreated from my awareness and thoughts vacated my mind. The grass felt cool against my arms. It formed a natural blanket beneath me, cushioning the hard ground. I began to hum, unaware of what I was humming, my mind drifting to another dimension where hopes and dreams lived.

"Alas, my love, you do me wrong—"

My eyes flew open, my heart thudded. A deep, masculine voice kept singing the lyrics to the tune I'd been humming, and I blinked up at the figure silhouetted in the opening of the arbor. Rory stood tall and erect near my feet, his face in shadow. Though I couldn't see his expression, his voice was gentle.

"What are you doing?" he asked.

"Don't you get tired of asking me that? It should be fairly obvious, anyway. I'm lying in the grass."

"I can see that." He sank into a crouch, and a shaft of buttery sunlight streaked across his face. "If you were trying to get away from me, I can go."

"Hiding isn't my thing. I wanted some fresh air, that's all."

Wary brown eyes studied me. "May I join you?"

"You want to lie in the grass?"

He concentrated on my feet. "I want to lie beside you, wherever that might be."

My heart, melting. As a tender warmth spread through me, I scooted over and patted the ground.

Rory stretched out beside me, his shoulder whisking against mine. We glanced at each other at the same instant, and something passed between us, something sweet and tender. He gazed up at the ceiling of roses and leaves and slipped his hand into mine. With our palms pressed together, he intertwined our fingers.

I admired the rose-covered roof too, succumbing to the lovely, unspoken connection forged in this moment.

"That's a sad song," he said softly, "the one you were humming. Greensleeves."

"Guess it is."

"The song and the look on your face earlier, they mean you weren't angry. You were hurt. It's worse, isn't it? Worse than if you'd shouted at me."

"I hate being angry. I hate being miserable too."

He kneaded the back of my hand with his thumb. "I've never done well with upset women. No idea how to respond to it."

"Congratulations. You're a typical man in at least one way."

"I have behaved like a bastard." He raised our hands to his face, laying my palm against his cheek. "I trust you, *m'eudail*, and I will make this up to you."

"Why did you have to point out I'd get nothing if I left you today?"

"It was—I don't know." He turned his face into my hand. "That will never happen again."

The longer we lay here together, the faster all my misgivings crumbled away. I wanted to believe him. My heart urged me to believe, but my head kept sending me flashbacks to the moment in his office when he'd reminded me, in that flinty tone, I wouldn't get one shilling of his money if I walked out now. I knew his coldness had been an act, and I'd seen his true feelings in his eyes, but I couldn't shake the worry he'd choose loneliness over me.

Rory moved my hand to his chest, over his heart, and rested his hand atop it.

I ached for him, deep inside, all the time—for him and for me and for what we might have if he could give up hiding behind that stoic facade.

"Listen," I said, "what you said really hurt me. I can't pretend it didn't, but I also realize this might be partly my fault."

"It isn't. I'm to blame."

"Let's call it ninety-ten, with you being ninety percent in the wrong." I wavered in my resolve for a brief moment before I added, "I never told you the real reason I married you. It's—"

His phone rang. He excavated it from his hip pocket and sat up, relinquishing my hand as he answered the call with a gruff hello. He stared into empty space for a moment, his focus on the caller.

I sat up too, squinting into the sunlight outside our little sanctuary.

"Yes," he said at last, "whatever you need. I'll pay any added expense. Let me know as soon as you find him."

Rory disconnected the call.

"Everything okay?" I asked.

"The investigator thinks he's found Sebastian Zegers. He needs to fly to Alaska. Your former love seems to be hiding in Anchorage."

"Alaska? Sebastian hates the cold."

"He's been in and out of psychiatric facilities for years, Emery. You don't know him anymore." Rory pulled me into an embrace, his cheek mashed against mine. "I want to fix this for you."

"I'm okay, even if you don't find Sebastian."

"But you worry the photos are still out there." He held me a little tighter. "What he did has affected you more than you think. I think it's why sleeping in separate bedrooms makes you feel like a concubine. I should've realized sooner."

The rightness of his assessment trickled through me until it suffused my being and I had no choice but to admit to myself he was right. His ability to see into my soul could be disconcerting but having one person who understood me so well gave me a feeling of…security.

He nuzzled my nose. "I have a call with a client, but I will see you for dinner. Won't I?"

"You will." I kissed him. "Don't work too hard."

We strolled back into the house hand in hand, kissing each other goodbye in the vestibule. Rory turned to leave but hesitated.

"For the record," he said, "I don't pay you to fuck me. I'm paying you not to leave."

He took two steps toward the stairs, but I called out, "Rory."

Shoulders tensing, he paused to glance back at me.

"I was trying to tell you earlier," I said, "before your investigator called. I didn't marry you for money or for sex."

"You did it for the adventure and excitement."

"Partly."

His gaze, sharp and clear, pierced me to my very soul. "You were lonely."

I drew back a little, struck by the rightness of his insight. Circumstances had taken my parents and my sister far away, I had no real friends, and my romantic relationships had either fizzled out or struck back with a vengeance. Though I hadn't voiced my loneliness, Rory had sensed it.

Because he paid attention. Whatever his faults, however blind he might've been when it came to certain feelings, he'd listened to everything I said since the night we met and deduced the truth.

"Yes," I said, "but that's not the main reason."

"Why, then?"

"Because you have potential."

His shoulders relaxed, but he gave a slight shake of his head. "Potential for what?"

"To break free of your past and become the best version of yourself. That's what I'm trying to do, to reclaim who I used to be, and that's what you want to do too."

He grunted. "You may be disappointed with my potential."

"Stop telling me you suck." I took a single step closer, never breaking eye contact. "I see you, Rory. Not just the parts you show everyone, but the pieces you try to hide. I *see* you."

He watched me with that piercing intensity, and a shiver of profound awareness rattled through me. I longed to go to him, throw my arms around his neck, and kiss him like nothing else existed in the world except us. I stayed put, though, uncertain of how he'd react to any display of affection after the day's events.

"Perhaps what you see," he said, "is what you want, not what I am."

With that, he slogged up the stairs to his office on the floor above.

"That's crap," I shouted up the stairwell.

He hesitated in his strides but then continued up the stairs.

I made my way to the sitting room, where I'd left my laptop, and logged in for a video chat with Hadley. She had the day off, so I knew she'd be available. I got the bonus of talking to my twin nieces, which always brightened my day.

Not that it needed brightening this afternoon. Rory wanted to find Sebastian so I would have peace of mind about those photos, and he accepted I didn't care about the money, even felt bad for suggesting I did. We had a long way to go, but our time under the arbor had given me hope. A future with Rory, a future beyond one year, no longer seemed like an impossible fantasy.

If only I could convince him he wasn't a cold, sucky bastard undeserving of love.

That evening, I loitered by my bed after undressing, my pink satin robe the only garment I wore. My discarded clothing lay in a lump on the bed. I secured the robe's sash around my waist, tying it into a little bow. Dinner with Rory had been...well, "fun" seemed like the most appropriate word. We'd made each other laugh and talked about our upcoming wedding, and Rory had regaled me with stories of the wacky MacTaggart clan, including the time when a teenage Lachlan had been caught with his pants down—literally—while showing his "dokey" to a pretty girl.

I'd figured out "dokey" meant penis without Rory explaining. The details of the story made it clear. Ever since dinner, I kept picturing Lachlan with his pants around his ankles, but the image failed to arouse me. Only my husband could turn me on these days.

I gathered my clothes in my arms.

The door burst inward.

I yelped and spun toward the door.

Rory stalked into the room wearing only pajama bottoms, moving like a jaguar on the prowl, his jaw set and his gaze scorching into me.

"What's up?" I asked, powerless to tamp down the desire sizzling through me.

He bent over, wrapped his arms around my waist, and slung me around his shoulders with my feet hanging over his chest on one side and my head and arms dangling down the other side. My midsection was crushed to the back of his neck and head. His arms lashed me to his front.

My clothes tumbled from my grasp, fluttering to the floor.

"Hey!" I said. "What's with the fireman hold?"

"I'm making it up to you." He strode out of my bedroom and down the hall to the door of the master suite.

With my head upside down and the blood rushing to my brain, I struggled to focus on my inverted view of the world. The door to his room hung open, that much I could see.

Rory walked inside and kicked the door shut.

"Put me down," I said, "before I pass out from too much blood in my brain. I'm getting tired of staring at your pajamas. Is that silk? Sheesh, for a guy who doesn't care about money you sure like the luxury comforts, don't you?"

"And you never stop blethering." He bent his knees and slid me off his shoulders, setting me on my feet. We'd wound up at the side of his bed, a king-size canopy number with golden-brown sheets that matched his eyes. "Are you angry I made another decision for you without asking?"

"Not this time." I took note of the spacious room. "You want to have sex in here tonight? I'm surprised you let me into your bedroom."

"Our bedroom." He snared the sash of my robe with a fingertip and tugged me closer. "You'll be sleeping here."

"Just for tonight."

"Forever."

My hands floated up to his chest. Even my appendages couldn't resist his body. "Are you sure about this?"

"Aye." He worked at the bow holding my sash in place, his big fingers fumbling to undo it. "I want to fall asleep beside you and wake up with you in the morning. Every day."

I grinned. "Sharing a bed. Now that's progress."

Head down, he focused on freeing my sash. "Progress toward what?"

"You fulfilling your potential." I batted his hands away and liberated the sash, letting my robe fall open. "Before you know it, you'll be doing me in the daytime and on every surface in this house. Maybe outside too."

He made a face. "Not certain I'll ever be like you."

"Don't be like me. Be yourself—the real Rory, the one who desperately wants to come out and play."

He swept his hands under my robe and pushed it off my shoulders. The garment tumbled to the floor, a billowing heap of satin pooling around my feet. "No sex tonight. Sleep only."

I feigned a pout.

As usual, he tried not to smile, though with less efficiency than normal. "It's been a trying day. Sleep is what we both need."

"Have you browsed your menu of fantasies yet?" I skated my palms over his chest and down to the waistband of his pajama pants. "Pick a costume, and I'll make you forget about everything in the world except for me."

"I'm sure," he said, grasping my hands, "but you were upset earlier, and it's clear you haven't slept well."

"Didn't realize it was that obvious."

He cupped my cheek. "It's my fault. I'm sorry."

"I know you are, and I forgive you."

Those amber eyes studied me, softening and glowing like whisky left in the sun. "Get in bed, *mo leannan*."

For once, I didn't argue or tease. I crawled under the covers and rested my head on one of the two pillows on the bed. Rory stripped off his pajama pants and joined me beneath the sheets. He lay on his back, one hand under his head, and raised the other arm in invitation. I cuddled up to him, my head in the crook of his shoulder, and he curled his arm around me.

"Why did you get naked?" I asked. "Since we're not having sex tonight."

"Hush." He stretched his arm out to turn off the lamp on the bedside table. "Time for sleep, Em, not talking."

A tiny giggle escaped my lips. "You called me Em. The man who hates nicknames called me by my nickname."

He grumbled.

I snuggled closer. "Maybe tomorrow you could take a break from work and do something fun with me."

He enfolded me in both his arms, his chin on the crown of my head. "Sleep, Emery."

"Promise you'll wake me up before you go downstairs in the morning, every day."

"If that will make you happy, I will."

"Thank you. Night, Rory."

He kissed the top of my head. "Good night."

For the first time in our home, the first time since our wedding night, I slept in the arms of my husband.

Chapter Twenty-Five

With the tips of my fingers, I swished the water inside the big claw-foot tub. My arms rested on the tub's rim, and I let the sloping wall of it support my head. The door to the ground-floor bathroom hung open so I could reflect on the sunset visible through the hallway windows. Streamers of clouds unfurled across the sky in shades of salmon and plum, inflamed by the glow of the setting sun. The warm water lapping around me and the beautiful vista lulled me into a semi-slumber, my lids too heavy to stay open.

"Emery."

I peeled my lids apart.

Rory observed me from the doorway, his body blocking my vista. His gaze roved from my face down to the slopes of my breasts, and to the waterline where the rest of me vanished beneath a skin of slippery white suds.

"A bubble bath?" he said, like I'd invented a new and bizarre use for a bathtub.

I dunked my arms into the water and raised them above my head. Suds drizzled off my skin along with the water, but a smattering of them clung to me. As I laid my arms on the tub's rim, I bent one knee to raise it above the water level.

"Bubbles are fun," I said, and hoisted my leg fully out of the water, my foot held high, toes wiggling. "Why not join me? It's warm and slippery in here."

"I don't lie in tubs." His eyes tracked the suds as they slid off my foot and dribbled down my leg. "I have showers."

"Mm, we could do that together too."

His fingers curled into his palms. "We can fuck later. I need to speak with you in my office first."

I pushed away from the tub's edge and stretched my arms out to him. "Give a girl a hand?"

Rory scuffed across the room, took my hands, and helped me stand inside the tub. He drank in my nakedness for a sizzling moment, moistening his lips once, twice, three times.

"Getting chilly," I said, though my stiffening nipples had less to do with the air temperature than his hungry gaze.

He nabbed a towel from the rack nearby and wrapped it around my torso. Sized for him, the towel draped down to my knees. He tucked in one corner of the towel to secure it, slung his arms around me, and lifted me out of the tub. Soapy water sloshed onto the floor.

Although my feet had hit the tile floor, he kept me bound in his arms.

"Thanks for the assist," I said. "One of these days, I will get you in a tub with me."

"Dry off," he said, "and meet me in the office."

"Sure thing, Rory baby."

He surrendered his hold on me, hurrying out the door.

Ten minutes later, I lowered myself onto the chair in front of the massive desk. Rory sat with his arms on the desk, at either side of a tidy array of folders and papers. With his reading glasses perched on his nose, glare on the lenses obscured his eyes. A pen lay beside the assortment of stuff, its gold surface gleaming in the light from his desk lamp. The cone of light shed a glow out into the room that dwindled the further it stretched from the desk, leaving the corners of the office cloaked in shadows.

I propped my bare feet on the desk in front of Rory, my ankles crossed.

He glanced up from his papers. His gaze flitted to my naked feet and meandered up my legs. He reclined in his chair, his mouth crimped at one corner.

"I said to get dressed," he told me in a patient tone. "A robe is not clothing."

"Sure it is." I wagged my foot. "Besides, you said dry off, not get dressed."

Rory fastened a hand over my energetic toes. His skin warmed my chilled foot. The hike from the bathroom up to the first floor had taken me across acres of cold wood floors, and I'd forgotten my slippers in the bedroom.

When I shifted my butt to get a better position, the halves of my robe skidded off my legs, uncovering my skin up to my hips. If I hadn't hooked my ankles, he would've gotten a stellar view of the curly hairs on my mound.

He rocked forward, tipped his head down, and peered at me over his glasses. "You are not a biddable wife, are you?"

"Uh, no." I shot him an overly chipper smile. "But I give you great sex to make up for it."

"Aye." He liberated my toes. "I have something for you."

He held out a sheet of paper.

I plunked my feet on the floor and strained to take the paper across the gap between us. As I perused the document, typed and organized with bullet points, I struggled to restrain my smile. His perfectionist tendencies delighted me, and oddly, made me want to crawl onto his lap and rub myself all over him like a cat in heat.

"What is this?" I asked.

"A list of my holdings."

"That like stocks and bonds?"

"No, it's an inventory of properties I own," he said. "I thought you should be made aware of this information."

"I'm definitely aware," I said with a teasing smile. As I read over the list of properties again, I realized it was indeed an inventory of real estate. The bullet points outlined details of each property. "This isn't a huge list for a rich guy. An apartment in Edinburgh, the castle here, and—" I squinted at the sheet. "You own property on Skye? The island?"

"Yes. It's a house."

"Cool." I set the paper on my lap. "How often do you go to Skye?"

"I've been there once, to buy the property."

"Once?" I couldn't understand this. If I had a house on a beautiful island, I'd go there as often as possible. Well, I kind of did have a house on Skye. "If you never go there, why did you buy it?"

He shrugged one shoulder.

"Don't try to convince me," I said, "you have no idea why you bought it. You don't want to tell me, that's all."

Rory arranged and rearranged the folders and papers on his desk, avoiding eye contact. "You'll see the property soon enough."

I bolted upright, hands on my knees, and the list of properties sailed down to the floor. "I will? When?"

"During our sightseeing holiday."

"Thank you, Rory." I clapped my hands, beaming at him. "Yay! I get to see the ocean and the famous Isle of Skye."

He gave me that baffled look, the one he wore so often around me. "It's not as exciting as you seem to think."

"Maybe to you." I swayed in my chair, my arms extended above my head, fingers fanned out. "This is awesome! Do you have any idea how long it's been since I took a vacation? Years. I mean, seriously, *years*. I should come over there and smack a big one on you."

He didn't respond, likely because he was ogling my bosom.

I glanced down.

The sash of my robe had come undone, and the garment gaped open. My breasts jiggled every time I waved my upraised arms. I dropped my arms and started to pull my robe closed, but I hesitated when I glimpsed Rory's expression.

Whoa, lava-hot.

My breasts ached for his touch, his mouth, his agile tongue. I let go of the robe, and cool satin glided across my skin. I choked back a moan, but the sensation had heightened my arousal until it pulsated through my clitoris.

Rory scrubbed his face with both hands, a tortured groan resonating from deep in his chest. "Ever since you mentioned it, I cannae stop thinking of—*bod an Donais*—taking you on this desk."

Excitement buzzed over my skin and fluttered in my tummy. I didn't want him to do it because I'd tempted him, inadvertently. If and when he threw me over that desk, I wanted it to be his decision alone.

I righted my robe and tied the sash. "Sorry. Didn't mean to flash you a full-frontal shot."

"Wasnae blaming ye." His eyes blazed with need. "I was enjoying the view."

"Oh, I knew that. It was written all over your gorgeous face."

His fingers, spread on the desk, curled and then straightened, curled and then straightened. "Ahm burning for ye, Em."

A shiver of electric awareness robbed me of any capacity for thought, speech, breath, movement. No man had ever beheld me with such wanton hunger or spoken his need aloud with so much intensity. I loved—in all caps with three exclamation points—the raspy way he'd called me Em.

His body seemed to melt against his chair. His arm remained on the desk, limp, and with his other hand, he gestured with one finger. *Come to me*, he commanded.

I went to him, sidling up to his chair.

He rotated the chair toward me, keeping his arm on the desktop, his face at the level of my breasts. The magnetic power of his gaze energized my skin, and my nipples shot erect, jutting against the satin of my robe.

He hooked a finger inside the sash and ever so slowly unfastened it. As the delicate strip of fabric fell away, my robe gaped open. He glanced at my groin and the thatch of fine hairs covering my mound and shut his eyes while he inhaled a long breath. His eyes flickered open. His lips curved upward just enough to convey his deep pleasure at the sight before him.

Moving both hands to his lap, he patted his thigh.

I climbed onto his lap with my knees straddling his hips and my sex poised over his thighs. "Do you need a special kind of cuddle?"

"Aye."

With a hand on each of his shoulders, I kneaded the bunched muscles until they softened under my fingers and he sighed with pleasure. I guided my palms up his throat, tenderly feeling the pulse point, measuring the beats of his heart as they accelerated. His lips parted, his cheeks grew ruddy. I slanted in, swept my palms up to his cheeks, and rubbed my lips over his.

A distinct lump had formed in his pants.

He cupped my hips, coasted his hands up my sides, brushed them against my breasts. "Yer bonnie, soft, sweet…perfection."

I swayed into him. "Kiss me. Touch me. Anything you want, please."

He held still for a long moment, his breathing uneven and harsh, his hands at the sides of my breasts, his thumbs lazily stroking the undersides. His hands wandered down to my waist, his thumbs sketching circles on my skin. One hand roamed down to cover my mound.

I rocked my hips into him, pressing my mound into his waiting palm. The heat of his hand, the firmness of it and the gentle pressure, felt so good a soft moan whispered out between my parted lips. When his fingers toyed with the damp hairs under his hand, I released another moan, this time low and throaty, evocative of the need rising within me.

"*M'eudail*," he murmured, his voice gone hoarse. He whisked his hands up to my shoulders, under the robe, and slipped it off. The fabric tumbled to the floor.

I was naked. He wasn't. This would not do.

Sinking into his lap, his erection trapped beneath me, I yanked his shirt out of his waistband.

The weight of his hand settled over my mound, his fingers molded to the swollen lips of my sex.

A potent cocktail of hormones intoxicated me, scattering my thoughts and searing my veins. I soared on a natural high, every sensation intensified. My fingers scrabbled to unhook his shirt buttons, even as lust compelled me to get him naked right now. *Screw this*. I grasped the lapels and tore his shirt open.

Buttons rained onto the rug.

Rory's eyes bulged, gradually narrowing as his lips formed a smile of erotic appreciation. "I love your enthusiasm."

"Too amped to be subtle."

I raked my nails down his chest, loving the way his body tensed and his dick twitched.

He shoved his hand between my legs, into the slick heat of my sex.

"Yes, baby." I rocked against his palm, finding a slow and sensuous rhythm, shuddering when he stroked me with his middle finger. "I want you so bad I can't think. Take me hard, do it fast, I need you inside me."

"Ah, *mo leannan*, yer so wet and hot." He rasped two fingers along my outer folds while his longest finger swirled around my entrance. "Ahm starved for ye, Emery."

He plunged his finger inside.

With a gasp, I latched onto his shoulders. As he pumped that finger in and out, the rest of his fingers chafed the insides of my folds and the heel of his hand rubbed my mound. My hips moved of their own volition, rolling in sync with the thrusts of his fingers. The storm of sensations had me panting and writhing, my breasts splashing against his chest. I raised onto my knees, placing my sex inches from his face, riding his hand while clinging to his shoulders.

"Rory," I gasped. "Yes, oh God, yes."

I clutched his head, and he buried his face against my belly, showering my skin with wet kisses, circling his tongue around my navel and then diving it inside at the same instant his finger pushed into my opening. I teetered on the verge of climax, about to careen over the edge.

"Oh shit," I whimpered. "Please, Rory, please, I need your cock inside me."

He snarled something in Gaelic.

I ground my body against his hand.

"Fuck," he growled, and yanked his hand away.

Bereft of his touch, my orgasm snatched away from me, I gaped down at him. "What..."

He launched out of the chair, dropping me down on my feet.

I wobbled a little as my brain, clouded by a thwarted climax, floundered to sort out the abrupt shift in our positions. Never had I experienced such an overpowering need to come, so I flailed for a way to encourage him. "It's dark out, but we can go to the bedroom if you want."

"Ahmno worried about the location." Breathing hard, he palmed his raging erection, imprisoned within his slacks. "Cannae wait a second longer."

He glanced at the desk, and I could almost see thoughts clicking into place in his mind. Rolling his shoulders back, he kinked his mouth into an expression of carnal resolve.

Oh yes. Gratification, here I come.

He swept one arm across the desktop, sending everything on it except for the computer toppling to the floor. Papers spewed across the rugs and wood flooring. Satisfied, he picked me up and laid me across the desk.

I grinned. "Rory baby, I love this new side of you."

His gaze pored over me, absorbing the sight of my nude body with an analytical squint to his eyes. The light from the floor lamp spilled over his bare chest, and I couldn't resist smoothing my hands over his pecs. He grasped my hips and dragged me closer, so my ass rested on the very edge of the desk. My legs dangled, and the coolness of the wood on my skin made me shiver, though not from cold.

Rory unzipped his pants and shoved them off his hips, along with his boxers. His cock sprang free, bouncing as it curled up toward his belly. Moisture beaded the rosy head. The mass of his clothing caught around his ankles, dammed there by his shoes, but he paid no attention to trivial things like having his legs shackled by his own slacks. With single-minded focus, he braced himself with both hands on the desk at either side of my head and positioned his erection between my thighs, the tip nudging my entrance.

He drew his hips back and plunged into me, penetrating deeply with one seamless thrust.

I gasped, my hands wrapped around his biceps. His length consumed me, the thickness of his hard shaft a hot and delicious invasion. I clasped my ankles behind his ass. "Oh Rory, don't stop."

"Say the other thing."

His request stopped me for a moment, until I realized what he wanted. "Rory baby, my Rory baby."

He plundered my mouth in a brutal kiss, his tongue lashing and his teeth scraping on my lips. I reveled in the taste of him and the velvety seduction of his kiss, lost in the overwhelming power of his hunger for me. I sank my fingers into his shoulders, scratched them down his back, gripped his ass.

"*Bod 'a chac*," he said. "Ye feel so fucking good, *m'eudail*."

I loved the way he said my name, but the rough tone of his Gaelic phrases sent me into a frenzy, head thrashing, hips undulating, my sex pulsating around his shaft.

He jerked his hips, withdrawing, then slammed into me again. And again. And again. I cried out, bucked my hips, clawed at his ass. My heart beat so hard and fast I couldn't catch my breath, and every punishing thrust pushed him deep inside me, so deep I had the crazy notion we'd become a part of each other in the most intimate, physical way possible. I flung my arms around him to bind his body to mine, my face mashed into his shoulder, my cries echoing off the walls and mingling with his grunts and shouts.

Our love-making grew so impassioned the desk jounced and thumped.

Rory grasped the desk's edge above my head, his hips pistoning in a frenetic rhythm. The room reverberated with the slapping of flesh on flesh until an orgasm thundered through me. My whole body convulsed around him.

"Oh God, Rory!"

"Emery, ahhhh!"

He punched into me once more, and his climax yanked his entire body taut.

I cradled him in my arms as he fell on top of me, both of us panting.

"*M'eudail*," he murmured in my ear, "I love—fucking you."

I stopped breathing for a few seconds, my mind straining to decide if he'd been about to say he loved me. His abrupt pause might've stemmed from the fact neither of us had fully recovered our breath yet. I longed to believe he'd almost spoken those three little words, but not in the throes of passion or the glow of a fading climax. I wanted to hear the words when I would know he meant them.

Did I love him? *Still deliberating that verdict.*

With his softening shaft inside me, I skimmed my hands over his back. "This is another milestone. We had sex somewhere other than the bedroom. Next thing you know, we'll be ravishing each other in broad daylight in the garden."

He raised his head to smirk at me. "Donnae hold your breath for that one."

"No need to hold my breath." I squeezed my muscles around his shaft, earning a wince and a slight gasp from him. "You take my breath away every time you touch me."

His penis was firming up.

I couldn't help smiling. "Again?"

"Mm." He ran a hand down my side, over my hip, up to my thigh still latched around him. "In the bedroom this time. The desk is too hard to do everything I want to do with you."

He pulled me up with him as he straightened, pulling out of my body with a wistful sigh. His gaze tracked down my body and then to his own where he stood naked from the waist down.

"Bollocks," he said.

"What's the matter?"

"Forgot to use a condom."

"Relax," I said. "I'm on the pill, remember? We're covered."

His face lit up. "We are, aren't we?"

"Mm-hm."

"Well then—" He scooped me up in his arms. "To the bedroom."

I pointed at his feet. "Might want to fix your pants first, or you'll dump us both on the floor."

"Ah. Yes. Can't have that."

He set me down and tugged his pants up, zipping them hastily, and carried me off to our bedroom. There, he shed all his clothes—and his inhibitions—making love to me again and again until we both lay boneless and spent on the bed, our bodies slick with sweat.

We fell asleep in each other's arms.

Chapter Twenty-Six

The sensation of cool air on my naked skin tickled me from head to toe, and tiny feet pranced around on my stomach. Tiny feet? As I roused from sleep, a vision of mice cavorting on my belly flashed in my mind. I jerked my head up to survey the length of my body, but there were no mice in sight.

Rory had pulled the covers off me and lay sideways to me with his chin on my hip. His elbows rested on the mattress, but he hovered his hands above my belly with the first two fingers of each hand forked like itty-bitty finger-people. They seemed to be performing some kind of jig on my skin.

"What are you doing?" I asked.

He aimed a sly smile at me. "Isn't that my line?"

"Usually." I tousled his hair, but it was too short to really get messed up. "What are your finger-people doing on my tummy?"

"Playing shinty." He made one finger-person run toward my belly button, then thrust his thumb out. "You have to imagine the caman he's swinging."

"The what?"

"Caman. The stick every player carries and uses to hit the ball."

I pushed up on my elbows. "What is shinty?"

"Something like lacrosse." He smiled. "Only better."

He was smiling. At me. Not a big, overjoyed smile like he'd given his family when they showed up in our garden. But still, he was smiling more than he ever had while looking at me.

My throat constricted.

The finger-people paused in the midst of their shinty shenanigans, and

Rory's forehead crinkled. "Are you all right?"

"Fine, yeah." I dropped back onto my pillow and waved a hand. "Go on. Don't let me interrupt your important shinty game."

"It's a match, not a game." He kissed my belly. "You'll learn the lingo when you watch the MacTaggarts play the Buchanans."

"You play shinty?"

"Aye."

"When will this game—sorry, match—happen?"

He shrugged. "We play whenever both families can get twelve members to join in. For the MacTaggarts that means our cousins need to be available. Lachlan may think he's the equivalent of ten men, but we need actual bodies on the field, not just his ego."

The humor glittering in his eyes and lighting up his face made my chest ache in a good way. I loved him like this, relaxed and happy, joking and doing goofy things on my body.

Loved him? I'd thought the words, but did I *love him* love him, or did I love the way he was acting this morning? Figuring out the answer could wait until another time, because in this moment I wanted nothing else but to watch my husband playing finger-shinty on my tummy.

A few minutes later, when he'd finished his match—the MacTaggarts won, of course, amid stage-whisper cheers from Rory—he lay back on the bed, his head next to mine. He threaded our fingers, holding my hand as we enjoyed a comfortable silence. In eight days, we would stand before God and all our relatives to vow our love and commitment to each other. He didn't love me, as far as I knew, and I wasn't sure how I felt. We'd have to lie to everyone, in public, in front of a minister.

"Do you think we'll be smote by a bolt of lightning?" I asked.

Rory feathered his lips over my fingertips. "Why would that happen?"

"Because we're going to take vows and swear we love each other."

He gave me a patient smile. "If everyone who married without love were smote down, hardly anyone would've survived the Middle Ages. Arranged marriages used to be the norm."

"Right, I forgot about that." I sat up and twisted sideways to look at him. "So, there won't be any smiting. That's good news. But we still have things to discuss, about our wedding."

He exhaled a perfect long-suffering-husband sigh. "Must we?"

"Yes." I swung one leg over him to mount his lap. Towering over *him* for a change, I planted my hands on my hips. "My family will be here in two days. We haven't talked about where they'll stay."

"I've made hotel reservations."

"You made a decision without telling me. Again."

His hands followed the contour of my thighs down to my knees, then retraced a path to my hips. "You didn't mind when I decided to carry you into this room without asking."

"That was different." I battled against the impulse to moan as he traced his hands up my inner thighs, his fingertips teasing the hairs at the apex. "Stop trying to distract me."

A naughty smile played across his lips.

I gave his chest a half-hearted slap. "That won't work, you sneaky, sneaky man. My family is not going to stay in a hotel. I haven't seen them in years. I want them to stay here."

Rory glanced around with feigned innocence and confusion. "I doubt we'll all fit in this bed."

I poked his chest with my index finger. "Figures when you suddenly decide to be playful, it's because you want to distract and confuse me in order to get your way."

"Am I succeeding?"

I commandeered his hands, where they lay on my inner thighs, and clapped them down on his belly. "Keep your hands to yourself, Mr. Mac-Taggart. No matter how cute and sexy you are, I am not letting you bamboozle me into having my family stay in a hotel. I want them here with us, in this ginormous castle. This place has enough bedrooms to host an army."

"I hope you're not implying your family has come to destroy me in battle."

"Only if you tick them off." I snaked a hand down to stroke his penis, surprised to discover it was hardening. "If you agree to let them stay here, I'll make it worth your while."

"In what way?"

"Any way you want." I caressed his length with easy sweeps of my hand. "Say yes, Rory baby. You have no choice but to bend to my will."

Which would be a refreshing change, seeing as I surrendered to his will whenever he flashed me that seductive, wickedly erotic grin.

And sometimes when he didn't.

Yeah, when it came to my husband, I was the easiest score on earth.

I massaged his cock with both hands until it was steel-hard and glistening with the evidence of his desire for me. His body tensed, and his face crimped in pained lust. His chest heaved. Pinkness speckled his cheeks and chest. He rocked his hips up into my strokes, his hands fisted in the sheets.

I bent low over him, my breasts swinging in his face, and spoke in my huskiest voice. "If you give me what I want, I'll give you what you want."

"Bargaining with your body?" He tried to smirk, but the rapturous agony of his need eradicated it. "Isnae that—too much like—ah God, woman. Yer killing me."

I licked at the seam of his lips. "Say yes and I'll use my mouth on you.

Don't pretend it's not what you want."

"Aye," he said, sucking in a breath. "Yer family stays here."

"Thank you." I waddled backward until my face hovered above his erection. "I've wanted to taste you since the night we met."

Despite his heavy breathing, his face blanked. "Emery..."

"Please don't tell me no again. You want me to do this, I can tell."

"I do, but—" He swallowed hard. "No one has ever touched me this way. Considering how much I want you, ahmno sure I can keep still. Donnae want to hurt you."

"Relax, baby, you won't."

"Better restrain me, just in case."

I set my hands at either side of his hips and looked up at him. "I am not tying you up. Stop worrying and tell me yes or no. Do you want this?"

He stared at me as the seconds ticked by in my head, counted by the beats of my heart. His blank expression gradually faded into a mixture of admiration and delighted surprise.

"Do you want this?" I repeated.

"Aye."

I lowered my head to kiss and lick his inner thigh, working my way up to the base of his cock. My breasts grew achy, the peaks stiff and tender as I grew more aroused the more I explored him. His breaths gusted from his open mouth and his eyes followed my movements, riveted to every swipe of my tongue. I flicked my tongue out to lap at his sac, slowly moving onto his shaft, lapping at his flesh as I made my way up toward the head.

His heels dug into the mattress.

My mouth watered as I marveled at the beauty of his sleek shaft and the blunt head. I laved my tongue over the slit.

He shuddered, his breathing ragged. "Please, Em, donnae go slow. Ahmno calm enough to take it."

"Whatever you need, honey."

I tucked my lips over my teeth and engulfed the head with my mouth, closing one hand around his sac. His head lolled on the pillow, his lids shuttered. I stroked my mouth up and down his length, kneading his thigh and moaning with pleasure at the flavor of his skin and the salty beads of liquid that gathered on the head of his penis. I kept the pace measured, alternately cupping his balls and skimming my hand along his thigh while he grunted and groaned and locked his hands around the headboard rails. I made hungry little noises in the back of my throat that seemed to arouse him even more, and he rolled his hips into the downward strokes of my mouth. His sac tightened and pulled into his body, and I knew he was close.

His eyes popped open. His gaze centered on me, on my mouth enclosing his cock and manipulating his flesh. His face twisted with the exquisite torture of impending climax.

I swiped at his flesh with my tongue, gliding my mouth up and down, maintaining a steady pace even as my clit throbbed and the urge to go faster beat at my willpower.

"Ah!" he shouted.

His release erupted in my mouth, salty and hot.

My clit pulsed. Despite my own mounting need, I kept stroking him with my tongue, tenderly, until his hand in my hair halted me. I propped my chin on his thigh, smiling up at him.

"God, Em," he said, breathless, his hand combing through my hair. "You are wonderful. I've never felt anything like that, it's almost as good as taking your body."

I levered up to sit back on my heels and take in the vision of my strong husband dissolved into a masculine puddle of satiated need. "Why wouldn't you let me do that before?"

"Donnae know."

"Baloney. You know as well as I do, but I want to hear you say it." I stretched out on my side next to him, twirling my fingers on his chest, the fine hairs tickling my skin. "This is part of your therapy. Tell me why."

He made an annoyed face and pinched the bridge of his nose. "I was afraid of losing control. When we have sex, I can't help losing it a wee bit. But your mouth on me...I knew I could never withstand the onslaught."

"How did it feel to let go and give in?"

"Extremely satisfying." He aimed a crooked smile at me. "You're a wicked little angel, *m'eudail*, and I love it."

"You're sinfully sexy yourself, Rory baby."

He curled an arm around me, his hand wandering down to my buttocks.

"We should get up," I said. "It's after six."

"In a while." He shifted his hand to my belly, sneaking it lower, and delved his fingers between my thighs to find the taut bud of my clitoris. "Once I regain my strength, it's your turn."

Desire shivered through me anew.

We wouldn't get out of this bed until long after his normal wake-up time, and he didn't care. Lounging in bed past six. Getting it on in his office, on his desk. Letting me pleasure him with my mouth. My husband had shattered so many rules in the past twelve hours.

Progress, progress, progress.

Chapter Twenty-Seven

On the following day, I convinced Rory to take a break from work and go outside with me. He groused, of course, but gave in without too much cajoling. That's how I wound up towing him by his hand out the vestibule door and toward the lush, green lawn Tavish had mowed an hour earlier.

At the edge of the grass, Rory dug in his heels like the stubborn mule he was. "What are we meant to do out here?"

"Dance on the grass."

"I don't dance."

"Well then, spin with me."

"Spin?" He virtually shrieked the word, as if I'd asked him to take his clothes off, spray glitter over his body, and prance around waving his arms in the air. He shook his head. "Emery—"

"Chill out, Rory." I let go of his hand to spin and skip my way across the verdant expanse, twirling my way back to him a moment later. I offered him my hand. "Give it a try. Please. For me."

He scrunched up his whole face.

I grasped both his hands, leaning back. "No skipping or prancing, I promise."

"But you expect me to spin."

"This one time. If you hate it, I'll never ask again."

He screwed up his mouth and sighed, resigned to his fate. "What am I meant to do?"

"Hold my hands, lean back, and then we both turn in a circle together. Slow at first, but faster and faster with each circuit."

Rory planted his feet on the ground opposite mine and canted backward.

As one, we rotated in a circle. At first, he wore a tight expression, but with every rotation he relaxed more, and as our pace increased, he seemed to get more into it. Faster and faster we whirled, my hair flying around my face and the centrifugal force stretching our arms. We spun and spun, first with only me laughing, but finally with Rory's throaty laughter joining mine. We twirled so swiftly the world around us blurred until all I could see was his face.

One of us tripped, I couldn't tell which, and we tumbled to the ground. I landed on top of Rory. He clapped his arms around me. We both kept laughing for a few seconds, but then the laughter diminished, and we simply gazed at each other.

Rory smiled. A brilliant, glorious smile that lit up his face—and lit up my heart. I grinned in response, breathless from the beauty of his overjoyed expression.

Overjoyed. My husband. Because of spinning, with me.

The clouds peeled back to admit a ray of sunshine. The light streamed down on us, igniting the golden highlights in his hair and glittering in his amber eyes. Yet nothing, not even sunshine, could glow with more brilliance than his smile.

A kind of laughter I'd never heard from him before, bright and unrestrained, tickled my senses and my heart, like a feather brushing over my soul. I laughed too, sprawled atop him on the lawn in the broad daylight, unable—unwilling—to relinquish this feeling one millisecond sooner than necessary.

I never wanted to give it up. If I could've stopped time, so we might live in this moment forever, I would've leaped at the chance. To keep him like this, happy and free. To revel in this without end. My head floated and swayed as if weightless, my heart lightened, and the world around us seemed more vivid and alive, suffused with the glory of his joy.

And that's when I recognized the truth. It inundated me, stunning in its fervency.

I'd fallen in love with my husband.

Helpless to deny the sheer bliss of my epiphany, I caught his face in my hands and kissed him. I poured all my love and passion into that kiss, transforming a simple meeting of the lips into a soul-searing expression of true and unlimited devotion. Whether he felt it, I couldn't say. The potency of it stole my breath, summoned nascent tears that pricked at the backs of my eyes, and set my heart to racing so fast I felt about to rocket into the sky.

He rolled us over, his body covering mine, and we kept kissing.

I hooked my legs around his, my arms around his neck, and dived into a shimmering pool of emotion.

He pulled away and hopped to his knees, sitting back on his heels with my feet beneath him.

Uncaring if I looked like an idiot, I gazed at him in rapt and unabashed adoration.

He regarded me without expression.

My heart rate slowly calmed, and I regained the ability to breathe. I couldn't stop looking at him. Love filled me, consumed me, energized me.

Rory coughed. "That was interesting, but I have—things to do."

My natural high fizzled out just like that. I lay there on the sun-warmed grass studying his face, but I couldn't tell if he'd been unaffected by The Moment, or if he was pretending not to have noticed everything had changed.

At least he hadn't said he had "work." I supposed "things to do" was an improvement.

But *everything* had changed—for me, anyway.

Rory rose and helped me up. "I'll see you at dinner."

He hurried back to the house and through the front door.

I rubbed my arms, suddenly chilled in spite of the warm sunshine and the temperate air. He acted like nothing had happened, but I'd seen him do this too many times to believe it. When we got too close for his comfort, he'd pull back into himself or turn into the cold bastard who liked to remind me of our contract and the temporary nature of this marriage. Maybe I was desperate to believe he shared my feelings. Maybe…

No, dammit. He must've experienced the same thrilling high, the same life-altering revelation, or else he wouldn't have gone stoic and run back into the house.

The rest of the day inched by, with my mood as cloudy as the sky. I hung out in the kitchen with Mrs. D until she had to leave to do the laundry. She refused to let me lend a hand with the task, and I didn't want to insult her by pushing. She commented I seemed "rather quiet" today but left it at that.

Since I didn't want to talk to Rory yet, the sting of his departure too fresh, I called everyone I could think of. First, I dialed up my sister in Germany. She was busy but promised to call back later. Next, I tried Erica but got her voicemail. Calli was busy at the office of the construction company she and Aidan ran together. I tried Jamie's number but got voicemail.

With nothing else to do, I resorted to the lamest activity I could find, staring blankly at the TV while sipping Ben Nevis. I'd felt like a thief for pouring myself a glass of Rory's favorite whisky without asking his permission, but this was my home too. Even *Captain America* on TV couldn't lift my spirits, and so I leaned my head back against the sofa and let the flavor of the single-malt scotch conjure a memory of Rory. Laughing. Smiling.

Beautiful.

When he found me asleep on the sofa later, he woke me but made no comment on the empty whisky tumbler on my lap. He informed me dinner was ready and ushered me into the dining room. We exchanged idle conversation over dinner, but neither of us brought up the incident on the lawn.

My chest ached every time I looked at him. It was stupid, this melancholy feeling. I'd succumbed to the fall without reservation, and I'd gloried in the moment when I realized I loved him, but as quickly as the joy had come it had vanished.

When we retired to the bedroom, neither of us wanted to do anything except sleep. Rory cocooned me in his arms and fell asleep, the ebb and flow of his breaths whispering in the darkened room.

He ran from me because he cared and it frightened him, I understood this. One day soon, though, he'd have to overcome his fears—if we had any chance of happiness.

Chapter Twenty-Eight

Our life went back to normal the next day. Rory didn't smile again the way he had on the lawn, and I wondered if he ever would. This morning, I'd resolved to enjoy my life in Scotland for as long as I lived here and to make the best of our marriage. No more moping because he hadn't declared his eternal love for me or announced I was his soul mate.

My family would arrive tomorrow. I refused to let them see me as a pathetic wreck in love with a man who would not allow himself to love me.

In the late afternoon, I waltzed into Rory's office armed with a new determination to work things out between us, even if that meant learning he didn't share my feelings.

"To what do I owe this honor?" he asked.

"Your own neurosis," I said, taking a seat on the front edge of his desk. "We need to talk about yesterday."

He flipped through a sheaf of papers. "Yesterday?"

"Come off it, Rory." I slapped my palm down on his papers. "You know exactly what I'm talking about. That moment when you actually had fun, out on the lawn. When you gave me a real smile for the first time in the history of us."

He plucked his glasses off his nose and tossed them onto the desk beside my hand. "I've smiled before. Many times."

"Uh-uh." I crossed my arms under my breasts. "You smirk. You almost smile. You kink your lips like you might be about to smile, but you don't go all the way. Not for me, at least. You grin and laugh with your family, but with me, you hold back like you think the universe will smack you down if you let on you like being around me."

"That's ridiculous."

"Ah, your favorite word," I said. "Case in point, that day in the garden when you were happy until you looked at me. Then you frowned."

He huffed. "I did not."

"You did." I leaned in. "Are you accusing me of lying?"

"Of course not." He twirled his pen on the desktop. "If I frowned at you that day, I apologize. I had no idea I'd done that."

"Apology accepted." I settled my hands on my thighs. "About yesterday…"

He rubbed his chest, wincing slightly. "What about it?"

"You had fun, admit it. Spinning made you smile." *Please say it was me, not the spinning. You were happy because of me.*

"I suppose it did," he said. "And I had fun."

Though my heart plummeted through the floor, probably landing on Mrs. Darroch's head in the laundry room, I realized I had to let this go for now. He'd admitted to having fun, which was itself a major step forward. Pushing him to admit his feelings for me, whatever they might be, wouldn't help.

At least I'd done it. I'd confronted him about yesterday, and I'd earned a confession of a sort from him.

"Spinning may have been enjoyable," he said, twirling his pen faster, "but it wasn't as much fun as the night before." He caught the pen, halting it, and spread his hand over the desktop. "When I shagged you right here."

His hand petted the wood.

And oh, how my traitorous body responded. Warming. Softening. Reeling backward in time to relive the sensations he'd evoked in me then.

He'd done it on purpose, naturally. Distract me from the real issue by getting me hot and bothered.

"I'm glad you had fun that night," I said, and hopped off the desk. "Maybe tonight we can reenact that pivotal moment on a different surface. Maybe someday we'll even do it in the daytime."

I swayed my hips, on purpose, as I sashayed out of his office. When I turned to pull the door closed, Rory uttered a single word dripping with sensuality.

"Perhaps."

I shut the door, leaving my husband alone in his office with the memory of that night, and myself with the dream of what might come in the future.

Alas, the previous night had not concluded with hot sex on his desk or anywhere else. I'd talked to my mom until one a.m., discussing the wedding, by which time Rory had gone to sleep. I curled up beside him and slept the whole night through without waking until he climbed out of bed at six o'clock. Per my instructions, he now woke me when he got up in the morning. We ate breakfast together before he retreated into his office.

Waking up with him and staying up until he went to bed would turn me into a daytime napper, for sure. Four hours into my day and already I was yawning, not to mention craving every kind of food the medical establishment scolded humans not to eat.

That's why I'd ended up in the kitchen, leaning my hip against the island and considering the items I'd collected and set on the granite surface. A few days ago, I'd mentioned to Mrs. Darroch how much I lusted for an ice cream sundae. This morning a note had awaited me on the fridge door, written in Mrs. D's efficient hand. It said, "Morning, *gràidh*. What you need is inside. Check the freezer too." Upon opening the freezer, I'd discovered three gallon tubs of ice cream—vanilla, chocolate, and strawberry—while in the fridge section I found an assortment of toppings.

As I gazed at my selections laid out on the island, my mouth watered. Hot fudge, caramel sauce, walnuts, and whipped cream sat in their respective containers alongside a tub of vanilla ice cream.

"In the mood to indulge your cravings?"

Rory's voice originated from the doorway, though I hadn't noticed his footsteps approaching. The man had a knack for stealth.

Turning toward him, I leaned back against the island and settled my hands on its rim. "I am jonesing for something decadent."

He gave me an appraising look, his eyes narrowing at the sight of my very short denim cutoffs and the short-sleeve, button-up top that exposed the swells of my breasts. The neckline just covered my nipples. My lacy pink bra peeked out from under the top.

"Ah, Emery," he said, his voice a silken rumble. He rubbed his jaw where faint stubble peppered his face. "Your erse looks divine in those shorts."

"I wore them for you."

"And I appreciate it." He sauntered across the kitchen to me, all masculine grace and power. His lust-darkened gaze flicked to the sundae fixings. "Donnae need food to be decadent."

"You have an alternate suggestion?"

"For a more satisfying dessert." He framed me with his arms, penning me to the island with his body and his hands on the granite. "A feast of pleasure."

He traced the shell of my ear with his tongue, following it down to the lobe, and tugged my tender flesh into his mouth. The full length of his body bore down on mine, the heat and firmness of him a temptation more decadent than any dessert. His cock had begun to stiffen against my belly, but a heady need overtook me, a need to drive him as wild as he drove me.

"Sex in the kitchen?" I said, and pushed my hand between our bodies to palm him through his pants. "And in the daytime, with Mrs. Darroch somewhere in the house. My goodness, Rory, you're tossing out all the rules."

"Hell with the rules." He rolled his eyes up, though not in complaint, but in response to my fingers fondling his shaft. He slapped a hand over the small of my back. "I'll be taking my wife whenever and wherever I please."

"So do it. Right here."

His fevered gaze landed on my neckline. "Do ye let your bra show in public?"

"No, baby. Only for you."

Rory crushed his mouth to mine, his lips yielding but hungry, his hot tongue ravaging my mouth while I ravaged him right back. I wrapped my free arm around his neck, loving the way he lapped at the roof of my mouth and slid his hand down to my ass. My body ached and grew slick in all the right places. I rasped my thumb over the slit of his cock, where the head peeked out of his pants.

His body jerked. He grunted into my mouth, and his fingers sank into my ass.

I was desperate to rip off my shirt and bra, along with his long-sleeve dress shirt, to rub my tits on his rock-hard chest, but I couldn't wrestle my other hand out from between our bodies. One hand couldn't get the job done.

Our kissing muted my frustrated whimper.

With his mouth latched to mine, Rory took hold of my behind in both hands and hoisted me onto the island. My butt rested on the granite, but my bare legs dangled at either side of his hips. I wriggled against him, lashing my tongue around his, starved for the taste of him—and more. I opened wider for him, inviting a deeper, rougher invasion, thrilled when he delivered what I needed.

Even in the throes of sexual hunger, he worked with precision to open my shirt. One big hand on my ass kept me in place while his fingers freed each button. He spread the halves of my top, and cool air ghosted over my skin. He molded his hands to my breasts, my bra no barrier to his touch, his thumbs stroking over my nipples.

I fumbled with the buttons of his shirt, nowhere near as agile at doing this as he was, especially with his tongue and his lips pushing me to the edge of sanity. By the time I got his shirt undone and my palms on his naked chest, he'd shoved a hand inside my bra to cover my breast. I raced my hands down his chest, over his sculpted abs, and straight to the button fly of his slacks.

He coaxed me down onto the island, flat on my back, then undid his pants and let them slump to his ankles. Naked except for his open shirt, he laid his body over mine. I moaned at the feel of his weight on me and of his erection wedged between us. He kissed a path down my neck and chest, making me arch into his mouth. When his lips found the lacy edge of my bra, he dove his tongue beneath the fabric, rasping it down the inner seam until he grazed my areola.

I hugged his head to my breast and slung my legs around his waist.

"Bloody hell."

We both froze. That exclamation had not come from Rory, though the voice was reminiscent of his. Rory turned his head, though I still clutched it to my bosom. He clamped his lips into a hard line, and I tracked his gaze to the kitchen doorway.

And I yelped.

Lachlan loomed there, his eyes large and his mouth agape. He swerved his head to the left and flung up a hand to shield his sidelong view.

"For Christ's sake, Rory," Lachlan said. "Put some trousers on."

Rory leaped backward and yanked his slacks up, hastily zipping them. The button hung open, but he'd lost all interest in his own state of undress, his focus on me. I lay there with my shirt gaping and one breast mounded up to expose everything except the nipple. He hauled me up into a sitting position, then struggled to button my shirt. Intense arousal mixed with humiliation made his large fingers clumsy.

I shooed his hands away. "Cool down, baby. I'll take care of my own clothes."

Lachlan chuckled. "Is he a sweetie-pie baby?"

Rory shot him a peeved look.

While I tucked my boob back where it belonged and buttoned my shirt, Rory stalked across the kitchen to aim a half-hearted glare at his brother. "Donnae be looking at my wife."

"I wouldn't have minded a good look at her," Lachlan said, lowering his hand and smirking at Rory. "Unfortunately, all I saw was you. Didn't need such an unobstructed view of your erse."

Rory's cheeks had turned a rosy shade. "Then maybe ye shouldnae be walking into our home like it belongs to ye. Havenae ye heard of knocking?"

Lachlan gave a careless shrug. "Mrs. Darroch let me in. She said Emery was in the kitchen and you were in the office."

Rory squinted at his older brother. "What do you want with my wife?"

"Calm down, man." Lachlan held up his hands, palms out. "Emery told Erica I could pick up the book she's borrowing today. Didn't mean to storm your castle while you were under your good wife's skirts. Isn't this a Wednesday, one of those days when medieval husbands couldn't bed their ladies?"

Rory's shoulders had bunched so tightly they looked about to split apart. I knew he wasn't angry at Lachlan, but rather embarrassed to have been caught in flagrante—in the kitchen, no less, and in the daytime. If he didn't calm down, he might shout something at his brother he'd regret.

Time to defuse my husband.

I hopped off the counter, my clothes righted, and trotted up to lay a hand on Rory's upper arm. He threw me a sideways glance. I slipped my other hand into his, though his fingers remained taut.

"Are you planning to pummel your brother?" I asked sweetly, with a matching smile. "Go ahead, if it'll make you feel better. But honestly, Rory, I don't think it's the most logical response. Lachlan got a gander at your bare ass, not mine."

"He saw you—on the—with your—"

Translation: Lachlan saw me sprawled on the island with Rory on top of me, my shirt open and my breast half out of my bra. Okay, I could see his point. I still didn't think a brawl with his own brother would solve anything. He'd stay embarrassed, probably more so for blaming Lachlan.

I squeezed his hand. "It was an accident. I'm not embarrassed, and you shouldn't be either. Tell Lachlan you forgive him and let it go."

The breath he'd held gushed out of Rory. His shoulders deflated, his entire body followed suit, and his hand folded around mine. He grudgingly told Lachlan, "Sorry. I may have…overreacted."

Lachlan's brows shot up, and he gave me an appreciative nod. "You are a miracle worker, Emery. Getting Rory to admit he was wrong is one of the signs of the apocalypse."

Rory huffed. "Didn't say I was wrong."

"Haven't heard forgiveness yet." Lachlan was smirking again, far too pleased with himself for getting Rory's goad.

My husband growled, then muttered, "I forgive you. Just donnae do it again."

The elder MacTaggart raised one hand. "I solemnly swear never to breach Rory's castle again without permission."

Rory looked to me. "Happy?"

"Yes." I boosted onto my tiptoes and kissed my hubby's cheek. "Thank you, Rory baby."

In the instant I realized my flub, Lachlan burst out in uproarious laughter.

"Rory baby?" he said between guffaws. "Wait till I tell Aidan about that one. He'll love it more than 'sweetie-pie.' "

My husband stretched his lips into a tight line, his gaze boring into me. "You promised never to speak that phrase in front of anyone but me."

"I'm sorry, I really am." I bit my lip, hunching my shoulders. "It slipped out."

Lachlan's laughter had died, but he still appeared vastly amused by his uptight brother's predicament. Clapping a hand on Rory's shoulder, he said, "It was bound to come out sooner or later. Can't keep something like this a secret in the MacTaggart family."

Rory's mouth warped into a half frown, half smile. "Not when we enjoy tormenting each other so much."

"I won't tell Aidan," Lachlan said. He winked. "Probably."

"Can I trust you to behave yourselves without me?" I asked. "The book Erica wants is in the bedroom."

"Aye, you can trust me," Lachlan said. "Can't speak for Rory, though. He seems to need his wife to keep him in line."

Rory pursed his lips.

I patted his cheek. "Try not to kill each other until I get back."

"No promises," Rory said with a slight smile. "Lachie might deserve a right skelping."

"Lachie?" his brother said with a chuckle. "Oh, I am for certain telling Aidan what your wife calls you."

Shaking my head, I jogged down the hall and away from the MacTaggart men. When I returned a few minutes later, the book in question held in one hand and sheathed in newspaper, the brothers were discussing shinty.

Lachlan accepted the package.

"Best get home," he said. "We'll see you two on Saturday. Your big day, as Erica calls it."

The wedding. Already? Time flew when your husband ravished you every day.

Rory didn't move until we heard the side door shut. Relaxing, he put a hand on the island and leaned into it. "What book are you lending Erica?"

"My copy of the Kama Sutra."

"What if I wanted to read it?"

"Happy to demonstrate my favorite parts for you." I bounced on the balls of my feet and rubbed my hands together. "What should we do now?"

Rory pushed away from the counter, scooped me up, and deposited me on the island beside my collection of sundae fixings. Grabbing the can of whipped cream, he touched its tip to my breast. "I have ideas. And we have time before we leave for Inverness to meet your family."

I smiled, locking my legs around him. "Show me, Rory baby. You always have the best ideas."

Chapter Twenty-Nine

The arrival of my family must've seemed to Rory like the invasion of Normandy. Four adults and a pair of twin toddlers poured out of Rory's jet, shouting their happiness at various decibels and various pitches. The twins squealed and flung out their little arms toward us. My sister, Hadley, confined one of the girls in her arms while her husband, Cole, had corralled the other in his. My parents waved and beamed at us.

What really baffled Rory was my sister.

Hadley threw her arms wide, shrieked, and bounded toward me. "Emmy!"

I shrieked too, my arms spread. "Haddie!"

We bolted for each other, colliding in a boisterous clinch. Compared to us, the twins had seemed tame.

Introductions followed, with Cole and my dad shaking Rory's hand. To Rory's bafflement, my mom hugged him and smacked a big kiss on his cheek. Madison and Mackenzie, Hadley's daughters, giggled shyly when Rory knelt to greet them.

Everyone acted like Rory and I were the perfect couple. My dad even spoke those words.

Right before he slapped Rory's back and announced, "I ordered a full background check on you, but it came back clean. Welcome to the family."

My husband's befuddlement only increased, and he looked to me for an explanation. I could only shrug and shake my head.

While the other adults shepherded the kiddies toward the limo Rory had rented for the occasion, my little sister sidled up to me and whispered, "Are you knocked up?"

"No," I said, making a somewhat rude face. "Why would you ask that?"

"Well, you did get married awful fast. Thought it might've been a shotgun wedding."

I rolled my eyes, startled to realize I'd done a Rory thing. "No guns involved. I love Rory."

True. I prayed she didn't ask about his feelings.

"Ohhh, that explains it." She bumped her shoulder into mine. "You're glowing because you're in love."

Her comment about me glowing got filed in my mental folder labeled Wacky Things Sisters Say, along with her subsequent claim I looked "happier than ever before with any other guy, no contest."

We got my family settled in at Dùndubhan, squirreled away in the guest-wing bedrooms, far from where Rory and I slept on the third floor. My brilliant husband had made sure we'd maintain our privacy, for those wild nights of love-making in our room. We did have to forgo sex in the kitchen, office, or anyplace where someone might stumble onto us in the throes. Rory was disappointed, but I assured him we could get naked in every corner of the house once the wedding was done.

The next day, we drove into Loch Fairbairn for a dress-hunting expedition. Rory went to his office while I wrangled eight women—my mom, his mom, my sister, his three sisters, and Calli and Erica. The kiddos had stayed home with their respective daddies. I bought a dress that cost more than my last car, recalling Rory's instructions from earlier that morning when he told me to "spend the bloody money, it's yours too."

Sorcha MacTaggart had offered to drive my family back to Dùndubhan so I could take my husband to lunch. After I bid all eight women goodbye, I traipsed down the sidewalk toward Rory's office. A block away, I passed the office of the *Loch Fairbairn World News*.

Graham Oliver shambled out the door and stopped, smiling at me with recognition and smug satisfaction. "Mrs. MacTaggart, are ye coming to see me?"

No way was I conversing with this guy. "Have a nice day, Mr. Oliver."

I took two steps down the sidewalk.

"Shame about those pictures," he said.

Paralyzed mid-step, I slowly turned my head in his direction. "What are you talking about?"

Graham tapped a rolled-up newspaper on his palm. "I hear Rory is very fond of you. Too bad it won't last. Your past will be too much for him once he sees it splashed across the newspapers for everyone to gawp at."

My past? Pictures, he said. He couldn't know about Sebastian and the nude photos. I'd told no one outside of Rory.

He'd hired an investigator to locate Sebastian. Might the investigator have tipped off Graham? To imagine a detective in America might collude with the owner of a tabloid in a small Scottish village, it seemed like the height of paranoia. What else could Graham mean by his comments?

I squared my shoulders. "I doubt you know a tenth of what you think you know, about me or my marriage."

The scandal-monger smiled again, with the certainty of a man secure in his superior position. "People talk to me, Emery. At heart, everyone is a gossip."

"My name is Mrs. MacTaggart, you slimy little maggot."

"Knowing how much I've seen of you, I feel entitled to use your Christian name. Ruining your husband's happiness will be my greatest accomplishment."

He strolled away, tapping the newspaper on his leg.

I sprinted to Rory's office and told him about my encounter with Graham. He told me to "ignore the goddamn scunner" and hustled me to our car.

For the rest of the week, we didn't discuss Graham or Sebastian. Our families and wedding preparations occupied our time during the day, and at night our voracious hunger for each other distracted us from everything else in the world.

The week zipped by.

Until the big day arrived.

I waited in the vestibule, before the open door to the outside, while my mom and my sister fussed with my hair and the folds of my dress's skirt. My stomach had wrenched into tight knots, each of them a hard lump in my gut. At the same time, though, anticipation zinged over my skin, lifted the hairs on my arms, and tingled on my scalp. What would Rory think of my dress? What would he be wearing?

When he spoke his vows, would he mean them?

My hand over my belly, I shut my eyes and fought to rein in my tumultuous emotions. I loved him so much, and I wanted him to love me, but I had no idea if he'd permit it. He'd sworn he would never let himself fall for me. If he thought he had fallen, how would he react?

Love. Fear. Hope. Dread. No wonder I was tied up in knots about tying the knot—again.

Hadley snapped her fingers in front of my face. "You okay, Emmy?"

"Yes," I said, straightening and rolling my shoulders back. "This is my first real wedding, that's all. Mumbling 'I will' in front of a magistrate isn't the same thing."

"No," my mother said, "it isn't. And it's normal to be nervous when you're about to stand up in front of two families to declare your love and commitment to a man you've known for a few weeks."

Two families. *Eek.* One of those families, the MacTaggarts, numbered in the dozens. Rory's parents and siblings had been joined by a multitude of cousins, as well as aunts and uncles. I could count my family on one hand—well, one hand plus one more finger. Couldn't forget my nieces.

Hadley squished her lips together. "Do you love him, Emery? I mean, really love him. Because if you're regretting this, you can leave him. We'll help."

"What makes you think I have regrets?"

She cast a meaningful look at my midsection. "You keep holding your tummy. So, either you're pregnant or you're nauseous from anxiety. You swear up and down you're not knocked up."

"I'm not." I dropped my hand to my side, but my fingers seemed to have minds of their own. They kept twisting into the folds of my dress. "I'm nervous, like Mom said. That's all."

My sister raised her eyebrows.

I understood the question in her eyes.

"Yes," I said, "I love Rory. I love him so much it scares me a little bit, because I never loved any other man this way."

Tears stung my eyes, and my throat went thick. People were supposed to cry *during* the wedding, not while waiting to traipse down the aisle.

I'd just marshaled the will to tamp down my emotions when my sister flung herself at me. She gripped me in a fierce hug, blubbering about how wonderful this was, how beautiful I looked, how happy she was for me, and on and on and on. She proclaimed I looked like a fairy princess, and I had to admit I felt like one. My designer dress featured miles of lace, from the figure-hugging bodice to the flowing skirts. The slender sleeves hung off my shoulders, leaving them bare, while the neckline showcased my bosom without veering into the unseemly. To top things off, my sister had pinned tiny silk roses into my hair, which flowed in loose waves over my shoulders, and clipped a dainty veil on with a barrette, letting it cascade down my backside.

I adored Hadley, but sometimes she got so overemotional she'd drag me into the cry-fest with her. By the time she let me go, the tears had come back and I was sniffling.

Mom handed me a tissue.

Dabbing my eyes dry, I took several deep breaths to calm my nerves. Oh yeah, that worked so well. I made my peace with the pain in the back of my throat and the tears pricking my eyes, because at least I wasn't crying. I blew my nose, tossed the tissue aside, and once more sucked it up for the long walk down the aisle.

The silvery-gray carpet that formed the aisle started at the vestibule doorway and curved rightward to the lawn, then took a straight shot between the rows of chairs. I lifted my chin and commenced my measured stroll down the carpet. When I turned onto the aisle between the chairs, I noticed three familiar faces in the back row—Luke, Pam, and Sabri. Rory must've flown them in for the ceremony, a surprise to make me happy. My heart clenched at the realization until I caught sight of Rory—and the vision of him robbed me of breath, even as my pulse quickened.

The sunlight shimmered on his hair and in his eyes. He'd dressed in a pristine white shirt with a black bow tie, a waist-length black jacket with shiny gold buttons, and the kilt he'd worn the night we met. The knee-length kilt exposed his brawny legs, but black leather boots—shiny ones that looked new, or at least well cared for—covered his feet and ankles. A matching black belt encompassed his waist, and a leather pouch in the same color hung from a gold chain around his waist to ride low in the front. A fringed length of plaid, the same tartan as his kilt, draped from one shoulder down his backside, suspended below his knee.

He was dashing. No, more than that. He was glorious, the model of a masculine, virile Scotsman.

Rory's gaze connected with mine and he went stiff, his unblinking eyes searching mine as if he'd never seen me before.

I tried to smile at him, but my lips quivered in the attempt. A riot of emotions overpowered me, stronger than when I'd realized I loved him. I had to concentrate on every step, or I might've tripped and collapsed to the silver-gray carpet that led me to my husband. When I took my place beside Rory, and we faced each other in front of the gray-haired minister, I wasn't at all sure I could speak my vows. My throat had tightened up, and I battled for each shallow breath.

Then Rory captured my gaze again, and everything changed.

In those beautiful eyes, somber yet glinting in the sunshine, I glimpsed tenderness. The stunned expression he'd worn as I walked toward him had softened a little, though he still seemed dazed. In spite of that, the gentleness in his eyes calmed me, calmed my racing heart and my frazzled nerves. I mustered a subdued smile, my lips no longer trembling. As the minister intoned the traditional spiel, I couldn't tear my focus away from Rory—and he never took his away from me.

At the minister's cue, I recited the usual vows. Love, honor, cherish. In sickness and in health. Till death do us part. I said them by rote, hardly aware of my own voice, and when I spoke those two words, "I do," I almost choked up. Every promise I'd just made, I had meant with all my heart and soul.

Rory mumbled his vows with that stark look on his face. He hesitated before saying "I do," like he couldn't quite bring himself to speak the words. When we exchanged rings, he glanced away from me only long enough to get the gold band on my finger.

Though I probed his face for an answer, I couldn't find anything to explain his demeanor. Did he hate saying the vows because he didn't mean any of it? Was he choked up with emotion? Had something else upset him?

If Graham had harassed him this morning, I'd throttle the maggot.

Next came the kiss.

I tensed in anticipation, like we'd never kissed before. We'd enjoyed each other's lips more times than I would even try to count. We'd kissed for long, long moments. We'd kissed slow and sweet, rough and hungry, lingering and steamy. Yet this lip-lock would happen in front of our families, in front of a minister, in the wake of meaningful vows we'd exchanged while gazing into each other's eyes.

Rory clasped my face in his hands, slanted toward me, and touched his lips to mine.

My arms hung slack at my sides as all the tension flooded out of my body. I swayed into him without conscious thought to do so, and my head angled up to meet his kiss. He pressed his mouth into mine with more conviction, his hands delving into my hair, his lips warm and soft, the kiss tender and imbued with a deep yearning.

He pulled away, his hands lingering on my cheeks.

Clapping erupted, but then someone whistled, and the clapping escalated into cheers and whoops from dozens of voices, male and female.

I rotated my eyes to scan our audience.

Aidan whistled with two fingers in his mouth, then grinned and pumped his fists in the air.

Oh yeah, my brother-in-law had instigated the ruckus, for sure.

I spotted my sister wiping tears from her eyes and my mom blowing her nose, her own eyes red and bleary. My dad's mouth was open as he—What the hell? My dad was whooping. I'd never seen him show so much enthusiasm for anything, much less for one of my significant others.

Rory lowered his hands, luring my attention back to him. He still had that stunned air about him, even when he brushed a thumb over my chin.

He sealed his hand around mine and led me back down the aisle.

Chapter Thirty

Guests milled around the first floor, availing themselves of the buffet in the dining room and spilling out into the great hall to chat and eat. The door to the library office was closed and locked to deter lookie-loos from poking around in Rory's private sanctum. Oddly, when I'd locked up the office on my way to the vestibule for my big walk down the aisle, I'd found the door ajar. Rory always kept it shut but unlocked. I'd brushed it off as wedding-day jitters making him forgetful.

After the incident with Lachlan in the kitchen, I figured my husband cherished privacy more than ever. What if Graham had those photos of me? How would Rory react to my nakedness splashed across the pages of a tabloid? The ultimate breach of privacy and decorum.

I shook off the thought, determined to enjoy this day.

Our mothers had decked out the great hall in wedding-appropriate fashion, with gauzy fabric hung artfully here and there, and other spaces festooned with silver and gold ribbons. Cute silver bells dangled from the chandelier. We'd opened the long gallery upstairs to guests as well, since many of Rory's cousins proved to be as large as he and his brothers were. They required extra space. The gallery featured the same decor as the great hall, but our moms had arranged for a wet bar there. They'd also cordoned off a dance floor in the gallery, using the same gauzy white fabric that decorated the walls to create a rope. A local band, comprised of MacTaggart relatives, would play both modern and traditional music for the guests.

Everyone wanted to congratulate me, tell me how happy Rory was, or regale me with stories of my husband the superhero solicitor who saved homes and businesses, even marriages. Pam, Sabri, and Luke stopped by to offer their felicitations and secure my promise to keep in touch, then they vanished into the melee.

After a while, maybe twenty minutes, I took advantage of a lull in the bridal greetings and sneaked outside for a bit of fresh air. I leaned back against the sun-toasted stones of the vestibule's outer wall. The sun, though descending toward the horizon, warmed my face as I turned it up to the golden rays, my eyes closed. I drew in refreshing lungfuls of clean Highland air, my thoughts circling back around to my husband.

"Mrs. MacTaggart, you're a bonnie bride."

I jumped away from the wall and glared at the figure whose familiar voice had spoken my name. "Graham Oliver? You were not invited. Get out of here before I kick you in the bawbag."

No need to ask how he got on the property. The new driveway gate was open to admit guests.

His lips warped into a nasty smile. "Sorry I missed the ceremony. I predict the marriage willnae last a week more."

I barred my arms over my chest. "Your predictions don't mean diddly-squat to me."

He scratched his chin. "But my next article will."

A shadow elongated over me.

"What the bloody hell are you doing here?" Rory's voice bellowed from the vestibule doorway. He stalked to Graham, seizing the man's collar. "Leave my wife alone."

Graham sneered. "Ye donnae know your bride as well as ye think, MacTaggart. I've seen sides of her bound to make ye cringe."

"*Dùin do ghob*, ye scunner."

"I'll shut the fuck up when I see fit."

Rory fisted his hands in Graham's shirt and hoisted him off the ground. Through teeth clenched hard enough to grind marble to dust, he snarled, "Go home to your sewer and *stay away from my wife.*"

He hurled Graham away.

The man crumpled to the ground, scrambled to his feet, and brushed grass from his pants. "I'll be seeing ye both. Soon."

Graham took off for one of the myriad vehicles parked in the vicinity of the drive.

Rory glared at the black sedan until the shadows of the forest engulfed it.

"Relax," I said. "Don't let him ruin this day for us."

My husband grunted, but the tension in his body lessened.

I slipped my hand into his. "Let's go back inside."

We tromped back to the great hall, entering hand in hand. I had my husband to myself for a whole five minutes before Lachlan and Aidan waylaid him to huddle in the corner talking about shinty and other guy stuff. My sister and mother cornered me at the opposite end of the room, though I lost track of their chatter, distracted by thoughts of Rory.

What was his problem today?

Just when I'd resolved to go talk to him, whether he liked it or not, my mom announced it was time for our first dance as husband and wife. With two sets of paired fingers in her mouth, she issued an ear-piercing whistle that made the great hall go quiet. She flagged Rory down and herded both of us upstairs to the makeshift dance floor.

My shell-shocked husband had relaxed a smidgen, and as he took me in his arms for a formal dance, his hand closed around mine in a gentle hold. I placed my other hand on his shoulder while his free hand settled over the small of my back. Rory and I floated across the floor together, swirling in elegant circles, our gazes bound to each other. Our world telescoped down to an invisible bubble encompassing us, a sanctuary where none of our problems existed and only this moment mattered.

Rory's expression had grown soft, his eyes shimmered.

A warmth blossomed in my chest. I must've smiled like a lovesick goofball, because I felt like one. When he looked at me that way, I had hope—for tonight, for the nights after this, for us.

He started, blinking rapidly. The frantic surprise gripped him once more.

My chest tightened, and my hope withered.

While Rory avoided looking at me, the guests meandered onto the dance floor in couples, gradually filling the space around us. I saw my parents dancing, Hadley and Cole too. Jamie had taken on the task of wrangling the twins for my sister so she and Cole could dance. I'd noticed Gavin Douglas seated beside Jamie during the ceremony, and now he crouched beside her aiding with the entertainment of Madison and Mackenzie.

Surrounded by all these people who loved me, I couldn't wallow in self-pity. I wouldn't.

I looped my arms around Rory's neck. "Did you fly Gavin back here for the wedding? Last I heard, he'd gone home to America. Jamie was bummed."

"I offered," Rory said, as he linked his arms behind my back, "and Gavin accepted the invitation to travel here on the jet."

"You wanted Jamie to be happy."

"For one day, if nothing else. What happens next is up to him."

"That was very sweet of you. And it was extra sweet to invite Pam, Sabri, and Luke."

"Your happiness is worth any cost."

I tickled the nape of his neck with my fingertips. "You want people to think you're a grumpy grizzly, but you're really a teddy bear."

"You have a strange opinion of me." He regarded me with guarded curiosity. "How can you call me sweet and a teddy bear, after the way I've treated you?"

"Sometimes you are cranky. On rare occasions, you're a jerk. I understand why you are the way you are, though, and I accept it."

He tried to pull his head back, but my hands prevented it. "Why would you do that?"

"Accept you as-is? Because I also know you want to evolve." I lifted onto my toes to look him in the eye, letting his arms carry me suspended above the floor. "Your therapy isn't over yet. You have potential, and I'll help you realize it in whatever way I can."

We lapsed into silence while his gaze turned distant and I rested my cheek on his shoulder. My feet touched down on the floor, but I let him lead me wherever he wanted to go.

I whispered in his ear, "You are the handsomest groom ever, very regal and sexy in your formal kilt-wear."

He glanced down at me but said nothing.

"Would it be rude if we snuck out of here?" I asked. "You slept in the other bedroom last night to make our mothers happy, but I'm feeling seriously deprived of sex and cuddling."

That strange, muted shock crept across his face again.

"What's the matter, baby?" I asked.

"Nothing." The word was clipped, his tone gruff.

"Baloney."

He loosened his hold on me, his gaze darting to the doorway.

"Hey." I snapped my fingers to regain his attention. "You haven't told me what you think of my dress, or whether I look pretty today."

"Well—I—" He gulped visibly. "The dress is fine. Rather flattering."

"Gee, don't gush like that. It's embarrassing."

He coughed, eyes averted. "You look pretty today."

"If you're resorting to repeating what I said near-verbatim, something is definitely up with you. Spill, Rory." When his face blanked, I added, "It means talk to me."

His gaze flitted around, the movements verging on frantic, until he seemed to spot the object of his search. "I need a drink. Excuse me."

Rory pushed away from me so fast I stumbled half a step. He bolted for the wet bar where Lachlan and Aidan loitered, sipping amber liquid from tumblers.

I gaped in mute confusion as Rory barked orders at the bartender, then grabbed the tumbler plunked in front of him. He swigged the contents in one mouthful and hollered for another, tossing it back in a single swig.

This was how every girl imagined her wedding day.

Our first ceremony had been rushed, utilitarian, and a total blur. Our second ceremony had proved beautiful and romantic—except for Rory's disturbed demeanor and the fact he'd run off to drink with his brothers. Was this how our entire marriage would be?

I clutched my tummy, struck by a sudden queasiness and a wave of icy dread. Our entire marriage would last less than a year from today.

A hand tapped my shoulder.

Startled, I turned to find a tall man with gray eyes holding a hand out to me.

The man turned out to be the first in a parade of MacTaggart cousins who each requested a dance with the bride. When the sixth cousin bid me adieu, I cried off any more dances. My feet ached, my legs ached, and every time I glanced at Rory stationed at the bar, a pang lanced my heart. I'd resorted to studying the black-and-navy striped tie of my last partner so I didn't have to witness my husband's steadfast attempt to get soused.

Yawning, I started for the bar—and stopped short.

Rory wasn't there.

Gavin Douglas was clomping toward me with a grave expression.

"Uh, sorry," he said. "They sent me to tell you. Your husband's wasted, and his brothers carried him up to your bedroom."

Despite the weight crashing down on me, threatening to plow me down into the bowels of the earth, I summoned a smile for Gavin. "They gave you the crap job, eh? It's all right. Thanks for letting me know."

"Sure thing."

I charged upstairs and straight to the open bedroom doorway. Lachlan and Aidan had hauled Rory halfway to the bed. The smacking of my footfalls on the wood floor attracted their attention. I stomped to a halt on the threshold, scowling at the scene, my skirts flouncing around my legs.

"We thought to drop him on the bed," Aidan said.

I drummed the toe of one shoe. "I'd say dump him on the floor, it's what he deserves for this." Despite my harsh words, I wanted to cry more than rage. "Put him on the bed."

With a bit of grunting and huffing, they hefted Rory onto the bed.

Lachlan nodded at my husband. "Should we, ah...undress him?"

"Don't bother. You can go." I moved inside the room. "Thank you."

The brothers filed out the door. As Aidan passed me, he said, "We tried to stop him drinking, but he wouldnae hear about it."

"He is a stubborn—" I bit off the word ass. "— Scotsman."

"Aye," Lachlan said. "But I haven't seen him drunk in twenty years."

Wonderful. Marrying me drove Rory to drink.

My brothers-in-law departed, shutting the door.

Since I had no hope of undressing Rory, given he weighed a ton, I changed into sweats and a T-shirt and laid down beside him. Across his body, I noticed an object on the bedside table.

My mini photo album.

I rose on one elbow. The album was open to a picture of me in the Egyptian dancer outfit. The album hadn't been there when we woke this morning. He must've gotten it out later to peruse the options for his wedding night feast of pleasure. I smiled down at my unconscious husband, caressing his cheek, loving the hint of stubble that prickled my skin.

Drool trickled from the corner of his gaping mouth.

Ah yes, the wedding night every woman dreamed of.

Chapter Thirty-One

$\mathcal{S}$eated cross-legged in a chair by the window, I reflected on the view of the castle wall and the woods beyond. The morning sun painted streaks of gold on the trees and the stone wall, and it shined through the window to warm my face. I might've gloried in the morning if I hadn't been so pissed at my husband.

Every thirty seconds or so, I'd shoot a glance at Rory passed out on the bed.

Green numbers glared on the bedside clock—seven fifteen, far past Rory's usual five o'clock wake-up time.

I propped my chin on a raised fist and stared out the window again. My thoughts had been scattered since I woke an hour ago to discover Rory still asleep, still clothed, and still lying sprawled atop the covers. He hadn't budged since his brothers dumped him there last night. His intermittent snoring assured me he hadn't drowned in his own drool.

What had happened yesterday baffled me. Something scared him. He'd seemed okay until he saw me walking down the aisle. What about me had freaked him out? I'd hashed and rehashed the options so many times the words in my head had stopped seeming like words. The night before, the last time I'd seen him before the ceremony, Rory had kissed me good night with all the scorching sensuality I'd come to expect from him. Nothing had been amiss then.

I frowned at his large, inert body and sighed miserably.

Answers would have to wait until he roused from his whisky coma.

The shapes of two suitcases positioned by the door caught my eye.

Would we make it to Skye? Or would our three-day honeymoon be canceled? Depended on the strength of his hangover, I guessed. Based on his behavior last night, he might not want to celebrate our marriage.

Clothing rustled. The bed creaked.

I targeted my sharpest gaze on Rory.

He grimaced, eyes closed, and rubbed his forehead.

"Good morning," I said with extreme, and extremely sarcastic, cheer. Jumping up, I padded around to his side of the bed and assumed a smile to match my phony tone. With a hand on the tall post at the foot of the bed, I spoke to my bleary-eyed husband. "Congratulations. You slept in for the first time ever."

He peeked at me between his fingers, with his hand clamped to his forehead. "What happened?"

"Are you serious? You don't remember?"

"Remember what?" He dropped his hand, his brows cinched tight over his nose, and peered at the canopy of the bed. Understanding dawned on his face like a blood moon inching over the horizon. "*Bod an Donais.*"

I flopped my butt onto the bed near his feet. "Yeah, you are a devil's dick."

"Emery…" His voice trailed off as he fixed his bloodshot eyes on me. "I ruined our second wedding night, didn't I?"

"Yep."

He spewed a string of Gaelic curses. "Christ, I'm an erse. Please believe me, I'm sorry for letting you down again. You have every right to be angry, so go on and shout at me. I deserve it."

I folded my arms over my belly, one hand atop the other, and rubbed my wrist furiously. "Not interested in yelling. Doesn't fix anything. You keep doing stupid things and then saying you're sorry. An ass you might be, but your apologies are wearing thin."

"What can I do?"

"Don't know." I scrutinized his face, the shame there making my heart hurt for him. Dammit, I did not want to feel tenderness right now. "I've got a revolutionary idea. How about you stop doing stupid things, then you won't need to apologize for them."

My wrist-rubbing mutated into scratching.

Rory pushed up on his elbows, his gaze drawn to my wrist. "You're not angry, are you?"

"No. Well, yes, but that's a minor issue at this point."

He squeezed his eyes shut, his body caving in. "I hurt you, again. Last night you said you accept me as I am, but I donnae see how you can overlook this. I behaved—I'm a selfish bastard."

"I don't overlook your faults or your behavior. I forgive it, usually, but—" I bit down on my lower lip. The first blur of tears in my eyes paid no attention to my command to cease and desist. "Not sure I can do it this time."

"Cannae blame ye." He winced as he shoved up into a sitting position and swung his legs over the bed's edge. His boots hit the floor with a *thunk*. He stabbed a hand into his hair and scrubbed his scalp with his nails. "I realize it isn't worth much, but I am so sorry, Em."

My heart sped up at his use of my nickname. *No, no, no, you are not melting for him because he called you Em.* Right, yes. No melting. None whatsoever.

Good plan, until he swiveled his face toward me.

Raw anguish, exposed by the faint quivering of his bottom lip and the starkness in his eyes.

Oh God, why did he have to look so pitifully apologetic? The pain of three failed marriages had carved deep scars in his heart. He needed my help, so maybe…

No melting, remember? Noooooo melting, no way.

My shoulders sagged, and my body angled toward his.

"Why did you do it?" I asked, my voice gentler. So what if I'd melted? I loved him too much to grind salt into his old wounds. "I suggested we have sex, and you scurried to the bar to drown yourself in whisky."

"I wanted one drink, but it…escalated."

"Why? Something scared you yesterday. Why you chose to deal with it by getting soused is beyond me."

His chin dropped to his chest. "I don't know why I did it."

"You mean you don't want to tell me." I slid off the bed. "Total honesty. You promised me that. Remember?"

Bleak brown eyes beseeched me. "I remember."

"Honesty means no lies, no evasions, no secrets. Lately, I feel like I'm getting all three from you."

I hadn't told him I loved him. Maybe I was guilty too. Though I longed to share my feelings with him, telling him now seemed like a recipe for disaster.

"Should I assume our honeymoon is off?" I asked.

He opened his mouth, but no words came out.

"Right." I spun toward the bathroom door. "I'm taking a shower."

I made it halfway there before he finally spoke.

"Wait," he said, heaving his body off the bed. "Have a bath instead."

"Why do you care if I take a shower or a bath?"

"Please, Emery." He shuffled toward me, grasping my upper arms. "Have a bath. Downstairs."

"Downstairs? Why?"

"The ground-floor bathroom. Please."

"Wh—" My will to argue crumbled away when I beheld the earnestness on his face. A torrent of meltiness gushed through me. He really, really wanted me to take a bath. On the ground floor.

"Ground-floor bathroom," he pleaded. "Will you do this for me, even though I bollocksed everything badly and haven't earned the right to ask anything of you?"

"Oooh-kay," I said. "I'll take a bath on the ground floor. Happy?"

"Not yet, but I am grateful." He lighted a tentative kiss on my forehead. "Thank you."

"Sure, whatever."

On my way to the bedroom door, I tossed confused glances back at him, unable to decipher his motivation for this request. I had to take a bath. Downstairs.

Why was I doing this? No mystery about that.

I loved him so much I would've done almost anything he asked.

Immersed in sultry, steamy water, I leaned back against the claw-foot tub and savored the arousing sensation of water lapping around me.

A knock sounded at the door.

I unleashed a whiny moan. "Who is it?"

"Your husband."

"Which one? I've got so many, you'll have to be more specific."

"Rory," he said, over-enunciating the syllables. "May I come in?"

"You may."

The door pivoted inward, and Rory sauntered inside wearing a dark-blue terrycloth robe. As he neared the tub, he shed the robe. It crumpled onto the tile floor, granting me an unobstructed view of his nude body and his thickening penis.

I waved at my body, submerged in the steaming water. "Your wish is my command. I'm bathing on the ground floor. Care to explain why?"

"This is the only tub large enough."

"For what? This thing swallows me—"

He leaped into the bathtub.

Water sprayed up around us, flooding over the rim and deluging the floor. He landed with his feet straddling my legs, then fell to his knees amid the swirling, sloshing water.

He smirked.

I grinned. "Rory baby, you're in the tub with me."

"Twice you asked me, and twice I said no."

His hands curled around my calves, exerting slight pressure, encouraging me to bend my knees. I drew them toward my chest. He lowered onto his butt, knees bent in front of him, our toes touching. "I wanted to join you in the jacuzzi that morning in New Orleans. I wanted it badly. And when you asked me to join you in this tub, I wanted it even more."

"Why didn't you?"

"It felt too intimate." Wrists balanced on his knees, he met my gaze without flinching, his eyes clear and bright. "Yesterday, when I saw you walking toward me in that dress…You were more beautiful than anything I'd ever seen, more beautiful than any masterpiece of Renaissance art. With the sun on you, your hair a glowing halo, you looked like an angel come down from heaven to bless this world with your incandescent beauty and life."

Holy shit. I struggled to sit up straighter, my insides quivering with anticipation.

"That was almost poetry," I said. "But I'm still confused about why you went all deer-in-the-headlights instead of telling me how beautiful I was."

"Are, Emery. You *are* beautiful, always, on the inside and the outside."

I couldn't speak for a moment, overwhelmed by what he'd said and by the maelstrom of emotion it incited. "That's the best compliment ever."

He shimmied forward until his feet were wedged between my hips and the tub wall. "I should've told you yesterday. But the enormity of the day— you, the ceremony, the guests—it overwhelmed me. I overreacted, for reasons I don't fully understand."

"Graham showing up didn't help." Why was I making up excuses for him? He'd called me an angel, said such beautiful things, and I couldn't hold on to the hurt in the face of his honesty. Honeyed words like those coming from any other man would've struck me as contrived. From Rory, they sang with truth.

"Never mind Graham," Rory said. He clasped me around the waist and lifted me half out of the water, only to set me down astride his lap. "Let's have fun in the tub."

I draped my arms around his neck. "Yes, please, let's."

He buried his face against my neck, showering feather-light kisses on my skin. "The honeymoon is not off. Once we've had a bath and a breakfast, we will get in the car and drive."

I strapped my arms tighter around him, smiling into his hair. "Remember when I said your sister worships you?"

"Mm."

"I was wrong." Tunneling my fingers through his short hair, I mashed my breasts to his wet, naked chest. "Worshiping you is my job, exclusively."

"You've got it backwards. Your body is my temple, and I worship inside you."

"Prove it."

Chapter Thirty-Two

The road unreeled before us in curves and straightaways, through countryside and villages, on a journey to nowhere in particular. Well, we had a destination in mind—Skye, and Rory's house there—but we had no specific plans for where to stop along the way. I drove this first leg of our sightseeing tour, so Rory could take it easy in the passenger seat.

"Enjoying your wedding gift?" he asked.

I inhaled the scent of new leather as I steered my red Jaguar F-Type convertible around a curve. With the top down, wind whipped through my hair. "I love-love-love it. And I'll give you a proper thank-you tonight."

"Amazed you're not violating the speed limit."

"Saving that for later."

For my uptight husband to relinquish control, letting me drive and agreeing to no set itinerary, showed how much progress he'd made. Our playtime in the tub had proved it.

Mm, the tub. While the Jag cruised down a straight stretch, I permitted my thoughts to travel back to the noisy, impassioned sex we'd shared in the bathroom. We'd splashed more water out of the tub than had stayed inside it, and we'd ignored the getting-clean aspect of bathing in favor of orgasms. Afterward, Rory had glimpsed the wet mess on the floor and responded by tossing every towel he could find onto it to soak up the water.

"Good enough," he'd said, then carried me to the large, multi-head shower. "Not done yet."

We'd gotten clean in the shower, sort of—but only after more playtime.

His throaty laughter, decadent and sensual, echoed in my mind.

"Emery." Rory's stern voice shattered my reminiscence. "Pay attention when you're driving, please."

I blinked at the road, but I hadn't veered off the edge or anything. "What's the matter? No bodies scattered on the asphalt, so I think I've done fine at multitasking."

"Not murdering innocent bystanders," he said, "is hardly an endorsement of distracted driving."

"You're right. Sorry, I'll keep my mind on the road."

"Maybe I should drive. You've been at it for more than an hour."

I pulled over so we could switch places, and so he could retake control of the situation. That left me free to relive our recent escapades of the erotic variety, from the kitchen incident to the splash-fest in the ground-floor bathroom. I also recalled our breakfast with my family, when everyone had been cheery, joking and sharing raucous stories from my childhood.

We'd reached Loch Linnhe before my mind drifted back to the present. We were preparing to board a ferry for the next leg of our journey.

"Where are we going?" I asked, leaning forward to watch the loch's waters go by.

"You wanted to see the ocean." Rory braced an elbow on his open window, the light glinting off his sunglasses. "I'm taking you there."

I whooped.

He gave me a perplexed little smile.

Not long after, I skipped across a sandy beach rimmed by outcroppings of dark rock. The sun drenched me with its enlivening heat, inspiring me to throw my head back and glory in its brilliance.

"Even the sun can't resist you," Rory said from his position at the beach's edge. "It shows its face more often since you came to Scotland."

Laughing, I twirled in circles, my bare feet sinking into the sand.

Rory's mouth cracked open and his forehead crinkled. He tracked my every movement with his eyes.

I leaped into the air to splash down in a tidal pool. My feet sank in deep. Cold water splattered on my calves, exposed by my rolled-up jeans. I faked an exaggerated shiver for Rory's benefit—his mouth fell open more—then spun and spun with my arms outstretched, laughing through every circuit.

Brawny arms cinched around my waist, halting me. Rory crushed me to his hard body and jacked me up to level our faces.

I gripped his biceps, marveling at how they bulged from the effort of holding me off the ground. Suspended in his arms, I grew breathless from more than spinning.

"The water's bloody cold," he said, casting a pointed glance at his sneaker-clad feet submerged in the tidal pool. "You'll catch pneumonia out here."

Hugging his neck, I glued my body to his. "Good thing I've got you to warm me up."

"Are you finished admiring the ocean? You'll see more of it when we make our way to Skye."

"Let's go. I want to see everything." I tickled his earlobe. "Absolutely everything."

"May not have time for everything in three days." He waddled as he turned us around, his feet mired in wet sand. "But I'll do my best."

He carted me back to the car, ever the chivalrous husband, and dried my feet with a towel he'd brought for the occasion. I'd made him promise to show me the ocean. Leave it to Rory to plan for the aftermath. He'd realized I'd want to at least wade in the water, because he knew me better than he had a right to after such a short time together.

Once he'd settled in behind the wheel, he laid his hands atop it and drummed one finger. "Should we continue up the coast, or go back to Corran to take the ferry? We could take the interior route to Skye, driving through Fort William and Invergarry."

"You're driving. You pick."

"This is your holiday, love. You choose."

My tummy did a flip-floppy thing that made me lightheaded for a second. He'd called me "love," though I doubted he realized he had. *Love.* He'd called me that.

"Um…" I floundered for a response to his question, but my heart had gotten stuck on that single syllable he'd spoken in passing. "Back to Corran."

After another ferry trip, we journeyed northeast out of Fort William past Loch Linnhe and Loch Lochy. Seriously, that's what it was called. Loch Lochy. Along the way, we stopped at various places to appreciate the scenery. Rory selected detours off the main road whenever possible, though it meant backtracking repeatedly, to let me see more of the Highlands. He described everything, in lush detail that almost made seeing the sights obsolete. I loved listening to his voice.

On a relatively even stretch of road, I sneaked a hand onto his thigh, down between his legs. "I know you have a wild heart, so let it show. Violate the speed limit, baby. See how fast this Jag can run."

He flashed me a shocked look. "I'd risk a fine and penalty points on my license."

I massaged his inner thigh. "How many points have you got so far?"

"None." He squirmed just a touch and cleared his throat. "Sixty isn't fast enough for you?"

"Kilometers are longer than miles, so you're not going as fast as it sounds."

"We use miles per hour here." He collared my wrist and plopped my hand on my lap. "We are going as fast as it sounds."

"Come on, break the speed limit for one minute. Floor it and see how it feels."

Rory glanced at me sideways, with a wry twist to his lips. "You are a sexy little devil whispering in my ear, luring me to sin."

"Is it working?"

He punched the accelerator. The Jag rocketed forward, engine roaring. The sudden momentum pinned me to my seat.

"Wooo!" I shouted and thrust my arms in the air. The wind battered them, so I locked my hands over the windshield's top edge. "Go, Rory baby!"

He grinned and laughed.

After precisely one minute, as gauged by the dashboard clock, he slowed to sixty miles per hour.

"How did it feel?" I asked.

"Good, but not as exciting as making love to you."

My spirit soared high above the car, detached from my earthbound body. He'd used that word again. Love.

With so many detours, and a stop for lunch, we didn't make it to Skye that day. After so long driving, to make sure I got the full experience, Rory was exhausted when we reached Invergarry. We got lucky and scored a room at a quaint farm that doubled as a bed-and-breakfast. Despite his fatigue, Rory rebounded after a homestyle dinner, and once we got inside our cozy room, he made love to me for an hour, with a reverence and tender care that took my breath away.

I slept better than I had in all my adult life.

On the second day, the sights blurred together because I had trouble concentrating on anything beyond Rory. He'd grown so animated while pointing out landmarks and explaining the history of this ancient land that I couldn't look away from him. Watching him made me smile and soften in the best ways. I twisted my torso to get a better view of his face, with my cheek against my seat's back.

A stop for lunch. More sightseeing. I saw nothing anymore, except for him.

Tonight, I had to tell him. I had to say the words even if it freaked him out. *I love you.* He needed to know, because I hated keeping it secret. After vowing we'd both be honest with each other, always, I felt like a hypocrite for not sharing my feelings.

The sun was lagging toward the horizon when we crossed the Skye Bridge over Loch Alsh. Fifteen minutes after setting wheels on Skye, we pulled up in the circular drive of a two-story home.

Rory parked in front of the door. "This is it."

I climbed out of the car, tilting my head up to survey the gray-stone building. "It's a mansion."

"A manse," Rory said, coming up beside me. "Not a mansion."

"What's the difference?"

"This was, at one time, the home of a clergyman. Houses like this are known as manses."

"Sure, whatever you say. I'm used to America. We have mansions and McMansions, but no manses I know of."

He pulled me against his side. "You're Scottish now."

We wandered into the manse, and I oohed at the intricate woodwork on display in every room, as well as the period-appropriate furnishings and decor. Rory informed me the house dated back to the 1800s. I might've thought I'd stepped through a time portal into the past, if not for the modern amenities tastefully blended into the historic elements. We had a modern kitchen with an old-timey feel and a modern bathroom upstairs.

Rory prepared dinner, which I gobbled up like I'd been starved for three days. Nerves made me eat too fast. Since deciding to confess my feelings to him, I'd developed an underlying sense of dread that frayed my composure.

How would he react? Would my confession drive him away?

I held out no hope—only the slenderest thread, at least—he might say he loved me too. I suspected he did, or maybe prayed he did, but he wasn't ready to admit it.

After dinner, we retired to the sitting room. I curled up on the couch with my knees folded and turned to the side. Rory reclined beside me, his feet on the coffee table.

D-Day had arrived.

I angled my body toward him and wrung my hands on my lap. "I'm a hypocrite."

He moved only his eyes to glance at me. "Why?"

"I need to tell you something." I anchored my hands on my knees. "Something I should've told you days ago when I realized it, but I've been afraid of how you might react. That's not like me, you know, to be afraid to speak my mind. I have to say this, even if you freak out."

He swung his head toward me, lips pinched. "What is it?"

My fingers dug into my knees. My mouth went dry. "I'm in love with you."

"I understand." Blank face. Flat voice.

"You understand? What does that mean?"

He faced forward, his body stiffening, and cleared his throat. "I need a drink."

Rory launched off the couch and hastened to the liquor cabinet. He brought out a bottle of Ben Nevis and a glass tumbler. When he decanted a precise inch of whisky into his glass, I jumped up and stomped to him.

I bumped my hip into the liquor cabinet. "I love you, Rory."

"Heard you the first time," he muttered between mouthfuls of booze.

"And your response is to get drunk again."

He slapped his glass down on the cabinet, sloshing the remaining liquid. "If you're expecting me to—"

"I'm not expecting anything from you. I'm telling you how I feel because we both promised each other complete honesty." I eyed his whisky, and a memory of our wedding night flared in my mind. "That's a lie. I do expect one thing from you—not to get wasted."

The corners of his mouth tugged downward. "I am not getting drunk. I'm having one drink."

"Because I told you I love you."

"Stop saying it." He nabbed his glass and downed the rest of its contents in one gulp. "Repeating the words ad nauseam won't make me say what you want."

Ad nauseam? He was freaked out, and I didn't have the energy to talk him through it, not this time.

"Do what you want," I said, whirling toward the doorway. "I'm going to bed."

I tried to storm off in dramatic style, but I was too tired for melodramatic gestures. Despite knowing he wouldn't say he loved me, despite not knowing if he did love me, I'd thought he learned his lesson on our wedding night. I'd believed he'd refrain from drowning his angst in a whisky bottle.

Ten minutes later, I shambled out of the bathroom into the master suite wearing a silky black nightie trimmed in black lace. It was the only item of sleepwear I'd brought on this trip. I didn't feel sexy in it tonight.

I made it to the bed, my gaze downcast, before I realized I wasn't alone.

Rory lay in bed, under the covers, his chest bare and the remainder of him concealed under the sheet and blanket. His head rested on a plush feather pillow.

I nudged the bed with my knees, mulling whether to get in.

He pinched the bridge of his nose. "I've been an erse again."

I snorted. "An eejit and an erse, I'd say."

"Aye." He gave the covers a hesitant pat. "Should I sleep in another room?"

"No."

He pushed up on an elbow. "I'm sorry, Emery. I reacted badly, again, and hurt you—again. But I am not drunk. I never intended to get drunk, please believe that."

I rocked back on my heels and then forward again until my knees met the mattress. "I believe you."

"Thank you." The words emerged on a relieved sigh. His eyebrows rose. "You're wearing a nightie. Didn't think you owned one."

"I have a few, but I don't sleep in them very much. Bought this one for—" I smoothed my hands over my nightie. "Doesn't matter."

"What did you buy it for? I'd like to know."

His gentle tone convinced me to say it. "For our wedding night."

Rory winced.

I raised a hand to stop his imminent apology. "You already said you're sorry."

"Will you sleep with me, then?"

As an answer, I peeled back the covers and crawled on hands and knees toward him. At his side, I sat back on my heels.

He fingered the hem of my nightie. "It's bonnie, but not as bonnie as you."

Melting. Again. Damn, sometimes I wished I didn't turn gooey for him so easily.

"What are you wearing?" I asked, picking up the edge of the covers to peek beneath them. "Oh. You're not wearing anything. Does that mean…"

"Too tired for sex, I'm afraid."

"Me too." I let the covers fall back over him. "Why the nudie show if we're not getting it on?"

"I like feeling your naked body beside me." He ran a finger along my nightie's hem, grazing my skin. "You've picked this night to wear clothing to bed, for the first time since I've known you."

"Not true. You made me wear your shirt on the second night we shared a bed."

"So I did." He shot a pointed look at my nightie. "You complained then, but now you voluntarily cover your luscious body."

"A problem easily resolved." I raised onto my knees and whisked the nightie over my head, tossing it toward the foot of the bed. "See?"

He flipped the covers up so I could crawl underneath and nestle against him. We slept through the night, cuddled under the covers, content despite the issues hovering between us.

I woke at eight thirty to find Rory slumbering beside me.

When he roused a few minutes later, I was sitting beside him smiling.

He arched one brow. "What?"

I pointed at the bedside clock. "You slept in, without being drunk. It's after eight thirty."

With a negligent shrug of one shoulder, he said, "I woke at five, but I couldn't bear to leave my wife lying here all alone, soft and warm and naked. I went back to sleep."

My smile broadened. "That's what I call progress."

Chapter Thirty-Three

After a breakfast cooked by me, Rory and I explored the area around our property. Maybe if I'd grown up in Scotland, I wouldn't have gotten so excited about Skye, but for an American like me, the island had a mystical aura. Ancient people built mysterious monuments here. The whisky that won Lachlan a wife had been crafted right here. Rory had bought a house here, though for reasons I hadn't yet coaxed out of him, he'd never visited it before.

Yes, okay, maybe I hoped Skye would work its magic on my husband the way it had for Erica and Lachlan. They hadn't set foot here. A bottle of Talisker single-malt cast the Skye spell on their relationship.

"You look pensive," Rory said.

"Guess the amazing view inspired deep thoughts."

"About what?"

"Whisky and men." *And you, my mercurial husband.*

He pulled me against him. "You do have the strangest thoughts. Here we are on the coast of Skye, on a beautifully sunny day, and you're musing about whisky."

I swept my gaze over a loch I'd forgotten the name of and the various craft navigating its waters, from tourist boats to dinghies to sailboats. The coast was rocky here, and I'd clutched Rory's hand as we trudged across the stone-littered shore so I could get a closer view. Across the water from us, craggy mountains soared up to the heavens. Behind us, a road wended its way around the coast and the jagged cliffs gave way to a flatter area that housed a tourist shop and a parking lot. Nearer to us, between the road and the shore, large black stones thrust up from the earth.

Pretty, puffy clouds dotted the azure sky.

I linked my arms around Rory's waist and snuggled my cheek on his chest. "Don't you want to know what men I've been musing about?"

"I hope it's not Luke, or that *bod ceann* before him."

"Mm-mm." I smiled, though I doubted he could see it. "Your brothers."

"I see." He had that amused lilt in his voice, the one I usually figured was him trying not to laugh. "Aidan, I can understand. We used to call him Don Juan, after all. But Lachlan?"

Rory made a disgusted noise.

"Oh come on," I said, and gave him a playful slug in the gut. "Lachlan's hot. As for Aidan…Whew."

Rory twisted in my arms until we faced each other. He secured me against him with both hands joined over my lower back and tipped his head down to narrow his eyes at me.

"It won't work," he said. "Trying to make me jealous. I have no worries you want someone else more."

"More than you? Never."

"Last night—" He flattened his lips, which normally indicated annoyance, but something in his eyes suggested a different emotion, a mysterious one that edged dangerously close to the thing he refused to talk about. "I warned you I can't give you what you need."

"You said you won't, not you can't." My forehead on his chest, I gave in to a weariness more emotional than physical. "Don't worry, I'm not trying to make you love me. I told you how I feel to get it off my chest, that's all."

His gusty breath fluttered my hair, the only way I knew he'd dipped his head near mine. "Whenever you want to leave, I'll give you the money."

I made a rude face only his shirt saw. "I'm not leaving. The only way you're getting rid of me is if you give me the heave-ho."

Another breath gusted over my hair. "The heave-ho sounds terrible, as if I'm pitching you over the side of a ship in the middle of the ocean."

"How this ends is up to you, Rory."

We huddled there for a while, ensconced in each other's arms but not speaking or looking at each other. Waves lapped on the rocky shore. Car engines grumbled on the road. Gulls squawked. I pressed my ear to Rory's chest and let the rhythmic thumping of his heart soothe me. Odd that I found comfort in the one part of him I couldn't reach. I might crawl over his entire body, licking and touching him from head to toe, but could I ever penetrate his ironclad heart?

Rory shrugged away from me and turned his haunted gaze to the dark loch.

"You asked me once," he said, "why I bought a house here."

I stuffed my hands in my jacket pockets, afraid to speak, sensing he might be about to confide in me.

"Three years ago," he began, his gaze remote though directed toward the water, "I came to Skye on business. Doesn't matter why. On my way home, I drove past the manse and saw the estate agent's sign. Something about the house made me pull into the drive and get out of my car. No one was living there at the time, and the grass and shrubs were overgrown. With sunset almost over, the house looked dark and forsaken in the twilight, and I stood there watching the shadows consume it."

Consume. The tone of his voice transformed that word into the most desolate thing I'd ever heard. Though I longed to touch him, my muscles refused to budge.

He rubbed a palm on his chest, eyes closed. "This was a few days after I learned Una had given birth to a baby girl. She and her partner had done in vitro with a sperm donor. I learned this from Lilias when I ran into her in Ballachulish. Somehow over the years, she and Una had become friends."

The impulse to speak, to ask questions or offer comfort, became so powerful I had to literally bite down on my tongue to restrain it.

Rory looked at me, his expression rife with a pain I couldn't understand—not yet.

"Lilias was excited," he continued. "She showed me pictures of Una's baby, and of the three children she had with the boy she'd—" An emotion akin to anguish flashed on his face, only to be eradicated by a stony expression. "The teenager she'd become involved with while she was married to me. He's an adult now, of course. They married and have a wonderful life together with their children. Una is equally blessed, Lilias said. She also mentioned Isobel, gossip she'd heard about her. Apparently, my first wife was never able to have children, but she's happily married."

I couldn't bite my tongue any longer without drawing blood, so I dared to light a hand on his chest and say, "That must've been hard to hear."

He nodded solemnly. "I'm pleased for them, of course. And I might not have minded hearing about their joyful lives if Lilias hadn't also said—She told me I looked sad. Lonely. She offered to arrange for me to meet a woman she knew."

"Your cheating ex-wife wanted to set you up on a blind date?"

"Aye." He peered out at the loch, bleakness creeping into his eyes. "I thanked Lilias for the offer but politely declined, then I excused myself. Said I had an appointment to keep. For days after, I kept wondering why my ex-wives seem happy while I'm…not." He stared at the horizon beyond the road, his whole face squinted. "When I saw the manse, forsaken and unwanted, I felt a kinship with the house. Ridiculous, I know. But it spoke to me, and I thought I might like to come here once in a while to…I don't know. Wallow in seclusion. I bought the manse the next day, over the phone, without ever setting foot inside it. I paid people to renovate and furnish it. I still pay people to care for the place."

"You never visited the house until now." He'd stopped practicing the caber toss three years ago, the same timeframe when he'd learned his wives were happy and realized he wasn't.

His smile was rueful. "Wallowing in desolation isn't as appealing as it seemed at first."

I eased my hands into his. "Why did you bring me here?"

"You wanted to see the ocean."

"Don't be deliberately obtuse. You know what I mean. Why did you bring me to Skye, to the house you bought because it looked as melancholy and forlorn as you felt?"

He tried to back away, but I held fast to his hands.

"What makes you think I felt melancholy and forlorn?" he asked.

"You just told me." I inched closer. "The house was forsaken, unwanted, consumed by shadows. You felt a kinship with it. Takes a real genius to figure out you were talking about yourself when you described the house."

Rory's lips twitched upward. "You are the cleverest woman I've ever met."

"I was being facetious."

His subtle amusement broadened into a warm smile. "I know. But you're still the cleverest."

I hopped up to give him a swift kiss. "Let's get off this depressing jaunt down memory lane. You've had fun with me, haven't you?"

"Cannae help it, you insist on making me do ridiculous things."

I tapped his chest. "You say it's ridiculous, but I've figured out that's Rory code for 'thanks for showing me a great time.' And you're welcome, by the way."

He fanned his hands over my back. "Never could fool you, could I?"

"Nope." My pulse jumped when I noted the gleam in his eyes and the way his entire demeanor had lightened. "Why don't we go back to that lonely, desolate house of yours and find ways to have fun there. Maybe we can turn its frown upside-down too."

"If anyone can make a house smile, it's you."

We wended our way back to the house in no hurry after relishing a meal at a local eatery. For the rest of the day, we enjoyed ourselves in every room in the manse—every room except the bedroom. Rory had wanted to save it for last. We made love, yes, but we also told each other silly stories, laughed for no good reason, and played an erotic version of hide-and-go-seek. Rory's idea, not mine. Seriously. I won, of course. Not many places for a big Scot to hide, so little old me had the upper hand. On our last go-round, I'd come upon him attempting to hide in a closet. He hadn't been able to shut the door, however, because his big feet wouldn't quite fit. Somehow, he managed to have his way with me in that very same closet, with the door wide open.

By the time we finished our evening meal and retired to the bedroom, Rory had long since shed any traces of the melancholia he revealed on the shore. His revelations had seemed like a momentous occasion, but I shied away from pestering him for more info tonight. The last thing I wanted was to spoil our final night on Skye.

He'd opened up to me, more than ever before. That was enough.

Those ex-wives of his…*Grr.* I wanted to hunt them down and give them a piece of my mind, or maybe a punch from my fist. I supposed Lilias hadn't meant to hurt Rory with her update on the lives of his former wives. She had, though, and I couldn't help feeling protective of him.

I sashayed out of the bathroom wearing my black nightie and twirled in front of Rory, who lounged nude on the bed with the covers thrown back.

"Here I am," I said. "You seemed to like this nightie the first time I wore it. Thought an encore might be in order."

"*Mo gaoloch,*" he said with sultry conviction, "you are a masterpiece of sensual beauty."

"You said that the night we met. I assumed it was a come-on line."

"It wasn't." He pushed up on one elbow, proffering his hand to me. "Come, and let me show you what I mean."

I crawled across the bed to kneel beside him as I'd done last night.

"Emery," he purred, as he skated his palms up my thighs, under the hem of my nightie, and swept them higher to cup my hips. "Even your name is sensual."

He slid his hands down, caught the edge of my nightie, and flipped it up and over my head. I raised my arms to let him pull the garment free of my body. He tossed it aside.

While I'd been focused on his face—on those scorching eyes, on the intoxicating depths of them, and on the suggestive curl of his lips—his dick had become engorged.

He lay back, raising his arms above his head. "Take me."

Liquid heat rushed over my sex, tingling and slickening my flesh. No man had ever asked me to take him. His deep and husky request had made my nipples go hard and my stomach flutter with excitement.

"Please," he said, his chest swelling with each heavy breath. "Take me, Emery."

How could I deny that request?

I mounted him, positioned astride his hips, and took his shaft in both hands. "Sure you can handle me being in control?"

"You've been in control since the night we met." He sucked in a breath when I palmed his sac. "I surrendered to you then, and I'm done pretending it's not true."

Was he about to say…No, no, no, I did not want to hear it while I had his dick in my hand.

I relinquished his balls to place two fingers on his lips. "Shh, baby."

He captured my fingers with his mouth, suckling the tips.

So I skated my thumb over the head of his cock.

"Ah," he hissed. "Stop torturing me, will ye? I need your soft, wet—"

"I know what you need." Another flick of my thumb. I took his sac in my other hand and tugged, grinning when he made a strangled noise. "Trust me to give it to you."

"Hurry, love. Ahmno strong enough to withstand your teasing."

Towering over him, I closed my hand around his shaft and lowered my body onto his length, inch by sensuous inch. He groaned when I'd taken him all the way inside. I couldn't catch my breath, with his cock deep inside me and my sex drenched in anticipation. I laid my hands on his chest. It rose and fell beneath my palms, his skin hot and dappled with a pink flush.

His hands caught my hips.

I rode him slowly, rising up and sliding back down his shaft, rocking my hips to make him gasp and grip me harder. My cream glistened on his skin and dribbled down my inner thighs. The scent of my arousal intensified my need, and when he thrust a finger between my folds to tease my clitoris, I cried out.

He muttered in Gaelic, between panting breaths.

The pace quickened with our desire, my body slamming down on his length while he pinched my nipples and rasped his finger over my clit. I moaned and rode him harder, faster, our bodies pounding into each other, and he arched his hips up every time I sank down on him. My moans became a litany of "Rory baby, yes, oh God, Rory baby, yes, Oh God."

"Emery," he said, his voice strained and his face wrenched in desperation to come. "I love ye, Emery, I love ye."

No time to process his declaration. I came in an explosion of white-hot pleasure, robbed of my voice by the power of my release. My nails scraped his chest. My body clenched his cock in ferocious spasms.

His body went rigid, then he thrust into me so hard I bounced on the bed. He bellowed my name as he spilled himself inside me.

Rory rolled us onto our sides, running his hands over my body as we recovered from the bliss. When our breathing had normalized, he eased me onto my back with his body covering mine and his arms framing my head. I tried to speak, to talk about what he'd said, but he sealed his mouth over mine.

And he kissed me. Forever and ever.

When at last he yielded my lips, he shifted to the side so he could run his hands over my whole body.

I cradled his head in one hand and murmured, "You're not alone anymore."

His eyes blazed into mine, the emotion in them fierce and indescribable.

Ask him if he meant it. I knew I should. I tried, but my voice refused to cooperate. If he disavowed his words, if he claimed he hadn't known what he was saying, I didn't know if I could handle it. Not tonight. Not after everything we'd shared today.

I let him enfold me in his arms and listened as his breathing shallowed. He fell asleep long before I could. Hours elapsed while I held him close, praying for the strength to deal with whatever came next. I wanted him even if he never allowed himself to love me. I would stay, for as long as he'd have me.

Because I loved him that much.

Chapter Thirty-Four

Two days later, I lay across the foot of the bed while Rory packed a suitcase which sat near my head. Rory kept his head down and concentrated on folding his clothes in neat stacks. As usual, he performed the task with purpose and precision, spreading each garment on the bed so he could fold it properly.

I would've done a slapdash job to get it over with and worried about steaming away the wrinkles later. I admired his precision, though, and had come to find it rather sexy. He applied the same skill and determination to every aspect of his life. *Every* aspect.

Applied to sex, that attention to detail was astonishingly erotic. Watching him prepare to flee the country…not so much.

The last day of our honeymoon had been bizarre. Rory acted like nothing had happened that night on Skye, like he'd never declared his love for me. I tried—really, I did—to participate in the sightseeing on that last day. He must've sensed my unease, though, because after lunch yesterday he'd suggested we go home right away.

And this morning, he'd invented a reason to leave.

I supported my head with one hand, and with my other one, I twiddled my fingers on my thigh. "We only got home yesterday, and this morning you announce you've got to leave the country on a sudden business trip to France."

"Thank you for the summary," he said without inflection and without glancing at me, "but I recall what I said to you twenty minutes ago."

"Do you realize how it sounds?" I sat up and tucked my feet under me. "On Skye, you told me about a painful time in your life. And oh yes, I said I love you." *And you said it too.* "Are you running away to avoid being around me?"

"Of course not." He finally lifted his head to frown at me. "I am not a coward."

"No, but you are freaked out. I can tell. You go all Robot Rory when you start to worry you've let me get too close."

"This is a business trip." He clapped the suitcase shut and fastened the latch with a sharp click. "Two days at a conference, followed by two days working with a colleague to learn about the French legal system."

I clambered to my knees and waddled closer. "Take me with you."

"To a conference on international law? You would be bored."

"Have you noticed boredom being a problem for me? I know how to entertain myself." I leaned across the closed suitcase to grasp the lapels of his suit jacket. "If you take me along, I can entertain you every night."

"Despite what you may think," he said, grasping my hands to pry them away, "I can survive four days without you."

He guided my hands to my sides and released them.

"Maybe that's true," I said, "but can you go four days without sex?"

"Yes."

"At least let me drive you to the airport, instead of making poor Tavish go all the way to Inverness."

"He'll be visiting his mother, who lives there."

Rory snatched up his suitcase and marched to the bedroom door. He turned slightly, and the sun filtering through the clouds and windows cast him in a desolate light. A white shirt set off his dark-blue suit, but as usual, he wore no tie and let his shirt collar hang open. He looked glamorous and sexy, not like a husband about to abandon his wife because he'd inadvertently admitted he loved her.

"I'll see you in four days," he said. "Goodbye."

With that, he spun on his heels and clomped out the door.

Oh, like hell he was getting away with that crappy goodbye.

Barefoot and wearing only leggings with a long flannel shirt, I raced through the house to catch up to him. Damn, the man could outpace me. His long legs let him take the stairs two at a time while I had to hop and skip down them to keep his head in sight. He'd reached the Mercedes parked in the driveway before I got out the vestibule door.

Tavish observed us from the driver's seat, worry in his eyes.

"Rory!" I shouted as I sprinted across the lawn, the most direct route to the car.

He hesitated, his hand on the passenger door.

I hurtled through the air, colliding with him, latching both arms around his neck. My feet suspended above the ground, I mashed my mouth to his.

He turned to stone against me, his posture giving the impression he didn't give a hoot about me plastering my body to his. His mouth told a different story. His lips yielded to mine, and he parted them in invitation.

His cock jerked, its length distending.

I smiled against his lips. Oh yes, I'd leave him with a perfect reminder of what he'd be missing the next four days.

Reluctantly, I gave up his mouth. "Call me when you get to your hotel, okay?"

He nodded.

I let my body slide down his, withdrawing my arms only when my toes had touched the ground. "Have a safe trip, baby. I'll miss you."

With a grunt, he swung the car door open and dumped his suitcase over the back of the seat into the rear. Once he climbed into the passenger seat, Tavish drove the Mercedes down the driveway.

Rory moved his fingers in a hesitant wave.

I blew him a kiss.

His gaze stayed on me until the trees obscured his view.

Rory called three times a day—morning, lunchtime, and evening. We talked about nothing of real consequence, just chatting and joking, though his sense of humor seemed to have waned a bit since our trip to Skye. I longed to talk about what happened there, about what he'd said during sex, but I couldn't do that over the phone. I needed to see his reactions and gauge his freak-out factor.

So, we chit-chatted. It was nice, but I wanted him home.

On the second day of his absence, I spent more time with Calli learning about cataloging. When we delved into the topic of electronic library catalogs, I felt at home with the coding aspects of library work. I wound up fixing Aidan's computer at his office, earning heartfelt thanks from both him and Calli. After that, word got around I was a computer guru.

Please. I was a programmer, not the messiah of computerdom.

Lachlan called and begged for my aid. I agreed to stop by the next day and see if I could cure his computer of a malware infection. MacTaggart cousins called, friends of MacTaggarts called, and finally, clients of Rory phoned to talk to me.

"They act like I'm Steve Jobs," I told Rory that night. "I could make a career out of resuscitating hard drives in the Western Highlands."

"Is that what you want?"

"Not sure. Finding your true calling in life is harder than it sounds."

"You'll figure it out. You're intelligent and determined." He added in a teasing tone, "Stubborn, some might say."

"Says the pigheaded Scot."

"Taking my stubborn wife is my favorite pastime."

Our phone conversations inevitably turned to flirtation. I loved it. The more flirtatious he got, the happier he was. Not that I wanted him to feel too happy without me, but I didn't want him despondent either.

"Wanna have phone sex?" I asked.

He spluttered as if he'd taken a sip of a drink right before I spoke. "What did you say?"

"Oh, I think you heard me just fine."

"While I appreciate the offer," he said, "I prefer the real thing. Besides, I'm not the sort to…do that."

"You're exactly the sort." I toyed with a lock of my hair. "You're an exciting, adventurous man."

"Emery, you are the only person on earth who would call me adventurous."

"Nobody else knows you like I do."

After a hesitation, he said, "You may be right."

"So, phone sex. Yay or nay?"

"In a minute." He paused, his breaths audible. "Emery, I noticed you transferred money into our bank account."

"Closed out my account in America."

"You're meant to spend money, not add it. All you've paid for is petrol."

"And the wedding dress." I twisted a lock of my hair around my finger. "That's all I've needed. Had to buy gas when I drove into town. If and when I need something else, I'll tap into our account."

For several minutes, I labored to convince him I wasn't being overly frugal. He wanted me to spend money, but I didn't need to yet. He eventually conceded the argument.

The next day, after three sessions of "save my computer," I drove the Mercedes into Loch Fairbairn to do a bit of window shopping and decompress. Maybe I could start a business providing tech services to locals. I'd liked traveling the area and using my skills to help people.

Whether I could save my marriage, I had no idea. No amount of coding could overwrite my husband's fears. Being his therapist had turned into more than I'd bargained for, but I'd promised I would never give up on him. What if keeping that promise wrecked me? Every time I thought we'd made progress, he panicked.

We would talk when he got home. *No wriggling out of it this time, Rory.*

After a moment of admiring the window display of a quaint gift shop, I wandered inside to browse their selection of novelty hats and T-shirts. A stack of newspapers lay on the sales counter. The front-page headline caught my attention.

Cold washed over me, like I'd dunked my body in a vat of ice water.

The words, I must've misread them. Backing up a few steps, I edged sideways toward the counter until I could see the newspaper's headline clearly. It was, of course, the *Loch Fairbairn World News*. The top headline read, "Local Solicitor Marries Prostitute: Rory MacTaggart Buys a Wife to Satisfy His Deviant Needs."

A rock congealed in my throat.

I grabbed the paper, unfolding it to read the story. Nausea churned in my stomach and bile burned into my throat. Graham had concocted a wild tale painting Rory as a sexual deviant who performed all manner of twisted acts with his "prostitute" wife. Though he'd wrapped it in fiction, the man somehow knew about the marriage contract and the prenuptial agreement.

My gorge surged into my throat.

The article stated, "A former lover of the new Mrs. MacTaggart described the woman's insatiable lust and predilection for perversion. 'Get her in front of a camera and she'll preen like a porn star,' said Sebastian Zegers."

That bastard.

Graham's article included a single photo. When I saw it, the room tilted around me.

The photo showed me. Naked. Posed like a porno actress. It was one of the photos Sebastian had taken of me, vowing it was strictly private, and then posted online. How had Graham gotten his slimy mitts on it? How had he found Sebastian?

I slapped the paper down on the counter. My fingers clenched, crumpling the top sheet.

Rory had told me Graham loved to dive into the muck. He had dreams of grandeur, of his rinky-dink tabloid becoming the next *National Enquirer*, but his divorce had cleaned him out. With no money to fund his sleazy dream, he'd decided to blame Rory for all his problems. Now, the dirtbag had smeared Rory in a very public way. I prayed no one would believe this trash because I knew how much Rory's reputation meant to him. How much propriety meant to him.

Oh God, Rory. I had to tell him right away, before he heard it from someone else—or worse, came home and saw Graham's gossip rag on display around town.

I stormed out of the shop, intent on one goal.

Throttle Graham Oliver.

The door to the offices of the *Loch Fairbairn World News* slammed shut behind me. I stalked up to the desk behind which Graham slouched, his hair and clothes scruffy, his focus on the laptop computer situated on his desk.

His head jerked up at the *whack* of the door shutting.

I halted at his desk, glaring across it at the man I'd come to ream.

A smarmy smile crept across his face. "Mrs. MacTaggart, what brings you to my establishment?"

I thwapped my palms on the desk. "You know damn well why I'm here. You slandered my husband with your slimy lies."

"Corroboration, sweetheart. Look it up. I've got it."

"Anonymous gossip is not corroboration." I leaned in, my eyes narrowed. "Who fed you that garbage?"

He rocked back in his chair, appearing quite pleased with himself. "A journalist's source is confidential."

"You are not a journalist." I stabbed a finger at him. "You're a sleazy toad with a score to settle. Rory got your wife the settlement she deserved, and you're pissed about it. You are nothing but a petty coward who probably has a dick the size of a green bean."

The toad shrugged. "It's in the court of public opinion now."

"Retract the story." I ground the words out between my teeth. "Or we will sue your ass off and you won't have one penny left to your name."

"You can try, sweetheart."

His smug smile made me grit my teeth harder, shooting a pang through my jaw. I bent so far forward I all but climbed onto the desk and grabbed a handful of his shirt. Our faces inches apart, I snarled, "Tell me who it was."

Though he kept his smug expression, his lower lip trembled. "Your husband should be more careful what he leaves lying around in his office. The almighty Rory MacTaggart doesnae keep his home very secure."

A chill shimmied down my spine. Graham had intruded on our home twice. We had a gate these days, but it hadn't existed when this creep sneaked onto our property with a family gathering as his cover. The gate had been open on our wedding day, making it easy for him to sneak inside.

I had to call Rory, to tell him about the mess my past had made for him. My shit had hit the fan and splattered all over his life.

"You'll get yours," I said. "Count on it."

I stormed out of the office.

As the door swung shut behind me, Graham's cocky voice called after me. "Everyone you see from now on will know exactly how bonnie you are. And how depraved."

I rushed back to the car, but once I got behind the wheel I had to take several minutes to calm down. My hands were shaking. My breaths were short and shallow. A ringing started in my ears, and little black spots speckled my vision. While I drew in long, slow breaths, I rested my forehead on the steering wheel.

What if Rory invoked the morality clause in our contract? He could boot me out—of his home and his life.

He wouldn't do that. He loved me.

I'd warned him about the photos, but this…He was an object of public ridicule because of me. When Lachlan interrupted us in the kitchen, Rory had been embarrassed. How would he feel about his wife's indiscretions adorning the front page of a newspaper?

My deep breathing had banished the dark splotches in my vision, but my hands still trembled. Waiting until I got home to call Rory would leave me plenty of time to get more wound up about it. Time to suck it up and do what must be done.

I dialed Rory's number.

He answered with a cheerful, "Emery, I was going to call you in a bit."

"Yeah, well, something's happened." I clenched the steering wheel with my free hand. "Trouble on the home front."

"What's happened?" His tone had sharpened, concern a knife's edge in his voice. "Are you all right?"

"Fine, physically." Tears spilled down my cheeks, and my voice came out quavery when I said, "This is all my fault. I'm so sorry, Rory. I wish—God, it's all my fault."

"Emery…" His voice had softened, the tenderness in it almost too much for me to take. "Whatever it is, I'm sure it was not your fault. Tell me, please."

I blubbered the whole awful story, tears streaming down my cheeks in hot little rivers of misery.

"I'm coming home," he said, his voice decisive. "Immediately."

"No, please, I don't want to ruin your vacation from me. There's nothing you can do." My tears had stopped flowing, but I sniffled from the runny nose they'd caused. "I thought you should know, that's all."

I desperately wanted him to come home, to comfort me and to beat the crap out of that sniveling weasel Graham. I didn't want him to come because he felt a responsibility to do it. I wanted him to…Shit, I had no idea what I wanted, because I couldn't control my mixed-up emotions.

"There's nothing you can do," I repeated.

His voice became a dangerous growl. "There bloody well is."

"Rory—"

"I am coming home." Noises followed, as if he were gathering his things and stuffing them into a suitcase. "I'll call when we're in the air."

"Okay." My voice sounded so weak and pathetic I hardly recognized it.

"Try not to worry, love," he said. "I will handle this."

We said goodbye, and I drove home.

That evening, Rory came back from France. I met the car in the drive-way, flinging my body at him as soon as he stepped out of the Mercedes. He clung to me as fiercely as I clung to him.

"I missed you, baby," I said.

He pressed his lips to my neck. "I missed you too."

My heart stuttered like it couldn't believe he'd admitted to missing me. He'd said he loved me during sex, leaving me to wonder if he meant it, but this new confession had no such ambiguity.

"I will deal with Graham in the morning," he said, a flinty edge in his voice.

Maybe Graham was right about my predilection for perversion, because I took pleasure in imagining how my husband would deal with the toad.

When Rory made a promise, he kept it.

Chapter Thirty-Five

W here's Rory?" I asked Mrs. Darroch the second I stepped into the kitchen where she was scrubbing the countertops with a big blue sponge.

She paused in her work to cast me a worried look. "He went into the village to have it out with Graham."

"What?" A whip of icy panic lashed me. "When?"

"He left two hours ago."

She glanced at my stomach. I followed her gaze there and realized I'd been clutching one hand to my belly. The whip of panic had mutated into steel wires knotted around my stomach. They snaked into my chest to cinch around my heart.

Mrs. D enveloped both my cold hands in her warm ones. "It's all right, dearie. Rory willnae do anything rash."

I wished I could've been so sure. Graham had disgraced Rory with that moronic article, and Rory hated feeling like a fool. Every time he talked about his ex-wives, I recognized his shame—misplaced, but still there—and how much he loathed talking about those times. Though Graham had fabricated much of the story, he based it on a foundation of truth. Rory might've thought he wanted a trophy wife and a marriage of convenience, but to have the world know about it…That must've been the worst kind of humiliation.

What would Rory do to Graham?

He tossed cabers around like matchsticks. Would he beat up Graham? I had no idea. Like last night, though, when I imagined the possibility I discovered I liked it.

The gossip-monger might deserve a good skelping, but I couldn't stand by and let Rory get in trouble. Graham—the lying, smarmy, sleazy subterranean insect—would at least try to have Rory arrested. I had no doubts about that. The creep couldn't resist any chance to dishonor my husband.

My worry for Rory, and how this debacle would affect him, outweighed my own shame. To have his wife's nakedness splashed across a tabloid…

"I'm going after Rory."

Mrs. D nodded. "Good luck, lass."

I raced out of the house, set in my mission.

The Jag got me to Loch Fairbairn way faster than the last time I'd come here, in the Mercedes, thanks mostly to my rampant violation of the speed limit. The minutes nevertheless dragged like an eternity before I swerved into a parking space a block from the office of the *Loch Fairbairn World News*. I sprinted down the sidewalk and barreled through the door.

Graham stood behind his desk, that smug look on his leathery face.

Rory loomed over the desk opposite Graham, bent forward just enough to intensify the menace he projected from every inch of his body. Eyes narrowed to slits, nostrils flaring with each blustering breath, he snarled through tightly clenched teeth.

"Last chance," he said, his lip curling.

"I stand by the truth," Graham said, folding his arms over his chest and lifting his chin.

Rory walloped his fist into Graham's jaw.

The gossip-monger's head snapped back. The crack of the blow seemed to echo in the tiny office, and droplets of blood spattered both men.

Graham staggered backward. His eyes went wide, his face went ashen. He pressed a palm to his jaw as he flailed for his chair, grabbed it with one hand, and toppled into it.

My husband reeled his fist back, preparing for another blow.

Graham cringed.

I rushed forward to grasp Rory's arm.

He startled as if he hadn't noticed me before.

"Stop," I said. "Please, Rory. He's not worth it."

I wished I'd slugged Graham but watching my husband do it had been plenty satisfying. Still, one punch would suffice.

"MacTaggart, you've lost your mind," Graham said, but the arrogance had fled his voice. "I should tell the police about this."

"Go on, then," Rory said in his most threatening voice. "I'm a solicitor, ye *bod ceann*. Do ye think I'll stay locked up?"

A wicked little thrill tingled through me, but Graham slouched deeper into his chair.

"I'm the only witness," I said, "and I'll testify you started it."

Graham blinked once, slowly, his gaze on me. "You'd lie?"

"It's as truthful as your article," I said. "And you did instigate this with your made-up story about us."

Rory squinted at Graham. "No one believes your article. Retract it and apologize, or I will file a defamation lawsuit that will divest you of any and all assets you have left after the divorce."

Graham's pallor deepened. "Aye, I'll print a retraction."

Rory opened his mouth to speak.

"And an apology," Graham hastened to add.

His face the picture of grim satisfaction, Rory nodded. "Good. You can start your apologies."

Graham swallowed hard, wriggling in his seat. He studied the mess of papers on his desk and muttered, "I'm sorry for what I've done to you."

Rory glanced at me as if waiting for my response.

I shrugged. "Great, he apologized. Can we go now?"

His brow furrowed, but he said, "If you're satisfied, I am."

Though I had no idea why he cared if I was satisfied with how Graham had apologized to him, I let Rory usher me out of the office with a hand on my back. While the door swung shut behind us, Rory stopped to scan the street.

"How did you get here?" he asked, his voice as emotionless as his face.

"In the Jag."

Rory spotted the vehicle and hustled me down the block to where I'd parked. Without a word, he pulled the driver's door open and waved for me to get inside. I did not move. He waved again. I stared up at his face, baffled by the instant switch from anger to vacancy. It was like his personality had separated from his body.

"Are you okay?" I asked.

"Fine."

No emotion. No inflection. Not even his eyes gave a clue to his state of mind.

"Go home," he said. "I'll follow in the Mercedes."

He pointed over my shoulder, and I tracked the line from his finger to the Mercedes parked a few spaces away from the door to Graham's office. I hadn't noticed the car before, what with a massive SUV squatting in front of it.

"How did Graham know about our contract?" I asked. "How did he find the pictures?"

Rory turned his face away. "I was careless, left papers on my desk on our wedding day. Graham slunk into my office before he hounded you, before the ceremony even began. The papers included the contract and a report from the investigator about Sebastian."

"Not your fault." *No, it's my fault.* "Why did you have the contract out?"

Rory jerked his head toward the Jag's open door. "Go."

I wanted to argue, to pester him until he told me what the hell was going on here, but I sensed he wouldn't respond well to my questioning. Something had flipped his switch from human mode to Rory the Robot.

So, I climbed into the car.

He shut the door and trudged back the way we'd come, toward the Mercedes.

That old thread of panic wound around my heart. I'd been the ultimate source of his humiliation, the reason for Graham's article. Rory had every right to blame me.

We got home in the usual length of time since I obeyed the speed limit. Once we walked into the house, weariness blanketed me. I sagged against the wall in the ground-floor hallway.

"I'm sorry," I said, "about everything that's happened."

My robot husband stayed silent for a moment, then said, "Go to bed."

"Shouldn't we talk? I mean—"

"Go to bed, Emery. It's been a trying day."

Too tired to argue, I trudged up three flights of stairs. Rory accompanied me as far as the first floor but veered off in the direction of his office, leaving me to mount the last two flights alone. In the hallway of the top floor, I hesitated. The bedroom I'd been sharing with Rory lay to my left, but to the right lay the room I'd slept in before I'd forced him to sleep with me.

I shuffled into my old room.

Give him space, let him decompress. Sounded reasonable, didn't it?

Without bothering to undress or remove my shoes, I curled up on the bed on top of the covers. The room was tomb-like—chilly, dark and silent, devoid of life. I lay on my side, knees pulled up, arms hugging them. My body trembled. My teeth chattered.

The door swung open. A wedge of light slashed across me.

Rory's silhouette appeared beside the bed. "What are you doing in here?"

"Trying to sleep."

"Why aren't you in our bedroom?"

I stared numbly at the rug under his feet and hunched my shoulders.

He slipped his arms under my body and lifted me off the bed. "This is not where you sleep."

My husband lugged me down the hall and into the other bedroom where he lay me down on the bed. A pillow cushioned my head. The covers were thrown back in haphazard fashion, so unlike Rory to do. Neither of us spoke as he stripped my clothes and shoes off and pulled the covers up to shield my naked body. Once he'd undressed, he crawled under the covers too, nestling me against him.

"Sleep," he said.

I tried to obey, but sleep eluded me. Long after his breathing grew shallow and slow, signifying slumber, I lay awake with his arm around my shoulders and relived the day in my mind, over and over, an endless loop of pain and dread. One fact kept taunting me, louder than all the rest of my whirling thoughts.

The contract has a morality clause. He can boot you out anytime.

Chapter Thirty-Six

I woke alone in our bed. No sunshine gleamed through the windows, and the dull gray of the sky recast the bedroom in a murky gloom. I had become the princess imprisoned in an ivory tower. Christ, I'd gotten maudlin. A night without much sleep would do that to a girl, particularly when I'd lain awake wondering if my husband loved me or simply tolerated me.

After washing up and dressing, I pelted down the stairs to the first floor and Rory's office. When I pushed the door open, I found the room empty. It was after eight, and Rory wasn't at work. *Bad, very bad.* Nothing could take Rory away from his office in the daytime.

Not quite true. I'd lured him away from work on several occasions. Sex in the kitchen, that was his idea. Sex on his desk, that was all me. On our three-day honeymoon, he hadn't done any kind of work.

Those things had happened pre-scandal. Now, he probably wanted nothing more than to escape me. I couldn't blame him, but I needed to talk to him. To get him to talk to me. To figure out if our marriage could survive this.

Rory's ordered world had been destroyed by a landslide from my past.

I searched the entire house and finally located Rory in the sitting room.

Seated in the chair by the window, he glanced up from contemplating his hands when I entered the room.

"Good morning," I said, loitering near the doorway, swinging my hands because I had no idea what the hell to do with them. "How did you sleep?"

"Not well." His voice was flat, his expression too. "Did you sleep?"

"Uh, not much." I stuffed my hands in the pockets of my fleece pants. "Could we talk?"

His remote gaze lingered on me for a moment before he directed it out the window, at the lowering gray clouds. "Nothing to discuss."

I edged a few steps closer and noticed the papers balanced on his thigh. Not a newspaper or a magazine. White sheets of paper with typed paragraphs on them.

"Rory, come on," I said. "We need to talk about things. A lot of things."

He blew out a frustrated sigh.

I planted my hands on my hips, which made my sweatshirt flap and the zipper go *chink*. "Listen, we need—"

Rory erupted from the chair. The papers flew off his lap to flutter onto the wood floor. He spun toward me only to freeze into Robot Rory, his back straight and stiff as a caber, his face blank even as his gaze drilled into me. The abruptness of his movement made a stark contrast to his indifferent attitude.

"Talk," he said in a crisp monotone. "If you must."

Fine. I'd talk, and he could listen.

I rubbed my arms, suddenly unsure where to start. "I'm sorry, this is all my fault. The scandal Graham cooked up, he invented a lot of it, but the truth gave him a head start. You were humiliated because of me, because of my past, because I was stupid enough to say yes when my boyfriend asked me to pose for nudie photos. And I was stupid enough to believe him when he said the pictures would stay private, for his eyes only."

Rory stared at me.

My eyes were gritty from lack of sleep, but now they burned with the threat of tears. "I never imagined my mistakes would hurt you. I wish I could fix this, but those pictures may never go away." I scratched my arms, but the itch originated inside, not out. "I wish I could erase all of it, so you never have to go through that. You were so upset you punched Graham and made him apologize to you, but that's not enough. How could it be? I brought this shame on you. It's my fault."

He said nothing, moved nothing.

I walked up to him, bent my head back, and met his gaze. "Please know I never wanted you to be hurt because of me. I love you, Rory."

His lips tightened so faintly I wondered if I'd really seen it. "I understand."

"Do you?" I searched his eyes for a sign of…anything. I found nothing. "I love you, but do you even like me? Or do you put up with me for the sex? On Skye, you said you loved me, but we were having sex and I don't know if you meant it. Did you? Do you?"

No response.

I ached to touch him, but I had no idea how he'd react to that. Instead,

I chewed the inside of my lip while I debated how much to say. "Do you want me? Or would you rather get rid of your annoying American wife? I'm in breach of that morality clause in our contract, for sure, what with naked pictures of me—" I choked on the last word but gulped in a breath and kept going. "Naked pictures of me in a newspaper, for everyone to see. The contract says if I shame you in any way, then you can end this, and I won't get your money. Not that I want it, I never did, but I'm not sure if you really believe that, if you want me around anymore or what."

Rory pivoted on his heels and paced to the fireplace, his back to me. He rested a hand on the mantle, but otherwise, his posture remained unchanged.

I regarded him from a distance, unsure whether he was listening to me or tuning me out. Unsure if this was his way of telling me to go away. I'd thought I knew him, but ever since he confronted Graham I'd lost any sense of connection to him.

Except when he'd carried me into our bedroom last night. How could he treat me with such tenderness and then turn away? How could he hold me while he slept and then shut me out like I didn't matter at all?

Tears pooled in my eyes, a stinging tide desperate to flow. I blinked back the tears.

My gaze landed on the papers on the floor.

I crouched to collect them, my hands shaking as I swept the pages into a stack. I glimpsed the contents of the papers, and a coldness flooded through me. Though the pages were out of order, I recognized the text on the top sheet. This was our marriage contract. I flipped through the pages until I found what should've been the last page, where I'd signed it. Beneath my signature, where Rory would've signed, I saw only a blank line.

Stunned, I couldn't move or look away from the page.

"What is this?" I asked, my voice weak and almost pleading.

Rory turned his head in my direction. Something flashed on his face—shock or fear or anger, I couldn't say for sure—but it evaporated in an instant.

"You didn't sign the contract?" I said, the words part question, part accusation. Heat bloomed in my chest, searing its way outward.

Rory took three halting steps toward me, one hand outstretched as if to rip away the papers I held.

I flapped them in the air between us. "How could you not sign it? You said you would. You let me believe you had. The contract was a promise, you said that. A one-sided promise, turns out."

He lowered his hand.

My fingers crooked into the papers, crumpling them. "Was this a big joke? Trick the stupid, silly American into marrying you. Is this your way of getting revenge on the gold digger? Except I don't give a damn about your money. I give a damn about you. The joke's on me, I guess."

His fingers twitched, curled toward his palms, then flexed straight.

A few minutes ago, I might've tried to puzzle out the meaning of the movements or find a sign in his eyes. None of that mattered now.

"You promised to be honest with me," I said. "But you lied. You know how I feel about secrets, and still you betrayed me. I poured everything I have into helping you because I believed you wanted my help, but you were just…What? Playing me? Using me? I don't understand what you hoped to gain from lying about the contract, I really don't."

I thought his shoulders bunched, though the movement was so slight I couldn't be sure. Tears flowed down my face, my cheeks burned with what must've been a crimson flush, and I couldn't seem to take a whole breath.

Words kept tumbling out of me. "You don't love me, do you? I pushed you to do things you never wanted. I swore I didn't mean to change you, actually believed it too. But that's what I did, isn't it? I tried to turn you into something you're not. Maybe I deserved to be lied to and treated like a trophy wife."

Did I believe that? I had no clue anymore. The anger emanated from pain, and the pain had stemmed from Rory's betrayal. Was I overreacting? I couldn't think anymore. Reason had fled the scene, leaving me with the carnage. If only he would speak, to explain, to tell me I was wrong.

I mopped at my eyes with the sleeve of my sweatshirt. "I never cared about the stupid contract, but you should've told me you didn't want to sign it. We could've talked about it and…God, I don't know. You should've told me why you didn't want to sign. Tell me now, please, you owe me that much."

His amber eyes told me nothing, and I held out little hope he'd answer me. He'd shut down and shut me out.

"At least tell me one thing," I said, uncaring whether I sounded pathetic and needy. "What was Skye about? The things you told me there. We got closer, a hell of a lot closer, and I don't think that was all in my head. It meant something, didn't it?"

Silence, except for the ticking of the grandfather clock.

His unblinking gaze was riveted to me.

Did I imagine the pain in those eyes? How could I know anything? I'd trusted him, and he lied.

I covered my eyes with the heels of my hands, my breaths hiccupping. When I let my hands fall away, I shook my head slowly. "You don't trust me. Nothing I say will change that. I spent so long trying to help you, to give you what you need, that I stopped thinking about what I need."

His lips compressed.

"Say something," I demanded. When he didn't, I shook my head again as tears streamed down my cheeks. "I'm exhausted. Fighting to get you to let me in, even a little bit, it's like trying to drill through a mountain with a plastic spoon. I can't do this anymore, I can't."

His fingers twitched.

I smacked my hands on his chest. "Say something, dammit, I'm begging you. Talk to me."

Nothing.

My lips quivered, my hands trembled, my eyes blurred with tears. "I can't do this anymore."

At last, he spoke. "You're leaving."

No hint of emotion in his voice. The only clue came from his fingers bent into his palms, but I had no energy left to decipher the gesture.

"I don't want to leave," I said, "but we can't go on like this. I need time to think. Time away from you."

Saying it made my gut wrench and my throat burn, but I had no choice. Maybe I'd turned into a desperate idiot, but I prayed my leaving would force him to reconsider his actions. And then, if he felt anything for me at all, maybe he'd explain why he'd never signed the contract.

This was about so much more than the contract, though. So much more.

I was taking the biggest risk of my life. Either he'd wake up and be the man I'd believed he was, or he'd prove me wrong and I'd lose everything.

Please, God, let me be right about him.

Rory took one step backward. "Leave, then."

I wrapped my arms around myself, overcome by a sadness so intense it gripped my soul. "If that's all you have to say…You've left me no choice, Rory. I'm sorry."

My feet felt heavy as I trudged toward the doorway.

"Where will you go?" he asked.

"I don't know. A hotel, I guess."

Several long seconds of silence followed. At last, I gave up and slogged up to the third floor and our bedroom. The further I traveled from the sitting room and Rory, the more the heaviness in my feet spread up my body. In the bedroom, I took out my suitcase and began to stuff clothes into it with all the vigor of a zombie. I didn't hear Rory approaching until he spoke from the doorway.

"I called Lachlan," he said. "He and Erica have offered to let you stay with them."

I dropped a half-folded shirt into the suitcase. "Thank you."

My voice sounded as dead as his.

"Tavish will drive you," he said.

"Don't bother him. I can drive myself, unless you're taking back my wedding present."

A muscle in his jaw pulsed. "Tavish will drive you."

I gave up arguing.

Ten minutes later, I watched in the side mirror of the Mercedes as the figure of Rory dwindled and vanished. Neither Tavish nor I spoke during the drive to the hills outside Ballachulish, where Lachlan and Erica lived on their farm. The clouds seemed to bear down on me as I followed Tavish into the farmhouse. He'd insisted on carrying my bag. If I hadn't been exhausted in every way, I would've kissed him on the cheek for his sweetness.

After depositing my bag on the wood floor of the entryway, Tavish gave me a quick, awkward hug and left.

Erica hugged me next, her face revealing a sympathy that made tears prick at my eyes anew.

Lachlan hugged me too, surprising me so much I could do nothing except gape at him.

My hosts led me into the living room where Nicholas played with a squeaky elephant toy. The toddler squealed when he spotted me. "Em-ree!"

I knelt beside him, tousling his chestnut hair. The hair matched his mother's, but the ice blue of his eyes echoed his father's.

Lachlan cleared his throat. "I'll give Rory a ring to let him know you're here safe."

"He was so worried," Erica said. "He made Tavish bring you because you're too upset to drive. He was afraid you'd wind up at the bottom of Loch Leven."

I froze in the middle of handing Nicholas a red plastic ring that fit onto a little treelike contraption. "Rory told you that?"

"Aye," Lachlan said. "He made me promise to let him know the minute you arrived. 'The very minute' were his exact words. He repeated it twice."

Lachlan hustled off to call Rory, and I threw myself into playing with a toddler to avoid pondering why Rory cared so much about my safety. He hadn't cared enough to stop me from walking out the door.

He does care, that's why, declared an irritating little voice in my head.

After a while, Erica insisted I "veg out" in front of the TV because, as she'd diagnosed me, I suffered from depression brought on by a fight with my husband. The argument itself had originated with the trauma of a scandal instigated by "that sleazebag," aka Graham Oliver.

Rory and I hadn't fought. Things might've turned out differently if we had. He'd refused to acknowledge anything I said until I told him I needed time away.

That night, I tossed and turned in a strange bed, haunted by the memory of Rory's blank face and his frigid tone of voice. Yet when I finally sank into a deep enough slumber to dream, I relived the night on Skye when he'd made love to me with the tenderness and passion of a man who cherished me more than anything.

Chapter Thirty-Seven

A baby monitor lay in the middle of the kitchen table between me and my hosts. I slumped in my chair, one arm slack on the tabletop, while Erica sat straight in her chair across from me. To her right, Lachlan lounged in another chair. He'd turned it toward his wife and draped one arm on the table, his fingers tapping an erratic beat.

Three bowls had been pushed to the side or toward the center of the table, the spoons balanced inside them. Erica and Lachlan had polished off their oatmeal, but I'd done little more than pick at it. Nausea plagued me this morning, making breakfast less than appealing.

A baby noise, something like a sigh, emanated from the monitor.

Lachlan tensed and asked Erica, "Should I check on him?"

"Nicky's fine. Sleeping."

Her husband relaxed back into his chair.

Though I aimed my gaze at the oatmeal bowl, my thoughts revolved around one thing—Rory. I'd thought of nothing else since the moment I walked out of the house yesterday. One day? Was that all it had been? Felt like weeks, months, longer. Rory hadn't called, texted, sent a letter, or stopped by. Okay, I could admit it. I'd suffered the silly romantic fantasy he'd rush after me, catch me before I got in the car with Tavish, and beg me to stay.

Nope.

When that didn't happen, I'd fantasized about him driving up to this farmhouse to sweep me into his arms, apologize with sweet words and sweeter kisses, and whisk me home.

Nope.

My last-ditch fantasy involved me waking up this morning to find him sleeping on the front steps, waiting for me to come outside and find him there, pitiful in his regret and profuse with his apologies. He would, naturally, beg me to come back to him.

Nope.

Erica leaned across the table to clasp my hand in both of hers. "He'll come to his senses. Rory's not an idiot."

"No," I said with a rueful little smile, "but he is stubborn as hell and terrified of getting hurt again."

Erica's empathetic expression made my stomach hurt. "Give him time. Aidan waited two weeks for Calli to change her mind, and I made Lachlan wait two months." She slung her husband a playfully chastising glance. "He deserved it, though. Didn't you, honey?"

Lachlan shook his head, his lips ticking up. "I fell to my knees and begged your forgiveness, but you still made me wait."

"A few days." Erica sat back and patted her husband's knee. "It all worked out in the end, just like it will for Emery and Rory."

Though I heard her words, my brain—my heart, actually—had gotten hung up on what Lachlan said. He'd fallen to his knees and begged Erica. My dreams of Rory coming to sweep me off my feet involved an identical act of supplication, but I doubted he'd ever do that. Rory was stubborn and proud and entrenched in the past so deeply I didn't know if he could excavate his way out.

Lachlan made a dismissive noise. "I've known Rory all his life, and I've never seen him so full of angst over a woman before."

Angst. The very word made nausea roil in my gut. I didn't think me making him angst-ridden was a good thing.

Erica flashed her husband an irritated look. "She's depressed, Lachlan. We're trying to cheer her up, not make her feel worse."

"I didnae—"

"You just told Emery she's the reason Rory's a mess."

Lachlan started to speak but stopped. After a couple seconds, he said, "I meant he's never been like this before because he's never cared so much about keeping a wife, and he has no bloody idea how to do it." Lachlan looked straight at me. "He loves you. He'll come soon, you'll see. Rory doesn't waste time."

That was true. Rory had steamrolled the legal systems of two countries to get us married and get me a visa. He'd steamrolled me into moving to Scotland. Hell, the night we met he'd convinced me to sleep with him in a matter of minutes.

He didn't waste time. So, where the hell was he?

"Rory will come," Lachlan insisted.

"I walked out yesterday. I seriously doubt I'm going to look out—" I slashed a hand toward the window above the kitchen sink that overlooked the driveway and swung my gaze in the same direction. "— that window and see…" My voice trailed off as I spotted a car rolling to a stop outside. "Rory's Mercedes in the driveway. Him getting out of the car. Marching up to the door and—"

A determined fist rapped twice on the front door, the sound echoing down the hallway.

Lachlan and Erica exchanged surprised glances.

"It's him," I said, my pulse racing.

Erica flapped a hand at me. "Go, go. Talk to him."

Adrenaline powered my limbs as I flew out of my chair so fast it toppled over backward. I hurtled out into the hall and to the door, but I halted with my hand on the knob.

"We'll be in here," Erica called from the kitchen, "in case you need Lachlan to whup his brother's behind."

"Aye," Lachlan said.

I took a deep breath and let it out. Then I opened the door.

Rory's body consumed the doorway. He wore that unreadable expression. "Please come home. I love you."

My mouth dropped open, but I couldn't summon words. His tone of voice, like his expression, gave nothing away. Oh how I'd dreamed of him speaking those words. The reality kind of, uh, fell flat.

Not entirely flat. My tummy fluttered a touch, but no butterflies took flight. What happened next counted more than his matter-of-fact declaration.

"Told ye," Lachlan shouted from the kitchen. "He doesn't waste time."

"Quiet," Erica chastised.

I shooed Rory away with my hands. "Outside. Please."

He shuffled backward, his brows knitting together, and kept backing up until I'd shut the door and situated us away from it.

"That's it?" I said.

"I thought you'd want to hear—you said—" He squinted his whole face and rubbed the bridge of his nose. When he met my gaze again, his eyes evinced a desperation I'd never seen before. "You wanted me to say it. I thought this would…fix things."

Oh jeez. Lachlan was right. Rory had no clue how to do this. Love had no rules he could follow, which left him floundering.

"If you'd said that a few days ago," I told him, "it would've fixed everything. But after yesterday…I don't know how we make this right. I'm sorry, I just don't know."

He rubbed the back of his neck. "Do you want to?"

"Want to what?"

"Do you want to work this out?" He pinned me with the bleakest stare I'd ever witnessed, on him or anyone. "Do you want me?"

A pang in my chest. A lump in my throat. I fought the impulse to throw my arms around him and kiss him until he stopped looking at me that way.

"Rory." I clamped my hands under my arms. "I love you. I want to be with you. But saying you love me doesn't resolve any of the problems I tried to talk to you about so many times. It doesn't erase what happened between us yesterday. You hurt me more than ever."

He raised his hands as if to touch me but let them fall. His mouth open, he gave a weak shake of his head. "I thought you'd be happy."

"That you're here? That you love me? It's all well and good but—" I winced at a pain that twisted around my navel. Too much stress, for sure. "You just stood there. Robot Rory staring at me like I was invisible."

"How could I stare if you're invisible?"

"Don't be obtuse on purpose. You know what I mean."

He hung his head. "Aye."

Scrubbing my cheeks with my palms, I tried to think in spite of the nausea and the weird pain in my gut. I wasn't cut out for drama like this. "I told you everything—*everything*—I was feeling. I told you how much I love you. And you said nothing. I cried, and I said I had to leave. You said nothing. While I walked out the door, you stood there watching like it didn't matter to you at all."

He lifted his head, and I knew he was about to object.

I held up a hand. "Even then, I knew you cared if I left. I'm not saying you don't love me. I'm saying you still don't understand how much it hurt me that you had no comment on the most emotional monologue I've ever delivered to anyone."

Exhaustion buried me under its weight. I stumbled to a wrought-iron bench and slumped onto it.

Rory knelt before me, eyes full of pain and compassion. "Emery, I wish I knew how to make things right, but this time, I have no bloody idea how. Please help me."

"I'm too tired, Rory."

"You said that yesterday. Taking care of me has drained you."

"Yeah." I shut my eyes for a moment. "I'm sorry."

"I'm the one who needs to apologize. Again and again, for all eternity if that will help." He tentatively laid a hand on my knee. "I miss you, Emery. I can't sleep without you."

"Did you not sleep when you were in France?"

"Not well, but that was different. I knew I'd be coming home to you. Now…" He drew in a breath, his lip quivering. "I no longer have the luxury of assuming you'll be there when I wake up in the morning."

I'd missed him so much last night, it felt like years had elapsed instead of a single day.

Rory rubbed his jaw. "Not signing the contract was a mistake because I broke a promise to you. But I don't regret not signing it, which I suppose is a contradiction. Can't help that. I never wanted to break a promise to you, but I couldn't bring myself to sign the contract. You told me you didn't care about the money, you didn't marry me for it, and I believed you."

"But?"

He inched his hand closer to mine, a finger's width away. "Part of me couldn't accept that anyone, especially a woman as vibrant and passionate as you, could want me without the enticement of money. Isobel cared for money and status more than love. I tried to become what she needed, tried until it had eaten up a part of me I may never get back, but it wasn't enough."

Unable to move, unwilling to move, I simply stared at him. Never before had he bared his soul to me like this, not even that day on Skye.

His fingers twitched as if he longed to touch me but feared I'd reject it.

I walked my fingers toward his until the tips of mine slipped between them.

The relief on his face made tears sting my eyes.

"You are not Isobel," he said. "I know this. You never needed anything from me but love, and I couldn't believe I deserved that. Mentioning the contract every time we grew closer…You were right. I used it as a wedge. I also used it as a sort of insurance policy, to keep you around even after you got tired of me. Not signing the damn thing, that was a sign I should've recognized sooner if I weren't such an eejit. I couldn't do it because I didn't want you to stay for money. I wanted you to stay for me."

"But I didn't know you never signed the contract." I shifted in place, unable to find a comfortable position on the bench. "Besides, it was the other stuff that mattered more. You don't trust me."

"I do."

"Really? You thought you had to pay me to stay. You wouldn't explain why you got drunk on our wedding night, or a ton of other things."

He nodded toward the empty space on the bench next to me. "May I sit beside you?"

"Do what you want."

He settled onto the bench, keeping a discreet distance between us. "I've been a bastard, I know. You have no reason at all to come back to me, but you are wrong. I trust you. The things I said over the past few weeks, they came from my fears and had nothing to do with you."

"Nothing? Come on, Rory."

"Well, they had something to do with you." He angled toward me, laying an arm atop the bench behind me. "The more time I spent with you, the harder it was to deny the truth. I fell in love with you, Emery. My behavior at the wedding, that was the day I realized how much you mean to me. When I saw you coming down the aisle toward me, in that fairytale dress with your hair gleaming in the sun like a halo. Your smile was so sweet and full of…love. And I knew I love you, more than I've loved anyone in my life."

I remembered his shell-shocked expression and the way he'd acted uncertain, confused, afraid.

"Getting buckled is a mistake I'll regret forever," he said, his voice soft and rife with emotion. "You deserved a perfect wedding, particularly after the way I bulldozed you into marrying me in front of a magistrate. Realizing I love you, it turned me into a bampot of the worst sort. I knew if you left me, and I was certain you would, I would never feel this way again."

He'd been certain I'd leave him? The statement sent my thoughts rewinding, replaying an assortment of conversations we'd had and the little things he'd said. When I complained about separate bedrooms, he'd told me, "Once you've lived with me for a while, you'll be glad of the privacy." After I inadvertently called him baby and suggested it meant I liked him, he'd replied, "You'll change your mind about that soon enough." Then there was his behavior, requiring separate bedrooms, locking himself away in his office sixteen hours a day to avoid spending time with me, not wanting to have sex until the wedding. He'd chalked that up to respect for our mothers, but I'd suspected at the time he wanted to keep his distance as a prophylactic against developing feelings for me.

So what had I done? Pushed him to be with me.

No wonder he'd gone a little crazy.

I wrapped my arms over my belly, feeling sick from a physical nausea and the sudden realization of my own role in this debacle. "This is partly my fault, I'm sorry."

"How on earth is it your fault?"

"You told me, in your own way, you weren't ready for a real relationship. I agreed to a marriage of convenience, then I demanded you care about me." I sank back against the bench, and his arm supported my shoulders. "I pushed you at every turn, tried to make you change. That's what Isobel did to you. I convinced myself I was your therapist." I snorted at my own arrogance. "And that you needed my help—wanted it, even. I drove you to drink. That's my doing."

"Emery…" He inched closer, his fingers grazing my shoulder. "Nothing is your fault. You put up with me no matter what I did, forgave me every time I acted like a bastard. Your love changed me, not because you forced me to do anything, but because I couldn't help loving you. I need you with me, and I have evolved."

"Just like that? It's been a day, Rory." With him so close, and his arm behind me, I longed to crawl into his arms and never leave. But had we really resolved anything? "Nobody changes overnight. You want me to come home, but that doesn't mean anything will be different if I do."

"I didn't change overnight." He brushed a lock of hair from my face. "You showed me how to love again. It took weeks. It took too much effort from you and not enough cooperation from me, but it happened. Last night without you, not knowing if you'll ever come home, I finally gave up being afraid of this. I will do anything for you. Please believe me, *m'eudail*."

Pain twisted around my navel again, and my gorge rose into my throat. I gulped it down, but the first beads of a cold sweat chilled my skin.

"You're unwell," Rory said.

He reached out to touch my forehead, but I batted his hand away.

"I've got the flu," I said. "Probably caught it from the chickens."

"Chickens?"

"You know, bird flu." I groaned. "Never mind, dumb joke."

He scrutinized me, lips tight, eyes searching. "Let me take you to a doctor."

"No, I'm fine, really." I heaved my body off the bench, and though I turned toward him, I couldn't meet his concerned gaze. "I need a nap, that's all. And you need to do more thinking before you announce you've overcome your fears. Please, go home. I'll call you tomorrow."

"I don't need more time, Emery. I need you." He unfurled his body from the bench, still inspecting me with a worried furrow in his forehead. "But I'm more concerned with your health today. You need a doctor."

"I need sleep." And a toilet or a bucket, because I felt on the verge of vomiting all over his nice leather shoes. "We'll talk more tomorrow, okay?"

Without waiting for his answer, I hustled into the house with a shuffling gait, my feet heavy, and tripped over the threshold. Though I glimpsed Rory galloping after me, I slammed the door shut. *Can't deal with this now, can't think about it.* I staggered forward a few steps.

A sharp pain sliced into me on the lower right side, piercing straight through my body. I gasped, doubled over, and emptied my stomach on the pretty wood floor.

"Emery!"

Footsteps punctuated Erica's exclamation. Her arms came around me.

"Sorry," I mumbled. "I ruined your floor."

"What? Oh for heaven's sake, I don't care about the floor." She laid her palm on my forehead. "Sweetie, you're burning up."

"Might wanna find a bucket."

Erica hugged me to her side. "Lachlan! Hurry, something's wrong with Emery."

Her husband dashed out of the kitchen. "Ambulance?"

"Get Rory," Erica said. "He can get her to the hospital faster."

Lachlan stomped to the door, flung it open, and hollered, "Rory! Get in here, man, your wife needs a doctor. *Now.*"

Footsteps pounding. Voices murmuring. Erica let go of me as a pair of larger, stronger arms hoisted me off my feet. I found myself in Rory's arms, clutched to his chest.

He cursed in Gaelic. "I'm taking you to the hospital."

I nodded.

My husband barreled toward the Mercedes.

Lachlan hastened to open the back door, and Rory laid me tenderly on the backseat. He swept hair from my face and kissed my forehead.

"Donnae worry, love," he whispered. "I'm taking care of you."

I lunged my head forward and threw up on the floor.

Chapter Thirty-Eight

I surfaced from unconsciousness with my eyes closed, groggy and confused, lying on a bed. The event that had brought me here replayed in my mind. The drive to the hospital. Rory carrying me into the emergency room. Nurses, doctors, questions. After a CT scan, they'd delivered the diagnosis. Appendicitis, they'd said. Need surgery, they'd said. Rory stayed by my side until they wheeled me off to the operating room.

Throughout the whole ordeal, he'd stayed calm and alert, asking questions I couldn't think of and ensuring the medical people had all the information they needed. He'd sat by my bed while we waited, combing his fingers through my hair, a reassuring smile on his lips.

Something creaked beside me.

I pried my lids apart and rolled my head in the direction of the sound.

Rory shifted in his uncomfortable chair again, eliciting another creak from it. His attention was focused on the badly creased home decor magazine he held.

"Hey," I said.

With a start, he dropped the magazine. "Emery, you're awake. How are you feeling?"

"Like I got sliced and diced." I managed a faint smile for him. "Thank you for coming with me."

"Of course I came." He scooted his chair closer to fold his hands around mine, the one with an IV stuck in its backside, careful not to put pressure on the needle. "I haven't taken care of you, but that changes now."

I shifted on the bed, feeling stiff and like I'd been cut open in several places. The incisions were small, the surgeon had told us before I went in.

"Easy," Rory said in that calm voice. "You've only just woken. Are you in pain?"

"Some."

He released my hand to scurry outside, returning a moment later to reclaim his place at my side. "A nurse will bring medicine for you."

"Thanks."

"Stop thanking me. I have more than enough to make up to you to fill several lifetimes." He focused on my hand, once again ensconced in his. "Will you let me look after you while you recover? I have no expectations of what will happen once you're well. But I'd like to care for you."

"Rory, about what I said earlier. I was sick, and I didn't mean—"

"Hush." He brushed the backs of his fingers over my cheek. "You're not to make major decisions for at least a week, two would be better. Anesthesia impairs your thinking."

"But I know what I—"

One finger on my lips, he silenced me. "No arguments this time. Wait two weeks. Then we can discuss things."

I knew better than to argue with the resolute solicitor. He wouldn't believe anything I said if I told him now, anyway. Maybe waiting a couple weeks was the right move.

He pressed a kiss to my forehead. "The surgeon says they'll release you later this evening. I can take you to Erica and Lachlan's if you'd feel more comfortable there."

"Oh Rory." I raised my unencumbered hand to his cheek. "I want to go home. With you."

A smile struggled to take hold, and his lips twitched and quivered with the effort until, at last, he mustered a vulnerable smile. "No more secrets, Em. I promise."

I nodded.

He held his cheek to mine.

No anesthesia made me want to go home and be with my husband. An epiphany accompanied by vomiting seemed strange, but I'd known the moment he scooped me up and rushed me to the car that I belonged with him, and that he had evolved. If he needed to prove it to himself, I could wait. In two weeks, I'd tell him.

I was staying, for good.

Two weeks sounded like a long time, in the context of our quickie marriage, but the days seemed to fly by too fast. I wanted to memorize every second of these days, because for the first time since I'd met him Rory was not obsessed with work. I woke every morning to find him beside me in bed, still asleep or lying there waiting for me to wake up. Every morning he did the same thing when he noticed I'd awakened.

He smiled, leaned in to kiss me sweetly, and said, "Good morning, *mo gaoloch*."

Sometimes he'd substitute the old favorite *m'eudail* for *mo gaoloch*. I had no idea what those words meant, and I didn't want to ask and risk spoiling the mood, though from his tone of voice and the softness in his eyes I knew they were endearments.

The first morning post-surgery, he whipped up a sumptuous breakfast for me. Blueberry pancakes with loads of butter and maple syrup, both bacon and sausage, and scrambled eggs to boot. I'd slept downstairs because there was no way I'd make it up three flights to our bedroom. Rory had offered to carry me, but I opted for sleeping in the guest wing instead. We opted for it. He refused to go upstairs until I could walk up with him under my own power.

When he'd laid that breakfast out for me on the dining room table, I'd grinned and laughed. "Wow, you sure know how to treat a girl. Not sure I could eat this much in three days, but I'll give it a shot."

"You don't have to eat all of it." He scratched his jaw, eying the spread with a sheepish expression. "I may have overdone things."

He kept overdoing a lot of things, in a good way.

Like the afternoon when we'd lounged in the sitting room. He'd dragged the sofa over to the windows so I could enjoy the view while taking it easy, with a fleece throw over my legs—Rory insisted I must stay warm—and a mug of hot cocoa clasped between my hands.

After a period of quiet relaxation, Rory left his chair to perch on the sofa beside my hip. "I love you, Emery. Do you believe me?"

"Yes, I believe you." With one cocoa-warmed hand, I stroked his cheek. "I love you too."

He covered my hand with his, fastening it to his cheek, and turned his face into my palm to kiss it. "About Graham…I didn't assault him for my sake. His ridiculous article didn't humiliate me, it humiliated you, and I could not stand for that. Before you walked into his office, I'd threatened him with everything I could think of to make him issue an apology—to you."

"That apology was aimed at me?"

"It was." Rory rubbed his thumb over the back of my hand. "Donnae care what the scunner says about me. But when he slandered you, I had to make it right. Would've skelped him bloody, if necessary. Graham has moved to Liverpool to be with his mother. As for Sebastian, he checked himself into a psychiatric clinic. The investigator determined Sebastian doesn't have the pictures of you anymore, and Graham admitted he found only the one image, on a website that archives other sites. The owners of that site complied with my demand they delete the image immediately. It's over, Emery."

Over? I had no idea how to process that fact.

"Thank you doesn't seem like enough, Rory. No one's ever fought for me before." I leaned forward to touch my lips to his. "You are my knight in a kilt."

"I've made too many mistakes to earn that designation." He twined our fingers, absorbed with the movements. "You were right. All those rules, I invented them as a means of keeping you at a distance. Didn't work. I think about you even when you're miles away."

"That a bad thing?"

"No." He aimed his beautiful smile at me. "It's wonderful."

On the second day, when I'd gotten sick of wandering the halls for exercise, I tried to walk outside. Rory had lunged between me and the vestibule door.

"Where are you going?" he demanded.

"For a walk."

"You can walk indoors. It's too soon to leave the house."

Stifling a laugh—really, his overprotectiveness was adorable—I'd tamped my humor down to a closed-mouth smile. "I can handle strolling around the front lawn. The doctor said I should get up and moving right away."

"He didn't say traipse into the wilds where you might break your stitches."

"It's staples, not stitches."

"That's worse. The staples might pop loose."

I took his face in my hands and pressed my lips to his. "Rory, you adorably silly man, I will be fine. Come with me. It'll make you feel better, and I'd love the company."

From then on, he'd taken me for a walk every day. I amused him with all sorts of descriptive phrases in the vein of "cute" and "adorable," some that made him roll his eyes and others that made his smile go steamy. On the fourth day of pampering, I'd finally asked him the question that kept niggling at me. I was reclining on the sofa in the sitting room while he kicked back in his big chair by the windows, ankles crossed, gaze on the vista beyond the glass.

"I think you've worked a total of three hours in the past four days," I said. "What happened to all that vital, important work that used to keep you busy sixteen hours a day?"

First, his lips puckered. Then, they twitched upward. Finally, a broad smile lit up his face. "Fuck work."

Though I couldn't resist smiling back at him, I had to push for more info. "I appreciate the sentiment, but that's not really an answer."

"You were right," he said. "I hid in my office to avoid spending time with you, to avoid loving you. It didn't work, and I'm done with that. I'll help people who need it, the ones who can't afford a solicitor, but otherwise, I'm retired."

Pretty sure my jaw dropped to the floor when he said that.

"Retired at almost-forty?" I said. "Are you sure you're ready to join the ranks of the idle rich?"

"I have no intention of being idle." He lifted his head to look squarely at me. "We can do whatever you want. Anything. Say it, and I'll make it happen."

"Anything?"

"Yes." He raised his eyebrows. "You wanted a new career, a new mission in life. I'll support you in whatever way you need."

"Well, I was thinking—"

He raised a hand. "Not yet. No decisions for two weeks."

I'd learned I couldn't argue with Decisive Rory, particularly when he was also in Protective Rory mode.

The next day, the MacTaggart clan descended on the castle. They had called to ask permission to visit me first, and Rory had asked me if I was ready for a gathering of well-meaning Scots and the American Wives Club. I couldn't say no to these people. They'd welcomed me into their family without reservation and made me feel like I belonged here. Besides, convalescing got really boring. The MacTaggarts didn't stay too long, a consideration I appreciated.

His family had assured me they didn't give a hoot about my arrangement with Rory, or our marriage of convenience. They'd realized we loved each other before Rory and I had. His reluctance to commit to a normal relationship hadn't shocked his family one bit. My family hadn't minded our unusual courtship either. After meeting Rory, they'd trusted him to take care of me.

Every day with Rory brought new revelations, new evidence of his change. He watched superhero movies with me, enduring the experience with aplomb, but he got to like it when I started comparing him to the muscle men in the movies. I'd squeeze his bicep and say, "Mm, yours are much firmer and sexier." Or I'd slide my hand along his inner thigh and say, "Your legs are so much more toned and powerful, perfect for driving a woman half crazy in bed."

He volunteered to watch every movie a second time.

The two-week mark arrived on his birthday, though I doubted he realized I knew it was his birthday. That evening, we loafed on the sitting-room sofa, me in the corner with my legs bent under me and him beside me with an arm on the sofa's back and his legs outstretched, his feet on the coffee table.

I rubbed my cheek against his arm. "I have a surprise for you."

He slanted sideways to fold his arm around me, his face a hair's breadth from mine. "What sort of surprise?"

"One sec." Without dislodging his arm, I sneaked a hand behind me to pull out the object I'd hidden between the cushion and the sofa's arm. My body had concealed the part of the object that protruded. I offered the gift-wrapped package to him. "Happy birthday, Rory baby."

He glanced at the package and back to me. He blinked slowly as if he couldn't comprehend what I'd said. "You haven't called me that since before—since everyone found out about our arrangement."

I tipped my head to the side. "Haven't I?"

"No." His brows lowered. "Is it a good sign?"

"Guess so." I thrust the gift at him. "Open it."

He accepted the package, tapping his fingers on it. "How did you know it's my birthday?"

"Oh please. I've got five sisters-in-law and two brothers-in-law, not to mention parents-in-law. Did you honestly think I couldn't find out when your birthday is?"

"I should never doubt your skills in uncovering my secrets."

"Yep, you should know better by now."

He tore off the wrapping paper with a single swipe of his big hand. The discarded paper crinkled. The gift—a rectangular book with a smooth, hard cover—glistened in the low light.

"What is this?" he asked, turning the book over in his hand.

"Flip it open and you'll see."

He flipped it open. A smirk tightened his lips as he eyed me sideways. "Interesting title."

I shimmied closer and pointed at the words on the page as I recited them. "The evolution of Emery and Rory baby, a pictorial history."

"Yes, I can read." He held me snug against his body. "Do I want to know what pictures you've got in here?"

"Be brave. Flip through it."

He ran his fingers over the writing on the title page. "Did you write this by hand?"

"Yep. And I had every picture printed out, so I could stick it to the page with my own little fingers. I handwrote the captions too."

"Captions?" He turned to the first page of photos and smiled when he read the line at the top. "Once upon a time, there was an uptight but very hot Scotsman who lived alone in his castle. Until, that is, he met a princess geek…"

He touched the first photo, the selfie I'd taken in Pat O'Brien's.

"That's me," I said, "right before you walked up and propositioned me. I left that part out of the caption."

"I see that." He moved his finger to the words beneath the photo. "Emery, thirty seconds before she met her solicitous solicitor."

My cheek on his shoulder, I asked, "Why did you pick me that night? I've always wondered. You could've had your choice of hot babes, professional and unprofessional ones. Why pick the girl in faded jeans and a goofy T-shirt who hadn't showered or brushed her teeth?"

He hooked a finger under my chin, tilting my head up to gaze into my eyes. "I saw you take this picture."

"I didn't see you."

"You wouldn't have. I was in the shadows near the doorway." He rubbed his thumb across my lower lip. "I saw you and then I saw nothing else. The way you smiled when you posed for your self-portrait, the way your hair shimmered in the light, you were the most radiant woman I'd ever laid eyes on. I had to have you."

I licked at the pad of his thumb. "Good answer."

"The truth." He lowered his hand. "I saw you rooting about in your bra as well. Hunting for cash, but I didn't know that. I thought you were a bit barmy, in the most adorable way, and I was enchanted."

"That answer's even better." I stuck my finger in his side. "Even if you did call me barmy."

"I love your unconventional nature." He returned his gaze to the photo of me. "When I watched you fiddling with your bra, I had no idea you were hiding the crown jewels in there."

"A hundred bucks isn't a treasure trove."

He lighted a finger on my breastbone, revealed by the low neckline of my blouse, and dragged the tip down into the valley between my breasts. "I wasn't talking about your money."

My breath hitched when his fingertip slipped under my breast. "And Aidan wonders why women like you. It's no mystery to me."

We browsed the album together, laughing over the photo of Rory eating pancakes with surgical precision, reading the captions that summarized our weeks together, and finally snuggling closer when we got to the wedding photos.

Rory tapped the picture of him at the altar with that dazed look on his face. "Who took this? Not you, unless you hid a camera in your bosom."

"Hadley took it. She said we needed to document how shocked you were by my effervescent beauty."

"You are effervescent, and beautiful. But I was stunned by how deeply I love you."

"Are you still stunned?"

"Every day." He whisked his lips across mine. "By your beauty, your intelligence, your never-ending positivity, your passion, everything about you."

"I adore you, Rory MacTaggart."

"And I worship you, Emery MacTaggart." He picked up the book and aimed it at me. "The last photo isn't of us. It's the house on Skye."

"Because that's where I told you I love you, and it's where you shared your feelings with me for the first time."

He shut the book and set it on the table. "I shouldn't have said it during sex. I love you, and I should've told you the day I realized it. I can't blame you for wanting to leave me."

"I told you I needed time to think."

"Time away from me." He bowed his head. "I used to believe I gave up on Isobel too soon, that I should've fought for her. Now I know I should've done the opposite and ended our marriage long before she left." He sagged against the sofa. "My worst regret is that I let you walk away without saying a word. I wanted to fall to my knees and beg you to stay. Instead, I let you go without a fight. I will never repeat that mistake. If you want to leave me now, I'll run after you. I'll make a bloody fool of myself in any way necessary if it will keep you from going."

"I'm not going anywhere."

"You left me once, and I deserved it."

"Oh Rory, you've got it all wrong." I climbed onto his lap, straddling him with my hands on his shoulders. "I asked for time, not a divorce. I needed to think, but I never had any intention of leaving you."

He rested his hands on my hips. "You came back because of your illness."

"Wrong again." I glided my hands up his neck to cradle his nape. "I wanted to tell you then, but you insisted I shouldn't make decisions for two weeks. Well, it's been two weeks and I can tell you. I came home because I love you and I need you and I want to live with you for the rest of my life. I came home because this *is* my home. Anywhere you are is where I belong."

His fingers tightened on my hips. "You mean it?"

"With all my heart." I spread my legs wider to sit lower on his lap. "I'm never walking out that door again unless it's with you."

"You weren't sure I'd changed."

"I was sure. You weren't." I cupped his face in my hands. "Do you believe it now?"

"Aye. I believe in you, and I believe in us."

With my hands holding his face, I leaned in until our lips skimmed each other. Our breaths mingled. "I've meant to ask you. There was something you said on our wedding night. It was Gaelic, I think. I'm dying to know what it meant. You probably don't remember."

"No, I remember." His smile turned steamy. "Yer so beautiful, ye make my *bagais* ache, *cho cinnteach is a tha bod's an each*. I want my face in your *camas*, my mouth on your *brillean*. The translation is you're so beautiful, you make my balls ache, as sure as a horse has a penis. I want my face between your thighs, my mouth on your clitoris."

"I'm on board for all of that." I grazed my tongue across his lips. "You haven't kissed me in weeks, not the way I want you to."

"Didnae want to overtax you."

"I'm fine, baby. Recovered and cleared for all activities." I sucked his bottom lip between my teeth and released it slowly. "And I do mean all activities. But let's start with a real, bone-melting kiss."

He gave me everything I asked for, and more.

The following day, with our relationship on a solid footing, Rory insisted we must visit the village for the sole purpose of having "a ridiculous outing packed with frivolous behavior and even more frivolous spending." He planned on teaching me how to blow pounds sterling on things I didn't need but simply wanted. My head came close to popping off my body when he announced *he* would teach *me* to be extravagant.

We drove into Loch Fairbairn in the Jag, and Rory committed a flagrant if brief violation of the speed laws just to make me smile. Before I could dash into a shop to browse their clothing selections, Rory caught my arm and informed me he had an urgent task to complete at his office. I was to meet him in the village square in fifteen minutes.

So, I shopped for ten minutes and then journeyed to the square. The two overstuffed bags of frivolous stuff I'd bought weighed down my arms. I set them on the stone-paved sidewalk, taking in the beauty of the historic stone buildings. I ambled toward the front windows of a little restaurant, my tummy grumbling at the sight of food. *Hubby, you better show up quick to buy me lunch.*

Movement in the image reflected in the glass drew my attention.

I grinned at my husband's reflection and whirled around. "Rory baby, finally. Your wife needs feeding."

He halted in front of me, his expression oddly determined, his fist closed around a small, square object. "Something to do first."

"What's that?"

Rory lunged backward two steps. He grasped the hem of his untucked T-shirt and stripped it off, pitching it to the stone sidewalk. In only his jeans and sneakers, he flung his arms out and broke into song, belting out a boisterous rendition of "You Make Me Feel So Young."

I burst into giggles and slapped a hand over my mouth. The giggles segued into all-out laughter that made my eyes water and my stomach muscles twinge.

Done with the first verse and chorus, Rory reached for the metal button on his jeans. He started to unhook it.

I rushed forward to stay his hand with my own. Between lingering giggles, I said, "What on earth are you doing?"

"Told ye I'd make a bloody fool of myself for you anytime, anywhere."

"I thought that was a thing you say, not a thing you actually do." I prized his fingers away from the button. "Besides, your nakedness is exclusively for my viewing pleasure."

A small crowd had gathered across the street. People pointed, smiled, shook their heads in amused disbelief. One person called out, "Never thought I'd see the day Rory MacTaggart goes barmy for a woman."

Heedless of the crowd, Rory dropped to one knee and raised the little velvet box he'd concealed in his hand. He flipped it open, revealing a diamond ring. "Will you be my wife, Emery?"

"Uh, I am your wife. Married you twice. How many weddings do you need?"

"Not a wedding." He thrust the box up at me. "You never got a ring or a proper proposal."

My attempt to quash laughter resulted in a snort. "This is proper? You half naked on the street?"

"For you, this is the most proper sort of proposal." He plucked the ring out of its velvet bed and lifted it to my left hand. "Will you be my wife, my Emery baby?"

"Yes." I grinned, my whole being suffused with joy. "Forever."

He slipped the ring on my finger, in front of the gold wedding band, and kissed my knuckles.

Then he surged to his feet and hollered, "I love my wife!"

"I love my husband!" I shouted.

Rory swept me into his arms, spinning us around and around.

And the crowd cheered.

Epilogue

Two Months Later

On a warm and sunny fall day, I wandered into Rory's office carrying a book and sprawled on the chair in front of his desk with my feet on the desktop. Sunshine beamed through the windows, spilling over my husband and burnishing his beautiful face with golden rays.

Without looking up from his work, he said, "I'll be finished in ten minutes, then we can play."

Yes, Rory MacTaggart now played—in the sexy way, and in the silly way. He loved it these days. Instead of making time for fun, these days he squeezed work in around everything else.

My tech support business had taken off, though I most often worked for free. Rory's generosity in taking on pro bono clients had shown me I wanted to do the same. People who wanted to pay me did. Everyone else got my skills gratis.

"That doesn't work for me," I said. "I want to play right now. To celebrate."

"Celebrate what?" He glanced up, and his eyes widened. Swiftly they narrowed as his mouth curved into a sensual smile. "It's a good thing we're the only ones in the house today."

We had welcomed many guests, on numerous occasions, over the past two months. His family. My family. Even my work buddies from Travellis got a free round-trip ticket on Air Rory.

"Don't know what you mean," I said, pretending innocence.

He dropped his pen, leaning back in his chair. "You are barely clothed, *mo gaoloch.*"

"Really? I hadn't noticed." He'd called me his dear in Gaelic. Sometimes he called me *mo leannan*, his sweetheart—or *m'eudail*, his darling. I loved anything he rumbled in Gaelic.

I stretched languorously and rose.

Rory drank in the totality of my appearance, from my ComicCon T-shirt to the black lace of my bikini panties, and down to the naked expanse of my legs and my bare feet. He exhaled on a guttural groan, the sound hungry and totally masculine.

Then he noticed the book I held.

"What are you doing with that?" he asked, his fingers stroking the desktop, the movements eliciting a warm shiver in me, as if he'd stroked my body that way.

I ambled to the desk and leaned against it as I handed him the book. "I added something to it."

He took the volume and flipped it open, smiling at the title page. "We're still evolving, then?"

"Absolutely. I hope we never stop."

"We won't." He thumbed through the pages of our photo album, past the pictures that represented every stage in our relationship. When he reached the final page, he stilled. "What..."

I tapped my finger on the picture of me as a baby. "A preview of what the next phase in our evolution might look like. Your little guys are strong swimmers."

"My what?"

"Your sperm, baby. They got the job done."

A breath exploded out of him, and he broke into the most radiant smile I'd ever seen, the truest expression of exultation. "It's true?"

"No, I thought it would be funny to trick you."

"We—" He pulled in a shaky breath and exhaled it as laughter. "We're having a baby?"

"Yes, my sweetie-pie, we are."

He leaped out of his chair, threw his arms around me, and hauled me across the desk. My feet had just touched down on the floor when he swooped me up, my feet swinging, and consumed me with the most wonderful, scorching kiss. He pulled away from my lips only enough to grin and say, "I love you, Emery."

"I love you too, Rory baby."

"You were right. We do need to celebrate." He set me down, then grasped me around the waist and flipped me to face the desk. "Donnae move."

I held still, facing away from him, while a series of zipping and swishing noises assured me he was shedding every scrap of clothing. I glanced over my shoulder.

Rory stood behind me, completely nude, his swollen cock waving.

"Time to play?" I asked.

"Aye."

He yanked my lace panties down to my ankles.

I kicked them off. Desperate to get started, I ripped my shirt off over my head and thanked the stars I'd gone bra-less.

"Palms on the desk," he said, his voice low and deep and resonating with need.

"Yes, my lord." I slapped my hands on the desktop and wiggled my ass. "I live to serve."

"Like hell you do." His lips ghosted over my behind, then his tongue traced the upper curve of each cheek. "You're obstinate and independent, and I wouldn't have you any other way."

He raked his hands up my sides, around to my tummy.

I spread my legs, excitement sizzling on my skin.

"You are so beautiful, so perfect," he said, his hands traveling up to fondle my breasts. As he plumped and kneaded them, scraping his thumbs over my nipples, he pressed the hard length of his erection against me. "You are the most precious gift I've ever received."

"You're so sweet," I said, and moaned when he slid his shaft between my thighs. "But for heaven's sake, say something dirty."

He chuckled, the sound soft and darkly erotic, as he shifted one hand to my mound. Two fingers dived between my folds. "Ahm going to fuck ye, Em, until my cock is slick with your cream and ye beg me to make ye come. Is that dirty enough?"

I opened my mouth to speak, but his fingers plunged down my cleft and inside my entrance. His thumb stroked my clitoris, and all I could do was moan.

Oh those fingers, those strong and agile fingers, they strummed my body like a virtuoso playing a Stradivarius. He swept his fingers up and down my cleft, settled the heel of his hand on my clitoris, and worked me into a frenzy of need. I bucked my hips forward and back with each stroke of his fingers, swirled my hips in a frantic attempt to rub my clit against his hand, but the pressure of oncoming ecstasy escalated higher and higher without release. I whimpered and dug my nails into the desktop. He kept me balanced on the edge of climax, teetering but unable to tumble over, and I loved every second of his delicious torture.

"Please, Rory," I pleaded. "Please."

He nipped my shoulder. "Cannae resist a warm, wet lass who begs."

He grasped my hips and drove his cock deep inside.

The bliss of penetration, the fullness of him buried within me, forced a breathless string of words from my lips. "OhGodyesohyesthankyou."

My orgasm rocketed through me, searing and convulsive. I cried out as my body clenched around his shaft, again and again, the pleasure so intense I finally lost my voice on a strangled scream.

He held onto my hips as he pumped in and out, his balls slapping on my ass with each inward thrust, and my wetness making a sucking sound with each withdrawal. I rocked my hips back to meet his thrusts, crying out every time his hard length sank into me. As the pace quickened along with our breaths, I threw my head back and plastered my body to his, lashing my arms around his neck while his grunts and groans reverberated in the room.

I came again, with a burst of pleasure that made my heart pound so hard it almost hurt. My sex clenched around him over and over until, with a vigorous thrust, he found his release.

"Oh God, Em!" he shouted, punching into me once, twice more. His body went still. He enfolded me in his arms, his hands over my belly. Gasping for breath, he murmured into my ear, "I hope our bairn is just like you."

I reclaimed my breath enough to say, "I hope our baby's like you."

He peeled his body from mine, leaving me aching from the loss of his hot shaft filling me. He turned me toward him. "Our baby will be the best of both of us, and better than either of us because our love made this bairn."

"This is one lucky baby." I looped my arms around his waist. "And the first of several, I hope."

"Several?" He smiled with a heat that reawakened my desire. "Best keep practicing for the next one, then."

By the time we finished practicing, we'd made our way up to the third floor and collapsed on our bed, satiated more than any living thing had a right to be.

Sprawled across my husband, I traced lazy circles on his chest. "In a couple months, we'll have our first Christmas together."

"Can't think of a blessed thing I need or want." He kissed the top of my head. "You've given me the two best gifts—your love, and our baby."

"I think we should throw a big holiday party."

"Anything you want, *m'eudail*. This will be the first Christmas in years where I've had something to be grateful for."

I lifted my head to gaze into the warm amber eyes of the man I loved. We would celebrate our first Christmas, our first New Year's, and soon our first child.

"Our life is amazing," I said. "Now, if I could just help Jamie and Gavin..."

"Matchmaking?" Rory groaned. "What can I do to dissuade you from that course?"

"It might be hard…" I glided my hand down to his groin. "But I'm sure you'll think of something."

Love the

Hot Scots

series?

Visit
AnnaDurand.com

to subscribe to her newsletter
for updates on forthcoming books in this series
&
to receive a free gift for signing up!

Anna Durand is a bestselling, multi-award-winning author of contemporary and paranormal romance. Her books have earned bestseller status on every major retailer and wonderful reviews from readers around the world. But that's the boring spiel. Here are some really cool things you want to know about Anna!

Born on Lackland Air Force Base in Texas, Anna grew up moving here, there, and everywhere thanks to her dad's job as an instructor pilot. She's lived in Texas (twice), Mississippi, California (twice), Michigan (twice), and Alaska—and now Ohio.

As for her writing, Anna has always made up stories in her head, but she didn't write them down until her teen years. Those first awful books went into the trash can a few years later, though she learned a lot from those stories. Eventually, she would pen her first romance novel, the paranormal romance *Willpower*, and she's never looked back since.

Want even more details about Anna? Get access to her extended bio when you subscribe to her newsletter and download the free bonus ebook, *Hot Scots Confidential*. You'll also get hot deleted scenes, character interviews, fun facts, and more! As an added bonus, you get bonus audio chapters too.